PREVIOUS BOOKS
BY DAVID POYER

Tales of the Modern Navy

The Cruiser

The Towers

The Crisis

The Weapon

Korea Strait

The Threat

The Command

Black Storm

China Sea

Tomahawk

The Passage

The Circle

The Gulf

The Med

Tiller Galloway

Down to a Sunless Sea

Bahamas Blue

Louisiana Blue

Hatteras Blue

The Civil War at Sea

That Anvil of Our Souls

A Country of Our Own

Fire on the Waters

Hemlock County

Thunder on the Mountain

Winter in the Heart

As the Wolf Loves Winter

The Dead of Winter

Other Books

The Whiteness of the Whale

Happier Than This
Day and Time

Ghosting

The Only Thing to Fear

White Contine

Stepfather Bank

The Return of
Philo T. McGiffin

Star Seed

The Shiloh Project

TIPPING POINT

THE WAR WITH CHINA—
THE FIRST SALVO

DAVID POYER

St. Martin's Paperbacks

This is a work of fiction. All of the characters, organizations, and events portrayed in this novel are either products of the author's imagination or are used fictitiously.

TIPPING POINT

Copyright © 2015 by David Poyer.

All rights reserved.

For information address St. Martin's Press, 175 Fifth Avenue, New York, NY 10010.

ISBN: 978-1-250-12326-8

Our books may be purchased in bulk for promotional, educational, or business use. Please contact your local bookseller or the Macmillan Corporate and Premium Sales Department at 1-800-221-7945, extension 5442, or by e-mail at MacmillanSpecialMarkets@macmillan.com.

Printed in the United States of America

St. Martin's Press hardcover edition / December 2015
St. Martin's Paperbacks edition / December 2016

St. Martin's Paperbacks are published by St. Martin's Press, 175 Fifth Avenue, New York, NY 10010.

10 9 8 7 6 5 4 3 2 1

All nations want peace;
but they want a peace that suits them.
—ADMIRAL OF THE FLEET SIR JOHN "JACKY" FISHER

1

Crete

Even the hills looked ancient. They stretched away mile after mile, bright green under the spring sky, patched with bleached rock where the spare soil had worn away. Over centuries, no, millennia . . .

Dan Lenson glanced at his wife. Her head was turned away, blond hair flickering in the warm wind from the open passenger-side window. The breeze smelled of sage, rosemary, cypress, a warm mingled scent blowing off the myrtle-covered hills. Blair had flown in the day before, and he'd left his executive officer in charge while he took two days' leave.

"My wife, the congresswoman," he murmured.

She pressed a finger to his lips. "Don't jinx me, okay? It's by no means a shoo-in."

The rented BMW was headed south, along a winding two-lane coast road lined with rustling olive groves, each a slightly different blue or green. Violet and cream

flowers bloomed along the verge, and the blue Mediterranean murmured on their left. No one seemed to
build near the water here. Maybe, Dan thought, they
remembered ancient disasters. Earthquakes, volcanic
eruptions, tsunamis . . . classical civilization had risen
atop a tectonic fault line.

They'd dined the evening before at a restaurant atop
one of those myrtle-choked hills. Cheese pies, Cretan
rice, slow-cooked wild hare with artichoke hearts, followed with phyllo-dough pastries and candied fruit.
He'd told her how the English word *candy* had come
from a town near where they were going: ancient
Candia. And she'd told him what she was doing at SAIC,
where a shadow cabinet convened when her party was
out of national office. She'd tried the raki, and sputtered
it out, to the amusement of the other diners.

They'd stayed overnight in Mperetiana, at a hotel
overlooking the sea. The bay was so narrow he could
look across to the gray speck that was USS *Savo Island*,
moored at the long pier at the naval base. A crane barge
lay alongside. It had extracted the remaining missiles aft,
both the live ones left from the brief but fierce engagement with an Iranian task force the month before, and
the dud rounds damaged in an electrical fire before that.
Now the whole magazine, wiring and controls, was being
refurbished by a Tiger Team from Norfolk.

But for a few hours, he'd almost forgotten his respon-
sibilities. Renewed passion and ripped-off clothes, along
with strange little arguments, quickly extinguished
flares of temper. But just as quickly, recurring.

They'd coupled again hungrily this morning, followed by an hour of sleeping in. Showered, and enjoyed a leisurely breakfast. Then back on the road, toward Heraklion, on the island's northern coast. He slouched in his seat, one hand on the wheel, the other on her shoulder. Now and then his skin stung, whipped by strands of her blowing hair.

"Knossos. One kilometer," she said, folding the tourist map and tucking it back into a worn cordovan briefcase. "So that was the right place to turn."

"You nailed it. Again."

She made a face. "Oh, shut up. That must be it, on that hill. My God . . . it's *huge*."

The asphalted lot they pulled into was nearly empty; only a few dozen cars. When they got out the air reverberated. Silent, except for the wind, and the chirrup of insects.

"I used to read about this place." She gazed up at the columns. "When I was a kid."

"We must've read the same books." He stretched the kinks out, examining the pillars. Bright red and blue, ocher and yellow, they tapered toward their bases, inflated-looking pillows of stone. Behind them the famous mural of the bull-leapers was just visible. "Looks like we'd better take some water."

Plastic half-liters tucked into their pockets, they joined a tour, and trailed the group up into the ruins. He saw now why so many of the reconstructions were porticoes, elevated roofs; they provided shade from that relentless sun. Halted inside, they listened to a long explanation of how the English archaeologist Arthur Evans had excavated what he interpreted as the ancient palace of the shadowy bull-king Minos. And then, later, decided to "reconstruct" it in reinforced concrete, with frescoes by modernist artists. The whole talk came first in Greek, then in French, and last in English. Then they moved on to the next stop, where the whole process was repeated.

Half an hour into the tour, he turned to see Blair lagging back. "We're going to lose the group," he called.

"Let them go on ahead. I want to say something," she murmured. "I didn't want to bring this up last night, and spoil our . . . reunion. But we need to talk."

"About what?"

"About the ruckus you've stirred up."

He blinked into the burning sun. The concrete trapped the heat radiating off the walls. Sweat trickled down his face. "What ruckus?"

"Your shooting down that Israeli missile. I've had to field questions about it. So far, I've managed to put them off. But at some point, I'm going to have to take a position."

Dan cleared his throat. He'd thought they were going to enjoy the day. See the sights. "Can't you just hand them off to the Navy? Say it's a military question?"

"This isn't just a military issue anymore. Anything that has to do with supporting Israel is political, Dan. Highly. And it's getting even bigger than that. Have you heard about the Lenson Doctrine?"

He frowned. "The *what*?"

"That's what Cal Thomas—that newspaper columnist—what he called it. In a very hostile piece, by the way. The 'Lenson Doctrine': If we have the capability to intercept a ballistic missile strike, at least one targeted against a civilian population, we have the moral obligation to do so. No matter whom the strike's against."

Dan said slowly, "I wasn't making policy; it was what my orders said. Priority three: offensive missiles targeted against civilian populations."

"That was NCA *draft guidance,* Dan. And it certainly didn't mean for you to intercept counterstrikes by our own allies."

"It didn't mention any exceptions. And I'd already knocked down an Iraqi missile."

"Uh-huh. Absolutely literal, like always . . . Is that the Academy mind-set? Or your own patented Dan Lenson blinders?"

"Sounds like a loaded question to me."

She blew out and glanced away. "It's getting hot . . . want some water?"

"Not yet."

"Anyway, whether you intended it or not, that's how your action's being interpreted in some quarters. And I have to say, knowing the way you operate, it wouldn't be out of character."

"What's that mean?"

"Your fucking idealism, or naivete, or whatever it is, gets in the way of your common sense."

"Now you sound like Nick Niles. But don't we oppose the use of weapons of mass destruction? Isn't that what Iraq was all about—toppling Saddam because he had that capability? And he didn't actually even use them. Except on his own people."

"You forget the Iran-Iraq war. He used gas then, too."

Dan shrugged. Ahead, the group had stopped before a fresco of a young man against a background of stylized lilies. The somniferous drone of the guide's canned lecture went on and on, like a fat fly's buzzing. First Greek, then French . . . Dan couldn't keep the irritation out of his voice. It was easy for pundits—or wives—to second-guess a decision he'd had thirty seconds to make. And he was still sure, or at least pretty sure, it had been the right call. "Look, let's discuss this later, all right? I'm sorry you're taking heat. Or that it's hurting you politically. If it is. But my decisions have nothing to do with you. If I screwed up, if they've lost confidence, the Navy will relieve me. If not, you've got nothing to worry about."

"Nothing to worry about." She looked away, pretending, he guessed, to examine the fresco. "Does that include Lieutenant Singer?"

"Singer . . . You mean Lieutenant Singhe? Amy? What about her?"

"The way she was looking at you. Aboard your ship. You don't find her attractive?"

"She's part of my *wardroom,* Blair. I don't get paid to rank the attractiveness of my junior officers." But even to his own ears, that sounded evasive. And Singhe was more than attractive; more like some Hindu goddess of erotic desire, in tight-fitting blue coveralls that outlined every curve . . . Damn it. "Anyway, I'm married."

"Nice compliment, Dan. Meaning that if you weren't . . . ?"

"It *is* a compliment. Or didn't last night convince you?"

She took his arm, but still didn't meet his gaze. "It was nice. So was this morning. But we don't see each other very often. I knew you'd be gone a lot, but I didn't realize exactly how long. Or how much I'd miss you. The Navy seems to be eating you alive. Even when you're around, you're not *here*. Like last night—"

He smiled. "You seemed to like it."

"I don't mean that." She punched his arm with a sharp knuckle. "I mean at dinner. You hardly looked at me. You just stared across the water, toward your ship."

He sighed. The group was out of sight. He wasn't sure where it had gone. The most likely way seemed to be down a long corridor. He took her arm, and they strolled toward a pool of cool shadow. Birds chirped overhead: swallows, nesting in the porticoes, their droppings like white paste on the bright ocher paint. "This'll probably be my last sea tour. Then, some twilight assignment ashore. Conning a desk."

"That wouldn't be so bad, would it?" She sounded hopeful. "And then what? I could put your name out in DC. In certain circles. If you wanted me to."

He shrugged. They came to stone steps leading downward, and took them. The shadows deepened, and a musty smell rose. "God, that's better," she said. "It's like an oven up there. And all that sparrow shit—yech."

"I miss you too, Blair. But I seem to be at my best at sea."

"You mean you like it best at sea."

This seemed to be one of the less-frequented corridors. The stone was rough ashlar coated with scarred plaster. It didn't look like the reconstructions. Here and there figures were inscribed, very faintly, on the surface. Maybe this *wasn't* the way the group had gone. They walked a few yards, turned right in the gloom. Something skittered away—a small gray-green lizard. She flinched. "You sure this is right?"

"No. Anyway, what're you getting at?"

"I don't begrudge you what you want to do, Dan, but we've had this conversation before. I thought once you had a plan, for life outside the Navy. They already offered you a medical retirement. Because of your lungs, right?"

"My lungs are fine." He coughed into a fist, wheezing dramatically.

She rolled her eyes. "Very funny. But I'm not the government-issue service wife you seem to need, Dan."

"No, you're much higher powered."

"Don't flatter me. I've spent a lot of time around generals' wives. They're usually the reason their husbands became generals. Shrewd, hardworking women, behind the scenes. We need to think about where we're going." She looked away. Then added, in a lower voice, "If we stay together."

He halted in the near darkness. "What does that mean?"

"Just that I'm coming up on some decision points of my own. If this campaign fails—"

"You're not going to lose. Not with Checkie pulling for you. And all his wealthy buddies." He looked back along the corridor, dark behind them, even darker ahead. "Crap . . . I don't think this is part of the regular route."

As they retraced their steps she murmured, "There are more voters in Maryland than my stepdad's friends. And the other side's going to put a bargeload of money against us."

"Uh-huh . . . Did we go right here, or left? I don't remember."

"Right, I think . . . There's a banking bill coming up. We've got to regulate the financial market more tightly, or there'll be hell to pay. For the whole economy."

"But aren't you taking contributions from the bankers?"

"I'm not sure what that's supposed to mean, Dan. But I don't like your tone."

He lifted his head, suddenly realizing that the dust they were walking on was unmarked, save for the curving arabesques of the lizards. "We never came this way. No tracks."

"We should've turned left back there, I guess."

"Maybe."

She laughed, a low, throaty sound. "Lost in the Labyrinth. Without even a lousy spool of thread to guide us out."

"At least we're together."

"Ariadne and Theseus?"

He pulled her close. "At least we're together," he said again, this time into the familiar scent of her hair, blinking back the sting of incipient tears. Holding her in the musty, close dark, breathing the dust of millennia. What had she meant, *if*? He couldn't ask again. She evaded questions she didn't want to answer. Was she talking about another man? He didn't think so. But he'd been wrong before, about women. About a lot, actually.

All things came to dust in the end. The fine silt beneath their feet had dreamed too, fought, hated, loved. Again and again, wearing different faces.

Someone was calling, from above. The guide sounded worried. "We're down here," Dan shouted up through a gap in the stone. And shortly thereafter they were trudging up time-hollowed stone steps, back into the blazing sun.

The ship lay at the end of a finger pier, the green and buff mountains rising beyond. It reared above them like a falling tower as Dan pulled into the space with the welded steel sign that read COMMANDING OFFICER USS SAVO ISLAND.

When he turned off the engine he could hear the steady roar of blowers and machinery, could smell the mingled scents of turbine generator exhaust and fuel and fresh paint and overcooked food. Below him seamen on a float wielded rollers on long poles. Fresh haze gray gleamed on the sheer. As he held the door for Blair, a welding arc sputtered halfway up the overlofty, top-heavy-looking superstructure. Flat squarish panels with truncated corners, not quite octagons, were set like breast badges just below the bridge.

The panels were SPY-1 antenna arrays. The Ticonderogas had been designed around them, mating a Spruance-class hull and propulsion to the most powerful radars ever put to sea. Within a radius of three hundred miles, an Aegis cruiser could detect and track over a hundred possible targets simultaneously, and reach out with scores of missiles to destroy enemy aircraft threatening the massive carriers that centerpieced U.S. or NATO battle groups.

The bells announcing his arrival bonged out. *"Savo Island, arriving,"* the 1MC said, the topside loudspeakers strident and metallic. The absentee pennant floated down.

The autumn before, Dan had stood by the window of the vice CNO's temporary office, looking out toward the Pentagon. He and Niles had staggered out together on 9/11, through burning fuel and collapsing ceilings, over torn-apart bodies.

"So, Lenson," Admiral Niles had rumbled, slapping his desk, "I keep my promises. Still want a ship?"

"Yes sir," he'd murmured. Someone had engineered his promotion, even after he'd been officially passed over. It wasn't supposed to happen, but there'd been "irregularities."

"You made captain. Sure you don't want to cash in your chips, go make some real money?"

He didn't answer, and Niles had slammed the desk again. "You might actually be a good fit . . . But you won't have long. She's out there on a national-level mission. If this ship doesn't turn around, and I mean on a dime, I've got another O-6 with his bags packed. And tread light this time, Lenson. No more *Gaddis*es. No more *Horn*s."

He winced now, inwardly, as he saluted the flag, then turned to face his officer of the deck. Blair stood at attention, hand over her heart. A small woman with a pointed face, chunky hips under dark blue shipboard coveralls, and blond hair smoothed back under her fore-and-aft cap stepped out onto the main deck and saluted. Staurulakis had been fleeted up from operations officer at Dan's recommendation when the previous exec had self-destructed. "Good evening, Captain. Mrs. Lenson. Hope you had a good trip."

"You remember Cheryl Staurulakis, Blair. Acting exec."

The two women shook hands. "Nice to see you again, Cheryl. But it's Ms. Titus, not Mrs. Lenson."

"Sorry, ma'am." Staurulakis said to Dan, "We're about to begin reloading the after magazine, Captain."

"What's going in first?"

"I asked if they could load the 4As first."

The Standard Block 4As were new, still-experimental antimissile rounds. The autumn before, just before this deployment, *Savo Island* had gone from a baseline Aegis 7 to a new mission: theater ballistic missile defense. The Navy's go-to antiaircraft missile had been grown with a higher-energy booster and a lighter proximity-kill warhead to gain the range and altitude needed to intercept a reentry body. This was its first deployment, and most of the experts said it was too early. Not only that, but when she was operating in antimissile mode, the ship was practically blind to other threats. He nodded. "And they said?"

"They wanted to load in a specified order given the cell layout. Said it might not get the 4As in first, but it'd be faster overall. I gave them the okay."

"All right, we'll let that stand." He checked the TAG Heuer Blair had given him as a wedding gift. "We set up for dinner? Got the word, the commodore'll be here?"

"Yessir, they're setting up in the unit commander's cabin."

"That's the suite?" Blair asked.

Staurulakis nodded. Dan told her, "Make sure the bed gets made up. The commodore will probably stay over."

As dusk fell the First Division rigged floodlights and the Tiger Team worked on. After he got Blair settled with a cup of coffee and the CNN feed in his in-port cabin, and scanned his e-mail, he went aft to check on the rearming.

The vertical launch system magazines had no launcher. Or, rather, each cell was its own, with the missile boosting vertically until it cleared the ship, then arching over to its departure azimuth. The upside was that a launcher casualty didn't put you out of business at a ticklish time. The downside was that rearming was slower than with the older systems, and required a crane, which meant you couldn't rearm at sea. Each of the square gray stenciled canisters that housed the missiles had to be poised above its cell, cables connected, connections tested, then lowered, very carefully, so as not to bend the loading rails.

He crossed the afterdeck to the open module. The coveralled, hard-hatted civilian technicians nodded. He waved back and looked down as gulls circled, crying out in the failing light. Forty feet, two levels down, nearly to the bilge. A narrow catwalk halfway down gave the gunners' mates access to the canisters. A stench of burned insulation and propellant welled up. When a missile had shorted out and lit off, he'd had to flood an entire eight-round module, ruining a few million dollars' worth of weapons. But if the others engines had ignited—or, worse yet, the blazing-hot exhaust flame had set off their high-energy warheads—there wouldn't have been much left of USS *Savo Island*.

Chief Angel Quincoches saw him and ambled over. In charge of the VLS, he'd been first to go in after the fire. Dan returned his salute. "Chief."

"Captain."

"These guys on the ball?"

"We checked behind them as they got the new cables and control units in. One set of control units had to be replaced again. Defective from the factory, far's we could tell." The chief petty officer checked his watch. "Been problems with the crane, too. A bent sheave."

"Fixed now?"

"That's what they tell me. Sir."

"Keep 'em moving. The commodore's coming

aboard tonight. We might get orders. Are we checking the hatches, the hatch components, gaskets?" They were one of the biggest failure items.

The senior enlisted nodded, short, as if Dan shouldn't have had to ask.

"What are we ending up with, loadout-wise?" He knew the numbers by heart, having thrashed it out in midnight sessions with the exec and the strike and weapons officers, with input from the squadron weapons officer, the type commander, and the COMNAV-SURFLANT Ballistic Missile Defense Readiness Office. But it never hurt to make sure you were getting what you expected. Especially the way tensions were running up with Iran and Pakistan, and China now, too. There'd been something on CNN moments ago, about massive capital outflows from that country.

"New totals aft are twenty-four of the new RIM-162s, four Tomahawks, and four regular SM-2 Standards. Twelve new Block 4A rounds total: two in the forward cells, ten aft."

Dan nodded. They'd left the States with only four of the experimental rounds, which he'd expended in two engagements. The Combat Systems Weapon Inventory screen in CIC loomed in his nightmares, counting down as whatever dream-battle he was fighting progressed. Until he was left with zeros, and cruise missiles incoming, and he'd wake shaking and sweating.

He didn't need imagination to guess what would happen then. He'd seen it, aboard USS *Horn,* and *Reynolds Ryan,* and *Turner Van Zandt.*

He didn't want his name associated with another

disaster. Not because of his career. That was over, after this tour. Especially after what Blair had said about congressional interest. He just didn't want more corpses on his conscience.

The chief corpsman, "Doc" Grissett, was leaning against the bulkhead in the passageway outside the unit commander's cabin. "You asked for a report on our cleanup, Skipper. We replaced all the air filters and disinfected all the ventilation ducts we could reach."

"Is that going to solve our problem?" *Savo* had been plagued by a flulike illness among the crew, especially in forward weapons berthing, though there'd been cases throughout the ship. One seaman had died in his bunk. They'd shipped the body back to Bethesda, but the cultures had been inconclusive.

"Hope so, sir. Scrubbed out with bleach."

The 1MC bonged. One, two; three, four; five, six bells. That would be Jenn Roald. He spun on his heel and headed for the quarterdeck, conscious, too late, that he was still in civvies.

The unit commander's stateroom was actually a small suite, first a large room with desk, terminal, and table, then a smaller bedroom, with a compact head and shower aft of that. On the rare occasions when an officer senior to the commanding officer was aboard, he operated out of here.

Or she, as was the case tonight. Fine-boned, thin-faced, Jennifer Roald held a cup of punch at the table, which was spread with white linen. To his relief, she was in civilian clothes too, a dark pantsuit that looked both dressy and as if she could inspect an engine room in it. He and Roald dated back to the West Wing, where she'd run the Situation Room. Now she commanded the squadron that *Savo* was, however loosely, attached to.

This was the first time he'd seen the silver service laid out. The old metal glowed with a soft light. The dishes were finer china than the heavy, thick wardroom settings. The food, though, would be straight from the crew's mess—jerk chicken, steamed green beans, brown rice, butterscotch ice cream—laid out by CSSN Longley. Dan's culinary specialist stood half at attention by the galley door, in a white jacket for once without food stains. The evening's guests were Blair, in a green sequined one-shoulder sheath that sparkled as she moved; Cheryl Staurulakis; Commodore Roald; and Dr. William Noblos, the acerbic, nay-saying rider from the Johns Hopkins Applied Physics Lab. Also, the commanding officer of Naval Station Souda Bay, Captain Nichols Blomqvist, and his opposite number on the Greek side, Captain Photios Stergiou, Hellenic Navy. They were in service dress blue. Stergiou handed over a bottle of wine with a smirk. Knowing, no doubt, that U.S. ships were dry. Dan thanked him and set it aside.

Circulating, he got involved in a discussion of the cracks in the superstructure with Blomqvist and Roald. Ticonderogas were aluminum from the main deck up, for lightness, but the whole class had been subject to cracks. His inspection had located two. "My welders tell me you'll be ready to go in a day or two, Commodore,

Captain," the shipyard commander assured them. "Do you have sailing orders yet?"

Dan deferred to Roald, who murmured, "Expecting them any day."

"Back to the protection-of-Israel mission?"

She glanced at Dan, who cleared his throat. "Um, actually, the Israelis seem to have a pretty good handle on the ABM role now. Iron Dome. Patriot, for the terminal phase. And their new Arrow system, for midcourse intercept." He swirled his glass of alcohol-free pineapple-and-Sprite punch.

"So you might deploy elsewhere?"

The commodore sidestepped the question. Dan understood why; Blomqvist should've known better than to ask. Stationing of the Navy's sole antiballistic missile asset was decided at the National Command level, Pentagon or West Wing. As his wife had pointed out that morning, it wasn't just a military question anymore.

When he glanced around, Blair, on the settee, had crossed those long legs she was famous for. The Greek couldn't look away. "And this lovely lady, she is spoken for? . . . Oh, the captain's wife. How unfortunate. I mean, for me." He bent to kiss her hand. Blair shot Dan a mischievous smile over Stergiou's bent back. He took a seat next to her, but spoke to Dan. "I understand you have a Greek exec."

"That's her over there, speaking to Dr. Noblos. Tall guy with white hair. Actually Staurulakis is her married name. She's not Greek by birth."

They were starting on the salad when someone

tapped at the door. A face showed at the circular view port. Longley hesitated, glancing at Dan, who nodded.

It was the duty radioman—the rate was IT now, information technician, but everybody still called them radiomen—cradling a clipboard. Routine messages came over e-mail via the ship's network. Important or time-sensitive ones got walked directly to the CO. Dan rose. "Excuse me, please."

"Sir? There's also a message for the commodore."

"Both of us?" Roald got up too, smooth forehead furrowing.

In the passageway, door closed, the radioman handed each of them a clipboard. The same message, apparently, addressed to Roald as squadron commander, Dan as commanding officer.

After a moment Roald murmured, "Dan . . . I'm sorry."

He sighed, finishing the terse sentences. Captain Daniel V. Lenson, United States Navy, was to turn over command of USS *Savo Island* and report as soon as possible to the CNO's office in Washington. A flight would be scheduled from Akrotiri in a separate message.

The door cracked, eased open, and a shining blond head emerged. "Something important?"

"Blair. I've been, uh, ordered back to Washington."

"Oh, no, Dan. No."

Roald put her hand on his forearm, but didn't say anything. He took a deep breath, fighting for control. "Guess I thought . . . but it's not something I didn't expect. Just figured it would happen faster. And when it didn't . . . well, never mind."

"I'll get your . . . placeholder aboard tomorrow morning. We can helo him in," Roald said. "But this doesn't sound like a relief for cause, Dan."

"It's hard to tell," Blair put in. She took Dan's clipboard and squinted at it. "It doesn't say, temporary or permanent?"

Roald shook her head. Dan took the clipboard back and read it again. The words didn't change. Bitterness seeped in, but he quelled it, lifting his chin. "Anyway, it's been a good command. A good ship."

"You're leaving her better than you found her," Roald murmured. "And as far as I can see, you fought her beautifully. Maybe they just want to pick your brain about tactics."

"They'd send somebody out to interview the Aegis team, or recall Bill Noblos, for that. I'm afraid . . . Oh well." He jotted jerky initials and handed the clipboard back.

"Want me to help you pack?" Blair said.

"Not that much to get ready, actually." Her dress threw green smears of light in the darkened passageway. He drew her close, then remembered where he was and let her go.

"I'll get back to our guests," Roald said. She handed her clipboard to the messenger, and opened the stateroom door. Murmured over one shoulder, "Let me know if you need anything. Just for the record . . . whatever happens in DC, your detachment fitness report from me will be two-blocked, Dan."

"Thanks, Commodore."

"Jenn. Make it Jenn."

He nodded, something in his throat hinting he'd better not trust his voice. It was the first time he'd ever heard her say anything not strictly objective. Blair was still clinging to his arm. He cleared his throat. "Well . . . we can fly home together, I guess."

"Actually, I think I'll stay with my original reservation. Keep the room tonight, and fly back commercial Tuesday. It's always a hassle, trying to deal with the military flights as a dependent."

No, probably not that appealing, after being the equivalent of a three-star in the Department of Defense leadership. "Yeah," he said unwillingly. "Okay. Whatever."

"Do you want a moment?"

"Maybe. Yeah."

Alone in the passageway, he braced his arms against the bulkhead, feeling through his bones the faint hum of a live ship. He'd barely gotten to know her. Her foibles, her capabilities, the little things that made her different from all the rest. Now someone else would sit on her bridge. It didn't seem fair. As far as he could see, he'd made the only decision possible.

"Good-bye," he told her, lips barely moving. Knowing it was sentimental, silly, talking to a mindless thing of metal and fuel and electronics as if it were alive.

Ridiculous, really.

But to a Navyman, it felt right.

I

THE DOCTRINE

2

The Pentagon

He took the Metro in. It was all right at first, but he had a bad moment coming off the subway up into the Mall. He'd expected security barriers, and there were more, but the gift shop and florist and candy store were still there, though the bookstore was gone. The bright lights were the same, and the wide, brightly lit, thronged corridors, filled with uniforms, nearly all hurrying, except for the civilian employees. Three men and a woman stood holding signs by the Taco Bell: the janitorial staff was on strike. Behind them trash was piled high, and shattered glass lay scattered across scuffed tiles. . . .

He started to shake, and felt like throwing up. Had to turn aside and stare into a storefront, pretending to be examining purses, while he got himself under control.

He'd left the Navy Command Center only seconds before Flight 77 had plowed into it. Had been standing in the first deck corridor, west, when a tremendous

explosion had quaked the floor and blown all the overhead lights down in a spray of glass, plunging him into
instantaneous darkness.

And after that fire, debris, screams, charred bodies
under tottering walls. The howls and weeping of
wandering, burned, blinded survivors. The stinks of
jet fuel and burning insulation. And the smoke and
toxics that even now threatened to close up his scarred
trachea—

"Sir, you all right?"

A security guard was eyeing him. Dan coughed into
his fist and swallowed. Took a long, slow breath. Another . . . He shook himself, nodded, and fished out his
ID. Held up his arms as he was wanded. His briefcase
was opened and inspected. Then he paced on in, past
the nail salon, the flower shop, into the shining wide
corridors once again.

He had eggs and toast and weak coffee in the noisy caf-
eteria, but kept checking his watch. At 0730 he got up,
leaving his copy of the *Post* for the next customer. His
orders were to report to the CNO, but a phone call the
night before had modified that to the director, Navy
staff, a couple of rungs down the chop chain. He found
the office easily. A receptionist seated him, but he didn't
actually get called in until 0820.

"Captain Lenson? Admiral Rongstad's respects, and
will you come in?"

The conference room was lined with blue-bound
books that didn't look as if they got used much. Two

men in dress blues waited at the far end. Dan squared off and came to attention. "Captain Lenson, reporting as ordered."

To his surprise, they both rose too. Then he remembered: the sky-blue ribbon with white stars that topped his decorations. "Take it easy, Dan. Grab a chair. Coffee?" The senior, a very tall, balding rear admiral with gaunt cheeks and a reasonable rack of ribbons himself, motioned to a carafe, a covered tray. "Had breakfast?"

Dan noted surface line wings, an Academy ring. "Yes sir, taken care of. Could use a cup of joe, though."

"Help yourself. Admiral Niles was called out of town. Asked me to take care of you. Thanks for returning on such short notice."

"Um—yes sir. It wasn't exactly voluntary."

"I understand. And for what it's worth, I'm sorry. We'll try to answer your questions, if we can. I'm Malon Rongstad. I guess you don't remember me, but we fought together once."

"Is that right, sir?" Dan asked, shaking hands with him.

"Abu Musa? The night attack. Operation Nimble Dancer. You were Ben Shaker's exec on *Van Zandt*, right?"

Dan nodded. A classic night surface raid with guns and torpedoes on a Pasdaran base. The frigate had hit a mine and gone down, and her crew had spent the night and the next day and the next night sliding up and down the Gulf with the tide, as the battle that had wiped out three-quarters of the Iranian navy and air force had roared over them. Every breath had been like drawing in superheated steam. The island had floated shimmering in the western sky. The captain had died, leaving him in charge of 115 men, helpless in the water . . . then the sharks had arrived. He shook that memory off, drew a breath. "You were aboard *Adams*?"

"Her exec. Hey, is it really true that you gave Stansfield Hart the finger that day you mustered your crew to go back?"

"Uh . . . it was juvenile. Uncalled-for. But you have to remember, we were all pretty wrung out. And we thought he'd forgotten us."

The second officer, a hatchet-faced four-striper wearing the gold oak-leaf-and-grinding-wheel judge advocate general insignia on his dress blues, said, "There are quite a few Dan Lenson stories told in the fleet. Did you actually hang a murderer, in the China Sea? And get away with it?"

"I don't think I've ever 'gotten away' with anything, Captain," Dan told him. "If the full story ever gets told."

After a moment's hesitation, the captain took his hand. "Schulman."

"Good to meet you, Captain Schulman."

"And I remember something about you and Ben Shaker," Rongstad said. "An unsettling story, actually. About that nuclear Asroc we used to carry. I always wondered about that—"

"Sea stories get embroidered." Dan drank off the coffee. "That isn't why I was recalled from command, is it? To catch up on sea stories?"

Rongstad seemed to stall out for a moment, then grimaced. "Okay, they said you were . . . blunt. One further question. Your exec. On *Savo*. He shot himself, right? Are there any loose ends from that?"

"By loose ends, you mean . . . ?"

The JAG murmured, "Pending legal action. Especially concerning you personally."

Dan said soberly, "Fahad Almarshadi had issues. Emotional, or mental, no one'll ever know. If one of the chiefs hadn't tackled him from behind, he could've killed a lot of people. No one else in the space was armed."

"But legal action?"

"The investigation was closed. No further action pending."

"Good. Just wanted to clear that up before we started. I'm gonna sit here and let my legal adviser bring you up to speed. Sy, you're on."

Schulman sat forward, extracting a sheet of paper from a briefcase. "As the admiral said, you've been called back pursuant to an official request by the House Armed Services Committee. You're scheduled to testify next Wednesday about what the media's calling the 'Lenson Doctrine.' Have you heard anything about this?"

"My wife told me—I mean, I've heard the phrase. But I'm not sure how my name got attached to it."

"It's the idea, or concept, that if the U.S. is capable of stopping a mass-destruction strike on a civilian target, we have a moral obligation to do so. Relevant statutes include Article 17 of the Fourth Geneva Convention, international humanitarian law, and several UN resolutions since 1946."

"I was just following orders," Dan said, not without relish. He bent to his own briefcase, and dropped a folder on the polished glass surface. "CINC and NCA guidance message for my mission. Draft guidance for employment of ballistic missile defense assets within a combat theater. ComSixthFleet rules of engagement."

"Well, there's a good deal of uncertainty about your rather . . . liberal interpretation of those orders."

"I'll be happy to defend myself. But it'd help to know what the official position is. Before I resign."

"There is no 'official' position," Rongstand put in. "And no one's mentioned resignation in my hearing. If you mean charges being preferred, or a letter of reprimand being considered, nothing like that's going on. At the moment."

"At the moment," Dan repeated. "Am I getting my ship back?"

"As to that," Rongstad said carefully, "it's not in my hands. We'll have to wait and see."

"Okay, but how about unofficially? The Navy's got to have some opinion. We're striking to be the major missile-defense stakeholder, after all. Is this too big a commitment for us to step up to? Or is this a mission we want? With all due respect, sir, I deserve to know if the CNO's behind me on this. Or if I'm hanging out there all by my lonesome."

Shulman said, "It would not be appropriate, at this stage, for us to take any position on your actions. But you might be interested to know you've been set up for a murder board before the hearing."

Dan nodded slowly. "Murder boards" were combination strategy sessions and third-degree grillings designed to prepare a witness to testify. He'd sat in on a few, when he'd been with Joint Cruise Missiles. Getting Admiral Willis and Niles, a rear admiral back then, ready to testify before the Procurement and Military Nuclear Systems Subcommittee about the high failure rate of the Tomahawk program and whether it should be terminated. The procedure had spread to preparing candidates for high office; Blair had had a mini–murder board before being appointed to DoD. "That sounds like a vote of support."

"If you want to interpret it that way. Here's the office address. A retired Marine general who specializes in prepping people for congressional hearings. Be there at 0700 Tuesday. On Wednesday afternoon, you testify."

"I get all Tuesday night off, huh?"

"And Wednesday morning." Schulman had such a deadpan delivery that Dan almost missed his wink. "I'll be there with you."

"Me too," said Rongstad. "Don't have to be, but I will."

"I appreciate that." Having other uniforms flanking him would make him less of an individual target, would make it more a case of putting the Navy on trial, rather than painting him as an individual rogue. Which, God knew, anybody who wanted to could dig up more than enough evidence for. "Seriously. And, can I ask: this general's retired? Who's picking up the tab? For the prep session?"

"The general's donating his time," the admiral said. "I didn't say this, but apparently he's a friend of your wife."

"Fantastic," Dan said. Torn between relief and resentment. If it wasn't Niles, it was Blair. Didn't anyone think he could fight his own battles?

"We're not *against* you," Shulman murmured. "But there'll be some heat generated over this. If we have to sacrifice a burnt offering, to keep the mission . . ."

"Say no more." Dan eyed the frosted buns again, and at last gave in. Pineapple. Not bad. "I've had a good career. If I have to go out because I saved some civilians, I have no heartburn over that."

"Let's hope it won't come to that." The admiral coughed into his fist, and stood.

Dan did too, a little confused. "We done, sir?"

"I think we are. Good luck. Oh, and one more thing." Rongstad reached inside his double-breasted blouse and extended a white envelope. "This request came in. The SecNav was going to preside, but he's going to China as part of a high-level party. The family had asked for you, but you were deployed. It's short notice, but we can provide transportation and a draft speech."

Dan nodded slowly, looking at the schedule of events. " 'Naming Ceremony, USS *Cobie Kasson*.' I'd be . . . deeply honored to preside."

Bright and fair, the day was warm as they strolled down Pier 7, Destroyer-Submarine Piers, Norfolk Operating Base, between towering gray ships toward the last one, outboard. An Arleigh Burke–class destroyer, she lay lower and wider than *Savo Island*. A band was playing "Anchors Aweigh." Dan was in dress whites, white cap cover, white shoes, the uniform that made Navymen look like ice cream salesmen. Beside him, Blair strode along in low heels and a cotton summer dress, elegant but self-contained. She'd seemed torn about today, but had at last said yes, she would accompany him.

The previous evening had not been pleasant. A continuing cold misunderstanding that left them injuring each other with small jabs. Overcome by remorse, hoping for some reconciliation, even if only physical, he'd reached for her in bed, but she'd pushed his arm away.

An official car had picked them up at dawn, complete with a lieutenant commander public affairs type as escort. It had whisked them to the helo pad at the Pentagon, and forty minutes later he was looking down at the silvery glow of Willoughby Bay.

Horn still lay across the Elizabeth River, surrounded by barbed wire. She didn't exactly glow in the dark, but remaining aboard her for any length of time still fogged radioactivity badges. He'd written Kasson up for the Congressional, but it had been downgraded to the Navy Cross.

The ship-naming process was hermetic and unfathomable, run not out of the CNO's office but the SecNav's. Once it had been straightforward—submarines named for fish, cruisers for cities, battleships for states. Now submarines were named for almost anything—states, presidents, admirals, politicians who gave the Navy money. The surface force, though, had maintained its standards. With one or two exceptions, destroyers and frigates were still named after Navy and Marine heroes. And in this case, one who'd served under him. Not that he'd known her well, but she'd been in his crew.

Their escort introduced him to the rest of the official party, gathering under a blue awning a few yards from the raised platform where the ceremony would take place. Standing apart were two short women with a family resemblance. After a second, he recalled why they looked familiar, though he'd never met them before.

"You must be Captain Lenson." The sixtyish woman had a deep Louisiana accent. A very thin teenager stood beside her, hugging herself. Both looked awed and out of place; the younger woman would not meet Dan's eyes. "We're Cobie's family."

"Of course, I recognized you right away. Mrs. Kasson. And this must be Kaitlyn? Petty Officer Kasson's— Cobie's daughter?" They shook hands, the girl's eyes still sliding away from his, her hand limp. "This is my wife, Blair Titus. Your mother was a real hero. Saved the ship, and the lives of the crew. You can be proud of her."

"I barely remember her," Kaitlyn said, voice almost lost in the renewed blast from the band, which had struck up "Under the Double Eagle." A tune he considered a waste of good notes.

Dan said, "She wasn't a standout at first. But when the pressure was on, we saw what she was made of." He was reluctant to admit he barely remembered her. She'd been lower-ranking enlisted, in Engineering, a deckplate snipe; he'd see her only during inspections, or when something went wrong and had to be repaired. Not the best opportunity for socializing.

"Captain? I can introduce you to the rest of the guests—"

"Yes. I'm sorry, we'll talk again." He bowed, and Blair took his arm; they moved on.

"They don't look like much," she murmured.

"Who doesn't?"

"The mother. The daughter. Surprising."

"What's surprising? They're just regular folks—"

"I mean, that they managed to get the ship named after their relative. That takes a lot of grassroots organizing. A lot of smarts, behind the scenes . . . Aha."

"Aha what?"

"Vacherie La Blanc. Over there. Their congressman. Third District. Be sure to make a good impression, Dan. He's going to be at your hearing next week."

Their escort led them on, to introduce them to Admiral Zembiec, COMSURFLANT; USS *Kasson*'s first commanding officer; the squadron commander; a shipyard representative from Bath; the rest of the official guests. Everyone seemed to know who he was. He shook hands, made small talk. La Blanc was short, friendly, almost obsequious, but he and the congressman didn't get to exchange more than a couple of words.

Dan was nervous about his speech. They'd given him a draft, but it was so full of clichés and inaccuracies, especially about *Horn*'s final hours, that he'd finally cut out everything except the intro and summary and rewritten the middle himself. Blair had looked it over, and suggested some grace notes. Cut a couple passages, where he'd let himself go. This wasn't the venue. Or the time. "You can save it for your retirement speech," she'd said.

When he stepped before the podium the faces turned up to him, expectant, open. A moment of breathlessness. He gripped the wooden sides and tried again.

"Admiral, Congressman La Blanc, distinguished guests . . . the Kasson family . . . the Honorable Blair Titus . . . Ladies and gentlemen.

"It gives me great pleasure to be here on this occasion: the accession to the fleet of a new warship, named after a hero I personally had the privilege to lead. Naming this ship after her is an honor to all the enlisted men and women who have made the Navy and Marine Corps what it is today: not only the largest, and the most powerful, but the most respected armed force in the world.

"You will hear a great deal today about the capabilities, armaments, and sensors of this new warship, built to survive and prevail in a hostile electronic environment. The Navy considers these new destroyers its most capable surface combatants. They incorporate advanced geometries and construction materials, to reduce the likelihood of enemy targeting. This tough, survivable ship will venture into high-threat areas to conduct antiair, antisubmarine, antisurface, and inland strike operations. Its designers and builders deserve the highest praise.

"But I will not dwell on that. Instead, I want to talk about the woman this ship is to be named after: Engineman Gas Turbine Mechanic Third Class Cobie Kasson.

"You will hear the official citation which awarded the Navy Cross to Petty Officer Kasson read later in this ceremony. To put it in perspective, she and I—we— were deployed off the coast of Egypt to intercept a suspicious trawler. Unknown to anyone, its hull was packed with explosives. When it detonated close aboard, the shock wave ruptured essential propulsion and machinery, rendering us dead in the water and with rapid progressive flooding.

"As part of the damage-control team, Petty Officer Kasson heroically fought to preserve ship and shipmates. Even after sustaining injuries, she continued to attempt to close the firemain suction valve, located under swiftly rising water. At last, she succeeded. At the cost of her own life. But she saved her shipmates. Greater love hath no man—and no woman—than she give up her life for her friends.

"The ship Cobie and I had the honor to serve on lies across the Elizabeth River, only a few miles from where we sit today. It testifies that even in times we regarded as peace, others intended war. The attack on *Horn,* as well as those on the Marine barracks in Beirut and on USS *Cole,* marked the beginning of the Global War on Terror. USS *Cobie Kasson* will be part of that war and, in her thirty-year life span, many other actions and operations as well. The thousands of officers, men, and women who will serve aboard her in decades to come will continue the tradition of their namesake.

"In the years I've served, the Navy has changed from a blue-water force, designed to prevail against the Soviet surface and undersea fleet, to a force designed to project power inland in support of national and international goals. It is evolving again now to protect us and our allies from ballistic missiles carrying weapons of mass destruction. USS *Kasson* will stand at the forefront of this new mission.

"I want to say, finally, again, how honored I am to be here for this ceremony. I share the pride of the Kasson family. The officers and enlisted are fortunate to serve under such an experienced, highly trained commanding officer. I wish him and all the crew good luck and good sailing."

That was all; he'd run out of words. But still, they seemed inadequate. He looked across the sunlit, sparkling river, out over the still-expectant faces. Took a deep breath, and tried one last time.

"A commissioning ceremony accepts a ship into the operating forces of the Navy. When we break the pennant, in a few moments, and the crew boards, she'll 'come alive' as a United States ship. Joining a roster that stretches back to the earliest days of our independence, in a chain that will extend for centuries into the future.

"Cobie Elizabeth Kasson is immortal now. She will always be a link in that chain as the ship bearing her name goes out into the seas of the world, to keep the peace and secure us against aggression."

When he looked down Cobie's mother, in the front row, had her face buried in her handkerchief. But the daughter stared straight up at him, skepticism, remoteness, in her doubtful frown.

They were booked into the flag suite at the Navy Lodge on Hampton Boulevard that night. Dinner with the commissioning party, hosted by the Navy League, at the Abbey, downtown. He begged off early, making sure to shake hands and say good night to La Blanc. Their escort dropped them back at the Lodge. After which he and Blair argued again, this time over something so inconsequential—the way he'd parked the car, so a bush had snagged her dress and almost torn it, when she got out—that even he realized that wasn't what they were really arguing about.

He didn't know how to respond. Was it the pressure of campaigning? His own recalcitrance and absence, like she said? In the room, he opened the little fridge, hoping for a Diet Coke, and found himself facing the ranked shining jewels of single servings. Whiskey. Brandy. Vodka. Shining like liquid platinum, liquid bronze, liquid gold. They even had his old favorite, Cutty Sark. He started to reach for it. Then redirected his hand, to the soft drink.

The book-swap shelves in the lobby had held a worn copy of Barbara Tuchman's *The Guns of August*. He was swallowing the last of the cola, stepping out of his white trou for a shower while reading the back cover, when the phone rang. "Can you get that?" Blair murmured, looking into the mirror over a desk she'd converted to a dressing table as she stripped her bra off. She was turned away, but he could still make out the burns and scars. He sighed and picked up the phone. "Yeah?"

"Captain Lenson? Will you hold for Edward Szerenci?"

"Is that for me?" Blair murmured.

He covered the mouthpiece. "No. For me. It's . . . the national security adviser."

"Szerenci? What does he want?"

"I don't know. You know he used to be my teacher, at George Washington."

"And he's now on *their* side. Be very careful, Dan."

"Dan? Dan Lenson?" A sharp, rapid, accented voice. Devoid of all doubt or self-questioning.

"Yes sir. Hello, Professor."

"Heard you were in town. Or at least, in country. Where are you now?"

"Norfolk, sir. At a commissioning ceremony."

"You're going to testify. House Armed Services."

"Correct, sir. Wednesday."

"I'd like to meet up before then. Can you stop by my office?"

He covered the mouthpiece again. "He wants me to stop by. Before I appear."

"No. You're busy."

"Uh, well, sir, my time's scheduled pretty solid before then. A murder board, and—"

"I know about the board. How about just before you go in to testify? I'll have my people set it up. Good to talk, Dan. I remember your paper on Tomahawk in the first-strike role. It's been too long."

Dan started to protest, but found himself instead talking to a pleasant-voiced woman. They made the arrangements, then hung up. He stared out the window, at salmon-colored streetlights, the passing cars of a late Norfolk night. This whole area had been Fiddler's Green. Pawnshops, tailor shops, strip joints, locker clubs. Now the base sprawled south and east until it was running up against the hospital and the university. The rowdy honky-tonks were gone, the locker clubs and used-car lots. What did it mean? Maybe just that things would always change, that you couldn't hold on to anything.

Her voice, still with that underlying sullenness. "Did you want the shower first?"

"I guess so." He felt sweaty and unclean, prey to a deep, sourceless unease. Taking a deep breath, he went into the bathroom and closed the door.

3

The Pentagon

Niles had come back a day early, and his secretary had called Dan to come in for a brief interview. He'd gotten his blues dry-cleaned, polished his shoes, made sure his ribbons were new and in the right order, every shoelace and button squared away. Blair was still in bed as he left.

The secretary looked up expectantly in the lobby of the vice CNO's office. He blinked past her through an open door at the green hills of Arlington. "Daniel Lenson, reporting in to—"

"Get in here, Lenson."

His old patron, turned enemy, then reluctant rabbi again, stood at the window, broad back to Dan. Never a lightweight, Niles had gained even more poundage since they'd last met. Rongstad, his staff director, was at a long, polished, glass-topped table devoid of even the faintest specks of dust, a folded newspaper by his elbow.

The windows had all been replaced after 9/11, with blast-resistant, shatterproof, slightly green-tinted glass two inches thick. The sky tumbled with dark, driving clouds, but it was empty of incoming airliners. An I Love Me wall held photos of a hulking young Niles with Victor Krulak, with Elmo Zumwalt, with Sam Nunn, with a bent, aged, irascible-looking Arleigh Burke. A photo of Niles on the bridge of USS *California,* gripping binoculars. Another with a youth group, all the kids looking up at Niles, in dress blues, as to some massive and inscrutable deity.

Their relationship went back many years. Then rear admiral Niles had cherry-picked him as a project officer at Joint Cruise Missiles, troubleshooting the crash-plagued "flying torpedo" that had become Tomahawk. Dan had submitted his resignation there, despite Niles's avuncular advice he was throwing away his career. After his fiancée's murder, Dan had changed his mind about resigning. But by then, Niles had washed his hands of him, pegging him as mercurial, cavalier, not a team player. For years Dan had wandered in the Navy's outer darkness. Only lately had the admiral seemed to change his mind, when they'd stumbled out of the ruins of the burning E ring together.

"I pay my debts," he'd muttered then. Maybe, in his mind, he had, arranging Dan's promotion to captain, then his command of *Savo Island.*

Who knew where that left them, or what the second most powerful officer in the Navy wanted now.

"Lenson," Niles rumbled, clearing his throat. He turned from contemplating the view. Nodded to Rongstad, who without a word opened the *Post* so Dan could see the second page. The headline read: NAVY IN QUANDARY OVER ANTIMISSILE STRATEGY, POSED BY ACTIONS OF ROGUE OFFICER.

"Read it?"

"Yes sir. On the Metro. But you note, it doesn't quote me."

"You're not this 'highly placed source'?"

"No sir. They called, but I haven't said a word. On or off the record." He stood waiting, hands locked behind him, until Rongstad nodded at a chair. Niles lowered himself, and he faced the flag officers across the expanse of polished glass over dark mahogany.

"Actually, that's not why you're here," Rongstad said.

Niles rumbled, "Remember Zhang Zurong? You were involved with him. Back when Bucky Evans and that Tallinger bastard were passing our secrets to him."

"Yessir. I recall that." He'd met the smooth-faced, pudgy Zhang in a Chinatown restaurant, at what had seemed at the time like a family party. But "Uncle Xinhu" had turned out to be a senior colonel in the Second Department, China's equivalent of Defense Intelligence. Dan had turned over elevator wiring diagrams disguised as top-secret terrain guidance schematics. The NCIS and FBI had nabbed the go-between, but by the time they showed up on Zhang's doorstep, he'd decamped, fled Washington for his homeland.

Where, by all accounts, he had prospered mightily.

Niles grunted. "General, lieutenant general, army chief of staff, then the political sidestep. Just like Putin and Bush—from chief of intelligence to president. Or at least, to chairman of the central military commission. Which, right now, is pretty much the same thing."

"He's always been a hawk," Rongstad put in, drawing idle diagrams on the dustless glass. "When we saw his name show up on the State Council, we knew it meant trouble."

Niles got up but motioned them to stay seated. He crossed to a flat-panel display on the side wall and picked up a remote. The screen glowed a stylized logo. Niles machine-gunned through PowerPoint slides, and stopped at one of a chubby face. Zhang, in a gray-green Soviet-style uniform. Niles let that burn on the screen for a moment, then went to the next image. The western Pacific.

"This is what I spend my day worrying about, Lenson. We have a strategic concept, handed down from administration to administration. Containment, until they integrate into the world trading system. But what if they don't want to integrate into a system that we, the West, designed? At some point, we'll lose our grip."

Niles's fat finger swept a scythe from Japan to Vietnam. "Think of growing national power like the shock wave in a detonating bomb. As it increases, it presses against any restraint. What Acheson called our defensive perimeter in the Pacific runs from Japan through

Korea, Taiwan, and the Philippines. West of that, we have an understanding with the Vietnamese."

Dan raised his eyebrows. "With Hanoi?"

"It's secret, so far. Fuel and basing at Cam Ranh, if the balloon goes up, and intel support. Drone and recon flights out of Kep.

"The Chinese have never been happy with the situation, especially being kept out of Taiwan. Up to now, they've probed, tested, but mostly accepted it. Now Zhang's lighting the fuze." Niles clicked to the next screen. Arrows pushed outward from the coast of Asia. They ended in dotted lines that, as Dan hitched his chair closer, enclosed massive areas of the southern seas. "You operated here. Correct? Ten years ago, in USS *Gaddis*."

Rongstad said, "Zhang calls his program 'restoration.' Harmless, right? But to the leadership he's appointed, that means hegemony over the South China Sea, Taiwan, Vietnam, and South Korea, based on the cruises of Admiral Zheng He during the Ming Dynasty."

Dan tried to look impressed. But none of this was news. There would always be threats. That was the nature of the human beast. Power expanded, until it met the increasing density of some competing power. And along that unstable, trembling fault line, all too often, war. Peace was like health: a temporary condition, maintained only by continued vigilance and lots of exercises.

Rongstad went on. "Since the Party's embraced capitalism, but not democracy, it's basing its claim to rule on nationalistic fervor. We've tried to keep the military-to-military relationship going. The SecDef and chairman went to Beijing in January, and invited Zhang to visit the U.S. We even promised him the spy charges were history. So far, no answer."

"Do we see war coming?" Dan asked.

Niles tilted a massive head, and prowled the office like an overweight panther. Outside, past the reinforced glass, clouds rolled, darker and more threatening. It would rain soon. "War? Probably not. Significantly increased pressure? Definitely. So far Japan, Korea, Taiwan, the Philippines, are sticking with us. We're coming to an understanding with India. The Vietnamese have always hated the Chinese. Which we should have figured out long ago . . . But Zhang's busy too. He's secured basing rights in Myanmar and Pakistan. What worries us more, though, is rice and wheat."

Before Dan had time to frown, the controller clicked. The next screen showed climbing graphs in green, red, blue. "Rice, wheat, and oil stockpiles. Notice how last summer they hockey-sticked up. So far this year, they've bought over ten million tons of corn and twelve million tons of wheat, and we're still uncovering massive rice purchases. They say it's to ensure stable supplies, but . . ."

Dan nodded, feeling a chill. This *wasn't* usual. "What are they buying it with?"

"U.S. long-term debt. At a sizable discount. So the Treasury's happy."

"Unloading debt, which we can nationalize, and

taking grain and oil in return," Rongstad murmured. "Also copper, aluminum, manganese, and tin. And they've cut back or restricted access to their own strategic exports—steel, rare earths, tungsten. We had DIA do a historical study. Almost every war we have data for was preceded by a stockpile buildup by the aggressor."

The next slide zoomed in to Southeast Asia. Niles spoke to the screen. "Fortunately for us, their balls are hanging down where it's easy to whack them. The energy corridors, from the Gulf, across the Indian Ocean, and into the South China Sea." Dan noted islands or bases hopscotched through the narrow seas: the Spratly Islands, the Paracels, Kra, the Cocos, Myanmar, Bangladesh.

"Mahan," he said.

"Not coaling stations, but the same idea. The big difference is that their allies are developing states, going along for the money. Or because they're already on our shit list for being dictatorships. While our allies have major regional navies of their own, especially India and Japan."

"And Korea," Dan put in.

"Right, you have this soft spot for them."

He nodded. "Good seamen. Good fighters."

"So are the Japanese. The Indians, well, that's yet to be seen. The couple times their army's gone up against the Chinese, it hasn't been impressive." Niles stepped back and turned the screen off. "But the balance of forces can look different depending on where you stand. If you ask me, is war imminent? I'd say no. If you ask me, is it *possible*? I'd say . . . maybe."

A second premonitory shiver gripped Dan's spine. "Is there some way I can help, Admiral?"

"I have to make some tough decisions. First. You ran the SATYRE exercises, right? Antisubmarine joint exercises?" Dan nodded. "And served with the Koreans. So you know their capabilities as well as anybody. Set any personal feelings aside, and give me an objective call?"

"Yessir. I'll try."

Rongstad skated a single sheet of paper across the glass. Dan took it in: a list. "If we provided them with a supplemental arms package—additional antisub aircraft, the new sonobuoys, upgraded torpedoes—could they hold the Korea Strait against Chinese submarines?"

Dan sat back in the chair, taking a second to process force levels, effectiveness, the geography of the strait. "Sir, in terms of antisubmarine skill sets, they rank near the top. Right now, they could seriously attrite any attempt to force the passage. But they're limited on platforms, and they've got two coasts to cover. Plus Pusan, if we have to reinforce or supply them."

"And?" Niles said.

"I'd say, if the Chinese try to ram through, there'd be a lot of floating debris. From both sides. Anything you can do to beef up the Koreans, they'll put to good use." He looked down the list again. "ASW aircraft and updated sonobuoys, that'd be where to put short-term money. The rest of this—it'd take years to get them air-independent propulsion. That's a nice-to-have somebody added up the line."

"About what Jack told you he'd say," Rongstad murmured.

Dan was about to ask if he meant Jack Byrne when Niles nodded. "Okay, makes sense. By the way, the Taiwanese have requested a supplemental for air defense. They're seeing the same trends. Specifically, a buildup of ballistic missiles and attack aircraft across the strait. That shifts air power in the PRC's favor.

"Second question. How effective are the Ticonderogas as antimissile platforms? Can I count on them to screen a carrier task group?"

This was a loaded question. How he answered might determine what happened to him from here on out. And for a moment he was tempted to obfuscate. He shook it off. "Sir, I have to say, in their current state of development, the upgraded Aegis and the new missile are marginal for the intended mission. We managed two hits out of four firings, but we got lucky."

Both Rongstad and Niles looked unhappy, and more so as he gave statistics. Finally Niles held up a broad hand. "I've heard enough. Malon, anything to add?"

"No sir, he's given you the view from the trenches. The Block 4's at the shaky limit of what you can do with that airframe."

"So we need to speed up the replacement program. Specifically, the two-color seeker head. I've got a captain in charge out there at Raytheon, but he's not cutting it. Dan, we didn't see eye to eye at Joint Cruise Missiles, but you nailed that problem with the cable cutter that didn't cut. The one that kept shredding the rudder, till

the missile went down. Maybe we need a new broom."
He exchanged glances with the director, who nodded
slightly. Niles turned to Dan. "Want to go to Tucson?
Take over the SM-3, get it back on the rails?"

Dan swallowed. "Well, I'm . . . I'd have to think
about that, whether I could do a better job."

Niles looked away. Murmured, "There might be a
star in it for you. If you came through in time to be
of use."

Dan gave it a couple seconds, as much to savor the
offer, and regret it, as to give the impression he was
considering it. Because Niles didn't tease. If he said
there was a promotion in it, there would be. "I wouldn't
do it for that reason, sir. But I'm not sure it would be
the best use of my talents."

Niles scowled. "That's a weasel answer, Lenson.
I didn't have you pegged for a fucking *weasel*."

"Sorry, sir."

"Lay it on the table."

"I've got a crew, and a wardroom, I just managed
to glue back together, mostly, after they took a serious
morale hit." He gave it a beat, then added, "I'm still,
on paper, CO of USS *Savo Island*. I'd rather stay there,
Admiral."

Niles looked away for a second. Then nodded,
once. "You took one for the Navy, after the assassination thing. So I'm inclined to let you have what you
ask for. As long as you understand what you're passing up."

He waited, but Dan didn't see the necessity for saying

anything more. Though he was wondering if he'd just shot himself in the foot in a truly historic way.

At last Niles clicked back to the CNO logo. The next slides were Joint Staff marked, not Navy. They were classified top secret SPECAT, and bore the code names Satchel Advantage/Iron Noose.

"Okay, we've gamed this to death up at Newport. If the worst comes to the worst, we expect any breakthrough attempt to take place via Taiwan. That's where they have the best claim, and holding the center of the chain gives them access to the whole Pacific."

"The Army's not gonna be in this fight," Rongstad said. "Us and the Air Force, along with the Taiwanese and possibly Japanese sea and air forces, will try to hold them off the island. At the same time, we extend the war horizontally by a complete energy and raw-materials blockade. Another possible step will be conventional strikes on the seaports and missile launching points along the coast opposite Taiwan. We hope to limit the conflict, keep it a naval-slash-air war."

"We couldn't win a land war with China in 1953. We sure can't win one now," Niles murmured.

Dan wondered how thoroughly they'd gamed the Red Team portion of the exercise, and whether they expected a nation with a nuclear deterrent to take strikes on its homeland lying down. "But what if—I mean, suppose the Chinese decide to, um, extend the war horizontally too? Maybe by letting the North Koreans off the leash?"

Neither senior officer answered. "Then we'll be looking at a protracted war," Rongstad said at last.

They all contemplated that for a few quiet seconds as the thunderclouds rolled outside, and lightning flashed, far off, over the alabaster needle of the Washington Monument. Then Niles wished him well on the murder board; and Rongstad swept his papers back into his briefcase; and Dan realized he'd been dismissed.

4

Capitol Hill

Wednesday morning it was still raining. His head was stuffy, and as usual before any kind of trial or hearing, he hadn't gotten much sleep. He and Blair seemed to be getting along better, though. Dinner at a Thai restaurant in Georgetown the night before had helped. They'd talked about fallbacks. Hers, if her run for Congress didn't pan out. His, if the hearing went badly. They'd agreed to sell the house in town and move to Maryland. She'd go back to work until something opened up in the next administration, then try to get a position for him, too. Meanwhile, they could build up the exchequer a little.

But right now his head felt like it was going to explode. His neck and upper spine hurt from the old injuries. He dry-bolted three Aleves. Shaved. Got his uniform together. Checked the clock again. Still early.

Suddenly he remembered: if it was seven here, it was

noon back in the east Med. He'd meant to call for the last two days, but kept missing the window.

Sitting on the commode in the bathroom, he hit the number. Rather to his surprise, Cheryl Staurulakis answered on the second ring. "Hey, Exec," he said, keeping his voice low, as if calling a mistress. "It's me."

"Captain. That you? Where are you? Sound pretty faint."

"Long as you can hear me. I'm in DC. Where are you guys?"

"Lucky you caught me, I'm out on the bridge wing. We just got under way."

He could hear the wind blowing, the whine of the turbines. Under way, without him . . . He cleared his throat. "All the repairs done?"

"Repairs and rearm complete, Tiger Team offloaded, and everybody got one night's Cinderella liberty. And get this, everybody's back aboard."

"Even the Troll? And Rit Carpenter?"

"Even Carpenter. Yes sir." She chuckled, about the first time he'd ever heard her laugh aloud. "I had him escorted. Buddy system."

"Probably wise. Um, how's everything going with the interim guy?" He couldn't quite bring himself to say "CO" or "skipper."

"Captain Racker? He's great. A real charmer. Seems to have a lot of pull with the logisticians. We got every part we needed, and Hermelinda ordered a truckload. Building up depth, in case we get caught short again."

Dan grimaced. He'd wanted to hear they were all

right, but not that his replacement was hot stuff. "Uh-huh. So, where we headed now?"

Staurulakis's voice became guarded, official. "We're on a cell, Captain. I can't pass operational details."

He thought of asking for a hint, but dismissed that. "Uh, all right, I understand."

A tap at the door. Blair's voice. "Who're you talking to in there?"

"Just on the phone. Sorry," he called.

Staurulakis asked, all but overlaid by the blustering wind: "Are you coming back to us, Captain? Will they let you return?"

"Um, I'll have to get back to you on that," he murmured, and shortly thereafter, ended the call.

"Want me to drive?" Blair was examining herself in a full-length mirror. She'd come out of the bedroom in a gray belted jacket and a skirt with pleats and black heels. Hair brushed back, and already made up. He'd never understood how she could do full makeup in less time than it took him to shave. In the morning light he noted crow's-feet starting around her eyes, the faint, sad signs of passing time. Her hair was swept to one side, to cover the withered, reddened bud of her reconstructed ear.

"Yeah, that'd be nice. Uh—thanks for appearing with me."

She came up close and fiddled with his ribbons. Flicked something off his lapel. "I'm not *with* you. That wouldn't be smart for either of us, Dan. We'll go in separately. I'll be third row back in the audience." She gave him a peck on the cheek and an air hug. "But I'll be rooting for you. Good luck. I mean that. What we were talking about last night?"

"Yeah?"

"That was worst case. I hope they give you your cruiser back. I really do. But after that, we've got to have that serious talk you keep promising me."

As she drove him in along Lee Highway he paged through the briefing cards from the murder board the day before. The general and his assistant, both retired marines, had set up the scene at the hearing, led him through the opening formalities, and helped him prepare a brief statement. Then they'd cross-examined him like not one but two bad cops. He'd come out sopping with sweat, but with these points memorized:

1. Don't say anything unless they ask you.
2. Don't argue back if they start pontificating for the cameras.
3. Don't show off.
4. Don't make news.
5. Don't advocate anything different from what the Navy's currently doing.
6. Don't act as if you know how the hearing will turn out.

"But above all, once you've answered the question, *shut up*," the general had said. "Just answer what they ask, in the simplest terms possible. Demonstrate knowledge of the issues, act happy to explain so they understand too, but don't get lost down in the weeds. Especially, beware of yes-or-no questions. They're usually setups, to make you look like an idiot. How does a fish get caught?"

"Um . . . what's that?" Dan had asked with a frown.

"He opens his mouth. Old Russian proverb. The longer yours stays open, the better the chance you'll come out with something asinine. Especially, Nick says, in your case. And he apparently has plans, or he wouldn't be going to the trouble of asking me to prep you. So write that on your hand if you have to. Let's hear it again."

"How does a fish get caught?" hissed the major.

"He opens his mouth," Dan muttered. Clenching his teeth, he visualized them laced shut with stainless wire.

The Intelligence, Emerging Threats and Capabilities Subcommittee met in the Sam Rayburn House Office Building. He'd been in this marble mausoleum before, during a hearing on Tomahawk appropriations. But it didn't feel welcoming. More than one military officer had torn his bottom out on these reefs. There wasn't really any visitor parking, but Blair had called in a favor from someone on the Armed Services staff, and they had a space for the day in the parking garage.

But first the car had to be searched. Standing there watching the cops wand its trunk, Dan wondered how many millions of man-hours the 9/11 terrorists had cost the taxpayer. He marveled at how thoroughly a few fanatics had transformed an America that had prided itself on its openness, its trust.

Blair pulled through and found the space, in a corner. They were headed for the elevator when a Hungarian-accented voice echoed. "Mr. Lenson."

Dan turned. Three civilians were strolling toward them between the concrete pillars. "Dr. Szerenci," he said.

His old professor was in a gray suit and a pale blue tie, with the American flag pin in the lapel that had become de rigueur for every right-thinking official, as if to dispel any doubts. His hair had platinumed at the temples; aside from that, he looked as he had in Defense Analysis class at George Washington. Hawk-like. Intent. And short. He also wore glasses now—retro, intellectual-looking horn-rims. The men with him stopped several steps back, gazes roving the garage. Szerenci inclined his head to Blair. "Ms. Titus. Good to see you again. Understand you're running this fall? You're here in support of your husband?"

"Hello, Ed. Nice to see you, too." Her tone was cool. "I'm just here as a spouse. Dan can stand up for himself."

"Of course." Szerenci turned to him. "Sorry we had to meet like this." They shook hands. "Congratulations, by the way, on winning the Medal."

Dan never knew what to say to this. The Medal of Honor wasn't "won," but awarded, usually because you'd died performing some heroic act. Or, if not, by all rights should have. In his case, several other people had, and he wore it for them. But it felt graceless to correct a

well-wisher, and explaining came across as either evasive or falsely modest. So he just nodded awkwardly.
"Bravo Zulu to you, too, Doctor. National security adviser, huh? That's really something."

"Come on, Dan. Make it Ed. Actually, you should
have seen the other names being considered. The president made the only smart choice."

Dan glanced toward the elevator, feeling surreal here
in the dusty echoing labyrinth. Szerenci smiled at Blair
and pressed the Call button. One of his escorts stepped
into the elevator, looked around, stepped out. Szerenci
turned to Blair again, as if debating asking her to step
aside, but she slid past. "You can take the next one,"
she told them, and pressed the Close button. "Dan, good
luck. See you upstairs." She blew a kiss off the back of
her fist as the doors began to seal.

But the steel tip of Szerenci's umbrella shot out,
and they opened again. "I have no secrets," he said
casually.

The car was large enough that his security team
could board too. They took positions at either side of
the door and faced it, backs to their principal, expressionless visages dimly reflected in the stainless wall.

Szerenci took off his glasses and polished them with
a handkerchief. "First, if there's any help I can offer
today, please turn to me, Dan. Blair and I are on opposite sides of the aisle, but you and I, we're both executive
branch. In fact, if you have no objection, I'd like to sit
with you while you testify."

Dan gave him a quizzical side-glance. What was
going on? But having a high figure in the current ad-

ministration in his corner couldn't hurt. "I appreciate that . . . Ed. Thanks."

"This subcommittee usually oversees counterterrorism initiatives, and works to prevent proliferation of weapons of mass destruction. I'm not sure what they have in mind calling you. But I wanted to lend what support I could." He lowered his voice, though his words were already almost lost in the hum of the elevator motors. "For old times' sake. And because, as the CO of *Savo Island,* you'll be in the front line of any conflict. Frankly, we need an immediate, crash upgrade to our antiballistic capabilities."

Dan frowned down at him. "I'm hearing—around the building—that we're looking at an increase in tension. In the Pacific."

Szerenci shook his head in wonder. "Increase in tension—is that what they're calling it? We're on the brink of war. Outside capital's fleeing the country. But I believe we're ready."

Dan looked at the ceiling. It was stainless too, and a blurred image of himself peered back down. First Niles, now Szerenci, and even more direly phrased. "War, huh? I've seen some of it, since we were at George Washington. It's not like the mutual-attrition equations you taught us."

Szerenci cocked his head, gaze sharp. "Force is always the ultimate arbiter. 'Only the dead have seen the end of war.'"

"No argument there, sir. And I respect the need for intellectual rigor. But some conflicts are different. Not so-called limited intervention, when we can pull out when we've had enough. We fight China, it'll be like World War I."

"Your illusions are almost amusing," Szerenci said coldly. "But very well, let's take your example. If not for that conflict, Germany would dominate the world. As it was, Britain and France waited too long."

"Germany chose that war. Not the Allies."

Szerenci waved a hand tiredly. "Who *chooses* a war? That's like saying you choose to lose a poker hand. There's always risk in the great-power game. We have no choice but to play."

The elevator came to a stop on the main floor. But instead of letting the doors open, Szerenci put that umbrella tip on the Close button. And held it there.

Blair said, "Imperial Germany could've been incorporated into a world trade system. If the situation had been handled better, not just from the point of view of each threatened nation. Isn't that what we should be doing with China?"

Szerenci snorted. "What have we *been* doing, since Nixon? But they've got to *want* to be integrated. Instead, the more powerful they get, the bigger their ambitions. And now this new guy—"

"General Zhang," said Dan.

"Yeah, another Tojo—he's whipping them up. I'm going to tell you something classified now."

"I'm not asking for classified information."

"You'll understand why." He lowered his voice still more. "Someone's been probing us for a massive cyber-attack."

"We've heard something about that," Blair said, though Dan wasn't sure who "we" was there—SAIC, or her former compatriots at Defense, or the banking community her stepdad was so tight with.

"Have you? I'm talking about major, ongoing probes of our most sensitive systems. We've traced the hackers, and they're out of the Second Department—Zhang's old outfit.

"So here's our reasoning, in the administration. Emotion must play no part. We look only at what the numbers tell us. Comparing growth rates, they'll out-produce us in five to ten years. You won't quote me on this, to anyone. But war now could be better than later, with a more powerful adversary that's already rolled up our weaker allies."

Dan took a deep breath. He'd forgotten how icy cold Szerenci could be. He could discuss megadeaths as if they were acey-deucey points, dissect and anticipate catastrophe and holocaust almost with relish. "Do we want to roll those dice?" he asked, trying to keep his tone neutral, as if they were back in class.

"It's the only rational way to deal with a rising adversary that won't comply with international rules."

"But what's the endgame? You can't occupy China, the way we occupied Japan—"

The door jerked, shuddering as if desperate to open; Szererenci jabbed the Close button again. "We won't need to. Defeat in war will trigger political change."

Blair shook her head. "How do you figure that?"

The national security adviser smiled. "Historical

precedent. Russia, 1905, 1917. Germany, 1918. Argentina, 1983."

Dan said, "And why are you telling us? Why are you even *here*, Ed?"

"Because—as I said—ships like yours will be in our front line. If you look good, even if for what I might consider the wrong reasons, that helps us toward the supplemental appropriation." He winked, and dropped his umbrella tip from the panel.

The doors whisked open, and they walked out into wide, brightly lit corridors, into a dazzling flicker of camera flashes, men and women jostling in to shout questions. Szerenci's boys shouldered through the scrum with professional ease, until they reached the hearing room.

HOUSE OF REPRESENTATIVES
Committee on Armed Services
Intelligence, Emerging Threats and Capabilities Subcommittee
Washington, DC, Wednesday, June 10

The subcommittee met, pursuant to notice, at 10:00 A.M. in the Rayburn Office Building, the Honorable Beverly Maclay, chairman of the subcommittee, presiding.

MRS. MACLAY. Good morning. Today, the subcommittee will consider funding of additional increment to national antiballistic missile systems. But also, significant issues that have arisen over the proper employment of current systems, notably our mobile defensive systems, such as the ABM-capable Aegis cruisers and destroyers slated to enter the fleet in the out years of the current funding plan.

To outline the issue, I have asked Dr. Denson Hui, director, Missile Defense Agency, to address us as a backgrounder, followed by witnesses from the United States Navy, including the vice chief of naval operations, Vice Admiral Barry Nicholas Niles. Admiral Niles, good to see you here again.

ADMIRAL NILES. Likewise, ma'am. Thank you for having us.

MRS. MACLAY. I see we're also graced with the presence of Dr. Edward Szerenci, the national security adviser. Welcome, Doctor. However, you are not testifying today, I believe.

DR. SZERENCI. I am here in support of the testimony, and to be available should you have additional questions.

Dan, Niles, and Rongstad took a long table in front of the congressmen, who were seated on a dais beneath a large seal. Niles looked taken aback by Szerenci, who bent to murmur into his ear. At last he nodded, but without enthusiasm. He pointed to a chair to Dan's left.

As usual, at least in Dan's experience, not all the subcommittee chairs on the dais were occupied. The subcommittee was made up of nine Republicans and eight Democrats. The chairman, Mrs. Maclay, was a moderate Republican from Kansas. Mainly because of her ready gavel, there were remarkably few partisan squabbles. She wore her gray hair in a schoolmarm bun, and spoke in a dry monotone. The others, mostly male, were in business suits, all with the same flag pin Szerenci was wearing. Dan wondered if they were issued, or if they all had to buy their own in some little kiosk in the Capitol.

The witness table was filling too, which surprised him—he'd more or less assumed he'd be on his own. But nameplates were being set out for an Asian-looking civilian in a severe gray suit and other uniformed attendees. Mostly Navy, but a few in Air Force blue and Army greens as well. When he glanced back, the rows were already filled with lieutenant commanders, majors, civilian aides. It seemed like only yesterday he'd perched back there, handing slides up to his principals as they squirmed under grillings about budget overruns, crashes, missed deadlines.

When he turned forward someone new was pushing her way onto the dais. A woman, her face not quite unfamiliar. Blond. Perhaps attractive once, but now bloated with too many Capitol Hill cocktail parties. As her blue-eyed gaze fixed on his she gave a small but unmistakable smile.

Dan sucked in his breath. He whispered to Szerenci, "Isn't that Sandy?"

"Representative Treherne now. Seventeenth District. Tennessee."

"That's right. I remember." He and Sandy Cottrell had both been students of Szerenci's . . . no, Cottrell had been more than just the prof's student . . . but their paths had diverged since. Hers, steadily ascendant, in both politics and an advantageous marriage, while his had bumped along the seabed. Sometimes literally. They'd met only once during the years between, at a party at the vice president's home. "I didn't know she was on this subcommittee."

"She isn't. Must be sitting in."

The gavel fell, and the room quieted.

DR. HUI. Thank you for the chance to present the progress of our interim ballistic missile defense system. Gentlemen, ladies, unfortunately, what I am going to present really *is* rocket science. So I am obliged to begin with a short definition of terms.

As you know, several nations which find it in their internal interest to present us as an adversary are developing, or have developed, short- to medium-range ballistic missile systems. These are what we refer to as "theater" ballistic missiles. The intercontinental ballistic missile is treated under a different legal and technical regime. The purpose of our defensive systems is not to substitute for our offensive weapons, but to strengthen deterrence by holding off a surprise attack until we can muster our offensive capabilities—to add flexibility to the range of our military and political responses.

It is difficult to exaggerate the technical challenge. We are required to guide a warhead at seventeen thousand miles an hour, intercepting a terminal reentry vehicle—the warhead—which is also traveling at around that velocity. We're trying to hit an object the size of a wastebasket seventy miles up, at a combined closing rate of thirty-plus thousand miles an hour. As you might imagine, this isn't simple. A lot of subsystems have to work perfectly, within a very narrow time window—what we call the latency period.

The flight path of the enemy missile takes place in three phases. The boost phase extends from the launch pad to engine burnout, at the edge of space. This is the point at which "ballistic" flight begins. The midcourse phase extends from burnout to reentry into the atmosphere. The terminal phase follows the reentry body, the warhead, to its target.

Our current state of the art in sensors limits us to interceptions within the two latter regimes, midphase and terminal phase. Terminal phase TMD systems comprise Patriot, THAAD, and the Israeli Iron Dome. Midcourse intercept systems include Arrow and the Navy's Aegis-based Standard system. It is this last system we are concerned with today, I understand?

MRS. MACLAY. This is correct.

DR. HUI. I will then hand off to Captain Widermann, for the Navy Missile Office.

MRS. MACLAY. Good morning, Captain. Again, let

me welcome you and the other DoD members who have come here today to testify.

CAPTAIN WIDERMANN. Thank you, Madam Chairman. The Navy has been entrusted with a growing role in national strategic-level missile defense because of certain inherent advantages naval forces bring to the table. These include ready deployability and redeployability, and the independence of host-country politics the open sea grants us. In addition, it has proven relatively inexpensive to upgrade preexisting Aegis antiair capabilities, embarked in the Ticonderoga- and Burke-class warships, to provide a TBMD capability in the terminal and midphase flight regimes. Needless to say, this is upsetting to those who believe their own programs constitute a means of coercion or threat to us. I believe this is about all that is wise to say in open session on that topic.

MRS. MACLAY. That's my cue to go into closed session, is it not? Before going further, let's make sure the room is secure.

Dan sat back, trying not to slump while accommodating the pain in his upper spine. When the room was reported secure and the mikes were off, the hearing resumed.

MRS. MACLAY. One point we wanted to get to today is recent Navy actions in the eastern Mediterranean. Though there hasn't been much press coverage, we've been briefed that two TBMs were intercepted and two were missed. Then, in a second . . . event, I guess you could call it, an Israeli missile was shot down and an Iranian ship was sunk. Some reports say two were sunk. Several members have called for clarification.

VICE ADMIRAL NILES. Madam Chairman, we will go as deeply into that action as this subcommittee desires. However, let me make one point first.

As you know, the Navy has a long tradition of allowing its commanding officers considerable latitude in how they fight their ships. We try not to micromanage them when they are deployed, especially in situations that require swift and decisive reactions for own-ship defense. Instead, we provide general combat guidance and rules of engagement.

The surface action against an Iranian task group falls under the ROEs for self-defense. I will venture the statement, to the extent I can speak for the Navy, that Captain Lenson, of USS *Savo Island,* acted properly in responding to actual weapon launch by the Iranians. In the subsequent action, although we're still sorting out "who shot John," the Iranian frigate took major damage and a gunboat was sunk. Once the threat was resolved, Captain Lenson took appropriate action to rescue survivors and tow the derelict frigate to a friendly port.

MR. HOLLIGER. This ship was captured by our forces, correct? Are you saying Captain Lenson then gave her back?

VICE ADMIRAL NILES. A state of war did not exist, and the Iranian authorities held that their missile launch was accidental. Thus, we had no legal right to retain the frigate as a prize. Captain Lenson kept us informed of his thinking in that regard, and we concurred in his actions.

However, to go on. Immediately prior to that engagement, *Savo Island* had engaged two Iraqi missiles targeted against Israel, utilizing a small loadout of experimental SM-2 Block 4 ABM rounds. She was the first ship to deploy with this nascent capability, and frankly, we did not expect much; both software and missile are still developmental.

MRS. MACLAY. So it's your opinion that Captain Lenson's conduct in this engagement was within the guidance the Navy had given him?

VICE ADMIRAL NILES. This indeed, ma'am, is the crux of the question. He is here with us. Perhaps it would be best to let him speak for himself.

MRS. MACLAY. Good morning, Captain Lenson. We're glad you could be with us today to clarify your actions. I understand from my staff that you are one of the most highly decorated naval officers still on active duty. And in fact, that you hold—and I am reading from your Navy Department summary record—the Silver

Star, the Navy Cross, the Navy–Marine Corps
Medal, the Navy Achievement Medal, the Navy
Commendation Medal, the Meritorious Service Medal, the Legion of Merit with a V, a
Defense Superior Service Medal, four Armed
Forces Expeditionary Medals and one Navy
Expeditionary Medal, six Navy Sea Service
Medals, four Purple Hearts, a POW Medal,
two Overseas Service Ribbons, the Southwest Asia Service Medal with two battle
stars, the Presidential Unit Citation, the National Defense Service Medal with one star,
and various other ribbons, some, I note, from
other countries—Indonesia, France, the Republic of Korea. I congratulate you on what
has obviously been a long and no doubt stress-
ful career.

CAPTAIN LENSON. Thank you, ma'am.

MR. LA BLANC. Is the chairwoman's summary essentially correct, Captain?

CAPTAIN LENSON. Um, if it is from my record,
probably. I would have to check before I could
say it was definitive.

MR. LA BLANC. Meaning you have been decorated
so much and so often you no longer are able
to keep them straight. I would submit that
Captain Lenson is a warrior. Unlike most who
testify before this committee, who are rear-
echelon figures.

MRS. MACLAY. Thank you, Mr. La Blanc. Captain,
would you summarize your actions this win-

ter, specifically those which led to your firing four antiballistic missiles?

CAPTAIN LENSON. Yes, ma'am. USS *Savo Island* was posted off the Levant on a defense of Israel mission. I have brought a copy of those orders for the record, if desired. They are classified. During our time on station several enhanced-range Scud-type variants knows as Al-Husayns were fired from the Western Operating Area.

On the night in question, three TBMs were fired simultaneously from the Al-Anbar area. We were cued via satellite and prepared to engage. However, I had only two missile defense rounds available at that time, due to a casualty in the after magazine. The impact point prediction for the first missile resolved to an aim point directly over *Savo Island*. Missiles 2 and 3 were targeted against cities in Israel. I directed that we take missiles 2 and 3 with Standard.

MR. LA BLANC. Not the first? The one that was aimed at you?

CAPTAIN LENSON. Doctrine assigned us a lower value than the defended area. This is actually pretty common, in that the mission of a cruiser, or a destroyer, is typically to defend a higher-value unit.

MR. LA BLANC. I see. Proceed, please. I take it that the first shot, aimed at you, missed.

CAPTAIN LENSON. The first reentry body, which

I believe was a terminal homer, disintegrated during its reentry phase.

MRS. MACLAY. What were the results of your own two shots?

CAPTAIN LENSON. We achieved one successful intercept and one miss. The warhead we missed impacted on a shelter in Tel Aviv. I have seen media reports that upwards of two hundred people died.

MR. PARKS. Were you satisfied with that performance? Captain Widermann, I would like you to comment as well.

CAPTAIN LENSON. I was not satisfied, sir, but it was consistent with the results we had seen up to then in the test series.

CAPTAIN WIDERMANN. Sir, Captain Lenson's statement is basically accurate. The Block 4 is not yet in the production phase. He was issued developmental rounds and beta software in order to respond to an emergent operational necessity at the strategic level. Given the limited resources devoted to the program thus far, I would say we were lucky to get the results he did.

MRS. MACLAY. I see. Then two days later . . .

CAPTAIN LENSON. Two days later, more or less, we received intel that a retaliatory launch was being planned. This was to be an Israeli launch of their Jericho missile against Baghdad. We followed this very closely.

MR. LA BLANC. Did you seek guidance as to how to react?

CAPTAIN LENSON. Yes sir. Via naval channels, and also directly from the West Wing via a civilian White House staffer who was aboard, a Mr. Adam Ammermann.

MR. PARKS. Was such guidance forthcoming?

CAPTAIN LENSON. Not in a timely enough fashion to guide my actions.

MRS. MACLAY. Let's go back to this civilian staffer. What was his function aboard your ship?

CAPTAIN LENSON. He informed us his mission was liaison with the administration.

MRS. MACLAY. Doctor, was this one of your people? This sounds very irregular.

DR. SZERENCI. Mr. Ammermann is not attached to my office. He is, or was, I understand, a junior-level staffer in the Office of Public Liaison. I am not aware of any orders to him through my office, which stands separate.

Dan ran his gaze along the row of faces above him. Some seemed interested; others, tuned out; one or two, hostile; most, impassive. Sandy kept staring down at him. Her head seemed to be weaving slightly. As their eyes crossed she smiled again, but it wasn't friendly. More like someone contemplating a tasty meal.

A nudge; one of the staffers passed up a note. When he unfolded it, it was Blair's handwriting. *Who is the woman on the right? She keeps staring at you.*

He pocketed it, then changed his mind. Wrote, *Knew her in Dr. Szerenci's class. You met her at vice president's house. Tennessee congresswoman.* Folded it, and held it behind his back until someone took it.

MRS. MACLAY. Back to you, Captain Lenson. Your actions vis-à-vis the Israeli counterstrike. That is the crux of the matter we want to get to.

CAPTAIN LENSON. Yes, ma'am. To cut to the bottom line, we detected the Israeli launch, and I took it under fire and destroyed it.

MR. PARKS. Without authorization.

CAPTAIN LENSON. Under the guidance provided in my orders. Specifically, the directive to safeguard civilian populations.

MR. PARKS. You were aware we were at war with Iraq?

CAPTAIN LENSON. With respect, sir, I understood we were engaged in regime change. This did not, in my view, change the intent of the orders.

MRS. MACLAY. All right. I think we have clarified Captain Lenson's view of the matter, as the commander on the scene. If I understand correctly, his position is that he made that decision based on his written rules of engagement. What we are concerned with here is, first, if he actually followed those rules, and, second, if so, whether those guidelines are sufficiently transparent and inclusive so as to avoid having our commanders subject to having to reinterpret them at short notice. Believe me, we here do not enjoy having to second-guess our military commanders. That is far from our intent. I would like now to have, first, Dr. Hui's, then Admiral Niles's position on those two questions. After that, if Dr. Szerenci has anything he would like to contribute, the subcommittee would be glad to have his input as well.

DR. HUI. Madam Chairman, you are entering upon questions of national security, questions as to the strategic employment of certain new weapons, that go to the heart of our alliance relationships, commitments outside my portfolio. As scientists, we can comment on the technical aspects of developing antiballistic systems. But you are asking a policy question that needs to be addressed at the military command level.

MRS. MACLAY. Your response is noted. Admiral Niles, it seems like the buck is on your desk.

ADMIRAL NILES. Thank you, Madam Chairman. I will answer both questions. First, Captain Lenson made, perhaps not the only possible decision he could logically derive from his guidance, but still, a rational decision under conditions of great pressure. Would I have made that same decision? Possibly not. But it is justifiable under the terms of his orders.

The answer to your second question will be unsatisfactory, perhaps. It has to do with the latitude one allows commanders in combat. As you recall, I began with the comment that Navy tradition allows its commanding officers considerable leeway in how they fight their ships. It is possible that his rules of engagement should have specified that they did not mean for him to forestall acts of war by our allies. However, that, in my view, would be a mistake.

MR. PARKS. That is a less than satisfactory answer, Admiral.

ADMIRAL NILES. Then I will have to say that if a more detailed guidance is necessary, it properly needs to come from the secretary of defense. Inasmuch as it concerns a conflict between our commitments to an ally, and relevant sections of UN treaty and international law, it should be studied at the highest political level.

MRS. MACLAY. All right, thank you, Admiral. Dr. Szerenci: you represent that highest political level, as the national security adviser to the president. We would be glad to hear your opinion.

DR. SZERENCI. With all due respect, ma'am, this is a question we are debating within the administration. I would not care to vouchsafe a personal opinion until we have had time to exercise due diligence and take legal counsel.

However, I would like to point out that the very fact we are able to have a debate like this—to discuss whether the United States should exercise some sort of international police power, to abort or strike down any ballistic attack or counterattack, by whatever country—is a source of considerable deterrent effect.

Deeper than this, however, lies a question of the limits of national power. Let's move past whether this officer acted rightly or wrongly, to a broader issue. I have heard the idea advanced that if we have technology to prevent a strike, we are bound by international law to stop it, irrespective of its origin. Certain quarters are even calling this—to Captain Lenson's outrage, I feel sure—the "Lenson Doctrine," and calling for its adoption as policy.

Though such a policy might be superficially appealing, I can hardly imagine a more dangerous course. It would place the United States in the position of an officer of the law on the most dangerous corners of the world, but without the legitimacy of that corner policeman. The only way to legitimize such a mission would be under the aegis of the United Nations; and this is unacceptable to large portions of our public. Also, many of our closest allies have or are developing such missile systems, for defensive purposes. Finally, it would require massive investments in equipment, sensors, and manpower. As the funding authority for our forces, Congress should tread especially carefully here.

Thank you for the opportunity to state my position.

MRS. MACLAY. Thank you, Dr. Szerenci. For the
    insight into geopolitical realities, and also for
    the reminder that we fund the armed forces.
DR. SZERENCI. I apologize, ma'am.
MRS. TREHERNE. Madam Chairman?
MRS. MACLAY. The chair recognizes Congress-
    woman Treherne as a guest of the committee.

Dan sat erect, skin prickling with a foretaste of
storm. Treherne's cheeks were flushed bright red. Her
hair looked as if she hadn't combed it. Niles beckoned
an aide to his side and whispered into his ear. Szerenci
sat frowning, twiddling a gold mechanical pencil.

MRS. TREHERNE. It seems to me that an important
    part of all this is being left out. That is, does
    everyone realize certain things about this
    man—Lenson?
MRS. MACLAY. Can the congresswoman please
    expand on her statement?
MRS. TREHERNE. I will be happy to do so. I have
    known this . . . officer for many years, and
    frankly, I am astonished his likes are still tol-
    erated in our armed forces. I'm sitting here lis-
    tening to this list of his medals and all this
    praise, but the truth is, this man is a closet pac-
    ifist. He was closely associated with antiwar
    elements in this city, including the radical
    Dorothy Day House, home of the convicted
    saboteur Carl Haneghan and the Griffiss Four.
    How did such a man get promoted? Is the sub-

committee going to take his anti-American activities into account?

MR. PARKS. These are surprising allegations. If true, they are serious indeed.

MRS. TREHERNE. They are both true and serious. They point to a dangerous penetration of peace elements, elements that desire the weakening and defeat of the United States, into our national defense. What exactly is Lenson advocating? I think Dr. Szerenci hit the nail on the head. Nothing less than turning our armed forces into some sort of Gestapo that enforces the will of the United Nations around the world, ending in tyranny.

"This woman knows you?" Niles whispered from behind a large hand. "She's drunk."

MRS. MACLAY. Admiral Niles, were you aware of such activities on the part of Mr. Lenson, Captain Lenson, before his being placed in command?

ADMIRAL NILES. Ma'am, I have known Daniel V. Lenson since he was a junior officer. I believe that at one time he dated a woman who was involved in those circles. However, he has rendered sterling service in very demanding circumstances. I have never believed all leaders are cast from the same mold, or that one step out of line, as long as it's for praiseworthy reasons, renders an officer unfit for command.

MRS. TREHERNE. Is that so, Admiral? Then he's pulled the wool over your eyes, that's for sure. Let me ask him one question. Lenson. One direct question.

MR. LA BLANC. Really, this is going beyond the prerogatives of a guest of the subcommittee. Did we come here to conduct a witch hunt, or to examine policy?

MRS. MACLAY. I rather agree, but in the interests of clarification, I would tend to let the congresswoman ask her single question of the witness. One only.

MRS. TREHERNE. Very good. Captain Lenson, then.

CAPTAIN LENSON. Yes, Congresswoman.

MRS. TREHERNE. You are in command of a ship that has these antimissile missiles. We, the Americans, launch a missile that's headed for an enemy population center. Not a military installation. A city. Will you shoot that down? Yes or no?

Dan took a deep breath. Beside him Niles was still as a mountain. Szerenci's proton-beam stare was scorching him from the opposite side. The national security adviser hissed, "Of course you wouldn't. Just say so." And Blair, no doubt, was glaring at his back.

MRS. MACLAY. Captain Lenson? Will you respond to the question?

CAPTAIN LENSON. To my knowledge, attacks on population centers are not part of our war planning.

ADMIRAL NILES. If I may? This is a speculative question based on a highly unlikely hypothetical. It's unfair to pose this as some kind of litmus test, without first providing the ROEs and guidance from higher authority we are discussing in this subcommittee.

MRS. TREHERNE. But we attacked cities in World War II. If we do it again, whose side will you be on, Captain Lenson? I ask once more, yes or no: would you shoot down our own missile?

DR. SZERENCI. I must protest. I understand this is closed session. But this type of discussion, on the record in any way . . . if made public, it could seriously compromise our deterrent posture.

MRS. TREHERNE. I see he's avoiding the question. Hiding behind his superiors. Or is he taking the Fifth?

Dan sat with his head propped on his right hand. *Answer the question, then shut up . . . and, by the way, don't make news.* Unfortunately, it wasn't turning out that straightforwardly. Each second seemed to stretch out even longer than it had when a missile had been burning its way down toward *Savo Island*. And only flawed engineering, or too-hasty assembly, had resulted in its not tearing through steel and flesh to explode at last deep inside her hull. He'd put his crew's life on the line, to defend others. Just like any cop on the street, any day, in any city.

There had to be rules. But there had to be something above, or behind, the rules of the job, too.

A poke and a note: *Don't answer this bitch. Don't fall for her tricks.* Blair's handwriting again.

But he couldn't just sit here. That would be admitting her accusations. Hiding behind silence.

CAPTAIN LENSON. I will answer the congress-woman's question.

MRS. TREHERNE. Good, at long last.

CAPTAIN LENSON. In the circumstances you cite, such a weapon would have to have been launched in defiance of established U.S. policy: that we limit collateral damage, that we don't target enemy populations as such. Therefore, the answer is: yes, I would shoot it down.

MRS. TREHERNE. You see? He'd sell us out, based on some kind of skewed personal softhearted-ness. What good are our weapons, when we have men like this in charge? There's a rotten-ness here. A lack of commitment to the prin-ciples that made this country what it is. And it goes very deep, into all kinds of—

MRS. MACLAY. The congresswoman is out of order. This is not the occasion for a stump speech. I would like to return to the issue at hand: de-fining national-level antimissile policy. Mrs. Treherne, I must ask you to leave.

Dan adjusted his tie, feeling sweat trickle under his dress blues, as Sandy Cottrell Treherne fired a last venomous parting glance down at him. She rose unsteadily, nearly knocking her chair over, and tottered off. He eased a breath out, conscious that every word they'd traded was now part of the record. He caught Niles's glance, resting on him like a lead carapace; Szerenci's elevated eyebrows, regretful shake of the head. The junior staffers stared with wide-eyed horror. Only Blair regarded him levelly; then, after a moment, winked and grinned.

MR. LA BLANC. Should we perhaps strike that exchange from the record?

MRS. MACLAY. I think it serves a useful purpose. Let's leave it. But it does seem that the executive branch needs to devote more attention to the guidance furnished to commanding officers in the field. Now, returning to funding of an additional increment—remember?—we will take a short adjournment, after which we will hear on the topic from the deputy undersecretary of defense for strategy, plans, and forces.

The gavel came down. Sucking air bereft of oxygen, Dan hoisted himself to his feet. His neck felt as if someone had been mining for silver between his cervical vertebrae. A worried murmur rose from the back of the hearing room. Edging between the chairs, he caught Niles's brooding glance as the admiral slipped a small object into his cheek, where it bulged. An Atomic Fireball, no doubt. Dan cleared his throat. "Um, hope I didn't screw the pooch, there."

Niles said heavily, "You were doing reasonably well until that woman started holding your feet to the fire. It would've been better to obfuscate, Lenson. Lay a little smoke and sneak away. Didn't the murder board tell you . . ."

"Don't make news. I tried not to, sir."

Blair slid through the crowd. She patted his back. Szerenci leaned in to shake his hand and offer a consoling word before heading for the door. It was like a party breaking up, almost.

"So what happens now?" Dan asked Niles.

The admiral sighed. He started away, shaking his head, then looked back. "You know, I think keeping you out of Washington was a good idea."

II

INTO THE
LABYRINTH

5

The Red Sea

The helicopter ride out was hot and smoky, the rising sun baleful on a bloody horizon. As they slid into position over the green-and-white turbulence of the wake, Dan reached for a handhold. Ever since he'd seen one explode in midair, helos made him nervous. From the cockpit, Ray "Strafer" Wilker glanced back, and mimed pulling his seat belt tighter.

Red Hawk 202, *Savo Island*'s SH-60, dropped from the sky in a weave that left Dan's semicircular canals tumbling. Some kind of evasive maneuver, but why execute it now? The violet line of land off to starboard was Egypt. Friendly territory, last he'd heard. Though in this part of the world, one year's enemy could be the next's ally.

A powerful argument for a navy that could shift its positions within days; off one coast one week, but thousands of miles away the next.

That was happening now. *Savo* was redeploying, part of an unannounced, yet undeniable, pivot of force eastward. Below the helo, the cruiser's stern came into view. The white circle-and-cross of the landing pad grew. The nose tipped up and the turbines whined, husbanding power for an emergency waveoff. Was the crisis both Niles and Szerenci had warned him about coming to pass? Probably not. There'd always be threats, and rumors of war. Nothing to do but be ready, as best he could.

But *was* he? Sandy Treherne hadn't seemed to think so.

Not for the first time, he wondered if he was really the guy for this job. His shiphandling was above average. And he was pretty sure he could fight the ship to her limits in a multithreat air-surface-subsurface scenario. But the great names they'd read about at Annapolis—Nelson, Jones, Farragut, Spruance, Nimitz—hadn't gone in for much self-questioning, at least according to the biographies. "Don't give up the ship." "Damn the torpedoes." They'd known exactly what to do, and had been utterly determined to do it. Gut fighters, bruisers, eager to close for the kill.

Survivor guilt, a civilian psychiatrist had called it. Maybe. Sometimes the faces of the dead, and their screams, startled him awake in the depths of the night. Had Farragut and Nimitz heard those screams? Did every commander have to wall off this self-doubt, and buckle the iron mask of command tight over the human features beneath?

A double thump, a lurch, and they were down. He

unbuckled the stinky cranial, checked that his piss-cutter was tucked in his belt, and grabbed his brief-case. Actually, Blair's; she'd given it to him, saying she needed a new one and he might as well replace his battered antique. Sunlight cut a rectangle from the fuselage. Wilker yelled something unintelligible and pointed to the exit. Dan groped his way down the wire that lowered the access ladder to the rough gray nonskid.

Into brilliant light, equatorial heat like a stoked furnace, a dusty tan sky pureed by whirling blades; in his nose the hot blast of ship exhaust, turbine exhaust; sandy grit in his teeth. And bent forward, advancing to meet him, Cheryl Staurulakis's chunky figure in coveralls and flight deck boots. "Welcome back, Captain," she shouted.

"Good to *be* back."

"Let's get out of this heat. Captain Racker's waiting for you in the wardroom." Making a keep-'em-turning twirl of her index to Strafer, she turned away toward the hangar, her blocky little rear end beckoning him on.

They had iced tea and day-old upside-down cake in the wardroom. The air was so icy he shivered. Wickie Racker, Jenn Roald's chief of staff, nodded amiably and stood. They were both O-6s; Racker was numerically senior, but Dan's decorations seemed to even them up. Racker didn't look reluctant to leave. As they shook hands he said, "Crew'll be glad to see you. How'd your testimony go?"

Dan shrugged. "Well enough I'm back, I guess."

"Let's be grateful for that. Some tea? This isn't bad."

Dan took the glass the XO poured, and sucked down half before coming up for breath. Staurulakis was saying, "Bird's on deck for a hot refuel, but the longer we wait, the farther they'll have to fly to get back."

"I'm packed. Dan, any questions?"

"Just, what's changed while I've been gone? Cheryl, you said on the phone we completed the rearm."

She handed him a clipboard and a Hydra, the intraship radio they used when the J-phones weren't convenient, and sometimes when they were. "Yes sir. Here are the eight o'clock reports, combat systems weapons inventory, and this morning's DSOTs and engineering reports. Three hundred and thirty-eight bodies including the air det. Chief engineer reports indications of water in the CRP; otherwise engineering's green. Inertial navigation was down yesterday, but repaired this morning. Captain's mast is scheduled this afternoon, unless you'd rather postpone."

"Might as well hold it now, while we're in transit. Current orders? Remember, I've been out of the loop."

"Proceed east, refuel in Djibouti, join up with TF 151 near Hormuz. Past that, participate in Malabar exercises and Hash Highway patrol ops in the western Indian Ocean. Then possibly Deep Saber."

He nodded. Djibouti was a routine refuel. Malabar was a multinational exercise he'd refereed before as a rider. Deep Saber would be new, an antiproliferation exercise out of Singapore. But nothing in this part of the world could be counted on to proceed as scheduled.

Which Racker confirmed when he added, "You should know, if you haven't already heard, the Iranians are threatening to close the strait again, over Yemen. I know, what else is new, but there it is."

"Okay. Thanks. Cheryl, when's our next self-defense drill? Damage-control-team training? We've got a couple of slow days before the Arabian Sea. Let's be sure we're up to speed." Racker cleared his throat and Dan swung to him. "Sorry, Wickie—you're still officially in charge."

"Not much to add. Ready to relieve?"

"I relieve you, sir."

"I stand relieved, sir."

With that handshake, those ritual words, proffered on U.S. Navy quarterdecks for over two hundred years, command had officially passed. He felt, almost physically, the weight of his ship descend once more. Whatever she accomplished or failed at was now his responsibility, and his alone. It was sobering, but at the same time, exhilarating. No, that wasn't the word either. There actually wasn't a word for how command felt. He coughed into a fist, the dust irritating his esophagus. "XO, I really should go back and see him off, but can you accompany Captain Racker aft, make sure he gets off okay? I want to get my bearings in CIC. While we have a breathing space."

The Combat Information Center smelled like an ice cave in some far northern glacier during the season of darkness. He shivered; his khakis were still soaked with sweat from the helo ride. But the electronics liked it cold.

In the dim light four rows of consoles, about half of them manned at the moment, channeled data to the four full-color large-screen displays, LSDs, that glowed to port. Dan strolled to the padded leather reclining chair stenciled CO and nodded to the lieutenant and the chief at the command desk. They murmured "Captain" but didn't rise. As was proper, since they were on watch.

His priorities were to operate, navigate, and communicate, in that order. He had to maintain both the ability and the situational awareness to fight and defend his ship at all times. If weapons, engines, or generators were degrading, he needed to regain those capabilities, to restore his warfighting capability.

He also couldn't do that if he collided with one of the scores of other ships that transited this international waterway each day. Along with safe seakeeping, he had to reach his next objective in a timely fashion. Getting where he was supposed to be, when he was tasked to be there, dovetailed with "operate." This was mainly a function of the engineering systems, though position-keeping and bridge watchstanding also factored in.

Finally, he had to communicate. Keep the crew, ships in company, and his bosses informed as to his location, status, and intentions, while not screwing the pooch in one of the many ways ships' captains had come up with in four thousand years of sailing the high seas, from being swallowed by Charybdis to inadvertently crossing some new UN redline.

He leaned against his chair, examining the screens

as printer paper fluttered from the air vents. The sub-freezing air always blew down the back of his neck, and after several hours in here, his headaches would be excruciating. The sailors had taped the paper to the vents to deflect the cold breeze away from their consoles.

The air display, with so many winking green lines pointing in every direction it looked like a surface of cracked ice, was superimposed on an outline map of the Red Sea. It was slaved to the satellite-downlinked Global Command and Control System. GCCS—usually pronounced "Geeks"—coordinated U.S. land, sea, and air forces, all the way from national command authority, to component commands, right down to every division, air wing, and ship. Updated and overlaid by data from *Savo*'s Aegis, the screen displayed air and surface activity from the south Med to the tip of the Horn of Africa. A second screen had the local surface picture up, fed from the radar and nav system. Read-outs showed each contact's course and speed, and predicted its closest point of approach to *Savo*. A glance reassured him they were clear. He checked the fathom-eter readout, and at last gave the helo "green deck"—the clearance to launch.

The 1MC crackled on, and four bells sounded. *"Captain, United States Navy, departing."*

The third screen toggled to video, a camera point-ing down from the 04 level at the helo deck, from which Red Hawk was lifting off. Racker was on his way. Above the displays, text readouts presented the status of the various combat systems, a weapons inventory, daily radio call signs, and computer status summaries.

The older displays were flickering green on black or orange on black. The newer ones had larger screens, in full color.

Dan leaned on the back of the reclining chair that would be his during general quarters. The days of eyeballing the horizon for an enemy sail, of hours spent maneuvering for advantage before carronades or turreted guns roared, were long gone. *Savo* had a little armor—hardened steel, lined with a Kevlar layer against spalling—but antiship warheads would punch through it. If an enemy ever got within sight, Dan would most likely already be dead, his crew blasted apart, drowned, roasted alive, or sliced into bloody bulgogi by flying metal.

A twenty-first-century cruiser's main mission was to knock down all the incoming weapons possible, until her magazines were empty. Then, position herself between the carrier and the threat, and soak up the final weapons with her own steel. Take the hit, protect the higher-value target . . .

"Hey, Dan. Good to see you back."

He turned to Donnie Wenck's blond cowlick and slightly mad blue eyes. The chief held up a green wool sub-style sweater. "Wanna borrow? Cold as the ass end of Pluto in here."

"It's 'Captain,' Donnie, or 'Skipper.' Not 'Dan.' "

"Sorry, sir, keep forgetting. Wait a minute, I heard something on the 1MC. Racker's gone, yeah? I didn't like that guy. Too fucking friendly."

"I don't need your opinions on the outgoing CO, Chief. How's the system?" Wenck, who'd come to the ship from the Tactical Analysis Group along with Dan, was the "SPY chief," in charge of maintenance and operation of the massive radars that guided her weapons.

Wenck turned back to the Aegis console, and a chubby-faced girl blinked vaguely up at Dan. "Hey, Petty Officer Terranova," he said.

His lead radar systems controller turned a dial, and the familiar five-pops-a-second audio of the outgoing beam echoed like a query from some extragalactic civilization. She tapped her keyboard, and the raw video came up on the rightmost screen. An orange, slowly fading beam, clicking, not sweeping, in a clockwise march across the face of East Africa. There was the Rift Valley, where the first human had made the first weapon. . . . She muttered, "Hinky CFA, and I'm gonna have ta replace one of the switch tubes."

Wenck said, "ALIS is being a hooker, as usual. Otherwise, you got about 98 percent. You know that Aegis math—one plus one equals four."

"Chill water system still tight?" The chief nodded, and Dan lowered his voice. "And has Lieutenant Singhe throttled back on pissing off the goat locker?"

Wenck shrugged, as if talking about human beings bored him. Dan lingered for a while, then undogged the door and climbed two flights of metal ladders up to the bridge level.

Brightness and heat. Scarlet dust fine as mercury oxide coated the chart table, the top of the steering console, the objectives of the binoculars. Outside the windows, the green sea, flat and calm today, and the purple land far off. Not a single cloud. Two ships in sight, a tanker, low in the water, and a high-piled container-ship farther off, both blurred by the invisible dust hanging in the air, the shimmer of heat boiling off the water. Both stern to, which agreed with the radar picture.

Matt Mills and Noah Pardees turned to salute. Mills, the tall lieutenant, had joined them from Jenn Roald's staff. Pardees, languid and almost too thin to be seen sideways, was the first lieutenant, in charge of the deck division. A golf fanatic, he'd practiced his putting on the pier every evening in Crete. "Welcome back, Captain. Glad to see you again," Mills said.

"Good to be here, guys." Dan looked past them, inspecting the horizon. "Keep your lookouts alert. Some of these little dhows are just about transparent to radar, and a lot of containerships go through here. We don't want to hit anything that fell overboard."

Pardees murmured an aye aye, and Dan wandered the bridge, greeting the helmsman, the quartermaster, the boatswain, the junior officer of the deck, and the gunner's mates on the remote operating consoles for the chain guns. "Good to have you back, sir," they murmured, though none seemed terrifically enthusiastic about it.

He understood why. He went out on the bridge wing and checked aft. Then gazed down into green water churned to white froth, listening to the steady roar of the bow wave as *Savo*'s stem ripped through it at twenty knots. Only then did he hoist himself into the leather command chair, grinning. With the drill schedule he'd directed, hardly anyone would get enough sleep in the next few days. They all knew by now; the word flew around a ship like telepathy. But a busy crew, even if they bitched, were happier than one with time on their hands. And far better a trained and tired crew on the screens and damage-control parties, than a rested, sloppy one.

A message he'd gotten loud and clear watching his own COs in the past, both those who'd driven hard and those who'd let the reins dangle.

"Coffee, Captain?" The gangling, pimply-faced Longley, holding a tray as if tempted to throw it overboard. Skippers no longer had stewards, per se, but they did usually have a culinary specialist to look after them if operations drove hard. He'd seen some men abuse the relationship, using the seaman as a personal servant. The essential thing was that he never show Longley any favoritism. So far it seemed to be working, but not because of any excessive effort on the kid's part. The steward looked as rumpled and sloppy as usual in a stained white mess coat. "Chili dogs today. You gonna want lunch up here?"

"Let's say yes for now. Especially if traffic picks up."

"I set your shit, I mean your stuff, up in the at-sea cabin. And your computer."

"That's good. How you been, Longley? Pull any liberty in Crete?"

"Went to the zoo. That be all, sir?"

"Yeah. I mean, no. Is the shower still—"

"It's unfucked, sir. Just let the hot run for a minute or so."

Bart Danenhower stepped up next. The chief engineer

was big and bulky, with shaggy Hagrid eyebrows. Fittingly, he was a fan of the Potter books, leaving them in the engine spaces and offices. The CHENG wasn't brilliant, but he worked hard and told the truth. They had a long conversation about the controllable reversible pitch propellers, which had some kind of leak or condensation no one had ever been able to locate the source of. "We change the filters, though, it goes away," Danenhower finished. Dan glanced behind him to see who was next. The ship's medic, HMC Grissett. "Oh yeah," Danenhower added. "We still got that bug going around. I'll let Doc Grissy bring you up to speed on that."

The chief corpsman said that the sickness among the crew, which had gone away during their time in Crete, had surfaced again. "Got three at sick call just this morning, same symptoms. Dry cough. Chills and fever, spikes to a hundred and four. Muscle pain, lethargy, malaise; diarrhea. Even the people who recover, they feel like shit. Mopey. Slow. There's some kind of ongoing syndrome here."

"What the hell? We replaced the filters. Scrubbed down all the ductwork. Bart?"

Danenhower spread his hands. "We did it thorough, Cap'n. If it was in there, it's dead."

"But it's not just up forward anymore," Grissett added.

Dan rubbed his face. "The anthrax inoculations?"

"Bethesda says they're safe. Anyway, a reaction to that wouldn't surface weeks, months later like this."

Was his ship itself somehow infected? Case after

case, fever, chills, lassitude . . . one man had even died, in forward berthing, without a mark on him. "Okay, we're not sitting still any longer. Draft another message for Bethesda. Info our chain of command. Outline the problem and the corrective action we took, and ask for immediate assistance on scene. Hand-carry that up through the XO. Clear?"

"Yessir."

Mast was scheduled for 1330. Longley brought chili dogs and cold fries up on a tray and Dan ate looking out over the sea, observing a white sail far off. *Savo,* the tanker, and the containership were maintaining nearly identical speeds, churning along down the coast. Sudan was coming up to starboard, and he checked on the security teams, 25mms, and port and starboard machine guns. No boarder threat had been predicted, but it was wise to be ready. Saudi Arabia slid past to port, tan and violet as the sun glared down and the very sea glowed and shimmered with heat.

At 1300 Cheryl and "Sid" Tausengelt, the command master chief, came up to discuss the mast case. Tausengelt was older than Dan, small and lean, with receding hair and a deep-harrowed, leathery face. Staurulakis handed Dan the defendant's performance record, then briefed. Arthur Peeples was an MMSN, a machinist's mate seaman. He was accused under Article 134.

"Remind me."

"Basically, indecent language, Captain."

Dan suppressed his first response, which was that

dinging a sailor for indecent language was like . . . anyway, that was Oldthink. "Uh, okay. Elements of the charge?"

Staurulakis read, " 'One: That the accused orally or in writing communicated to another person certain language. Two: That such language was indecent. Three: That, under the circumstances, the conduct of the accused was to the prejudice of good order and discipline in the armed forces or was of a nature to bring discredit upon the armed forces.' "

"All right, three elements: that he said it, it was indecent, and it impaired discipline. Got it." Dan leaned back, considering. Each week the command master chief, Tausengelt, convened a disciplinary review board in the chief's mess. The DRB's recommendations went to the XO, who conducted an inquiry and decided either to dismiss the case or to forward it for the CO's nonjudicial punishment, or as the Navy had always called it, captain's mast. "Did he admit saying it, Master Chief? What was his defense?"

"Sir, he admitted saying it, but he told us at the DRB it was a joke. Also, that the words didn't mean anything."

"Yeah, I'm not exactly sure why this case had to come up to me," Dan told Staurulakis. "The way I read his records here, Peeples is a solid worker. A little rowdy ashore, but not enough to not rate a good-conduct stripe. Don't we have some bilges somewhere that need scrubbing?" When she didn't answer he added, "What exactly did he say?"

She looked off to starboard, squinting against the

glare. "He called his supervising petty officer a 'hucking skunt.'"

"Um . . . a what?"

She repeated the phrase, deadpan. Dan stared at her, then at Tausengelt. The master chief shrugged microscopically and averted his eyes.

"So, I assume his petty officer is female."

"Correct. MM3 Scharner."

"And this is symptomatic of something ongoing?"

"Peeples has a rep for blowing off authority," the exec said. "Especially if that authority has a double X chromosome."

"Okay, I guess . . . But what worries me is element two. They could reverse us on the grounds 'hucking skunt' is not actually indecent language."

"Basically, he made that point, yessir," Tausengelt murmured.

"It was intended as indecent," Staurulakis said, but as if she was advancing it as an argument, not an assertion. "Therefore it's indecent. If he calls the master chief here a rucking fetard, is that indecent?"

"It's certainly offensive," Dan granted.

"And prejudicial to discipline, if we let him get away with it," the officer of the deck put in. Noah Pardees had come on at eight bells, noon. Tall, laid-back, dark as any inhabitant of the land to starboard, he honchoed First Division, usually the roughest gang aboard ship. By all accounts, the boatswain's mates worshipped him. Dan and the XO stared at him. After a moment Pardees cleared his throat and strolled back to the far side, where he buried his face in the radar hood.

Dan's next question was, "If it's a sexual harassment thing, why aren't we charging him under Article 93?"

The exec said, "We considered that. But according to the UCMJ, you can't sexually harass someone senior to you. 'Any person subject to this chapter who is guilty of cruelty toward, or oppression or maltreatment of, any person *subject to his orders* shall be punished as a court-martial may direct.' I know, that doesn't really make sense, but the specifications and elements haven't caught up yet."

Dan checked his watch against the clock over the nav table. "Look, we convene in five minutes. I need a shower. This guy's a decent machinist. Possible career material. Bart's gonna be there to vouch for him, right? But they call masts 'delayed admin discharges' now. With nonjudicial punishment in his record, he's going to find it hard to get advanced. Or even to stay in, if his rate's overmanned."

"He should have thought of that before he called her names."

He looked away from the exec's flat gaze, sighing inwardly. Solomon would have shaken his head at some of the cases that came to mast. "Okay, let's go on down."

Ticos didn't have a space well suited to holding a legal proceeding. In port, he used the bridge, but that was impossible under way. The wardroom had been cleared, and a fresh tablecloth laid. Staurulakis had set up the varnished lectern at which Dan presided so that he would be backed by the large canvas of the Battle of

Savo Island that Tom Freeman, the artist, had donated to the ship. Dan ran down the laminated pages in the binder, making sure he had the names right. Checked the alignment of his ribbons on the fresh short-sleeved tropical white uniform. Glanced at the exec. She ran her eye up and down him, shoes to cap, and nodded. He cleared his throat. "Bring in the accused."

The master-at-arms, Chief Hoang Quoc "Hal" Toan, thrust the door open. "Accused: forward, *harch*. Right turn, *harch*. Accused . . . halt. Come to attention. Uncover . . . *two*."

They halted facing Dan, swaying with the very faint roll of the ship. Behind Dan stood Tausengelt and the exec. Behind the accused, others filed in: the injured party; the accused's division officer and department head; and, an unexpected addition, a dark-haired, dark-eyed woman so curvaceous it was hard to look away.

Lieutenant Amarpeet "Amy" Singhe. His strike officer, in charge of *Savo*'s offensive power. To his surprise, Singhe stepped up beside Scharner. Maybe he was imagining it, but he was pretty sure he could smell sandalwood even across the space between them.

There hadn't always been that much of it. Space, that is. After dark, in his at-sea stateroom, she'd leaned forward, explaining her plans to flatten the ship's hierarchy, modernize its management. He'd only just managed not to tumble her, he was fairly certain not unwillingly, onto his bunk.

He tore his attention off her breasts and focused on the tall, thin young man in front of him. He was white, as was his accuser, which removed one possible complication. At attention, but his eyelids drooped. His pale chin showed dark stubble. Haircut, within current regs. Shoes, polished. Whites, neat and clean. The fingers holding his cap next to his thigh were white too. With tension?

Dan said, "Seaman Arthur Peeples, you are suspected of committing the following violations of the Uniform Code of Military Justice: Article 134, in that you did use indecent language to a senior in your chain of command, to the prejudice of good order and discipline. You do not have to make any statement regarding the offense of which you are accused, and any statement may be used as evidence against you. Has the accused been notified of his rights?"

"Here, sir. Signed and witnessed." Staurulakis placed pages on the lectern.

"You are advised that a captain's mast is not a trial and that a determination here is not a conviction by a court of law. Further, you are advised that the formal rules that apply in courts-martial do not apply at mast." When Peeples nodded Dan held up the paper. "Is this your signature?"

"Yes sir."

"Do you understand this statement? And were your rights personally explained to you by the exec?"

A hesitation; then a firm "Yessir. I understand."

"All right, good." Dan gave it a beat; looked around the wardroom. Holding mast was the least favorite part of his job. Being judge, jury, and executioner. But he had a pretty good idea what punishment was in order here, or at least what the typical "award" was and thus what the crew would expect.

The purpose of mast wasn't justice. As Melville had made perfectly clear in *Billy Budd*. Discipline first, consistency second—no one liked a capricious captain, or one who played favorites.

Dan focused on the now-perspiring young face in front of him. "Peeples, it's essential we know exactly what happened, both from your point of view as well as that of your senior, Petty Officer Scharner.

"Now, both the chiefs and the XO felt her accusation warranted bringing you up before me. I will advise you personally that what is best for you right now is to come clean. Equivocate or lie, and life can get unpleasant very fast. Understand?"

A hesitation, then a nod. "All right," Dan said, trying for a friendlier tone. "Now what's your side of the story?"

"Well, sir . . . the petty officer, she always gives me the dirtiest jobs. I'm not sure why. I just came off watch, and I was tired, and I had the *Savo* crud—"

"The *what*?"

"That's what they call it, Captain. Anyway, we're shorthanded in the gang, and I'm headed for my rack when she tells me I've got to tear down the fucking . . . tear down the damn coolant pump. That's a twelve-, fourteen-hour job, tear down and rebuild. And she wants it by tomorrow morning. I said, how about Petty Officer Alonso, and she said, she's busy. And that she doesn't want any back talk, she just wants that pump back on the line. I admit, I lost my temper. But I didn't call her what she said I called her."

"What did she say you called her?" Dan asked him.

"A fucking cunt," Peeples murmured.

Dan cleared his throat, trying hard not to laugh out loud. "The charge sheet doesn't say that. It quotes you as calling her a, um, hucking skunt. Is that accurate, Seaman?"

"Uh, yessir, that's pretty much accurate."

"Is it, or not?"

"Uh, yessir, that's pretty much it. That's what I said, sir."

A beam of sun leaned in the window and explored the carpet. Dust motes milled through it. Sand, from the deserts of Arabia, the wastes of the Sudan. Was what he was doing here any more important than the milling of those motes? "What exactly is a 'skunt,' Seaman Peeples?"

"Sir?"

"You called her that. What is it? I am unfamiliar with the terminology." God, he sounded so stuffy.

"A skunt's like a low-class, um, bitch, sir. Sort of like a skank."

"So there is such a word?"

"I don't know if it's in the dictionary. . . ." Peeples glanced at Tausengelt, as if for corroboration, but the senior enlisted's visage was iron.

"Let's set that aside for the moment, and focus on the fact that you intended it as an insult. Is that correct?"

This was the come-to-Jesus moment Dan had calculated on, and to his relief Peeples rose to it. How does a fish get caught? He opens his mouth. The seaman said, shamefacedly, "Yessir."

"And it referred to her, specifically, as a female?"

Again the seaman said, "Yes sir," looking at the deck.

Dan said briskly, "If you intended it that way, the specific wording, seems to me, is beside the point. Petty Officer Scharner, anything to add? Specifically, on the assertion you habitually award him the dirtiest jobs?"

The petty officer said, "He's junior guy in the work center, Captain."

"Chief McMottie. Any substance to the accused's statement that Petty Office Scharner habitually awards the scuzziest jobs to male crew members?"

The senior engineering chief said, "Not to my knowledge, Captain. But we all had to work long hours, there in Crete."

Dan polled the division officer, then Danenhower. Neither supported Peeples, though Danenhower added he was a conscientious watchstander and equipment operator. "He does have a smart mouth on him, but when he signs off on a maintenance job, it's done right."

Dan asked the exec, for form's sake, if this was Peeples's first appearance at mast. She said it was.

He looked at his notes, letting silence fall, to give the appearance of deliberation. A chipping hammer clattered somewhere far aft. To dismiss the case wouldn't help discipline. He could assign extra military instruction, which would make the kid work extra hours. But that didn't mean much when you were pulling eighteen-hour days anyway. Plus, usually the chiefs or the exec awarded EMI; it was below the CO's pay grade. And restriction to the ship didn't mean squat when they were under way.

The harshest punishment he could impose was thirty days' restriction and extra duty, reduction in rank to seaman recruit, and dock half Peeples's pay for three months. Any of that could be suspended, and he'd normally suspend the bust and pay. This way he could give the guy a second chance, and if he screwed up again, he knew he'd get hammered.

The key was consistency, and Dan cleared his throat. "In previous cases, my predecessor as CO awarded hefty punishments for violating this article. And rightly so. This being my first time holding mast aboard *Savo*, I don't see any reason to veer . . . I mean, vary from that precedent. However, as this is Seaman Peeples's first time at mast, there may be grounds to—"

"Excuse me, Captain. If I may?"

He glanced up, taken aback. "Lieutenant Singhe?"

Singhe took a step forward, leading Scharner with her. "With all due respect, sir, the typical punishment will not suffice in this case."

Dan frowned. "Explain why not."

"This isn't just a case of a seaman mouthing off to his petty officer. However phrased, the fact remains he called her, let's speak plainly here, a 'fucking cunt.' It typifies a widespread and growing problem on this ship: a lack of respect for authority, when that authority happens to be female. We need to make it crystal clear the command supports its female members."

The wardroom suddenly seemed a lot quieter. Dan

looked from her, to Peeples, to Staurulakis. The exec's eyes were narrowed, but she wasn't disagreeing. Then back to Singhe. "Are you acting as some sort of prosecutor here, Lieutenant? Because there's no such position at a captain's mast."

Singhe said, "I'm acting as a spokesperson for Petty Officer Scharner and the other women in the crew. Since no one else seems to be standing up for them."

"There's no position for female spokesperson, or ombudswoman, or whatever you want to call it." Dan curbed his angry tone too late, but the comment about "no one else" had stung. He said more evenly, "I'll take your comments under advisement for the command policy board."

"Aye aye, sir," she said, stepping back. Lifting that goddesslike profile, widening her eyes and lifting her gaze, as if calling on some higher authority as witness.

He looked down again, seething. Singhe had wrecked his plan. He'd been going to award Peeples restriction and dock him three months' pay, and not suspend any of it, making clear that the reason was the slur he'd used wasn't just a general insult, but a specifically sexual slur. But if he did that now, he'd look as if he'd given in to Singhe, caved to feminist pressure. While if he went easy, it would look as if he were supporting any male crewman who felt resentful about having a female boss.

Damn it. . . . He cleared his throat again and rasped, "I just came from commissioning a destroyer named after a woman who died under my command. USS *Cobie Kasson*. Any idea we're not supporting our female members is flat wrong." He gave it a beat, then went back to the formula. "Are there any more witnesses you'd like to call, or additional statements or evidence you would like to present?"

Peeples shook his head, looking enervated, but beside Dan, Tausengelt stirred. The senior enlisted adviser growled, "Captain, a comment."

"Speak your piece, Master Chief."

"Basically, I agree with what you said and all, the command policy about supporting female members. But on the other side, it's not really fair to try this kid on how politically correct he is when he loses his temper. Or give him some kind of extra punishment because of it."

Dan sighed again, inwardly. Now he had Tausengelt, McMottie, and the chief master-at-arms, the three most influential chiefs on the ship, glaring at Singhe and Scharner, while beside Dan, Staurulakis was staring at him expectantly. He harrumphed and they all looked at him. "I appreciate everyone's input. After due consideration, I am imposing the following punishment: sixty days' restriction to the ship and half pay for three months, the half pay to be suspended for a period of six months. To clarify this, Peeples, you'll serve the EMI and restriction. If you succeed in not repeating your offense for six months, your pay will not be docked. But if you screw up like this again, I'll revoke the suspension and your pay reduction will start then.

"I strongly advise you to take this opportunity to revise how you interact with your seniors. Petty Officer Scharner, you are reminded to exercise fairness and restraint in dealing with your juniors, just as you expect fairness from those above you in the chain of command." He paused, but got only weak "Yessirs" from them both. He snapped, "Dismissed."

"Accused: Cover. Ready . . . two. About *face*," said Toan. "Forward . . . *harch*."

When the door closed on them Dan snapped the binder shut and handed it to the exec. She looked remote. Singhe, angry. Danenhower, puzzled. The chiefs left quickly, speaking to none of the officers.

The chief engineer, still frowning, went to the sideboard and valved coffee into a heavy mug. "Uh, what just happened?" he muttered.

"You think that was a fair sentence, Bart?"

"For Peepsie? Oh, sure. Pretty much what they usually get, right? For a first-time fuckup. But what was all that from Amy?" He lowered his voice, glancing toward the exec. "And the XO nodding, agreeing with her?"

Dan didn't answer. He'd hoped this whole Singhe versus the Chief's Mess fight was over, but it looked like it was on again. He raised his voice. "Cheryl, we need to talk. About the exercises. We're heading into dangerous waters. I want us to be ready."

"Yes sir. Certainly, sir," his exec said, expressionless, gaze eluding his. She flipped her PDA open. "Let's see what we have planned."

6

The Gulf of Aden

Despite the wind, the clouds never seemed to move. Since dawn, they'd been visible only now and then through low plaques of fog that hugged the sea. Beyond them a burning sky should have belonged to some hellish planet much closer to the sun. Six- to eight-foot seas were locomotived by winds from the southwest of twenty knots, with gusts to thirty. The bulwark of the bridge wing that Dan leaned on was too hot to touch with bare skin. The arid wind spasmed his throat; after the icy air in CIC, the heat made his temples throb. Right now they were in one of the gaps in the fog. The blue sea rolled, streaked with foam but otherwise empty, for ten thousand yards in the direction they'd be firing.

He lowered the binoculars. "Check again with Combat."

"Combat confirms: range clear, both radar and visual."

"Very well." He coughed into a fist and screwed bright yellow foam plugs into his ear canals. "Batteries released."

The phone talker repeated the command, and the first rounds cracked out of the chain gun, followed by light gray smoke that blew aft as the ship left it behind. Dan followed the projectiles in the binoculars by the furrowed instantaneous trace they left, like a crease in reality itself. The target rocked and rolled amid blue swells, a lashup of empty oil drums and scrap dunnage daubed fluorescent orange. Gray-helmeted, life-jacketed, the gunner's mates took turns at the pedestal-mounted gun, fitting their shoulders to the yoke to trigger bursts of five to seven rounds. Spray fountained up, obscuring the target. He braced his elbows, watching. The 25mms seemed more accurate, or maybe just easier to aim, than the 50-cals. And the rounds would hit harder, though a .50 was nothing to sneeze at.

He lingered on the wing as control was shifted to the remote operating consoles, just inside the doors. The operators twitched joysticks, watching screens. This time the rounds perforated the target. Within seconds, as the white spray subsided, it rolled over and disappeared beneath the blue.

"Target destroyed."

"Very well. Come back to base course." Dan crossed the pilothouse to his chair, stowed his glasses, and climbed up. And once again, resumed flipping through, and worrying about, that morning's messages.

After a five-hour refueling stop in Djibouti, then exiting the Bab-el-Mendeb, *Savo* had reported in to

Commander, Task Force 151, the antipirate coalition that patrolled the Arabian Sea. Since then she'd been trolling the Gulf of Aden and east coast of Africa, what the Navy called the "internationally recognized transit corridor" or IRTC. Maritime Trade Operations was reporting dozens of attacks each month on commercial vessels, and not long before, a private yacht had been hijacked and four Dutch nationals killed. A Russian combat tug, patrolling off Socotra, had reported boarding and sinking a confirmed pirate. So far, though, no one on *Savo* had glimpsed Edward Teach, Johnny Sparrow, or indeed any pirates whatsoever.

Meanwhile, the Iranians were threatening again to close the Gulf to foreign, meaning Western, shipping. He reread the top message: a maritime advisory for vessels transiting the Strait of Hormuz, southern Arabian Gulf, and western Gulf of Oman. It warned about swarm attacks by the Revolutionary Guard Corps, or Pasdaran, an ideological force separate from the regular Iranian navy.

He fidgeted, annoyed. That was their mission. Not hanging out here inspecting sixty-foot fishing dhows. But the shortage of frigates, now that the Perrys had almost all been retired or given away, meant the Navy had to use high-value ships in low-value missions. "This saves money?" he muttered.

"Sir?" Max Mytsalo, the cherub-faced officer of the deck. He was new to the job, but so far, Dan liked the way he stood his watches. A little overanxious, but better that than bored.

"Nothing. Just talking to . . . nothing."

He caught the glances from around the pilothouse, and cursed. Exactly what he wanted them to pass around the ship: that the skipper was talking to himself. Still, their patrol area had been shifted farther east, closer to Socotra. Hormuz was only a thousand miles' steaming from there.

He was in his in-port cabin with the light off, trying to conduct a quick eyelid inspection, when the ship heeled in an unscheduled turn, superstructure creaking to a new rhythm. His eyes snapped open. Two seconds later the cabin J-phone and his Hydra went off simultaneously. He got to the radio first. "CO."

Pardees, for once sounding not totally carefree. *"Captain, got a report from a ro-ro in the IRTC. Shadowed by two boats acting in a suspicious manner. Now under attack with antitank grenades. Plots twenty miles to the east. Coming to course to intercept, increasing speed to flank."*

"Okay, good. Sound general quarters, surface action, and call away the boarding team. I'll be right up."

He leaned on the splinter shield, in life jacket, flash gear, and the gray helmet stenciled CO. The bridge team was buttoning up. Down on the main deck, the five-inch train warning bell began ringing.

"Chain guns, manned and ready."

"Phalanx in surface mode."

"Mount 51, manned and ready."

"Mount 52, manned and ready."

Pardees leaned out. "All stations manned and ready, Captain. Time: one minute, fifty-two seconds. Material condition Zebra set throughout the ship. Boarding team and boat crew manned and ready."

"Very well." Dan glanced aft, to a raised hand from the boatswain's mate chief, back by the boat falls. The RHIB was swung out; the boarding team, in combat gear, helmets, carrying shotguns and M16s, stood with duffels at their boots, swaying in unison as *Savo* rolled. It was rough for boat ops, but within the margin of acceptability.

First, though, he'd check these guys out visually. If they showed hostile intent, he'd deal with them out of range of the Kalashnikovs and RPGs that typically formed pirate armament hereabouts. He leaned on the coaming again, binoculars searching through the heat shimmer, the red haze. The wind was behind them, and their exhaust added to the seethe of the atmosphere. He hadn't caught sight of the pirates yet, though radar had two faint pips astern of their assumed quarry.

The tremendous squared-off blue-and-white box was slogging along at ten knots as the fog blew past it like a cavalcade of specters. Dan had talked to its bridge on channel 10, and had messaged MSCHOA, UKMTO Dubai, MIRLO, the NATO shipping center, and CTF 151 that he was going to the assistance of M/V *Mons Neptune,* a Japanese-owned, Caymans-flagged ro-ro. It was enormous, a supership at least a quarter mile long. Ro-ros—roll-on, roll-off—carried anything with wheels, though he guessed this one would be carrying gleaming new Toyotas and Hondas and Lexuses. The pirates would be more interested in what portables and cash they could steal from the crew or by breaking into the safe, as he'd observed off Ashaara, when he'd been deployed to help protect and rebuild that failing country.

"Small-boat contact. Two small boats," a quartermaster shouted from the flying bridge, above him. He was on the Big Eyes, huge pedestal-mounted binocs with objectives the size of dinner plates.

"Where away?"

"About zero-two-zero relative."

He refocused and caught one, then the other, as they rose on a swell. Just specks, through haze. But something odd . . . they were headed in different directions. "What's CIC say about their course and speed?"

"Wait one . . . sir, they hold them essentially DIW."

Dead in the water. Dan frowned. Not what you expected, if they were carrying out an attack. On the other hand, if they'd caught sight of *Savo Island,* they might be turning tail. "Bump her up to flank. Designate to guns, but weapons tight until I give the word."

Over the next ten minutes they made up so swiftly on the tossing boats that it was clear neither had way on. They grew into dark craft with complexly curved, lofty prows, not a bit like the high unwieldy dhows of the Gulf. No masts, and apparently no deckhouses either. The housings of outboard motors gleamed at their sterns, but cocked up, propellers dipping into the water as the bows rose and fell violently, throwing spray. At Dan's direction, Pardees made an upwind pass at five hundred yards, while the Big Eyes and Dan's own binoculars studied them. Five souls in one craft, six in the other. Bare-chested, dark-skinned men, in white turbans or headdresses. They waved frantically.

"Sucking us into range?" the exec said, beside him. The issue helmet was far too big on her and looked faintly silly. Her holstered 9mm looked less jolly, though.

Dan had been wondering the same thing, and fighting apprehension. This was how *Horn* had died, sucked in close to a small ship that had then, inexplicably, detonated into light too hellish for the human eye. How to separate emotion from logic, experience from fear? "Maybe. Noah, let's do another pass. No closer than two hundred yards."

"Aye aye, sir."

On the second pass Dan, on the flying bridge now, bent to peer through the mounted optics. He could see the crews now as well as if they were beside him. They looked emaciated and desperate. No weapons, but they could be lying in the ceiling boards, or otherwise concealed. The tanker had specifically mentioned an RPG being fired. According to his ROEs, he could take them under fire and sink them based solely on that.

He took a deep breath, aware he was asking men to run a risk. When he looked up, the clouds were fleeing across the sky, and a squall grayed the horizon to the southwest. "Cheryl, I want you in CIC. Maintain a three-sixty awareness while my head's in this situation.

And make sure we're taping from the gun cameras. Noah, park us upwind, and put the boat in the water."

Savo rolled two hundred yards off. As the gray rigid-hulled inflatable motored past, the first few heavy drops of cool rain spattered on the deck like thrown pebbles. Dan looked down. At young Max Mytsalo, the boat officer. SK3 Kaghazchi, their designated Farsi speaker, who'd admitted a few words of other local languages. Braced at the stern, Seaman Peeples. They were hanging on as the RHIB skipped across the waves, rising and falling on the swells, then altering course to circle the nearest boat. The whine of the engine dropped, and the RHIB fell from its plane and its bow wave rolled on without it. The hulls surged in off-rhythm, then, for the briefest moment, matched. At that moment the squall-line swept over *Savo* and they vanished in a downpour that cascaded all around Dan, cold as a mountain stream, wetting him to the skin.

The noise all but blotted out the next radio call. *"Matador, this is Matador One."*

Dan retreated into the signal bridge, clicked his Hydra as the windshield wipers flailed and jerked. The rain was noisy in here, too, and he turned the volume up. "What've you got, Gene?"

"Five skinnies. Extremely agitated. Screaming and crying. No guns I can see."

"Take up the floorboards. Conduct a thorough search. Look for ladders and grapnels, along with weapons. You got rain coming your way. We're in a heavy downpour right now."

"Not much to search, sir. Pretty bare bones. They might have dumped them overboard when they saw us coming."

That was possible. Or they might not have been armed at all. Dan kept his eyes on the other boat, just in case. Too close for the five-inch, but below him on the main deck, and beside him on the wing, the 7.62s, 50-cals, and chain guns rose and fell as the crew kept the sights on their targets.

The ensign again. *"One of these guys talks a little English. He says they had a rifle, to defend themselves, but they threw it overboard when they saw us. He says they're out of water and gas. They've got a flare pistol. One of those plastic things."*

"Smell it," Dan said. "Over."

"Sorry, sir? Over."

"The pistol. Smell it."

"Got it, sir. Yessir, it's been fired. Recently. The guy here is nodding like hell. Pointing to it, then the sky. Over."

"All right. Good." He clicked off, reconstructing the scene. The boats adrift, out of gas, out of water. The massive ro-ro shouldering up over the horizon, first a blue-and-white dot, then filling the sky. The pistol had been their last despairing chance. Unfortunately, the bridge team on the tanker had taken the lofting flare for the launch of an antitank grenade. He was a little in awe of these guys anyway. Two hundred and fifty miles out at sea, in a thirty-foot boat without even a deckhouse?

The downpour eased and he strolled out again. Staurulakis joined him, tucking her hair under her cap. "Take them into custody, sir?"

"Cheryl. Um, no, I don't see any need to do that." He ambled to the side of the flying bridge and looked down. Rainwater gleamed, bent streams rainbowing from the scuppers. Pardees looked up from the wing. "Noah, bring us alongside. And ask Hermelinda and Ollie to come up."

The stench of unwashed men and fish and heaped damp nets rose from the boats. The dark wet faces stared up with hope, fear, awe, resentment. Dan surveyed them as Jacob's ladders went over. It looked like a hard way to make a living. Watching the huge powerful ships parade past . . . He could understand why a penniless and desperate fisherman might turn pirate.

The boatswain yelled orders, and blue plastic water containers and bags of rice and beans went down into the boats. Also a compass. Unfortunately, Ticos no longer carried any gasoline, so he couldn't help them with fuel.

Dan clattered down the ladder and back into the bridge to check the radar picture, keep from being sucked into the micro. The wind was kicking up. As soon as Uskavitch reported water and food offloaded, Dan ordered the RHIB back aboard.

He went out onto the bridge wing and looked down again. A very tall Somali was standing in the prow of the nearest boat as it pitched heavily.

Dan pointed south. "Three hundred kilometers," he shouted down. The Somali squinted, then grinned unpleasantly. He pointed, as if mimicking Dan, but to the southwest. "Okay, you don't need a compass," Dan muttered. He raised his voice into the pilothouse. "Let's get back on track. Fifteen knots."

When he looked back, the boats were specks again under a swiftly darkening sky. Then the mist, or fog, moved in again, freight-trained on the endless wind, obliterating them.

The room was small, square, low-overheaded. A green curtain hung across the door to the berthing area. By long and honored tradition, no one entered the Chief's Mess, also known as the Goat Locker, unless invited. Including the skipper.

Ushered in, Dan shook hands with Tausengelt, Wenck, Van Gogh, Quincoches, Toan, Anschutz, Zotcher, Grissett, McMottie, and others. He knew them all, though some, like the chief corpsman, the sonar chief, the quartermaster, and the assistant navigator, he worked with more closely than others. He slid onto the picnic-style bench, taking in the bug juice machines, the patriotic posters, the swimsuited near-nude that skirted official acceptability. *Savo* had no female chiefs yet. He needed to look into that.

A messman brought in aluminum trays. Italian day:

caesar salad, spaghetti and meatballs, cheese, tomatoes, fresh hot bread with crunchy crust, butter in ice. Everything was piping hot, and as soon as it hit the table the chiefs dug in like starving wolves, hardly talking, though perhaps his presence cast a pall.

The U.S. Navy was built on its chief petty officers. The sobering thing was that now, when he looked around, their faces seemed unmarked, young, nearly childlike. Only Tausengelt was Dan's age, and compared to the E-7s, the master chief looked ancient as lava. Did he look that old too? Was he the Old Man in fact as well as in name?

He asked Grissett, "Chief, how's our binnacle list?"

"The, uh, crud seems to've slacked off, sir. Maybe getting out of that fucking dust helped."

"It knocks you down for a long time. You feel like lying down every couple of minutes," Zotcher said. The little sonar chief, who looked like Doenitz, had always struck Dan as less than a hard worker. He'd actually caught the guy asleep on watch, though he'd pleaded illness, and kept finding reasons to mention it. But Zotcher had taken a bullet for the ship when the former exec had cracked, started waving a pistol and threatening people in CIC. "We headed for Hormuz, Captain?"

"Waiting for word. But get your people ready for shallow-water work. And some strange currents."

"That's what's giving us this fog. The Ekman Spiral. A monsoon phenomenon, east of Socotra. The southwest winds push the surface water offshore. The cool water comes up from below. You get boundary layer saturation and fog and low stratus development. Extending the mixed layer, and pushing the thermocline down."

Dan nodded, registering its impact on possible submarine detection ranges. "Be there in two days, at flank speed," Van Gogh said. The quartermaster.

The ship's channel was rebroadcasting a baseball game. "Who's playing?" Dan asked.

"Orioles and Tigers."

"Wait a minute. How the heck are we getting that?"

Donnie Wenck said, through a mouthful of meatballs, "Pulled it off a commercial satellite. There's some DC-2 encryption you got to unscramble, but—"

"Captain don't need to know that," Tausengelt put in.

"I didn't hear a word," Dan said, helping himself to the pasta.

He was here to smooth whatever feathers were ruffled from his mast case. To eat with them, signal that he stood with them.

A smart CO led less by barking orders than by building a consensus. The wardroom was the most directly responsive to the commander, as might be expected. The crew seldom acted as a unit, or felt as a unit; but when it did, the mood was usually negative, and meant a skipper was in a death spiral unless he could pull out fast. The chiefs were always supportive of the command, unless the CO was seriously off the rails; but their commitment could be grudging, especially if they felt their position was threatened.

Which Amy Singhe had been doing, establishing a

no-chiefs policy on her discussion groups. Dan had heard her talking to Matt Mills, Hermione Henriques, and the other midgrade officers. She was brilliant, but she seemed to believe the business-school methods she'd learned at Wharton could be transplanted intact to the Navy. That cooperative work groups outperformed hierarchies. That technology could dispense with middle management.

Her article in *Defense Review* had been scathing. It had taken courage to publish it. That, he could admire. And the Navy needed shaking up. But when it came to specifics, what a modern naval organization might look like, the piece had been vaguer. He'd come away with a fuzzy picture of strong, wise commanders, and maybe execs, and apparently the rest of the ship at more or less the same level; skilled, certainly, but without much required in the way of leadership.

But what happened when strong-willed sailors didn't want to cooperate? When "digitally mediated work circles" were disrupted by fatigue, troubled individuals, casualties, battle damage, death? He didn't believe tradition was sacrosanct. But he was leery of throwing it overboard without a more convincing case than he'd seen so far.

The chiefs exclaimed in disgust at the play on the screen, pulling him back to the messroom. He sighed.

"Ice cream, Captain?"

"No thanks, Red, I'm trying to stay in my size 32s." He glanced at his watch and rose. "Better get back, I guess . . . see if we got that message yet."

He didn't notice, as he eased the door closed, that he'd left his cap behind.

He reigned on the bridge for an hour, then went down to his sea cabin to try to nap again. His throat was scratchy. He read a few more pages of the book he'd picked up at the Navy Lodge in Norfolk and taken along. He hadn't made much progress, but it was gradually pulling him in. Barbara Tuchman's *The Guns of August*. But all too soon his eyelids were sagging, and he switched the light off at last.

For once, no one called him, and when he finally regained consciousness he blinked into the dark, confused. His watch said five but he wasn't sure if it was morning or evening, local or Zulu. Finally he clicked the reading light on: 1700, by the twenty-four-hour clock on the bulkhead.

Afternoon, then. He pulled on coveralls, went down two decks to CIC, and worked at his command desk for a while. Caught up on his e-mail, though nothing was super hot. Anything flash came up hard copy, hand-carried. Routine material was scanned automatically in Radio for key words and routed on the ship's network. He also had a secure intership high-level chat function at his battle station.

He was there when an update scrolled up. A Republic of Korea frigate had been hit by a torpedo, or possibly a mine, in the South China Sea. He came to

attention in his seat and searched for a name. Hoping
it wasn't *Chung Nam,* wasn't Commander Hwang or
Captain Hung or Commodore Jung. They'd hunted the
tiger together, when SATRYE 17 had turned from an
exercise into a live-fire barrier operation. He didn't get
a name for the ship, but the Chinese premier, Zhang
Zurong, had issued a statement: China would defend its
ally, North Korea, against Western aggression.

Topside the rain-laden clouds were darker, the squalls
passing north and south of them. The wet decks gleamed
like varnished lead. A huge chemical tanker was passing, looming through the patchy mist, then fading back
into it. More contacts stretched behind it on the radar,
lined up to enter the IRTC like airliners stacked up to
land. Van Gogh was the officer of the deck. Dan had
only reluctantly approved the quartermaster chief as
one of his OODs, but so far, he hadn't done badly. He
and Dan and Matt Mills, the operations officer, discussed the Somali Current, which hit six knots just a
few miles east of here.

"If we get orders north, we can ride it up and save
fuel," Mills said. Tall, blond, good-looking enough
to star on the cover of a steamy romance, he'd been
loaned to *Savo* from the squadron staff. The loan seemed
to have become permanent, and Dan had slotted
him in as ops when he'd bumped Staurulakis up to
exec.

"So far, they just want us at the eastern entrance to
the IRTC."

"Why, when most of the pirate activity's farther west? Shouldn't we be edging that way?"

Dan nodded rather grumpily. "Yeah, but we don't want to anticipate commands. If there's a piracy event to the west, it could take us too long to get there."

Someone cleared his throat behind them. "Captain?"

When he turned, the radioman presented the clipboard with the red-and-white-striped cover sheet. "Flash message, Skipper."

It was from CTF 150. The news he'd expected. The Iranians had announced the strait was closed. But not to commercial vessels and tanker traffic, their usual assertion.

Their diplomatic note quoted the UN Convention on the Law of the Sea, and argued the Iranian position with fine logic. It even agreed that Hormuz was open to transit passage, which permitted warships to cruise through territorial waters, as long as they remained within an area used for international navigation. The Iranians, though, stated that the UNCLOS-protected right of passage could legally apply only to nations that were actually party to UNCLOS.

The United States had never signed. Therefore, though it wasn't stated explicitly, it was implied that U.S. warships could enter the Gulf only after securing permission from Iran.

There was more to it, Dan was sure. And the diplomats were no doubt arguing the fine print. But as it stood, the declaration was tantamount to closing the Persian Gulf to the United States Navy, unless it stood hat in hand at the door. Since there was no other force capable of countervailing power in the region, that meant Iran would hold 50 percent of the world's energy traffic hostage.

National Command Authority—meaning, no doubt, Ed Szerenci—had decided to send a high-value unit through to assert the right of passage. *Savo* would be relieved on station by an Italian frigate, and rendezvous with USS *Mitscher* off Hormuz. Dan would take command of both ships as commander, Task Group 151.7.

He scribbled his initials, and lifted his gaze to find both Staurulakis and Mills regarding him. "Read this, Cheryl?"

"Yessir. It doesn't say so, but this will be an opposed transit."

"I agree. Essentially, a combat operation," Dan said. "I know we've been training hard, but if there's anything remaining to spin up or tune, we've got forty-eight hours. Chief Van Gogh! As soon as we're clear of this next guy, come to a course for the rendezvous and kick us up to full. Cheryl, set a meeting, mess decks, twenty hundred. Brief the weather, course in, choke points, enemy order of battle, the whole schmear. I want everybody to know exactly what kind of hornet's nest we're sticking our head into."

"I'd like to convene a combat systems working group before that," the exec murmured as the bridge started to bustle. "Maybe have Amy chair it, as strike officer—"

"Make it so," Dan said. "Weps, Strike, Wenck, Terranova, whoever else Singhe needs. Schedule a damage-control locker inventory too. Have the chief engineer see me as soon as possible. The last fuel state I heard was 82 percent. Cheryl, draft a reply, asking for an un-rep before we go in. I want to be above 90 percent when we hit Hormuz."

The duty quartermaster said from the nav console, "Course to rendezvous, zero-two-eight true."

"Where will you be, sir?" said the exec, head down over her BlackBerry. "CIC?"

Dan nodded as the 21MC said, *"Bridge, Combat: Skunk Oscar bears zero-five-five, range seven thousand yards. Closest point of approach, close aboard to port. Recommend come right to zero-nine-zero."*

"Shit," Van Gogh muttered. Dan stood back as he dipped his face into the hood. When the chief lifted it he said, "That's gonna take us way to the south, when we need to come northeast. Okay if I cut left in front of him, Cap'n?"

Dan glanced out the window. Nothing but fog, sewn by dancing silver needles of rain. "As long as you put on enough speed." Crossing in front of an oncoming contact was frowned on, but warships had enough reserve power and maneuverability that some risk could be accepted. "But keep a close eye on him."

Mills hit the 21MC. "Bridge, Combat, coming left to cross Oscar's bow. Putting on power to get across expeditiously. CO concurs."

"Combat, aye," said the watch team supervisor, sounding doubtful.

He'd intended to go below and start getting read in for the linkup, but lingered. Both Mills and Van Gogh had their binoculars leveled out the window as the wipers flailed like dying cicadas. The light was dimming as the monsoon sealed off the sky like wax on a jar of preserves. The whole Indian Ocean would be this way for months: high winds, mist, heavy seas, rain.

What would it be like at Hormuz? If it was this socked in, he'd have trouble detecting, much less engaging, the small craft the Iranians stationed there. The Navy had war-gamed their tactics. In some games, the Red side had won. In others, American firepower had mowed them down like infantry advancing against Maxims in the Somme. Success or failure mainly depended on how closely the attacks could be sortied from different ports and concentrated on a single, though in this case moving, *schwerpunkt*: the U.S. penetration.

The rain increased still more, drumming on the overhead, sheeting the windows. The wipers labored, but didn't help much. The junior officer of the deck was off to starboard, binoculars aimed into the fog. Dan glanced that way. "See him yet?"

"No sir."

"Radar range?"

"Four thousand," Van Gogh said from the repeater. "Good strong return. Big guy, but we'll pass at least a thousand yards in front of him."

"Confirm that, Combat?"

The CIC phone talker spoke into his chest-mounted set as Dan paced the length of the bridge. Not a distance he was comfortable with, but acceptable in the interests of getting up north without delay. If for some reason they had an engine glitch, and *Savo had* experienced occasional shorting in the engine controls, he could still angle left and open the range.

The Iranians had learned from their last clash with the Navy, when their major units had been wiped out. The Pasdaran had married suicidal commitment, light missiles, and mass wave tactics to reach for an asymmetrical advantage over the numerically inferior Americans. Dan could appreciate why *Savo* had been chosen to lead the transit. Aegis was designed to track hundreds of small, fast-moving targets. She could reach out hundreds of miles, but her close-in defenses were dense and prickly as well: the automatic five-inches, Harpoon, and last, Phalanx, for any leakers. His EW team could decoy and jam most missiles.

The real question wasn't capability. It was magazine capacity. Reduced, in his case, by the fact that so many of his cells were filled with BMD-optimized Block 4s. Given enough numbers, any defense could be overwhelmed. He couldn't help thinking of Thermopylae. Isandlwana. The Little Big Horn. And *Savo Island*'s namesake battle, where the Navy had been surprised, outnumbered, and outfought.

He didn't want to add the Battle of the Strait of Hormuz to that list.

"Forward lookout reports: large ship, bow on, one-three-zero relative," the talker said.

Dan and Van Gogh went out on the starboard wing and huddled for shelter in the pilothouse corner, lifting their binoculars like a synchronized team. The rain-fog seethed past like fine grist from some gigantic mill. "There it is," the OOD said.

Dan steadied the glasses as a gray form took shape. The bow loomed high over *Savo*'s pilothouse. A bulbous bow pushed up a taut green bulge of sea, which broke as it washed aft into a seethe of vanilla-ice-cream foam. An ultralarge tanker—no, ore carrier—bound, probably, for the furnaces of Germany. Christ, it looked close . . . though that might just be the fog. He slid the ring of the pelorus to bisect the bow. Watched tensely for a second, then blew out. The angle was drawing right. *Savo* would clear the oncoming behemoth by a comfortable margin, just as the management console's plot had predicted.

"One blast?" Van Gogh asked.

This signaled that *Savo* intended a starboard-to-starboard passage. Dan nodded and the horn droned out its incredibly long, incredibly loud note. Seconds later, an even deeper, more prolonged monotone answered.

"Combat's getting a second return," the CIC talker said, out of nowhere.

"Say again?" Van Gogh snapped, wheeling around.

Fighting a sudden shortness of breath, Dan snapped his binoculars to his face again but saw only seething silver mist, and the fog moisture had built on his objectives. He dried them hastily on the sleeve of his coveralls. When he got them back up, the tanker's bow was centered, aimed directly at them. But even as he watched, it continued to drift aft, seeming to rotate slowly as *Savo* emerged on its starboard side.

The junior officer's near shriek from inside the pilothouse broke the stillness. "Another contact! Behind it!"

The rain fell harder, solid roaring sheets, soaking them, obliterating even the sea. But just for a second,

Dan had made out a dim spark through the falling dusk. And the faintest shadow. Close behind the ore carrier, but smaller, *another* ship had pulled out to the right of the inbound channel, as if intending to pass the bigger vessel ahead, and was coming up on its quarter. But the huge mass of steel and ore between it and *Savo* had masked its radar return.

"All ahead flank!" he shouted. Van Gogh shouted it at exactly the same moment, as if they'd rehearsed. But Dan barely noticed. His brain raced. Rain blasted his face. The spark winked out, and the silhouette faded. But, to judge by its relative motion, it and *Savo* would arrive at the same point on the surging sea at the exact same moment.

He shuddered, suddenly gripped by a perverse apathy. For a second he seemed to hear voices, lifted on the wind. Screams. Dear God, no. It could not happen *again*.

"Hard right rudder!" Van Gogh shouted, and Dan, at the same instant, yelled, "Belay that. Belay that! Hard *left* rudder. Emergency ahead flank! Belay your reports! Hard *left* rudder."

The bridge babbled with a cacophony of shouts, through which the helmsman's clear tenor penetrated, calm as an accountant. "My rudder is left hard, sir. Passing zero-one-zero. Engines ahead emergency flank."

Dan breathed out. Van Gogh's instinctive response had been to keep to his original course. Try to fit the cruiser between the two oncoming ships. It might have worked, but he suspected not. His way was more prudent, but they still weren't out of the woods. "Very well. Combat, are we clear out at two-seven-zero? JOOD, port side, binoculars."

"Passing zero-zero-zero . . . rudder hard left. No course given."

The squall slackened. He raised his glasses again, focusing on the emerging slate-gray bow of a smaller ship, ro-ro or containership. Yes, there were the boxes piled high, the colors washed pastel pale by the fog that writhed around them. He bent to the bearing ring. Zero-five-four. *Savo* heeled into her turn, ten thousand tons of aluminum and steel leaning and straining as the plowing rudders levered it around, as centrifugal force tilted the deck and things started to slide.

When he bent to the bearing circle again, it was the same. Locked as if welded to the oncoming prow. "Range to Skunk papa," he muttered.

The nav console began to peep, a shrill electronic warning he didn't really need. "Range to new contact, twelve hundred yards and closing. Constant bearing, decreasing range . . . collision warning."

"Passing three-five-zero."

"Combat reports: range clear to port. Two-seven-zero is a good course."

When he bent again the bearing had changed just the slightest bit. Drawing right. They should pass clear. Unless the merchant, startled by the sudden appearance of the cruiser dead ahead, had swung his own wheel right . . . in which case they would still collide. "Continue left to three-zero-zero," he snapped to Van Gogh, beside him. "We'll put our stern to him, then figure out what to do next."

The ships drew together massively as colliding planets. *Savo*'s wake broke against the immovable reef of the containership's side. They stood watching helplessly as the distance narrowed. The merchant didn't seem to have changed its course at all. Probably astonished, Dan thought, at having a gray warship suddenly materialize ahead, then slam on power and spin away. He studied the stained rusty bow, the blunt cutwater, the indentation of the anchor well, only a hundred yards distant, until he could have drawn it from memory.

As *Savo*'s powerful turbines surged her ahead, the gap began to widen.

A minute passed. Another.

The distance kept increasing. The hull behind them paled as the fog pushed in.

Van Gogh cleared his throat. "Captain, about that right rudder order—"

Dan slumped against the bulwark. He clutched his binoculars, so no one would see his hands shaking. "Uh, we might have made it, Chief. But given the, um, circumstances, it wasn't the most prudent response."

"Steady on three-zero-zero," the helmsman stated.

"Very well," Dan called. "Let's get well clear, make sure this is all sorted out. Then come back to— Quartermaster: new course."

"Coming up with a new course, sir . . . zero-three-four looks good."

Dan cocked his head into the corner of the pilothouse, gesturing the OOD aside. Their heads together, he murmured, "Don't fucking *apologize*. Just tell me you understand what just happened."

"I gave the wrong order. Sorry, Captain. I mean—"

Dan wondered how best to tell him. "It's a little more than the wrong order. Ever heard of *Reynolds Ryan*?"

"The destroyer? That got cut in two by the carrier?"

"That's the one. I was on the bridge. JOOD. Know how it happened? At a critical point, like today, the CO gave 'left rudder' instead of 'right rudder.' I don't think he even realized, until it was too late."

The little chief's head was down. "I—I didn't know."

"Look, Teddy, you're a decent officer of the deck. Conscientious. Alert. All I'm saying is, when you're at an inflection point, that's when you need to take that couple of extra seconds and make absolutely certain of the order you're giving. That your brain, or your tongue, isn't on automatic, or you're replaying some old tape. So next time you're faced with a big decision, one that can kill people . . . slow down. Make what you decide as right as you can make it. Understood?" The chief nodded. "Now take the conn and get us back on course."

Dan clapped his shoulder and turned back to the pilothouse. The helmsman, quartermaster, phone talkers, instantly looked away. "This is the captain. Chief Van Gogh has the deck and the conn."

He waited as each watchstander reported his status to the conning officer. Until the bridge, overhead lights snapping off, going to darkened status now, settled back into the somnolent routine of night watch. Until they were on course for the rendezvous, and he'd double-checked it, made triply sure it passed near no reefs or headlands or other hazards to navigation.

Then he strolled out onto the wing.

Alone at last, both hands claw-gripping the dew-coated, varnished teak of the bulwark, he let himself freak out.

The mist cooled his cheek like an open freezer after the heat of the day. No stars gleamed through the overcast. Even the channel behind them, stacked with the lights of incoming and outgoing ships, was only a glowing band, fuzzy as the Milky Way. And all around, above, ahead, lay darkness, into which *Savo*'s cutwater drove with a continuous roar, her bow wave waxing and waning as the cruiser rolled, creaming out coruscating and flashing into the dead and returnless velvet black.

The shaking eased off, leaving nausea, and a stabbing agony in his knotted neck. By any standard, that'd been too fucking close. Five seconds' hesitation, a few screw-turns slower, or if he'd let Van Gogh's erroneous rudder order take effect . . . they'd have collided. Sailors dead, maybe. For certain, *Savo* damaged, her mission unfulfilled. The billions of dollars and millions of man-hours invested in her lost, squandered, wasted.

The chief was doing the best he knew how. So were Cheryl, Ollie, Hermelinda, Max, even Amy Singhe, who after all was just trying to fix something that all too often seemed deeply broken. But no one could do his or her job alone. They needed each other, and *Savo* needed them all.

And at the top, solitary . . . Really, who was *he* to lead them? Most Navy careers, successful ones, ascended as gracefully and predictably as a curve of ballroom stairs. Winding upward to greater responsibility, greater honor, greater rank.

While his own had been tossed by downsucks and updrafts like a glider in the mountains, heading for the ground one minute, the sky the next. Questionable decisions. Courts of inquiry. Awards. Letters of reprimand. Dangerous assignments. Unexpected promotions. The one sure thing he could say was, he'd had an eventful career. Yeah, if experience came through bad judgment, he *had* it, all right. In spades.

But by all rights, he should be on the beach, living the dreary aftermath of an active career. An engineer at a shipyard, a consultant, real estate, insurance, dabbling in local politics or charity boards or docenting at museums. Knowing, all the while, that the apex of their lives lay behind them.

A tentative cough behind him. "Captain? Meeting on the mess decks. They're standing by for you."

A sardonic smile curved his lips. He nodded into the dark, thanking it, at least, for staying with him. Before turning away, back to his duty.

7

The Strait of Hormuz

Emergency breakaway," Dan told Amy Singhe, and the pilothouse filled with shouting and the drone of the ship's whistle. Five short blasts. The distance line was hustled in hand over hand. Aft and below, the refueling gang danced their intricate pavane. The boatswain tripped the pelican hook with a clank audible even high on the bridge wing. The heavy black hose through which *Savo* had sucked as at some massive teat withdrew up its supporting cable in spasms and starts. As the ships began to pull apart, the linehandlers paid out the inhaul line, faster and faster, as it snaked back to the departing oiler.

Two days after the near collision, late in the afternoon, he reclined in the leather chair on the port wing under a cloudy low sky. Ceiling two hundred feet, winds southwest, seas four to six feet. Engines 1A and 2B on the line, generators one and two, steering unit B. Singhe had taken the conn for the replenishment. She'd arrowed in too fast, making them all hinky as the massive swollen stern of USNS *Kanawha* had loomed too suddenly. At his cautionary murmur, though, she'd slowed, and dropped them into the refueling slot fifty yards off the oiler's starboard side with seasoned aplomb.

He stole a glance at the strike lieutenant as she crouched, peeping through the bearing circle. "Watch your stern," he cautioned. "She's gonna swing fast if you put a hard rudder to her." Every word sounded like a double entendre.

She spared him one cool glance, eyebrow lifted, full lips curved in an equivocal half smile, then bent to the pelorus again. "Come to course two-seven-zero. Engines ahead standard, indicate pitch and turns for fifteen knots."

"My rudder is right, coming to course two-seven-zero." Dan's gaze locked with the helmsman's. Was that half a wink, as the seaman suppressed his own chuckle? "Engines ahead standard, fifteen knots."

He leaned back, opening the focus of his attention as *Savo*'s fantail, with the outboard-slanted canisters of Harpoon launchers, cleared *Kanawha*'s bow. The whipped-cream white of her wake frothed a curving path on pristine sea.

A mile away, another leaden shadow lurked in the haze: nearly as large as *Savo,* but her profile less lofty, more rakish, radar panels set lower on her superstructure. USS *Mitscher* was an Arleigh Burke–class destroyer. Nine thousand tons full load, five hundred–plus feet long, with much the same sensors and weapons, but without *Savo*'s antiballistic capability. Slightly faster and more heavily armored, with a stealthier radar profile, *Mitscher* would be riding shotgun for him as CTG 151.7 penetrated the most heavily traveled, fiercely disputed strait in the world. Dan didn't know her skipper, Frank "Stony" Stonecipher, but had downloaded his bio and discussed him with Jenn Roald on the "red phone," point-to-point secure satcomm. Roald said he was a good guy, one Dan could depend on. *"My N4 says HM&E and CS are both readiness status one. She has a full ordnance loadout and her Aegis is at 98 percent. If you have to fight your way in, you're both as ready as we can make you. If, that is, nobody's been gundecking his reports. Over."*

"No gundecking here, Commodore, but I could use some horsepower on those aux gen parts. Plus, we never heard back from Bethesda on assistance on those recurrent infections. Over."

"You're sure these aren't just dust? I get a lot of reports of dust infections when we're operating in the Gulf. Over."

"No ma'am. People don't die from dust. We need some expert advice. Over."

She'd promised to buck the issue up the line, but said that if it was getting to be an operational issue, he should look to his local chop chain for help.

He'd ended the conversation with a sense of the growing distance between them. He belonged to Roald for spare parts and manning, but out here, his sailing orders came from Bahrain. Commander, Fifth Fleet, directed operations in the Gulf, Red Sea, and Arabian

Sea. In theory, parts, manning, and administration followed you seamlessly, no matter who your operational commander was. But in practice, the farther from home port, the more interruptions and delays along the way.

He leaned back, taking advantage of a break before heading back to Combat to review what exactly they were sticking their heads into. The flurry of messages was getting overwhelming, just like before every major flap. He glanced out at *Mitscher* again. Both ships were coming to a course for the eastern entrance to Hormuz. The destroyer's station during the first part of the transit would be one thousand yards to starboard of *Savo Island.* This would place her between the cruiser and the coast. Carrier Strike Group One, centered on *Carl Vinson,* and Strike Group Nine, with *Abraham Lincoln,* would take turns providing continuous air cover.

Just that morning, as if to ratchet things up another notch, the Iranians had announced five days of major naval maneuvers. Both sides had put out Notices to Mariners, so it was hard to believe any commercial skipper would sail unaware of the brewing confrontation.

"Captain?" Cheryl Staurulakis, with Mills behind her. "You asked us to scrub down the Fifth Fleet ROEs against our combat doctrine. Got the results, if you have thirty minutes. Or we can give you the thirty-thousand-foot overview, and just leave the marked-up copy."

Dan accepted the document and relaxed back into the chair, digging at the tension in his neck and back. The sky ahead was smudged and obscured by the nearly invisible dust that in July and August rose from the deserts. The Iranians liked to pull the eagle's tail. Test American resolve. If it ever flagged, the rickety, artificial structure of monarchies and emirates lining the west side of the Gulf, inherited from the British Empire, would crumble. Iran would control the Middle East, and the world would change.

"Okay," he murmured. "Let's get to it."

They gathered over a chart laid out on the dead-reckoning tracer, in the antisubmarine plot area back of Combat. Staurulakis, Mills, Chief Van Gogh, and Bart Danenhower. Exec, operations, navigation, engineering. Maybe he should have invited Wenck, Singhe, and the ship's senior cryppie, but he'd always felt the smaller a meeting was, the better. He shuddered in the frigid air and leaned over the paper chart with its soft blues and tans, sea and desert. "I want to hit our most exposed position no later than eleven hundred. I need daylight in the Knuckle, and through the hundred-mile transit." He waved a hand over the deep Gulf of Oman, their current position; then swept it westward, into the Gulf.

Heading in, the Strait of Hormuz kinked left around the Omani Peninsula. The International Maritime Organization had set up two transit lanes, each a mile wide. The southern lane was for outbound ships, the northern for those inbound to the refineries and terminals of the Gulf. The Knuckle was only twenty miles wide, with the Iranian-garrisoned Qeshm Island to the north and the (more or less) friendly Oman to the south. Then it bent southwest toward Dubai.

Dan had navigated here before. It was another labyrinth, a twisting, obstacle-littered gut of shallow sea dotted with production facilities, pumping stations, on-load facilities, desert islands, barely awash reefs, and abandoned, cut-down drill platforms that stuck up to within a few feet of the surface . . . not to mention a ship every six minutes heading in as a like number exited. Just navigating would be a challenge. Doing so at full alert would test crew and sensors to their limits.

He turned to Van Gogh. "Chief, first thing, make sure we have all the Notices to Mariners entered. Matt, I need the boundaries the Iranians promulgated for— what are they calling it?"

Mills said, "There are actually two exercises. The regular navy maneuvers are announced from the strait to the quote 'northern part of Indian Ocean.' Missile live fires and ASW free play. No geographic limits promulgated yet."

"And the Pasdaran?" Staurulakis asked.

"The Islamic Revolutionary Guard Corps announced the 'Velayat-e' Exercises in the southern part of the Gulf. Here." Mills straight-edged it in.

Dan leaned in. A rough rectangle about twenty miles wide by thirty in depth. But not at the Knuckle. Instead, lodged deep inside the strait, like a pebble in a windpipe. It began at the thirty-meter line off the Forur Shoal and extended seaward, cornered by four islands, all Iranian or Iranian-claimed: Forur, Sirri, Abu Musa, and Kuchek.

Dan swallowed. He knew these desolate sandy islands all too well.

"Right across the shipping lanes," Van Gogh observed.

The operations officer said, "And they advise commercial traffic to stand clear."

"Which effectively closes the strait." Dan straightened, set his palms to his back, and stretched. "All right, that makes it simple. Plot us a course right through the square. We won't be alone, with dedicated F/A-18 coverage from the carriers. Now . . . battle orders. This is the last chance we'll have to look over them. So let's make sure there are absolutely no holes."

He didn't get much sleep that night. Traffic was heavy coming out, as if eager to beat a deadline. Tankers by the dozen, containerships, oceangoing tugs plodding along with rigs in tow, liquid natural gas tankers with bulbous white tanks, like floating bombs. He'd left word to be awakened when they passed 26 degrees north. But when the call came, he was already up and dressed, showered and shaved.

He met his own gaze in the mirror of the sea cabin. Whether he felt up to it or not, men and women would depend on him today. He'd have to make the right decisions. Reach beyond what he felt he could do, and then do even more.

He stared into tired gray eyes mitered by wrinkles. Then closed them, and asked for help.

* * *

0500. He stood flipping through the morning traffic on the bridge. Van Gogh had calculated local dawn at 0532, but already the east was brightening and the temperature rising. The swells were gentling as they moved in between the ramparts of land. *Mitscher* was on station four hundred yards ahead. Oman was off to port, the terrifyingly vertiginous cliffs of the northern peninsula and islands jumping straight up out of the sea. One headland behind the other, they were still dark, but shortly would illuminate in hues of rose and ocher.

The 21MC announced, *"Stand by for on top."* A growing roar drew him out on the bridge wing. Two black arrow shapes howled over, no more than three hundred yards up, tail cones glowing bright orange in the half light, and dwindled, peeling off toward the strait.

"I'll be in Combat," he told the pilothouse at large. As the door slammed behind him the boatswain announced, "Captain's off the bridge." Then the 1MC, also in Nuckols's voice but much louder, said all over the ship, *"Flight quarters, flight quarters! All hands man your flight quarters stations. Remove all covers topside. The smoking lamp is out on all weather decks. Muster the crash and salvage team with the team leader in the helo hangar. Now flight quarters."*

Combat was frigid, as usual. But this time, anticipating hours in the chair, he'd brought his foul-weather jacket and a pair of uniform gloves. Donnie Wenck waved; Petty Officer Terranova barely glanced up from her SPY-1 console. The rest of the stations were manned, and a murmuration of voices and a rattle of keyboards underlay the constant hiss of the ventilation.

He settled into his seat with a sigh, booted up, and ran through the priority traffic while keeping half an eye on Red Hawk's launch, clicking to follow comms with the helo through his headset. Aegis was already tracking eighty contacts in the strait area, but he wanted the SH-60B out ahead. The Seahawk had night vision, onboard electronic eavesdropping, and a data link, extending his radar, and ESM horizon, and giving him the option of visual checks on any contacts that seemed threatening. He gave permission for a green deck.

"Helo away," announced the 1MC. *"All hands secure from flight quarters."*

"Clear, coming to zero zero zero," "Strafer" Wilker drawled, reporting to the air control supervisor eight consoles behind Dan. *"Man, it's just paved with fuckin' ships out here."* "Storm" Differey was the copilot, with two crewmen. Four souls he had to remember, if things got dicey. *"Okay, got a little trouble here . . . red light on number one DLA."* Wilker and the controller discussed it, concluding that since the forward data link antenna had just gone tango uniform, Strafer would have to keep the nose pointed away from the ship for the data link to work at ranges over thirty miles.

Dan filed that away too. The helo also had some strike capability, with machine guns and laser-guided Hellfires, but it would be dangerous to pit it against anything with a real air defense. Dan planned to keep him in the air for three hours, recover for refuel and rest, and have him aloft again as they approached the IRGC exercise area.

A silent Longley placed a covered tray and carafe on the table. Dan acknowledged with a nod, focusing now on the large-screen displays. The F-18s were just outside Iranian territorial waters, angling west at five hundred knots. Loitering speed, for them. He was noting the commercial air corridors, prominently displayed on the LSDs, when two threat symbols lit. Wilker called in, the display locating him over the entrance to the Knuckle. *"Two gatekeepers hanging out here. Look like Combattante fast attack. I'm gonna moon you so you can—"*

Dan cut in: "Red Hawk, this is Matador Actual. Don't let your data link positioning affect your tactics. Just make voice reports. Over."

La Combattantes, or Kama/Sina–class missile patrol boats, were regular Iranian Navy units. They were fast, displaced about three hundred tons, and were armed with automatic guns and antiship missiles. But they were deficient in sensors and not data-linked. A threat at close range, but with the fighters streaking overhead, Dan figured, they'd stand clear. At least while he and *Mitscher* went in. Coming out, with magazines depleted, maybe damaged and low on fuel, might be a different story. So far, he didn't have a port of call inside the Gulf. Manama was apparently leaving that up in the air, seeing which way the cat would jump.

To his right at the command desk was the general

quarters TAO, Matt Mills, in the seat Cheryl had used to occupy. Now, as exec, she'd be Dan's alternate, and supervise on the bridge. Past him Wenck was at the OS chief's station. Donnie could turn in his chair and talk to the Terror, at the Aegis console behind him. Dan's antisubmarine staff was behind him to his left; his surface strike team, headed by Amy Singhe, directly behind; to his right, the air control people and his electronic warfare sensor operators.

All in all, almost thirty people in CIC and four more in Sonar, next door through the traditional black canvas curtain.

Dan pulled the napkin off the tray. French toast, scrambled eggs, bacon. He made himself take ten bites, chew, and swallow, to keep the blood sugar up.

Over the next hour they closed the Knuckle. Traffic was light going in, but outgoing was bumper to bumper, ships spaced every mile. Red Hawk gave the Combattantes a wide berth, then orbited over the great sweeping bend in the waterway, relaying back radar that showed small boats maneuvering deeper in the strait. Dan and Mills discussed the enemy order of battle, trying to work out who was where. Dan kept *Mitscher* and *Savo* in the middle of the incoming lane, so no one could accuse them of violating territorial boundaries.

Electronic warfare data started coming in, both from Red Hawk and from *Savo*'s and *Mitscher*'s own eavesdropping. Aegis correlated them with radar and cross-bearings to show where the Pasdaran was gathering. C-802 batteries were lighting up on Larak Island, and on the Iranian mainland behind it.

Chin propped on his fists, Dan mused on the murky history of the C-802. The missile had originally been a Chinese design, but the Iranians had reverse-engineered it with North Korean help. They were near-supersonic sea-skimmers with a pop-up maneuver at the end of their flight profiles. Dangerous, but his EW team had trained for hundreds of hours to jam them. And when they'd faced Syrian 802s in the Med, Wenck and Dr. Noblos had come up with a way to hijack the missiles' link to their launching point, and reprogram their targeting. "Backseat Driver" had proven its worth off Israel. And if jamming, spoofing, and chaff didn't work, he could shoot them down.

But if they overwhelmed him, in dozens stagger-fired from different locations to converge with a single time-on-target . . .

Lounging in his seat, shivering, he wondered if *Savo* had been sent in as a deliberate provocation. After all, they'd nearly sunk an Iranian frigate last winter. And Dan personally had tangled with Iran several times.

Or was that paranoia, megalomania, persecution complex? Surely no one cared.

On the other hand, it could be just enough to convince the other side they were being deliberately goaded.

As he'd expected, the Combattantes stood off as the U.S. warships passed. Red Hawk reported that the small contacts spaced along the northern boundary of the international strait were dhows. Dan suspected these were transmitting targeting data to the missile batteries, which remained locked on. Wenck asked if they should do some decoying drills, but Dan put a foot down. This was no time for simulations. The potential for misunderstanding, or simple fuckup, was too great. He maintained a steady twenty knots, covering ground while not burning too much fuel.

Unfortunately, after the task group had passed, the missile boats drifted south, then fell in astern, following them in. Staying in their wake, but maintaining a standoff of about ten miles.

If they were the gatekeepers, the gates were swinging shut.

By the time the clock above the LSDs read 0700 he was exiting the Knuckle, passing south of Larak Island with four antiship missile radars locked on *Savo Island*. The exterior cameras were picturing a gentling sea, a blood-scarlet, cloudy horizon beneath the risen sun, when Lieutenant Singhe leaned on the back of Dan's chair. "Sir. A word."

"Shoot. I mean—guess I shouldn't say that just now."

She didn't crack the slightest smile. Just leaned in, dropping her voice. "You wanted us to spin up Tomahawks on every C-802 battery we identified. How about a warning shot?"

This was a surprise. *Savo* could do limited land-attack mission planning onboard. But he couldn't "spin up," or prelaunch program, a TLAM without Fifth Fleet authorization. Still, he *had* ordered Mills and Singhe to do engagement planning. "Uh . . . you're not really spinning up, are you?"

"Well, no. Just building the missions."

"That's better. But, you're proposing a first strike? On the Iranian mainland? I don't think so, Amy."

"They're illuminating us in firing mode. That's a hostile act, according to our rules of engagement."

Dan cleared his throat. "There's something you have to learn about ROEs, Amy. There's the 'ought to be' and 'what they say it is,' and then there's 'how it's interpreted.' And after all that, there's 'what we do anyway.'"

"I'm beginning to see that, sir."

"But regardless of any and all of the above, I'm not out here to kick off a war."

"Sir, with all due respect, that's idiotic. As soon as we detect one launch, we should pull the trigger on every site we have localized."

Dan tensed, suddenly angry. *Idiotic?* "I'm not disagreeing with you, Amy, but I don't have that authority. I could release an overwater strike, on a surface unit. But a strike on the mainland, no way. I appreciate your aggressiveness, but you need to stand down. And reread your battle orders."

She was frowning, those luxuriant eyebrows knitted. Seemed about to say something more, but Dan spoke first. "Let me make something clear, Lieutenant."

"Yes sir. Listening."

"We're not out here alone. Us and *Mitscher*. Along with our Tomahawks, we have over a hundred more dialed in from the battle group, on every airstrip, tank farm, naval base, and barracks along the coast. Two wings of strike aircraft on fifteen-minute alert, and B-52s out of Diego Garcia behind that. We're just the cheese on the mousetrap, see? If the Iranians feel like taking a bite, they'll regret it." He hesitated, eyeing the long strip of Qeshm. Not for the first time, he imagined how easily the Marines could take the whole island and, with two miles of water between it and the mainland, wall Iran itself off from the strait.

That would mean all-out war, of course. But it might come to that, if both sides kept pushing chips into the pot.

She nodded slowly. "But do *they* know that?"

"Believe me, they do. This is a ritual dance, Amy. Like bees do, to send a message. It's complicated. If anybody gets the steps wrong, things can go south fast. But all we have to do is steam in and then steam out. This is a freedom-of-navigation operation. A transit passage. And nothing more. So we're not going to initiate *anything* that could be portrayed as an aggressive action. Understand?"

She hesitated, then nodded again. Straightened, and went back to her station, leaving a quick glance of dark eyes and the scent of sandalwood.

Cheryl Staurulakis came in at 0900. Dan got up and stretched. "XO, I'm going up to the bridge, have a look around. Let me know if anything starts."

"Yessir."

He stopped in his cabin and took a leak. Glanced out the little forward-facing porthole at a flat, dusty, light-filled sea. Still shivering; even with the foul-weather jacket, CIC had been freezing. At least on the bridge, it would be warm.

The pilothouse was so quiet he could hear the chronometer ticking over the nav table. Everyone had flash gear ready: hood, gloves, goggles, gas masks buckled to thighs. He paced from the starboard side, where Iran was visible as a low, sere coastline, to port. Where four tankers spaced out toward the west, growing smaller and smaller, like old photos of the Great White Fleet. The sea had smoothed, though the monsoon wind still blew. The sky was still overcast, but now with a queer reddish tinge to the slate, from all the refineries, plus the ever-present sand.

He nodded to the 25mm remote console operators. Wondering if what he'd told Singhe was totally true. About this being a message . . . that was clear enough. But the part about everyone knowing the steps . . . that was less self-evident. Especially when the Revolutionary Guard were involved. They were known to act independently of the regular navy, and sometimes, even, of the political leadership.

His Hydra beeped. "Captain," he snapped.

"Sir, Weps here. Got a train issue glitch in Mount 22 . . . the port CIWS."

"What's up?"

"Not sure yet. Failure in the train mechanism, or possibly the card that controls it."

Dan tried to keep his voice level. If a C-802 popped over the horizon, near supersonic at twenty feet above the water, and jamming and decoys failed, the Sea

Whiz was the last card he could play before seeing what three hundred pounds of armor-piercing high explosive did to an aluminum superstructure. "This is a bad time for gremlins, Ollie."

"Realize that, sir. Got the first team up there doing fault isolation now."

"Get it fixed. Report back." He snapped off, realized everyone on the bridge was watching, and tried to look unconcerned.

But it wasn't easy.

Back in Combat, he juggled a too-hot paper cup at the electronic warfare stacks, reducing the blood content in his coffee stream. The leading EW petty officer was plotting each jammer and fire-control radar that brushed its fingers over them. A golden opportunity to refine the Iranian order of battle. In the intelligence sense, his mission was already a success. The jamming was annoying, but the petty officer assured him it wouldn't affect their ability to detect launches.

Hoping he was right, Dan strolled to the command seat again. Staurulakis glanced up, looking haggard, hair straggling out of her ponytail. As well she might; she and Dan were standing watch and watch, and the exec had too much to do on her off-hours to waste them sleeping.

"We're past the Knuckle," she murmured. "No hostile action yet, but numbers are still building. Think it's just a bluff?"

Dan stared at the large-screen display, which showed

a steady increase in small contacts along the Iranian coast. The exec muttered, "They have to know what we did to their frigate. I wonder if that's hurt their confidence in their great new missiles."

"They have more than just 802s," Dan said. "They've got that rocket torpedo. The Shkval-K. And mines. But I worry about all these small craft."

Staurulakis eyed the screen. "Over two hundred of them . . . a lot North Korean built . . . with multiple rocket launchers, missiles, and torpedoes. Plus, yeah, mines, if we let them get in front of us. We don't have a great detection rate on those."

"I'll take it. Thanks, Cheryl." Dan resumed the command seat, warm where her bottom had just left it, and zoomed in. He keyboarded and moused, pulling out data. Four of the faster contacts might be hovercraft, but as he did the arithmetic his fingers slowed. Sixty contacts out there. Impossible to say which classes without a visual ID from the helo, but he wasn't sending Red Hawk in among scores of small boats, every one of which probably had Misagh shoulder-fired anti-aircraft missiles.

If they swarmed him . . . A Pentagon war game two years before had free-played just that tactic, with horrendous results. He didn't plan to repeat the mistakes the Blue commander had made. The most essential lesson was that, like a fight in a dark alley, he had to keep the enemy at arm's length, where better U.S. sensors, data, and long-range weapons could attrite their numbers. In other words, keep them inside his kill zone, while he stayed outside theirs.

The classic strategy against overwhelming forces was to defeat them in detail. Use maneuver and cunning to isolate a portion, wipe that fraction out with superior firepower, then move on to the next engagement with an improved force ratio. Napoleon had used that tactic to perfection.

But two huge ships couldn't outmaneuver high-powered speedboats and hovercraft skimming over the calm strait. They'd be surrounded, like a wagon train circled by Plains Indians. Then, on signal, all the boats would turn in to attack.

His gaze fastened to the Weapons Inventory screen above the Aegis display. The numbers weren't tactically satisfying. Even assuming one kill for one shot, and engaging eleven targets per minute, that would leave more than enough boats to overwhelm them . . . Or, wait . . . he'd forgotten *Mitscher*. The destroyer was data-linked and tactically merged with *Savo*, was for all intents and purposes the same ship, only with double redundancy on sensors and weapons. And he had the F-18s overhead, two low, four more stacked above them, mainly in case the few Iranian jets still operational decided to get into the act, but also on call to help suppress a mass attack.

Okay, things weren't totally dark. But he couldn't assume the other side had the same Big Picture, were operating as information-rich as NATO or U.S. forces. Certainly not once *Savo* and the EA-6B twenty thousand feet up started jamming them. After the Iranian radars blanked, they'd be limited to line of sight, and dust and haze plus comm jamming would make even

visual targeting and own-force coordination difficult.
He clicked to the air controller's circuit and asked for
each flight of fighter/attacks to make a low pass through
the Pasdaran exercise area. And to keep on doing that,
to give the impression of endless streams of F-18s
screaming in.

"Captain?" Van Gogh, brandishing a rolled-up chart.
"You said to keep you posted. See these islands to port?
The big one's Bozorg. The small one past that, Kuchek.
Once we pass those, we're in their op area."

Dan checked the paper chart against the nav screen,
matching longitude first, then latitude. If shots started
flying, he had to be absolutely certain they were in
the international straits. That would be the first thing the
Iranians would accuse him of—violating territorial
waters. "Okay, that's consistent with what I have on the
verticals, Chief. Thanks for backing me up."

"We really gonna call them on this?"

"Absolutely." Dan wondered why he was even asking.

"So you want this guy now, right?"

The navigator stepped aside. Behind him was SK3
Kaghazchi, the ship's go-to for translation. Dan murmured, "Hey, Bozorgmehr," and, after a moment, pointed
to the unit commander's chair. What the hell.

The emigre slid into it, smiling. He was mustached,
dark-skinned, in his mid-thirties; his long, closely
shaven skull gleamed in the overhead light. Dan was
never sure how far to trust him—storekeepers didn't
undergo the toughest clearance requirements—but he
had a deep, authoritative bass that sounded like Allah
himself on the radio. Dan picked up the Navy Red

handset. Time to pimp everybody. Especially *Mitscher*. "Matador actual for Anvil actual. Over."

"This is Anvil actual." Stony's voice, all right. He must have been sitting by the handset.

"See those small boats ahead? I make sixty of them, in two waves. Over."

"Copy, concur. I hold them."

"I'm having the Hornets sweep ahead of us. My intentions are to close up so we can put more fire on target if we have to. Also it'll make things easier for the air. So move in on me. Interlocked defense."

"Got it. How close you want me, what direction?"

"Five hundred yards. On a bearing of"—he hesitated—"due north."

"Coming to station. Over," Stonecipher said.

"Mitscher's turning to starboard," Mills muttered.

Dan signed off and nodded. The enemy had already split his forces, about two-thirds of the boats to the landward of the channel, the other third to port, south of the oncoming Americans.

Time to let them know what he expected, and what would happen if they didn't comply. He gave Kaghazchi his instructions, making sure the guy understood what he wanted to communicate. Five miles' standoff. No illumination by fire-control radars. A clear warning he'd open fire if any surface craft closed in. "Tell 'em we want innocent transit, as defined by international law. Let us through, stand clear, and no one has to die for his country."

The bushy eyebrows lifted, but Kaghazchi nodded. They went over the phrasing, then Dan called Radio and warned them to start taping. He switched to International Call and passed the storekeeper the handset.

As the Persian intoned the warning, Dan concentrated on the twenty miles ahead. The pips to starboard had divided again. That made three groups now, two to starboard, one to port. Like a gauntlet the Americans would have to run.

Now he had to step back. There was always a temptation to fulfill a scenario, to make reality square with what you expected. Like it or not, now he just had to wait. Ceding the initiative, but that was how it had to be.

"Any response?" he asked. The translator shrugged and waggled his head. Dan took that for a no, and reached for the red phone.

"Anvil, this is Matador. Copy us going out to them on VHF?"

"Loud and clear. Over."

"We're not hearing anything back. You?"

"Nada. Weapons tight here. Over."

"Concur," he said. "But stand by for tactical maneuvering. Matador out."

He drew a slow breath, running it all through his mind again. Someday computers would do all this. Evaluate, plan, then maneuver ships in battle. Someday soon, most likely.

But not just yet.

Above all, he wasn't going to the mat with these guys. If they wanted a battle, they'd have it. But on his terms. Only a fool fought a fair fight.

Donnie Wenck leaned over. "Something you wanna

see. We don't have it on the screen, because it ain't painting regular—"

"What is it, Donnie? I mean, Chief? I'm kind of busy here—"

"Just come over and look."

At the SPY console he peered over Terranova's shoulder for several seconds before he saw what she was pointing at. The merest flicker. It didn't register with every sweep. Sometimes several beams swept past before it painted again, like a luminescent jelly, deep underwater. Only this, if it was there, was *way* up there.

"How high *is* this?" he muttered.

"When it paints, I get around seventy thousand feet," the Terror murmured.

"Holy shit. What the hell is it?"

"A UFO." Wenck smirked.

"You shitting me?"

"Well, maybe some kind of upper-atmosphere disturbance? There's something called a 'sprite,' but they're associated with major lightning storms. The course and speed . . . hard to calculate, and it drifts this way and that, but overall, seems to be about two-two-zero."

"How fast?"

"Hard to calculate, like I said . . . sixty knots?"

Two-two-zero was close to their own course out of the Knuckle. Was it following them? Tracking *Savo Island* through the strait? That seemed unlikely. Seventy thousand feet was where the high-altitude recon birds lived, the U-2, the SR-71. And they were fast burners. That high, that slow, what could it be? "A rogue weather balloon, or some kind of upper-atmosphere physics experiment, is all we could come up with," Wenck said. "Anyway, figured you oughta know."

"Pass it to ComFifth. Probably nothing, but they need to know if it's some kind of local environment thing."

Dan patted Terranova's well-padded shoulder, cleared his throat, and pulled himself back to the problem at hand. He couldn't just wait. On the other hand, he couldn't pick a fight. He went over it all again in his head, hoping he wasn't getting ready to really screw up, then grabbed the handset. "Red Hawk, Matador Actual."

"202, over. Hey, Skipper."

"Hey. Confirm, you hold altitude limitations on Misaghs. Over."

"We have angels three on Misaghs. Over."

"That's correct," Mills put in from the TAO's seat.

Glancing over, Dan saw the redbound book open in front of him. "Um, confirm angels three on this end. Now listen up. We talked last night about maybe trailing some bacon in front of these guys?"

"Coming left, to conform to your base course."

Dan checked the pip that was Red Hawk 202. Five miles ahead, with the speed vector out front. Good. "Okay. Run the ball up the middle, but stay above angels four. No . . . make it five. And keep your finger on that flare button."

"Giving them a sniff?" Donnie Wenck muttered.

Dan didn't answer. The leftmost screen changed, became hurtling waves: in black and white, jerky, because of the bandwidth limitations, but real-time video from the helo. It flinched right, left, then steadied on four boats skipping white trails across black water. In classic line abreast, like the old movies of World War II PT boats. They looked closer than they ought to from five thousand feet, but that might just be the magnification. Dan murmured, "Matt, get our speed up. Also, pass to EW and the EA-6B, to start jamming their radars and comms." He picked up the red handset to *Mitscher*. "Matador actual. Stand by."

"Anvil, standing by."

From one of the speeding boats, a point of light ignited. The next frame showed it lancing upward at the tip of a cone of shining cloud.

Dan said, enunciating clearly, because this was being taped and would be gone over many times: "This is Matador. My helo is taking hostile fire. Execute form one. Flank speed. Interval five." Out of the background noise he registered the CIC watch officer passing the same order over fleet tactical, then over the HF blower to the fleet commander.

"Roger. I see them. Maneuvering now." And simultaneously over the other circuit, from the destroyer's OOD, *"Form one, speed three zero, roger, out."*

Dan pressed the 21MC lever. "Bridge, CO. Exec, execute Bacon Sandwich. Ahead flank emergency. Left hard rudder, pull us out to port."

On the screen, the picture jerked, then banked crazily as Red Hawk tilted away. Sky filled the screen, then was replaced by video from the ship's own forward gun camera. Wenck was thinking ahead, feeding Dan information via the screens. The flat, nearly calm sea. And above it, in the distance, a fleeing speck, striding away on what looked like immense spider-legs of flame-tipped smoke that spiraled slowly downward. "Strafer" Wilker, crapping flares as more missiles climbed after him.

The EW operator called, "Racket, racket. Heavy jamming, R band, correlates with EA-6B."

Dan said, "Okay, but are we jamming too? I don't want these guys to be able to coordinate their movements."

Mills said they were, at the same moment the air controller stated, in Dan's headset, *"SAM, SAM! Red Hawk reports taking fire. Initiating evasive action."*

"Tell him to clear to the west and circle to his port. Pick out a target, but hold fire."

The order went down the line. Dan studied the screen as *Savo Island* shuddered as if in orgasm, leaning into the turn, then out again as the rudders bit deep and the engines, full out, pushed her faster and faster. He wasn't going to outrun a hovercraft, but he could remold the tactical situation. Three small islands lay south of where the leftward cluster of boats milled. He had just enough water to go between two of them. The major unknown was going to be, first, if whoever was in charge of the southern gaggle tumbled to what he was doing, and second, if that commander could communicate his countermove fast enough to forestall Dan's.

"Matador, this is Anvil. In your wake five-hundred-yards interval. Conforming to your movements. Over."

Dan acknowledged, and added a sentence explaining his aim. Beside him, Mills was passing the information to Fifth Fleet and Strike One. On the big screen, the southern group were still milling around, not moving in one direction or the other. As if they couldn't use their tactical radio channel anymore . . . since the Prowler, far above, was broadcasting enough jamming power to light up a small city.

Time to further isolate the battlefield. "Air Control, CO. Pass to the F-18s. Our helo's been fired on. He's clearing to the west. Focus on the boats to the north of a line between the islands Forur and Kuchek. That is, the formation closest to the mainland. If any cross the transit lane heading south: warning shots, then take them out. But *weapons tight* on anyone moving north." He made the petty officer repeat that, then clicked his Hydra on. "Cheryl, CO."

"XO, over."

"Got the picture here? Between the shoal area to port and the low island bearing about one-niner-zero true. Keep Van Gogh on the GPS. Watch the fathometer, but take us through at flank. *Mitscher* will follow. When we're clear, we'll come right, and weapons free at that time."

She rogered. Dan made sure Mills had that too, and the orders rippled away. He gripped the chair arms. The whole ship was shaking, vibrating as sheer power wedged the sea apart. The speed indicator trembled just short of 35. "Start designating targets," he told Mills. The Aegis picture jumped forward as the combat system began selecting targets and assigning ordnance. He checked on the helo. Still out to the west, completing a lazy circle as the first two F-18s dived, their altitude readouts spinning downward, toward the transit lane.

So far, so good. With eight Hellfires hanging off his pylons, Wilker would hit the enemy from the west, while *Savo* and *Mitscher* slammed the door to the south. The islands and shoals would pen the Pasdaran in to the west and eastward, and the F-18s would polish off anybody who tried to come to their aid. On the other hand, for anyone who felt like retreating, the back gate was open. He clicked the Hydra again. "Hold the bubble up there, Cheryl. I'm gonna be too busy to talk. Keep an open channel to Sonar for torpedo warnings. Hold speed once you pass the shoal."

"XO, roger."

Mills said, "Southern element's turning toward."

"I see it," Dan told the TAO. "Take with Harpoon." The screen zoomed, and four pips turned red and began to pulse. Missiles weren't all he had to worry about. Peykaaps and Tirs carried torpedo tubes, too. If they had Shkvals, they could really be dangerous, but according to intel they didn't have big enough tubes for it. He hoped that was right.

"Matador, this is Anvil actual. Interrogative: Who's taking these first four? Over."

Dan told Stonecipher, "Matador will take first wave. Anvil takes second wave. But keep an eye out behind you for those Combattantes. Out."

Mills said, tone as even as if this were just another drill, "We have a Harpoon solution. Request batteries released."

Dan nodded, flicked up the red cover over the Permission switch, and clicked it to On. "Batteries released."

A distant roar signaled departure of the first Harpoon. A moment later the second left. The third. Then the fourth. They came up on the screen, swiftly departing, with the next clicking rotation of the SPY-1 beam. It would be a short-range engagement, no more than twenty thousand yards. "Anybody we miss, designate to guns," he told Mills. The five-inches would reach out fifteen thousand yards, with seventy-pound shells proximity-fuzed to burst above the oncoming boats.

"Vampire, Vampire, Vampire!" the EW petty officer yelled. "Missile in the air, X-band emitter, correlates with Sackcloth antiship missile . . . Vampire number two, in the air."

Two weapons were headed their way. One from the southern group, the other, with farther to travel, from the north. The NATO reporting name "Sackcloth" was the C-801, the version before the 802. So the Pasdaran had inherited the older missiles.

Sharp bangs echoed through the superstructure as the chaff mortars went off. Someone nudged him; held out a flash hood, gloves, goggles. Dan almost pushed them away, then took them, pulling the heavy fabric over his head. If jamming failed, if the chaff and flares and rubber duckies didn't decoy it, that missile was coming through the side. He donned the goggles, too, but left the gloves off, to be able to address his keyboard.

On the display, twin carets pulsed red, clicking toward the blue cross of Own Ship with each sweep.

"Take with Standard?" Mills asked. Dan shook his head. Their EW team should be able to cope with the earlier-version seeker heads.

"What the *fuck* is he doing?" Mills breathed, beside him.

Dan glanced back up at the screen, to see the TAO's pointer highlighting the readout for Red Hawk. The SH-60B was in a tight turn to port, down at two hundred feet. "What's he *doing*?" Mills breathed again.

"Vampire, Vampire, Vampire. Two more incoming. Tracks—"

Aegis classified threats and assigned weapons without human intervention. Dan didn't see any need to interfere with the watch team as they ran the intercepts. To Mills he said, "I'm not sure." He clicked to the helo coordination net to hear Wilker say, *"Tell the Old Man—"*

"The Old Man's on the line."

"Uh, yessir. Danger close. Madman, Madman. Smoke away. Mark, on top."

"Streaming the Nixie," Mills said, beside him. The antitorpedo noisemaker. Not totally dependable, but better than nothing.

Dan sat frozen as the screen showed the first C-801 curving to port, away from *Savo* and *Mitscher*. *Savo*'s electronic warfare team had hijacked its guidance, spoofed it to think they were where they weren't. But the helo, on its way in from the west to attack the southern gaggle, had just detected a magnetic anomaly in the sea beneath. Dan had gone over the chart carefully before the engagement, looking specifically for wrecks, and there weren't any marked. At the same time, another part of his brain noted that several boats were organizing out of the gaggle into what looked like a wheeling movement. Even in the absence of communications, someone was trying to coordinate a preplanned attack.

But rehearsing it in drills was nothing like executing it under fire, with your comms jammed, missiles headed at you, and five-inch shells going off overhead in instantaneous blooms of black high-explosive smoke that boomed shock waves across the water like the crack of doom.

"This is Red Hawk. Prosecute, or attack? Over."

He decided. "Attack as ordered. Stay high. Take out the ones turning south. If they turn north, let 'em go." He clicked to the Sonar channel. "Zotcher. Copy that datum from Red Hawk?"

Instead he got Rit Carpenter. *"On it, Skipper. Designate Goblin Alfa. But we got nothing there. If it's a sub, he's doggo on the bottom."*

When he looked at the screen again the semicircle that denoted Red Hawk was passing just to the south of the gaggle, low, at two hundred knots . . . close to never-exceed speed. Spitting out those sixty-pound homing Hellfires. The contact ahead displayed as a possible submarine. If *Savo* kept on the course he'd planned, north of Sirri Island, she'd pass within range of its torpedoes. If it *was* a sub. But if he turned to slide south of Sirri, he'd be in among the rigs and pipelines of the Fateh oil field.

"Red Hawk reports: Eight Hellfires expended. Four

detonations, one secondary, lots of smoke. Winchester, Winchester." Which meant, all ordnance expended.

"Sir, do you need me anymore?" the Persian beside him asked, very politely.

Dan flinched; he'd forgotten Kaghazchi was there. "Um, you can stand by . . . but stay in CIC, please.— Very well," he said into the helo net. "Clear to the east, but stand by to light off jamming and spoofing as required. Fuel state?"

"Bingo fuel time twenty."

Christ, he'd have to recover them soon. He'd boxed his enemy in, but now he was getting boxed himself. And time was running out. He was processing this, with the still-turning missile boats next in line, when Mills breathed, "Bandits."

When Dan looked up there they were: three, then four tracks just winked into existence above the mainland. The callouts went up: Su-24s. Not the latest and greatest jets, but more than adequate to threaten surface ships. The top cover F/A-18s could deal with four, but if their numbers kept building, the situation might turn dire.

"Matador, this is Anvil. Stand by . . . Salvo. Taking second assault wave. Over."

"Roger, out," Dan muttered. *Mitscher* was taking on a new wave of boats, but to judge by their ragged intervals, and the fact that several were lagging the leaders, the warrior spirit was flagging. One boat was already fleeing, heading north across the transit lane. If the F-18s let it go, as he'd directed, there'd be more.

Mills was blinking at him. "What'cha think, Matt?" Dan asked him. "Something in your eye?"

"The IIRN bases its Kilos outside the Gulf. The navy and the Pasdaran don't exercise together, according to a brief I heard. Not a lot of mutual trust."

"Uh-huh. I heard that too. So our contact's probably not a Kilo."

"I'd say, doubtful. But the Guard operates those minisubs."

"I don't think it's a sub at all," Dan said. "There's all kinds of metal under the water here. Pipelines. Abandoned drilling structures. Wrecks, from Operation Praying Mantis—we hit the Iranians before, right about here." He clicked to the ASW circuit. "Rit, Dan. Anything yet on that possub? Goblin Alfa?"

"Not a peep, amigo. I'd let you know."

Dan let the "amigo" go by. For now. "Can you ping him?"

"Tried, but it's too shallow to get an active return. Suspect shadow zones, too. Like I said, shallow as shit."

"At only eight thousand yards?"

"Like I said, Cap'n—"

He clicked off, as the screen showed *Mitscher*'s Harpoons mowing the oncoming boats down one after the other. *Savo*'s five-inches were slamming away. So far nothing had gotten into range of the 25s or the Phalanx. Dan had expected to expend several Standards, but so far his electronics were proving a better shield.

An antiship missile had to be smarter than the average weapon. It navigated not to a fixed geographic point, like a cruise missile, but to an area where the target was expected to be. It then had to pick a maneuvering warship out of the sea return and surface clutter, select the real target out of perhaps several ships in range, calculate the most survivable approach geometry, and home in. At any point, it could be foxed. Sea-skimmers were particularly vulnerable to having their radar altimeters pulse-doubled, which aimed them into the sea at six hundred miles an hour . . . fatal to the missile, but to no one else.

But this was an engagement he couldn't totally win. He'd hoped to take advantage of the enemy's dividing his force, hit hard and keep going. By and large, that was a done deal. The gun cameras showed smoke plumes on the horizon, along with the puffs of high explosive as *Mitscher*'s and *Savo*'s guns planted a hedgerow of shellbursts in front of any renewed attack. The remaining boats in the southern gaggle were roaring in circles, more and more withdrawing to consolidate with the larger group up along the Iranian coast.

He had no interest in taking them on. Right now, he had to extricate, before the air forces got involved. But the only graceful way out led across the possible submarine. The guy didn't even have to torpedo him. If he'd quietly shat eight or ten mines across their line of withdrawal, *Savo* and possibly *Mitscher* too were toast.

The repetitive *whump . . . whump* of five-inch rounds going out ceased. The gunnery officer reported all targets beyond effective range, bores clear, forty rounds expended, no casualties. Dan rogered. Then flinched as Mills touched his elbow. "Um, we got a message on chat," he muttered.

Dan lowered his gaze reluctantly; this wasn't the time to screw his head into a computer screen. He'd assumed that once the lead started flying both Fleet and Strike One had been monitoring his tactical comms. Mills had been feeding them information too. So he grunted "Huh?" now as he read.

DARK HORSE: Point of this operation is to establish free passage through SOH transit lanes. Is it commander's intent not to complete transit?

"Fuck," he muttered. Dark Horse was Fifth Fleet, in Bahrain. From the wording, it was some staff puke assigned to monitor the op, not Fleet himself. But he'd have to answer, and from the phrasing, a simple "yes" wouldn't suffice.

It had been his intent, given the possible sub contact, and the increasing number of aircraft beginning to swarm like aroused hornets over the mainland, to cut south. From there, he could either put in to the U.S. naval facility in Jebel Ali to refuel, or else proceed, at a lower speed, up the Gulf to Bahrain. He typed back.

MATADOR: Enemy air activity increasing. Intent is to withdraw south out of the transit area and await orders.
DARK HORSE: Your orders are to quote complete passage unquote through SOH transit lanes. You have not completed passage unless you exit via the western entry/exit point of the traffic separation scheme.

"Oh, fuck me," Dan muttered. Was this guy for real? Wasn't transiting the Knuckle, and blasting the shit out of the Pasdaran, enough? With a sinking heart, he realized it might not. If *Savo* and *Mitscher* didn't complete the full passage, tomorrow the Iranians would be crowing they'd driven them off, held the ground, and won the battle.

He scanned the displays, making sure he wasn't fumbling the tactical picture. Two more missiles had been splashed, one by jamming, the other by a Standard from *Mitscher*. As he watched, a third Vampire continued inbound. They were coming in on the starboard quarter, overtaking, and popping up in such a way that he couldn't tell even from Aegis where they'd been fired from. They just appeared, about twenty miles out, barely enough time to get EW on them before things got really interesting. He snapped his IC switch to the antiair circuit, to hear his own coordinator speaking swiftly, voice overlain at times by the EW operators'. *"Correlates C-802. Jamming ineffective. Seeing a hard turn now to bird's port. Crossing engagement—"*

"Stand by to take with birds."

"Outside Matador engagement envelope—"

"This is Anvil. We'll take with Phalanx."

He tensed as, on the screen, the incomer neared *Mitscher,* and the babble of voices attained a new intensity. A quarter minute later Mills murmured, "Splash track 8617 . . . but *Mitscher* may have damage."

"What kind? How serious? Get a report."

"Wait one . . . They engaged with CIWS. Main

warhead exploded prematurely, but airframe elements impacted aft."

"Roger. Damage assessment as soon as possible." He contemplated asking Stonecipher for it, but didn't; the other CO would have enough on his plate without Dan riding him.

He sucked a deep breath, and with it the unmistakable scent of sandalwood. Then hands were on his back, his neck, digging in, loosening the knots locking up his neck and upper back. Despite himself, he leaned back, sighing, closing his eyes. Letting the tension ease, just for a millisecond.

Then opened them again, to catch Mills's astonished stare, and Wenck's, and most everyone else's at or near the command desk, too. He mumbled, "Uh, thanks, Amy. I mean, Lieutenant. But you . . . It felt great, but that's enough of that, I think."

"It's Healing Touch. Looked like you needed it, Captain." She patted his shoulder, then headed back to the Strike console.

Jesus. Okay, back to business . . . check the display again. He rubbed his face as the display flickered and renewed, as GCCS and the SPY-1 and Sonar and NTDS and the aircraft overhead flooded him with seamless torrents of data. His opponents didn't have anywhere near this information, this fast, but it was overwhelming him. The southern group had broken. Boats were streaming back across the lane. The northern group, on the other hand, seemed to be holding position, absorbing the fleeing units and turning them around in a chaotic, uneven, but partially reorganized line.

If he was going to go past again, he couldn't give them time to re-form. If an enemy starts to buckle, you don't let him catch his breath. He murmured to Mills, "Maintain course, but drop speed to twenty. Make sure *Mitscher* gets that."

Four seconds later, the 21MC clicked on. "CO," he snapped. At his elbow, Longley was trying to pour fresh coffee. Dan waved him away impatiently. Then changed his mind as the CS set a plate with two doughnuts beside it. Plain but sugared, just the way he liked them.

"Captain, exec, on the bridge. Just got the order to drop to twenty. We still headed south?"

Everybody was a step ahead of him today. Well, that was good. "Reconsidering that decision as we speak, XO. Why d'you ask?"

"Got a merchie coming down the pike toward us. Still on the horizon, but looks like he's headed out-bound."

Dan checked the vertical display again. Astonished, first, that he hadn't picked it up. Second, that some idiot was so far out of the loop he hadn't gotten the word that war was breaking out in the strait. But there it was, fifteen miles out, a fat, dumb, doubtlessly happy tanker bopping along at eight knots toward the outbound traffic lane. Which lay empty at the moment, except for the pulsing diamond of the still-stationary suspected submarine. Dan keyed Sonar again. "Rit, I really need an updated classification on that fucking datum."

This time he got Zotcher's voice, though. *"Working on it, Captain. It'd help to have another MAD pass, though. And a sonobuoy drop."*

"We don't have time for another pass." He had to decide. As if goading him still further, when he looked down again, lines had popped up on his chat.

DARK HORSE: Please advise intentions re completing assigned mission.

Dan typed,

MATADOR: Prefer to divert to Jebel Ali. Possible submarine contact in southern TSS.

Stonecipher came up on the voice circuit. *"Anvil here. Okay, back in business. Debris impact aft took off one of the comm antennas and the starboard Harpoon launcher. Fortunately the canister was empty. Two guys with minor burns from fuel splash. Redundancy on the antenna. Ready for combat. Over."*

The computer screen scrolled up to read,

DARK HORSE: Clear transit corridors of hostile forces. Use necessary means.

"Did he really say that?" Mills breathed, beside him. " 'Use necessary means'?"

Dan shook his head, hesitating for one more second. Blew out, shaking his head again. Then typed,

MATADOR: Coming NW to 310. Flank speed. Will reenter inbound lane E of Bani Forur and exit at established western check-in point.

He repeated this over the red phone to Stonecipher, adding, "Follow in my wake." Then spun in his chair and shouted across the compartment, "Bingo fuel, Red Hawk?"

"Bingo, ten minutes."

"Plant a sonobuoy on Goblin Alfa. Then vector back here for hot refuel."

The antisubmarine coordinator told him 202 had launched with a full loadout of ordnance but no sonobuoys. "We didn't expect ASW, Captain. Made the decision to load up with extra bullets instead."

"That's okay—well, fuck."

"Another run isn't going to tell us anything we don't already know," Mills said.

"*Skipper, Sonar,*" the 21MC at his desk blared, deafeningly loud. Dan turned it down and pressed the Transmit key. "CO."

"*Rit here. A MAD run's not gonna tell us anything we don't already know about this turkey.*"

"Mr. Mills was just saying the same thing."

"*He's right. But instead of charging on in, how about we squirt a couple 46s out on that bearing? Let the fish do the work?*"

Dan rubbed his chin. The Mark 46s were lightweight homing torpedoes, their digital brains programmed to hunt down submarines in shallow water. Ticos carried them down on the damage-control deck, aft of Medical, to eject with compressed air though tube doors just above the waterline. "What's the speed differential? Those aren't fast torpedoes, Rit."

"*They'll get there ahead of us. And if that's a minisub*"

sitting on the bottom, he's gonna do something when he hears those high-speed props headed his way. Pop a bubble decoy, at least."

"Makes sense. Join us on the ASW circuit, Rit." Dan snapped his selector. To the ASW officer, Lieutenant Farmer, and out of the side of his mouth to Mills, he muttered, "Okay, waterspace management. There's not the slightest chance this could be a friendly?"

Mills shook his head. "We don't operate subs in the Gulf. Nor do any of the trucial states."

"Uh-huh. Winston?"

The ASW officer agreed with Mills. Dan rasped, "All right, set up. Two Mark 46s out along the bearing, set for circular search around the datum. Get 'em out there ASAP."

"Copy weapons free, two-shot salvo."

He confirmed, then leaned back, easing a breath out, looking up at the display. The never-sleeping beam swept over the southern Gulf, the Arabian Sea, the eastern Indian Ocean. He saw and knew with the wisdom of Athena. Wielded the thunderbolts of Zeus. Yet still, obeyed the iron commands of Mars.

Through the fatigue and fear a sudden disenchantment surfaced. Out there, his shells and missiles had torn men apart. Burned and drowned them. His side called them fanatics. They called themselves patriots and believers. But the ineluctable realities of the energy markets meant they had to die, and that sailors had to risk their lives killing them.

He could almost hear Nick Niles grunting *Above*

your pay grade, Lenson. Eyeing him with that amused disgust the vice admiral reserved for him alone, it seemed. He imagined Blair shaking her head too. He took another deep breath and scrubbed his face with a palm, stubble and grit and oil grating on his skin.

The double thud of compressed air shuddered the compartment. *"Fish one away . . . fish two away. Mark, start of run. Time to target, time one five."*

The Mark 46 ran out at over fifty knots. *Savo* would arrive at the datum twelve minutes after the torpedoes began a circle search, pinging and listening. Either they would sense a submarine and attack, or declare the area clear.

A third possibility existed, of course. That the other skipper could fox or evade his weapons, and loose his own as *Savo* and *Mitscher* passed close aboard.

A shiver ran up his back, and his neck knotted. Each breath took an effort, drawn against a narrowing in the throat, a weight on his chest.

But he had his orders. To throw the dice, and let the god of war decide.

He told Mills to have *Mitscher* open the interval, lag back two miles, and directed Red Hawk to vector to the destroyer for a hot refuel. If the worst happened, they'd be safe, at least. Then he clicked to the General Battle circuit and tried for a confident tone. "This is the Captain. All ahead flank. Indicate turns for thirty knots. Come to course for the Western Entry Point. And stand by."

* * *

Two hours later he sagged in his seat, soaked with cold sweat turned to liquid ice by the air-conditioning. Wenck had the helo deck camera up on one of the displays. Black columns of smoke stained the dusty horizon: the sinking, burning boats they'd hit during the first attacks.

His torpedoes had completed runout, circled, but detected nothing. Then, ending their brief consciousnesses, had self-detonated, raising huge plumes of white water to port and then starboard as *Savo* and, miles astern, *Mitscher* passed through. Either there was no submarine, or it was keeping its head down. The northern gaggle had made short threatening dashes as if to charge, but were turned back each time by low passes of the carrier air. They'd launched no more missiles, and taken no action as the huge, deep-laden tanker, a Chinese flag, as it happened, churned past. Maybe they'd already made their point: that they could close the strait anytime they liked. And weren't afraid to die doing it.

He remembered how during previous interferences with navigation, the Iranian state oil company had sold heavily as the price of oil futures peaked, then sold short as the West cleared the sea lanes again. Cashing in as the price rose, then again on the fall.

As corpses drifted in the warm Gulf, tossed by the waves, their sightless faces caressed by the dust-laden wind.

"Secure from general quarters?" Mills asked. Glancing at him, Dan saw awe. Respect. Saw the same expressions around him, from the consoles and watch stations. How strange, that they should look at him this way, while he himself felt only relief they'd survived.

Without a word, he nodded. Unbent, and lurched to his feet. Staggered once, weaving, as his calves cramped. Then stalked silently through his silent crew, until he could dog a steel door between him and them.

8

The United Arab Emirates

Jebal Ali, in the United Arab Emirates, was a gigantic commercial port, larger than Norfolk or Long Beach, with square miles of baking asphalt, mountains of containers, dozens of offload cranes. Then more square miles of petrochemical tanks, all shimmering in a baking sun that hit Dan like a red-hot bullet as soon as he stepped outside the skin of the ship. In deep summer, everything was shrouded in the shamal-borne dust, fine as triple-X sugar, that at times made it hard to see a softball-throw distant.

It was also only about twenty miles from Dubai City. But after a talk with the husbanding agent—and how Mr. Hamid loved to talk, droning on eagerly about all the flag officers he knew, all the U.S. ships he'd serviced—Dan decided, reluctantly, against granting liberty. The crew deserved R&R, and he wouldn't have minded seeing the fabled city himself. But there was just too much to do—inspecting the damage to *Mitscher,* then getting his after-action report sent off. After that, arranging for sewage disposal, fresh food, currency exchange, line handlers, fenders, refueling, repainting the scorch marks from the launches, and offloading garbage and onloading ammo. Plus taking generators and pumps down for maintenance and maybe getting a freshwater washdown, if they could get enough water pierside.

Not to mention a thousand other details . . . all to be completed in forty-eight hours. Fifth Fleet wanted them under way again as soon as possible for a transit the other way, outbound. He didn't look forward to that. The Revolutionary Guard had been able to study his tactics. Now they could game it out and, maybe, come up with something unexpected.

Also, after what had happened to USS *Cole* in a supposedly safe port, Dan was loath to leave his command half-manned, no matter how secure the locals assured him the place was. Aside from a UAE gunboat, he and *Mitscher,* moored on the far side of the basin, were the only two gray ships there. The security net, and the RHIB patrols both ships had out, made him feel a little safer. But if a terrorist decided to kamikaze alongside in a speedboat loaded with explosives, *Savo* wouldn't be hard to find.

After a talk with Cheryl, he'd agreed to let the guys and girls spend down time in the Sand Pit, a fenced, air-conditioned, U.S.-only facility where they could phone home, listen to music, and play video games. Surrounded on three sides by oil field supply yards,

tank farms, and container warehousing, it was un-
glamorous, but there was a pool, a shaded picnic area,
a volleyball court.

And a bar, with American and local beer, below even
commissary prices. That should cheer them up a bit.

He went over the last evening in port, maybe for a
burger and fries that didn't come off the mess decks. It
was only three hundred yards from pierside, but he
stopped a few steps up the shore and stood with fingers
tucked under his belt, watching the water. Under the
frosting of dust and scum it looked inviting. Small silver and black fish flickered in and out of the riprap. Familiar, but he couldn't put a name to them. He lingered
for several minutes, sweating, mind echoing as hollowly
as a house after the movers have left. Just watching
the fish.

By the time he got to the Pit his khakis were soaked
and the airborne grit sticking to the sweat made every
step a chafing torment. Rit Carpenter was sprawled
with several chiefs and first class in lounge chairs in the
bar. Some he didn't know, likely *Mitscher* men. They
fell silent as he came in. The yeasty, malted smells of
booze and beer didn't feel entirely comfortable. He'd
had to stop drinking years before. But he didn't feel out
of place, the way he had when he'd first gone on the
wagon. The idea of voluntarily ingesting a toxic chemical just seemed weird now. He said, only half joking,
"Telling on me again, Rit?"

The old sonarman waved a longneck. "Hell, Skip, we

been through some shit, right? I can't tell a sea story, what's a deployment for? Hey, guys, it's oh-beer-thirty. What say, let's buy the skipper one."

"Maybe in a minute. After I check out the store."

"We'll be here." Chief Slaughenhaupt looked drowsy, already half in the bag. "Hey . . . Lois says she got your message out to the dependents. They appreciate it."

Dan nodded. "Thank her for me, Chief. I'm gonna check out the store, then grab a burger. Join you after, if you're still here."

"Where else could we go?" Carpenter muttered. He drained the longneck and signaled for another. Dan took the slender, ponytailed bartender for a girl at first, then realized at a second glance he wasn't.

He checked out the little store, bought postcards. Looked over the tourist-trap trinkets, the heavy gold jewelry. Not Blair's style, nor his daughter's, either.

Then he noticed, against the wall, stacks of colorful cloth.

Shemaghs, desert-style cotton head-wraps with distinctive stitched designs. The clerk, who was Pakistani or Bangladeshi, spread them out on the counter, said they'd just come in. He explained how they protected the face from sun, the lungs from dust. Dan asked what the various colors and designs meant, and got more explanation than he needed, plus a demonstration of the various ways to wear one: a turban, a face-wrap, a bandanna.

There were bales of the things, and the prices were reasonable. He bought one in olive and black, after the clerk assured him this didn't belong to any particular nationality or tribe. The postcards went to his brothers and his daughter, a few words apiece on the back of a glossy colorful shot of Dubai. When they were stamped and in the blue U.S. Mail box he slid into a diner booth and ordered a cheeseburger and fries. The waiter talked him into a Lebanese nonalcoholic beer. At the first taste, he grimaced at the unexpected bite of lemon. Well, he wouldn't have to worry about scurvy.

He kept glancing at the phone booths. On most the handsets dangled, the international signal for "out of order." He'd e-mailed Blair almost every day, though of late his messages had been short, as had her replies. But all at once, he yearned to hear her voice. He checked his watch as he sipped the lemon beer . . . okay, so it grew on you. The time difference was eight hours . . . so it'd be around seven. She was usually an early riser.

To his surprise, his Verizon card worked. She picked up on the third ring. "Who's this?"

He smiled, picturing her lying in tumbled sheets. A little grumpy and disoriented, the way she was first thing, before her coffee. Maybe in the black silk pajamas he'd given her, practically see-through, breasts and nipples and the swell of her mons all perfectly outlined in glossy, sheer fabric. Shit, he was getting hard.

"Dan? I almost didn't pick up. Where're you calling from? God, there's a huge delay."

"Someplace hot and dry. Here for two days. Under way again tomorrow."

A pause, which he broke with "How've you been doing? Any progress on the fund-raising?"

"Oh, we're all right . . . ugh, the fucking fundraising. I spend two hours every morning calling people and asking for donations. They all want something for their money. Guess I can't blame them for that. They're talking about redrawing the district . . . oh, let's not talk about that. I guess the big news is we have a new member of the family."

Dan blinked. "What?" Had Nan gotten—

"He's black and white. And cute as hell."

"He's a . . . what? A puppy?"

"Puppy? No, you've always got to be there for a dog. I learned that from Checkie, and his Labs. So fucking needy. No, a kitten. I got it from Ina."

Ina was her English girlhood friend, who lived several miles away in Maryland. "Well, I guess that's good. Has he, she—has it got a name?"

"It's a 'he,' and his name is Jimbo. How's your cough doing? Your throat?"

"Not too bad. The dust irritates it, though. You remember what it's like out here."

"Yeah. How's your crew?"

"Oh, fine . . . We're still seeing that respiratory bug. But they're holding up. Actually, I've been trying to think of things to weld them together better, give them a little more esprit."

"Oh! You made the *Post*. Third page, continued from the second. 'Renewed Friction in Strait of Hormuz.'"

"Friction, huh? It was more than that."

"What do you mean?"

She sounded surprised, and he checked himself, wondering. Were both sides close-holding accounts of the action? He checked outside the booth; the senior enlisted were still talking and drinking. Outside, in the falling dark, lights were coming on, and it looked as if a drunken volleyball tournament was starting. "Um, well, more than I want to discuss on the phone. I'll send you a detailed e-mail. You still have that covered account through SAIC, don't you?"

"Yes. I'm still listed as a consultant."

"Look, I'm putting stuff out to the dependents through Chief Slaughenhaupt's wife, but if it's in the papers, it might be good to reassure the families. Have them get something personal from you. A note, or an e-mail. Think you could take up some of the slack? Maybe—"

"Dan, I understand, the CO's wife is supposed to do that stuff. But I'm not a traditional captain's wife. Running for office is like having two full-time jobs. Unless you really, really have something you desperately need me to do, I'd rather you stayed with your regular ombudsperson, or whatever."

He glanced out again, pulled the sliding door shut. Not a cheering answer, but pretty much the response he'd expected. And maybe it wasn't smart to ask the next question, either. The mid-deployment phone call . . . so much had to be crammed into these minutes, so much else left unsaid . . . . "Look, are we still good? You and me?"

A pause. "We still need to talk. What you're going to do, if I'm a sitting member of Congress. And what *I'm* going to do, if I lose."

"That's about our careers. What about *us*?"

She sighed. "I'm still thinking. Maybe it's just, I don't know, getting older, losing my looks—"

"Good grief, Blair. You haven't lost anything! If this is about your ear—"

"Not really. I'm not *that* shallow—"

He said, "I didn't mean to say you were," but the delay made it awkward and she was speaking again by the time his words reached her, leaving them talking over each other in a not-quite-argument, not-quite-friendly exchange that petered out into silence. Until there was nothing more to say but an awkward good-bye.

When he went back into the bar the chiefs looked him over, tsk-tsking. "Rough call home?" Zotcher said. When Dan shrugged, he beckoned the barkeep. "You like those lemon pops? I saw you makin' a face."

"I guess they're all right."

"Another of those for the skipper," Carpenter called.

Dan opened the plastic bag the clerk had given him. He pulled out the shemagh and unfolded it on the table. The chiefs frowned at it, then at him.

"Let me run an idea past you," he said.

They got under way just after dawn, beneath a sky the color of a sander belt and a wind that blew banks of airborne grit past them like mist on some haunted moor. Then steamed in six-knot squares through the morning, as the supertankers they were to escort were delayed getting under way.

At last their monstrous shadows loomed through a

pale red half-light as if some lander were televising it from Mars. *Mitscher* fell in astern as they joined up off the Great Pearl Bank. The tankers eddied in and out of sight in a ruddy, tricky haze that closed in with a rising wind. Dan placed his task group to the north, intending to transit the outbound lane with *Mitscher* ahead this time, *Savo* bringing up the rear. He went to general quarters an hour from the western entrance, developing a thorough air and surface picture.

Face taco'd in one of the shemaghs, he leaned back in his wing chair, coughing. The very air hurt to breathe. The sun microwaved through the haze. The bridge wing thermometer stood at 125 degrees. He wouldn't be able to stay out long. The only other person outside was the mine lookout, up in the eyes of the ship. He stood motionless as a figurehead, one hand on the wildcat, staring ahead.

But he didn't want to go inside. Since the battle, he'd felt depressed. In there, the line would form. Messages. Reports. Decisions. He'd told Cheryl to manage the routine stuff. Only if something hot came in would she route it out to him. She was taking hold. Which wasn't easy—the XO's basic job description being to act as the leading asshole. To demand more than anyone could offer, and keep driving standards upward. It had broken the previous exec, and come close to breaking Dan, back when he'd had the job. In some ways, being the skipper was easier.

Aside from making those life-and-death decisions, of course.

He shaded his gaze into the wind. The sand, the dust,

the scarlet sky, the sheen of brown scum on the weirdly still sea, reminded him of Earnest Will. The escort mission that had ended with *Turner Van Zandt*'s sinking. But also where he'd met Blair, on a fact-finding mission for the Armed Services Committee.

For a long time, the relationship had been on and off, passionate when they were together, but comfortable apart, too. Then they'd gotten married. And for a time it had all seemed fine.

But now . . . His first marriage had gone into the same kind of death spiral. He'd seen it over and over; deployments were hell on both sides. There was so damn little he could *do* from here. His daughter from his first marriage didn't need him anymore; she had her own life now. Maybe it *was* time he thought about getting out. A fucking cat . . . it was sad that Blair felt the need for company. If that was what it was.

And there she was, Staurulakis, not Blair, at the window in the port wing door. Checking him out, then undogging the door. Unsightly red grooves engraved her cheeks. The duty radioman fidgeted behind her, a clipboard over his crotch. Dan sighed and pulled his shemagh tighter.

"Sir? Update from Fleet. The Pasdaran announced the end of their exercise. Iran lifted the Notice to Mariners. Also, chief corpsman wonders if you can spare a minute."

He sighed again, and swung down. Took a last look around. Through the low churning haze, he could see fuck-all. Something could be bearing down on him right now, and he'd never know. Except through radar, of course. Thank God for radar. He couldn't imagine trying to navigate, much less fight, around here without it. "All right, let me read that. I'll see the corpsman in my sea cabin."

Grissett looked upset. Dan pointed to the spare chair, wedged into the corner of the tiny compartment. "Grab a sit, Bones. What'cha got?"

"Not good news, sir, I'm afraid." The chief medic handed over stapled sheets. "Today's sick list."

"Some of the troops overindulge at the Sand Pit?"

"No sir. Well, maybe a little. But mainly, I'm getting a big uptick with the crud."

Dan studied the list as the chief corpsman went on, "On the next page, I made up a graph. Trying to figure out what this thing correlates to—port visits, whatever. And it does seem to correlate with in-port periods."

"Is that right? We get more cases in port?"

"Yessir—I mean, no sir. The opposite. Look at the graph." Dan flipped to it. "It's a negative correlation. The numbers go *down* when we're in port, like in Crete."

"Not sure I see it."

"It's only about minus zero point two, but it's there."

"What's minus zero point two?"

"The correlation coefficient of the two variables, in-port time and reporting cases."

Dan whistled. "Are you telling me you calculated the correlation coefficient?"

"Well . . . yes sir. Just divided the covariance of the

variables by the product of the standard deviations. I brought along my calculations—"

"That's interesting, Chief. I didn't know you were into statistics."

"A lot of medicine's based on it nowadays," Grissett said stiffly, as if Dan had insulted his competence. "It's basic stuff."

"I see. Sorry, you just took me aback there. I'll look over your figures. Point two is a pretty weak correlation, but still." Dan flipped through a couple more pages, groping for a connection. "Anything from Bethesda?"

Grissett said no, aside from anomalous antigens in the urine samples he'd sent, and waited expectantly. Dan scratched his neck, trying to come up with something. "We scrubbed down the ducts and changed all the filters. Maybe the sequence of events? Did the new filters go in before or after the duct sterilization?"

"After, sir. And I supervised the duct cleaning, with the Top Snipe."

"Meaning Commander Danenhower, I take it." Dan regretted the reproof immediately, and hastened to gloss it over. "Yeah, the Top Snipe. Think his guys did a thorough job?"

"If hot water and bleach could've killed it, we'd have wiped it out, Captain." Grissett nodded at the sick list, still in Dan's hands. "But five new cases this morning. Added to fifteen already off duty. And what worries me is, people don't seem to be fully recovering, like with a flulike illness. A couple even developed pneumonia."

Dan's eyebrows lifted. "Pneumonia!"

"Yessir. I dosed them heavy with cipro, and I think

we got it, but even the ones that recover just drag themselves around like zombies. You've heard them coughing."

He had indeed. Pushing his hand back over his hair, he searched his mind. "And it correlates negatively with in-port time . . . but it doesn't live in the ventilation. Could we have picked up a brand-new bug? Some Middle Eastern bad boy nobody's seen yet?" Another possibility occurred, uglier than he wanted to voice, but forced himself to. "It couldn't be, um, sexually transmitted, could it?"

Grissett said, a touch patronizingly, "Most viral infections can be passed by close physical contact. But that's not sexual, in the way I think you mean."

Dan sighed. He seemed to be doing a lot of that lately. "I don't have any direction for you, Doc. We can't divert. This is a national-level mission. I can ask again for a medical team, but we don't seem to be getting much support out here. Let me talk to Fleet medical, see what they think."

"I've already done that, sir, but maybe the additional horsepower can jar something loose."

Dan nodded. He glanced at the door, and the corpsman stood. But hesitated, not yet leaving. "Feeling all right yourself, Skipper? I've seen you coughing. Wrapping that scarf over your nose."

Dan shrugged. "I sucked some smoke on 9/11. The dust out here doesn't help. Could the crud be related to dust? The commodore mentioned dustborne illnesses."

"Right, bronchiolitis, and dustborne asthma."

"Could we be picking up some kind of toxics in the dust, on the wind?"

Grissett's gaze went distant. "I don't think so. But I'll run the numbers, see if there's a correlation with the rates that spend a lot of time outside the air-conditioning envelope. Boatswains. Lookouts."

Dan got up, and unwrapped a bundle of thin stitched cotton. "I might have something we can try."

He passed the word about the Official USS *Savo Island* Shemagh via the chiefs. Hermelinda's storekeepers handled the issuing. He'd bought three hundred with the CO's discretionary fund (and documented that the ship's store price equaled what he'd paid, so he couldn't be accused of profiteering). On the mess decks, Kaghaz-chi demonstrated how to wear them. The exec made her policy clear: they weren't uniform items, or a replacement for flash gear, but something to wear on a voluntary basis, when you were on lookout or on watch. The crew seemed doubtful at first, but by that evening, when he went up to the bridge, everybody was wearing his or hers, sometimes in novel ways. The women especially liked them; their eyes, peering out from folds of cloth, seemed alluring and mysterious.

They headed for the channel out at 1700 local, with CAP and SUCAP en route from *Vinson*. According to Fleet, Tehran was crowing about how they'd "damaged two warships of the Great Satan." No one there seemed to have made much of a fuss over the butcher's bill: four boats missing, presumed sunk, five more damaged. At least that'd been Dan's estimate in his after-action report, and his numbers had lined up with Stonecipher's, as seen from *Mitscher*.

Settled into the pocket of his command chair in CIC, he stared at the displays, puzzled. Aside from a few scattered contacts along the coast of Qeshm, the waterway looked normal. Commercial traffic was resuming, to judge by the string of merchants on the surface picture.

Could it just be . . . *over,* with nothing really settled? But no radars locked onto him as they steamed past Jaziriyeh-ye Forur and reported in to Omani traffic control. The Omanis had been conspicuous by their absence during the entire fracas the week before. Preserving a careful neutrality by looking the other way. Well, they had to live next door to the Iranians. In this part of the planet, just staying out of trouble was an all too elusive goal.

Mills nudged him with the handset, rousing him from reverie. The call was a Dr. Somebody, from Bahrain. Dan drew a blank, then recalled: the Fifth Fleet medical officer. They discussed *Savo*'s problem. Dan pointed out they'd been reporting the same syndrome for months now, had already had one unexplained death. At last the medico agreed to ask for an epidemiology team from Bethesda. He couldn't promise when they'd get to the ship, though. "Until then, I recommend focusing on basic sanitation, on the food handlers and meal preparation." Dan doubted that was the source, but vowed to hold additional training, and inspect for cleanliness.

Mills cleared his throat and nudged him. A new contact had popped up, sourced from Silver Ghost, the Air Force AWACS out of Oman. Seconds later *Mitscher* reported it too: Track 7834, out of Abu Musa. The island was disputed between Oman and Iran, but had been garrisoned by Iran since the days of the shah. EW detected a radar corresponding to that of a PBF. These were modest-sized gunboats based on the North Korean Chaho class. Dan kept an eye on it as they passed, and had his surface warfare coordinator develop a gun solution. But the C-801s and 802s were the real threats—plus, of course, any Iranian air.

But nothing rose to challenge them. As they steered for the Knuckle, more small craft popped up. The supertankers churned serenely on. Presently the C-802 batteries began illuminating as well, though none locked on. Dan set his team to correlating them, trying to figure out if they'd relocated during the days between the transit in and the way out, or if they were parked in the same locations. They also passed four dhows that the cryppies picked up as verbally transmitting targeting data.

But aside from that, there seemed to be no massing of forces. "They're backing off," Staurulakis murmured, standing beside him with arms crossed. "Letting us out."

She looked frazzled, gaunt, a little unsteady on her feet. He eyed her doubtfully. Execs could burn out . . .

as her predecessor had, all too spectacularly. "I wouldn't let down our guard just yet, Cheryl. Still a couple hours until we're out of missile range."

"Right . . . right."

"Feeling okay? Get any sleep while we were in port?"

"Not much. We had to get those Harpoons onloaded, and coordinate everything with the port security people." She coughed into a fist.

"You're not coming down with this thing, are you?"

"Nope. Just tired. I'm okay."

He glanced around, abruptly realizing that almost everyone else looked just as hollow-cheeked, just as red-eyed. And equally apathetic. The port visit should have helped, but they'd had so much to do. He cleared his throat. "Look, we need to get out of GQ as soon as we clear the strait. Condition three, but only until we're over the horizon. Then, the normal steaming watch, so the off watch can catch some Zs. And maybe a rope yarn Sunday."

"A what?"

He blinked. "Never heard of a rope yarn Sunday?"

"You're losing me, Captain."

"Well, it's old Navy . . . a half day's work, to catch up on your mending, pick oakum, that kind of thing. Tomorrow's Sunday, right? What've we got scheduled?"

"I wasn't sure where we'd be at that point. So I didn't really—"

"Let's leave the afternoon free. And what else could we do? To sort of let everybody's hair down. Swim call?"

"I don't think that's a good idea in these waters, Captain. Sharks. Snakes—"

"How 'bout a steel beach picnic?" Wenck put in. Dan swiveled to face him. "And a beer call," the chief added. "We earned it."

Dan nodded slowly, gaze drawn back to the displays. Where the lumbering behemoths they escorted were turning the corner, bound for the Indian Ocean. The Combattantes they'd passed on the way in, and which had trailed them up to the exercise area, were still out there. He was keeping an eye out for them, and for any bogeys rising from the new airfield farther south, near Chabahar. East of that was the Chinese-built port in Pakistan, Gwadar. He'd love to take a look at that, see if he could pick up any electronic intelligence. If they made it out without further incident.

He nodded slowly. "Steel beach it is. Good suggestion, Donnie. Cheryl, let's get our heads together, see what we can do."

"Captain. Captain?"

He wasn't really sure, for a moment, if he was still dreaming. No. In his bunk. Having finally, *finally,* gotten his eyes closed. He coughed, hard, bringing something sticky and thick and gritty up from inside his chest. Under way . . . *Savo Island* . . . Arabian Sea. He groped for the Hydra. "Yeah . . . yeah. What is it, Chief?"

"We got some kind of light low in the water. Bearing zero-four-zero. No radar contact."

Fuck. But you couldn't say that, or betray in any way that you resented being woken. Or they might not call you, next time, when you really ought to be there. He muttered reluctantly, "I'll be right up."

The pilothouse was utterly dark. He groped his way around the helm console, barking his shin on something steel. Muttered, "OOD?"

"Here, sir. Chief Van Gogh."

"What've we got, Chief?"

Van Gogh led him out onto the port wing, where Dan stared into one of the blackest nights he'd ever seen. The warm wind blustered in his ears. "What am I looking at?"

Hands gripped his shoulders and aimed him. "Out there, sir. Right below the horizon."

What horizon? But he caught, just for an instant, what might've been a flicker of yellow. Van Gogh said, "Port lookout reported it. Young kid. Good eyes. Otherwise we'd have missed it. Zip on radar. I slowed and called you. We're at five knots."

"Okay. Where's *Mitscher*?"

"Astern, Captain. CIC put him there to do some kind of beam calibration."

A pair of binoculars was pushed into his hands. Dan found the lights of the destroyer, well astern, then searched off to port again until he picked up the flicker once more. But the 7x50s didn't give him much more than his naked eyeballs. "Phosphorescence?"

"Look down, sir."

He looked straight down, to a greenish flicker, along the turbulent layer where the steel skin of the ship slid through the sea. "We have luminescent organisms, but they're green," Van Gogh said. "That's yellow out there. Almost like a flame."

"Check with Sonar?"

"Yessir. Nothing on that bearing."

"How far are we from land?"

"Hundred and twenty miles, as of eight o'clock reports."

"All right, let's come around. Inform *Mitscher* what we're doing. Have them stand clear." He stared through the glasses again, but the spark was gone. Or he couldn't pick it up. "Go in slow. And better man up the lights."

The dazzling beam from the signal bridge picked out debris from the blackness. Low black dots, a dark line. Dan slowed to a crawl, came left to put the wind behind him, and let the ship drift in.

"Three guys, on a raft," the junior officer of the deck said, balancing binoculars on the tips of his fingers.

A few minutes later they were looking down at them. The wet black heads sagged and lolled. The men didn't look up, or wave. There was no raft. They were lashed to a long wooden timber, some kind of beam or spar.

This was what the Navy called a SOLAS event. Saving life at sea. Not that he wouldn't have anyway, but *Savo* was legally obligated to render assistance. Dan debated putting the RHIB in the water, but at last just bumped ahead and lowered the boat ladder midships.

Grissett and two boatswain's mates went down to help the men out of the water.

The first lieutenant and the chief corpsman reported to him on the bridge an hour later. "Three dudes," Grissett said. "Lucky as hell. One kept showing me a Bic lighter. That was probably what we saw."

"Okay, who are they? Where are they from?"

"Iranian. Not super coherent at the moment, but Kaghazchi says he thinks they're saying they're refugees. Baha'is. One was condemned to death for proselytizing. Disrespecting Islam, whatever. The other two are his cousins. They broke him out of prison, or bribed him out—that's not real clear, but who cares—and they were trying to escape in a boat. The good news: they made it out. The bad news: the boat came apart and sank. There were two others. They swam away, and these guys never saw them again."

"Hundred-plus miles from shore? Headed east? Where'd they think they were going?"

"I don't get the impression these are seasoned travelers."

Van Gogh put in, "This is where the prevailing wind and current would take them, from the coast. Pretty fucking lucky, I'd say."

"Absolutely agree," said the corpsman. "One more day without water, they'd have been DOA."

Dan leaned back against leather, unutterably fatigued. "Yeah—to get seen at night, way out here. *Somebody's* looking out for them. Okay, so they're claiming religious, political refugee status, I guess. That right?"

"We didn't get to the legalities yet, Captain. I was just trying to get 'em rehydrated, and checking eyes and airways. Two of 'em inhaled gasoline when the boat went down, in the slick. Think they're gonna be okay, though. You can talk to 'em yourself if you want."

"Maybe tomorrow," he said, envisioning his bunk again, looking at his watch. 0300. He might be able to get another couple hours in.

If they didn't call him again.

9

The Arabian Sea

Chicken, steak, and burgers were grilling over charcoal in torched-apart fifty-five-gallon drums. The smells of barbecue mingled with those of baked beans, coleslaw, chips, and stack gas. Gulls darted overhead, shrieking with rage and envy as *Savo* rolled eastward at a casual ten knots, barely fast enough to push a bow wave. Two hundred and fifty miles out of Hormuz, the atmosphere was nearly clear of sand. Still cloudy, still monsoon weather, and the wind still kicked up a blue sea.

Dan, holding a laden plate on the helo deck, studied *Mitscher* steaming in company a mile off. Incredibly, no one had woken him again until 0730, and he felt almost rested, though his throat was raw and the cough worse. Around him the crew chatted and chowed down at folding tables, squatted cross-legged on the nonskid, or dangled legs through the deck-edge nets. Most wore trunks or bathing suits, predominantly issue gear, but some in colorful civilian attire. Especially the girls, a few of whom lay garnering what ultraviolet they could facedown on blankets on the hangar roof.

Looking down, Dan couldn't help noting the tire marks and eroded surfaces where the helo had scraped the rough black nonskid off. They'd have to resurface the flight deck again.

"Bug juice, Cap'n. Orange or blue?"

"The orange, please."

Hands full, he stood eating with a gathering of the chiefs, listening to "Red" Slaughenhaupt tell about the time he'd been on a boarding team deployed out here. They'd been doing maritime intercept operations with a Canadian frigate when they'd intercepted a heroin shipment. "We found two tons of brown powder, in plastic bags," the lead fire controlman finished. "I had to witness the destruction. Felt pretty wasteful, dumping all that good shit over the side. You gotta wonder, it's worth that much on the street, why don't we just take it home and sell it? Buy ourselves another carrier battle group or something." The other chiefs grinned, glancing from him to Dan.

He wandered from there into the hangar. Red Hawk squatted, folded-back blades nodding with the ship's motion. The helo mechanics were disassembling equipment. "Thought this was a rope yarn afternoon," he said to Strafer, who'd strolled over when he came in.

"You want us in the air tomorrow, gotta maintain today." The lead pilot rubbed his crew cut. "Not to bring up business, but . . . we put a lot of hours on this bird. Coming up on Interval Two fast." Wear was accumulating, and the bird would need serious attention soon. Wilker looked out to sea. "We have to put flight hours into this exercise? What's it called?"

"Malabar."

"And who else—"

"U.S., Australia, Japan, India, Singapore. This year, they're gonna focus on ASW. So, yeah, you're gonna be tasked. Plus, if we have to put you in the air to check out any questionable surface contacts." Dan glanced at the worktables, where burgers and Cokes had been set aside. "We're all getting tired. If there's any way we can lighten your guys' load, let me know. And if we're getting close to the hairy edge on safety, let me know. I mean it. Don't push any envelopes, just for an exercise."

He wandered out onto the flight deck again and stood looking down on the fantail, eating baked beans with a plastic fork. Three dark-haired, swarthy men squatted on their haunches on the afterdeck. The Iranians they'd fished out the night before. They were looking out at the sea, not speaking or interacting, just staring, as if hoping to spot someone they knew was out there. The after gun was centerlined, threatening a distant, slowly rolling horizon. The wake unscrolled behind them, a smoothed path that gradually vanished as it approached the distant, jagged waves at his sight line. Several crew members stood along the lifeline, spaced like sparrows on a wire, holding poles or tending handlines. Seabirds whirled, making him shield his plate with one hand against errant squirts. Now and then a gull left the milling swarm to dive toward where the sailors' bait skipped along the surface.

Then, from high above, a greater shadow descended. The gulls parted, shrieking and crying. Dan squinted up into the opal light, not quite believing what he was witnessing.

The thing's wings were wider than a man was tall. It balanced on the wind like a Romanian gymnast. A black eye examined him from a cocked head. A hooked beak opened and closed. For an endless moment he met that dark soulless gaze. Then a wing tip twitched, and the great bird angled off, lifting without effort on some invisible draft Dan couldn't even feel. But still, gazing down.

He suddenly became aware of others standing behind him, also goggling at the bird, and watching him. The crew, holding plates and cans.

Tausengelt stepped up. "A good omen," the leathery old master chief said drily. "Or a warning?"

"Oh, they're good luck." Dan glanced over his shoulder and raised his voice. "Albatross. Good luck to a ship . . . unless you harm one. Let's just make sure we don't."

The anglers murmured assent, looking up. The great bird soared far above, gradually dropping back until it hovered over their wake. And stationed itself there, motionless, as if pasted to the cloudy sky, until Dan turned away, and carried his plate to the plastic bins.

He was in some kind of boarding school. Run on English lines, but somehow in Pennsylvania. He and some other boys were siphoning gasoline from what seemed to be a swimming pool.

The Hydra woke him. A furious-sounding Cheryl Staurulakis was on the other end. *"Captain? We have a situation."*

He blinked into the dark, the dream still inhabiting his mind. Shaking it off, he jumped up in his boxers and jerked the blue curtain from over the forward porthole. It looked out over the bow, but the night sea lay empty of lights. Not an impending collision, then. "What've you got, Exec? I was trying to get my head down—"

"A situation," the XO repeated. *"In my stateroom."*

"In your . . . stateroom. You want me to come down there?"

"If the captain pleases."

He didn't like her tone on that last, but bit back a snappish reply. If she thought it was important, it would be. He checked the bulkhead clock. Just past eight o'clock reports. "Let me pull my coveralls on."

"Khakis might be best, sir."

With lifted eyebrows, he signed off.

Five minutes later—the uniform races at the Academy had been, after all, a good preparation for eventual command—he knocked at her door. "Come in," said a muffled voice.

He closed the door to a flushed, sweaty Staurulakis, swinging a leg from a perch on her fold-down desk, and a seated, slumped Petty Officer Terranova. The girl raised tearstained cheeks. Her usual presentation, of a junior high school band student, was gone. The chubby face looked more like that of a child who'd fallen and skinned her knee. Dan restrained his first impulse, to put an arm around her, as when his daughter had been little, and fallen off her bike. "What happened?" he murmured.

"Tell him," Staurulakis said. Just from the speed at which her leg swung he could tell she was furious.

Dan's leading SPY-1 fire controlman, the woman he depended on during general quarters, described in broken sentences how, back in Crete, she'd ordered a new bikini swimsuit from a Soft Surroundings catalog one of the other girls had. It had come in in their mail delivery at Jebel Ali. "And I thought, we're having the picnic, I'd wear it. Sure, I'm . . . a little heavy, but I could get a tan. In CIC all the time, we all get pasty white."

"I know," Dan said. "Take your time."

"Anyway I got in line and had a salad. Then took my blanket up on the 03 level. And Heather and Ashley and Reagan and I, we laid there and talked, and drank Cokes . . . and I bummed a cigarette off Reagan. Then after the bird came—"

"The albatross?"

"Yessir. The, um, albatross. The sun started to go down, and they packed up. But I didn't want to leave. You never get to be alone. So I stayed. And it got dark. Finally I got everything packed up and I left too. I was going down the port side, in through there, in my flip-flops, carrying my blanket—"

"Go on," Dan said, though from the exec's bouncing leg and the Terror's averted gaze he had an idea what was coming.

"Anyway, somebody . . . grabbed me, there, inside the helo hangar passageway, and pulled me behind the darken ship curtains. Where they fold against the bulkhead. And put a knife to my throat—"

"A knife?" Dan repeated. "A *knife*?"

"That's what I said. I felt it—it was fucking sharp, too." The petty officer gulped and straightened. "He pulled me behind the curtain, there, and felt me up. Stuck his hand under my top, and down the back of my—bottoms."

"I see. Was there actual—"

"There wasn't," Staurulakis said, flat-faced. "We already discussed that."

"I see. Well . . . then what?"

"I felt him . . . jerking off. Then he whispered in my ear to stay there for five minutes, or he'd cut me when I wasn't expecting it. In the mess line, or wherever." She took a deep breath. "So I did. And got myself back together, then came—"

"Then came to me," Staurulakis said. "You did exactly right, Beth."

Dan cleared his throat. "That's right, Terror. You didn't mention this to any of the other girls? En route? Straight here, to the exec's cabin?"

"I asked Donnie where the exec was. He said, probably in the combat passageway, observing eight o'clock reports. But I didn't tell him why I wanted her."

"Where did you see Wenck?" Staurulakis asked.

"On the way down to berthing. I would've come right here, ma'am, but I was still in my swimsuit and—"

Dan said, "Exec, we need the chief master-at-arms

in on this. Terror, you said he, um, hand-jobbed himself. Did anything get on you? On your suit, or your
blanket?"

"I didn't look."

"We need to sequester them, inspect for semen."

The exec murmured, leg slowing a bit, "Yessir, we
can do that. But about the master-at-arms . . ."

"What about him?"

"Can we, um, talk offline?"

Out in the passageway, door closed, Staurulakis
murmured, "Toan's not going to be that interested. You
heard them, when we took Peeples to mast over what
he said to Scharner."

"Oh, he'll be interested," Dan said. "This isn't verbal
harassment. Calling somebody a kunk, or whatever it
was. This is assault with a deadly weapon. A threat of
bodily harm. If he doesn't take this seriously, I'll recali-
brate him. I won't have my sailors terrorized. Also, I
want to know where Peeples was during the picnic and
afterward. Who he was with. And if he owns a knife."

"All right, sir." The exec hesitated, then added, "But
you have to realize, just about everybody on the ship
owns a knife."

"I asked whether *he* owns one, XO." He nodded
toward the door.

Back in the stateroom, Dan told Terranova, "Okay,
we're going to get the sheriff up here, fill him in on what
happened. He'll take an official statement. Anything
else you can remember, Terror? What he smelled like?
Was he big? Fat? Thin? Could you tell what uniform
he had on?"

"I couldn't tell much . . . I was sort of in shock . . . and he was behind me, feeling me up, and we were behind the darken ship curtains, with the door closed. The lights were off."

He was turning to go, but halted. "Wait a minute . . . the door was closed, but the lights were off?"

"Yessir."

Staurulakis was frowning too. "But when the doors giving onto the main deck open, the lights automatically go off. And on again, when they close. You're sure the vestibule light was off?"

"Check and see if the switch was broken, or maybe fucked with," Dan said, then immediately regretted the last phrase. "I mean, interfered with. If so, this wasn't spur-of-the-moment. It was planned."

Staurulakis said she'd check it out with the compartment petty officer. Dan hesitated, was contemplating where this could go, when she said, "Shouldn't we add some . . . horsepower to this, Captain? To, you know, help the chief master-at-arms with the investigation?"

"Um, I guess so," he said reluctantly. Remembering ex-USS *Gaddis,* the mutilations and murders that had followed her from port to port. And how fruitless his own investigations had been, and why. "What d'you suggest?"

"A joint investigation. Chief Toan and a female officer. Somebody sharp. With an inquiring mind. Say . . . Lieutenant Singhe."

"Amy," Dan said slowly. True, she was one of the keenest minds aboard. On the minus side, she'd already estranged the senior enlisted, and something like this could get messy fast. "Okay, but warn her not to play bull in the china shop . . . throw around blanket accusations, accuse people of sexism, et cetera. This is an assault investigation, not a chance to work an agenda. Or write her next article."

Staurulakis nodded, and Dan patted Terranova's shoulder. "We'll get this asshole, Terror. Like the XO says, you did the right thing, reporting it. But just for the present . . . try to stay with your friends, or in your work spaces. No more hanging out alone."

The exec's expression made him feel as if he'd just said something wrong. He was about to try again when Staurulakis's Hydra beeped. *"XO, OOD. Know where the captain is? I buzzed his at-sea cabin and tried his Hydra, but no joy."*

"He's here with me."

A hesitation."Discussing ship's business," Staurulakis added in an icy tone.

"Yes ma'am. Commander, just tell him we have USS Pittsburgh, *reporting in VHF voice."*

The exec double-clicked. "Did you get that, Captain?"

He nodded. Youngblood was early; the sub wasn't supposed to join up until tomorrow. And the day after, they'd start the exercise, though he'd barely glanced at the op order.

But that wasn't his major problem. Not now. As of today, he had a molester in the crew, one not afraid to use a knife. And every male was a suspect.

Just fucking great. He only hoped they could find him before Singhe split the crew down the middle.

He climbed heavily back to his sea cabin, undressed again, coughing, limbs feeling like waterlogged wood and his eyelids lead-loaded. He rolled into his bunk. Then stared at the overhead, his anxiety program rebooting. He rolled over, snapping it off. Remember the albatross. The castaways they'd rescued. Both seemed like good omens. Maybe they'd find the molester. Lock him down, get him off the ship. It could happen.

The creak and sway of a seaway, the muffled voices, the hiss of radios, faded. And gradually, imperceptibly, he became one once more with the blackness that surrounded them all.

III

10

10

On the Hash Highway

Several days later, and five hundred miles farther out. Monsoon season still, with sealed-off skies and growing seas. *Pittsburgh* was in company, making three units under his tactical command. His empire would be short-lived, though. *Carl Vinson* was on its way, to join up en route to the Malabar exercise area. U.S. participants would be *Savo, Mitscher, Pittsburgh, Vinson,* an oiler, *Tippecanoe,* plus antisubmarine aircraft out of Djibouti and Jamnagar. Mills and Staurulakis had put together an exercise package to get them spun up, and sonar runs with the sub would feel out the hydrography of the western Indian Ocean.

He was catching up on traffic in his in-port cabin. A long analysis by the Defense Intelligence Agency said that India was abandoning its traditional defensive orientation. It had just concluded a major exercise, Divine Weapon, testing its ability to mobilize forces if another flare-up occurred over Kashmir. The plan was to rapidly destroy Pakistan's military potential, without a lengthy period of preparation or warning.

It sounded eerily like the Schlieffen Plan Tuchman was describing in *The Guns of August*. Rigid, aggressive, depending on speed and shock to occupy territory and destroy an adversary. But Pakistani counterexercises in Sialkot, Cholistan, and Sindh had mustered heavy tanks and drilled self-protection procedures after use of a tactical nuclear weapon.

He scratched his chin, staring into space as *Savo* rolled and something in his closet went *clunk. Clunk . . . clunk.*

For half a century, the U.S. Navy had served as a balancer between Pakistan and India, to be thrown into the scales one way or the other to preserve peace. But the subcontinent's economic growth, plus the drawdown in the fleet, meant it mattered less and less.

At some point, the U.S. would finally have to choose. One ally or the other. And the spurned partner would automatically become an enemy.

In international news, Premier Zhang had warned "outside powers" against interfering in the South China Sea dispute with the Philippines. As Blair had said, the financial markets were getting nervous as the Chinese continued to liquidate and transfer their U.S. debt holdings. The dollar had dropped against the renminbi, and the stock market was tanking.

His J-phone beeped. It was Cheryl. "We're ready for you, Captain."

He coughed hard and long into his fist, until he had to pant for air. "Be . . . be right down."

In the passageway outside the mess decks, he flicked lint off his coveralls and made sure he had his Black-Berry. Coughed again, cleared a thick throat. Checked his Hydra. Fully charged.

When he pushed the door open Chief Toan cried, "Attention on deck!" and the ranks of men and women surged to their feet. The food service attendants had cleared, but a tang of disinfectant lingered. He waved them down, muttered, "At ease," and took a seat in the front row with the department heads. One of the mess-men brought a paper cup of bug juice; he nodded thanks and sipped at it, though he didn't really care for the pink flavor.

Matt Mills started. The first slide was the western Indian Ocean. An enormous blue triangle, with the Pakistani and Indian coasts at the top, Saudi Arabia to the west, India to the east. Five thousand miles of empty sea rolled to the southward, reaching down to the Ant-arctic.

The ops officer began with the weather. "The South-west Monsoon sets in towards the end of May, shortly after it establishes over the western Arabian Sea. Con-ditions persist through June, July, and August. South-southwest winds. Typically ten to sixteen knots to about 52 degrees east, becoming 22 to 27 knots in the area of 52–54E. As the exercise moves east, around midocean, we can expect increased wave and swell heights, the farther toward India we operate."

Dan sat back, massaging his neck, half listening—he knew this already from the pre-exercise messages and the briefing book Cheryl had put together—while he stared at Amy Singh's erect head. She'd braided her hair. His gaze trailed down the smooth long neck, to firm shoulders . . . he jerked his eyes away.

As he'd expected, and half dreaded, Singhe had taken hold of the Terranova investigation with a death grip. She'd interviewed every woman who'd been on the steel beach that day, along with the compartment petty officer for the access trunk, the electrical officer, even the laundry personnel. (They'd complained to the supply officer about being asked to log semen stains on coveralls.) She'd reinterviewed Terranova, trying again to come up with anything that could lead them to the groper.

But all, so far, without success. He shifted uncomfortably. They had to file a follow-up report today. If they made no progress, there'd be an NCIS investigation the next time they made port.

But the guy was still out there. Sex crimes had a way of escalating, as the perpetrator sought to re-create whatever twisted kick he got from humiliating and frightening his first victim. Next time, he might not be satisfied with holding someone at knifepoint and ejaculating on her.

The deck rolled. The steel around them creaked. The crew shifted and coughed. Mills was explaining the scenario. "Exercise Malabar 10 grows from exercise 9, which explored responses to extremist threats to shipping during the assembly of a multinational convoy. Building on that, this year's exercise will validate procedures and tactics in assembling a mixed-nationality naval force in response to a major Pacific crisis, and moving it through a narrow strait against surface, air, and subsurface opposition from Orange forces."

Dan stopped his leg from bouncing. It was obvious who Orange was meant to be. He was reminded of the bastion-penetrating exercises NATO had done in the eighties, testing ways to get through Soviet defenses. But Malabar 10 would be conducted while real-world tensions to the north, as per the DIA message, were escalating by the day.

"Also, we may have an audience," Mills droned on. "A three-ship Chinese task force is heading our way. The overt justification is to provide security for their merchants in the Gulf, like that tanker that went through at the end of our freedom-of-navigation, uh, exercise." The next three slides showed the three modern, high-tech surface combatants.

Dan lifted a hand. "Address the Iranian involvement, Matt."

"Yessir. *Savo*'s been the subject of hostile comment on Fars, the Iranian news agency. They say the castaways we picked up are escaped murderers. They demand them back for execution."

That was interesting. Given that the trio claimed to be fleeing religious persecution, CentCom and Com-Fifth would not have given out which ship had picked them up. Dan half turned, scanning the faces behind him. Usually they'd have offloaded any refugees stat, but given the time frame and the upcoming exercise, it hadn't happened yet. Hermelinda had them scrubbing out pots in the scullery for now. The refugees had asked to be taken into the crew, but certain of the chiefs had balked, saying they might be spies. One dude in particular, Behnam Shah, had seemed more inquisitive than his sea daddy had felt comfortable with.

Mills said, "So this reignites the Hormuz transit issue. They've personally dared us to try it again, and threatened that if we do, they will destroy USS *Savo Island* with a, quote, new weapon, unquote."

"We're not turning them over, of course," Staurulakis said calmly. "These threats are probably just the usual bluster. But we'll have to keep an eye over one shoulder while we're operating in the IO."

Mills sat down, and the ASW officer, Winston Farmer—a colorless guy, old for his rank, who looked a likely candidate for early baldness—took over.

Modern ASW wasn't like the World War II movies. Active sonar, pinging, gave away your own location, and only worked at short ranges. Machinery noise from a submarine propagated by three pathways: direct path, convergence zones, and deep channels. "Direct path" meant straight from the source to the receiving hydrophone. But over long ranges, sound curved up toward the surface.

So that after about thirty miles, the sounds hit the surface and bounced down again. If you had good equipment, a trained team, and proper positioning, you could hear your quarry thirty, sixty, ninety miles away. The "deep channel" could extend the range even more. But Chinese nukes were getting quieter, and their latest conventional boats were often less noisy than the sea around them.

Farmer said, "So our major job in this exercise will involve keeping Orange subs clear of the transit lanes through which the convoy will move. The IO's new territory for us. Personally, I'm looking forward to seeing how well we can pick up *Pittsburgh* today."

Dan nodded; the sub would be running slowly in on the ships at varying angles and depths, letting them calibrate sensors and estimate detection ranges. He sipped bug juice and massaged his neck. If he could break away and lie down, that would be great. He hadn't slept well since Hormuz . . .

He suddenly realized everyone was looking at him. "Excuse me?"

"Sir, I asked if you had anything to add."

"No, Winston, nothing. Just keep careful notes for the hot washup." He coughed into his sleeve. "Okay, let's get to the transit phase. XO?"

Staurulakis stood, and a laser pointer pulsed red. "This slide shows the entry point for the transit of 'Yellow Road' to the destination port in the country 'Oz.' As you can see, given constructive depths along the route, there'll be numerous opportunities for Orange force interdiction . . ."

"Sir."

Dan flinched at a nudge. The duty radioman, holding

the aluminum clipboard with the red and white stripes that meant top secret. Staurulakis fell silent. Dan rose. "Uh, go ahead, Exec. I'll take this offline."

He read the message leaning against a stanchion by the juice bar. It was from Fifth Fleet. CentCom Intel reported that M/V *Patchooli,* Pakistani-flagged, was reported to be carrying a hidden cargo of drugs from Karachi to Europe. The same ship had been boarded the year previously by an Australian destroyer on anti-drug patrol, but nothing had been found. Since the *Savo* task group was operating in the smuggler's transit area, Dan was directed to board and search, if it didn't interfere with ongoing operations.

He checked the coordinates, course, and speed. Then plucked the J-phone off the bulkhead for a conversation with CIC.

He didn't have far to go to lay the task group athwart *Patchooli*'s track from Karachi to the Mozambique Channel. The motor vessel was already up on GCCS, though still over *Savo*'s radar horizon. He was tempted to send Red Hawk out for a visual, but didn't, mindful of Wilker's caution about airframe hours. Since the sonar exercises hadn't started yet, he just shifted them thirty miles west and proceeded as planned. *Pittsburgh* began her runs, first on *Mitscher,* then on *Savo.* Dan stopped in to watch the sonarmen but was reminded, once again, what ASW really stood for: awfully slow warfare.

He'd seen the poppy fields in Afghanistan with TAG

Bravo, trying to localize and kill bin Laden in the aftermath of 9/11. Hashish and heroin were the cash crops of those remote and lawless highlands. When one conduit was turned off, the stream flowed another way. Right now, it seemed to be moving by sea, from Pakistan down the east coast of Africa to South Africa, Amsterdam, and New York.

He was on the bridge with his feet up when the sun crashed into the sea in a blaze of flaming debris. The cloud cover had thinned—not for long, Van Gogh assured them—and one bright planet, Jupiter, was even visible. The intercept would occur at night. Down on the forecastle the VBSS—visit, boarding, search, and seizure—team was running a drill. Back aft, Pardees was checking the RHIBs they'd use for boarding while *Savo* stood off.

He sighed, fighting the old apprehension. This was how *Horn* had died. Intercepting what looked like a soft target. The bomb had left her a radioactive wreck. But he couldn't let that paralyze him. No two situations were ever the same.

Feet up, drawing slow deep breaths, he waited for the night.

He detached *Savo* after dusk and ran north. If anything went sour, it would be better to limit the damage to one ship. He wasn't sure if he was being prudent or paranoid. It was only a freighter, for God's sake.

Still, he lingered on the bridge, reading over the protocols for boarding. In the old days, you fired a gun to order a ship to heave to. Now you needed probable cause, flag country permission, a warning, and a properly phrased request. You had to reconcile UN ROEs, NATO ROEs, JCS ROEs, and theater ROEs, and the battle group staffs got into the act sometimes too. But in general, the UN Convention on the Law of the Sea—UNCLOS—prohibited boarding on the high seas without permission of the flagging nation. There was wiggle room in the case of suspected smugglers, though, and if the ship's master gave permission, Dan could do a consensual boarding even lacking flag nation permission.

The interesting thing tonight was that the shipowner claimed Bangladeshi registration, but according to Fleet's message, the Bangladeshi government hadn't been able to confirm it. They might just be unable to find the documents, or the shipowner could be lying. Fifth Fleet wanted him to make it consensual if possible, but weasel-worded whether he was to proceed if permission was denied.

Mills made the initial call on Channel 16. "*M/V* Patchooli, *Motor vessel* Patchooli, *this is U.S. Navy warship ahead of you on bearing one-nine-zero. I am closing you for visual inspection. Please acknowledge. Over.*"

They got a garbled answer in halting English. Mills went on to ask for identification and flag. The answer came back that it was Pakistani-flagged.

The 21MC, by his feet. "*Captain, you following VHF?*"

"Yeah, Matt. I got that. Interesting. Let's get in there,

let him see us," he instructed Pardees, the officer of the deck. "And get those searchlights on."

"How close we want to be, Captain?"

"Make it . . . five hundred yards. And let's go to general quarters."

"General quarters, sir?"

"I don't like to repeat myself, Noah." He regretted his tone instantly, but refrained from apologizing. Pardees was a little *too* casual, sometimes. "And I want everyone on the bridge in flash gear. Matt, give us four minutes to close in and light him up, then ask for permission to board."

Someone hawked and cleared his throat on the darkened bridge, but he didn't hear any voiced questioning. Just the clank and scuffle as lockers came open, gear was distributed and pulled on. Maybe it *was* overkill. But still . . .

He climbed down from his chair and felt his way out onto the wing. A waning moon that barely penetrated the overcast. Four-foot seas. Boat ops were always risky, and these conditions were marginal, especially at night. He unholstered the Hydra and went over risk-reduction procedures with Mytsalo and BMC Anschutz, back on the boat deck. The freighter grew, red and white running lights, and a row of lit windows.

Savo's lights came on, swung across the dark sea, and pinned it. Black hull, white superstructure, a shelter-decked break-bulker with pilothouse aft and booms forward. At a guess, three hundred feet, and by no means new, by the streaks of rust along the scuppers and anchor well. She flew no flag.

"About ready for the scrap heap, looks like to me," Noblos said, beside him.

Dan almost winced, the guy's appearance was such a surprise. "Bill . . . I mean, Dr. Noblos. Don't see you up here much. In fact, I think this is the first time."

"I heard GQ being passed." The reclusive scientist was a tall shadow. "What're we doing?"

"Intercepting a smuggler. Want to go over with the boat, take a look?"

"Ha-ha! I think not. Can we talk about your cross-field amplifiers on the forward transmitters?"

"Uh, Doctor, I'd love to, but right now I'm kind of preoccupied."

"It's important. If you want to keep your Aegis on the line."

"Sure, but can we make it some other time? Soon, but right now."

"I've been trying to have a conversation for some time, Captain. As I've said before, several of your radar parameters are degraded. Others are merely nominal. Your operator proficiency is actually dropping, it seems to me."

Dan said, "I don't think you're saying my operators aren't trying hard enough. Or are you?"

Noblos shrugged. "The reasons are not my concern. But I'll advise you now: I'm drawing up a recommendation that your BMD mission area certification be suspended."

Dan said evenly, "Thanks for the heads-up, Bill. But as I just said, can we make this some other time? Right now I'm trying to run a board and search."

Noblos smiled coldly. "Absolutely, Captain. Whenever is most convenient for you. Just let me know."

Noblos felt his way to the door, knocking something off the nav table. Dan filed him away and got his binoculars back on the nearing ship, gripping the radio handset awkwardly too. "Five hundred yards," the OOD reported. "Matching course and speed. Ten knots, one niner five."

"All right . . . *whoa*!"

Under their lights, the freighter had swung her rudder hard, rotating her stern out toward *Savo*. It neared and neared, looming. Pardees ordered his rudder left, but Dan cautioned him that might smash their sterns together as both ships pivoted apart. "Steady as you go. He's gonna just miss you."

The 21MC: *"He's not going to cooperate."*

"Yeah, he just turned away . . . Let me talk to him." Dan pulled down the gray handset, clicked to the International Bridge to Bridge, squeezed the Transmit button. "Motor vessel *Patchooli,* this is commanding officer of U.S. warship. Request to speak to captain."

"This captain M-V Patchooli. *Go on."*

"This is U.S. Navy warship. What flag do you sail under, Captain?"

"Bangladeshi flag vessel."

"Bangladesh does not acknowledge your registry. What is your true ownership and home port?"

The answer came back scrambled and cut off, but might have been "Pakistan." Dan cradled the handset, frowning. Pakistan, not Bangladesh? Well, he wasn't going to wait around with his thumb up. "*Patchooli,* this is Navy warship. We are boarding under provisions of UNCLOS Article 108 and the Convention on Facilitation of International Maritime Traffic. Come to course one-nine-zero at five knots and stand by for boarding on your port side aft."

"No, Captain. You are in violate of 1988 SUA convention. Boarding us without permission is piracy under international law."

"Jeez," said Staurulakis from the dark. He wondered how long she'd been there. "This is new. A smuggler quoting international law."

Dan grinned. "A real 'sea lawyer' . . . Okay, let's try this again." He lifted the handset once more.

This time he got a different voice back. An oily, smooth spokesperson with a much better command of English. She said, *"This is* Patchooli. *I am speaking for the master. You are in violation of international law. We are beyond territorial seas. A warship may ask us questions, but you may not board us without our permission."*

Dan cleared his throat impatiently. "This is Navy warship off your port side—"

"This is Patchooli. *Maritime law insists you must identify yourself properly."*

Dan said unwillingly, because the woman did have a point, "This is U.S. Navy warship *Savo Island.* I say again, *Savo Island."* He gave her his hull number and said, "Request you cease maneuvering and slow for boarding."

"This is Patchooli. *The Convention for the Suppres-*

sion of Unlawful Acts Against the Safety of Maritime Navigation makes it a criminal act to unlawfully seize or exercise control over a foreign flagged ship at sea. You have no right to stop us. Therefore we will not heave to.

Dan snorted. In the not too distant future, every ship would have to sail with a full legal team. Beside him the officer of the deck murmured, "A shot across his bows?"

"Just give me a minute, okay, Noah?"

The 21MC. *"Bridge, CIC."*

Pardees hit the lever twice to say "Go ahead" and a petty officer said, *"Sir, we have a distress call going out from our guy alongside. He's saying he's under attack by pirates."*

"What the fuck?" Staurulakis stamped her boot.

"Mitscher's answered up asking for his position."

Dan said, "Get *Mitscher* on a secure circuit. Advise them there's no attack, just this little prick jerking our chain. Tell this asshole, stop screwing around and cooperate."

He slid down from his chair and crossed the pilothouse, bumping into someone but not apologizing, just shoving on through until he'd undogged the starboard door and was out on the wing. He looked across to where the searchlights still illuminated the freighter. It was headed away. Froth at the rounded stern showed he was cramming on power. A heavy, oily smoke bit his nostrils, and the beams above became solid shafts, turning coffee-brown as they plunged into obscurity.

Did this idiot really think he could make smoke and run away? He shouted into the pilothouse, "Come around to follow him. Bump up to ahead full. But don't get too close, and watch his stern." That was where they'd see motion first, if the freighter tried to squirm away again.

Back on the radio. "Motor vessel *Patchooli,* this is *Savo Island,* astern of you and closing. You are placing yourself in danger by attempting to avoid a legal boarding. This is your second verbal warning. Log that, and the time," he told the junior officer of the deck. His ROEs were clear: he had to offer a graduated series of nonlethal warnings before resorting to lethal force. But verbal cautions didn't seem to be having much effect. He picked up the sound-powered circuit and snapped the dial to Gun Control. "CO."

"Guns here, sir."

"I may need a star shell. And break out a couple rounds of BL&P just in case. But so far, weapons tight. Can do?"

"Aye aye, sir. Mount 51, load one illumination round to the transfer tray." The forward five-inch gun suddenly tilted its barrel up, then snapped it down again. It rotated left and right, testing the train mechanisms.

"Report on 21MC when ready." Dan snapped off as his own bitch box said, *"CIC, bridge: he's going out on HF."*

"Say again?"

"M/V Patchooli *is going out on high frequency to 'any vessel this net,' reporting attempted piracy."*

This was too much. He told Pardees, "Six short blasts," and waited as the horn droned out. He followed it with another warning over VHF as the cruiser, responding to increased power, surged up alongside the fleeing freighter. Huge black clouds were pouring from its stack, and a bow wave glowed in the searchlights' beams.

"Am I missing anything here?" he asked the exec.

"External loud hailers. So they can't say their radio malfunctioned."

"Okay, right." He had Nuckols repeat his warning on *Savo*'s loudspeakers. The other still didn't alter course. She was making about fifteen knots, which had to be close to her maximum speed, but *Savo* could easily double that. Dan kneaded his face. Where did this fool think he was going?

"Bridge, Gun Control. One round illumination to the transfer tray."

Dan said, "Mount 51 in local control. One round illumination. Load. Thirty degrees left of his bow light. Double-check bearing. Report when ready."

"Mount 51, ready and standing by."

"Batteries released, one round," Dan said.

The gun thumped and flashed, and a red-hot comet arched out into the night. It ignited into a magnesium brilliance that illuminated the undersides of the clouds and glittered white off the waves, so bright he had to squint. As the rays gleamed across the water he brought the binoculars up until he was looking at the pilothouse. Through one window, just for an instant, he made out the cutout of a human figure. And behind it, what looked very much like an armed man pointing a rifle at the back of its head.

The flare declined slowly, and the pilothouse grew dark again. He lowered the night glasses, frowning. "Did you see that, Cheryl?"

"No, what?"

"Rounds complete," said the 21MC. *"One round expended. Bore clear. No casualties. Refire?"*

"Negative, cease fire," Dan said. He fingered the binoculars. Had it really been someone being held at gunpoint? Or had he taken the outline of some piece of equipment for a human figure? If there were armed men over there, this wasn't a situation he wanted to send his boarding team into without some more advantages: such as daylight, his helo in the air, and reinforcements on tap.

All of which meant delay. He didn't like it, but sometimes you had to do what was prudent. He coughed. "All right . . . open the range, about a thousand yards. Take position off his port quarter."

"We're backing off, sir?" Staurulakis sounded disbelieving.

"Until dawn. Tell Ops we need a message to Fleet, to see if there's an M/V *Patchooli* in the Pakistani registry. Maybe they sold it, or transferred flag . . . but I'm not sending guys over at night, into a possibly hostile environment, without backup."

He sneezed. Someone murmured, back in the darkness of the bridge, and men stirred. The OOD gave the helm orders in a subdued voice. "Secure from general quarters, sir?" someone asked. And slumping back into his seat, bone tired, but resigned to staying there all night, he muttered, "Yeah, go ahead. Secure."

11

The East Coast
of Africa

He snorted himself awake several times during the night. Each time, he muzzily thought of going below, but stayed in the chair instead. Each time he woke he peered out, checking the freighter's stern light. It rode always in the same place, a yellow star low off their bow, glittering and reeling beneath clouds that were closing down again.

The last time he woke the sky was gray. A little after 0500, and Hermelinda Garfinkle-Henriques, wilted in the half-light, was at his elbow, the radio messenger beside her. They murmured good mornings. Dan grunted and coughed, hitched himself up, glanced out—the freighter was still there. He sighed, and reached for the clipboard.

It was from Fifth Fleet, info everybody on earth. Karachi had returned no response to the inquiry about registry. In the absence of confirmation, Dan was directed to carry out a noncooperative boarding, having regard to the warning provisions of References A through F and his ROE. He was also reminded to carry out a risk analysis of the boarding process.

"One more thing, Captain," the supply officer said. "We have a closing contact from the east. You might want to check it out in CIC."

"It's on GCCS?"

She said stubbornly, "You might want to check it out for yourself, sir."

There was hot coffee in Sonar. He got a cup and a sticky bun en route to the command desk. CIC felt deserted with only a steaming watch. Empty consoles, and half the lights on, while a compartment cleaner jockeyed a broom across the deckplates and progressive jazz warbled from the EW console. He blinked up at the displays. Highlighted the contact, and studied the callout. Its extended track met *Savo*'s later that day. He powered up his work station and scrolled through the intel.

PLANS *Wuhan* was a Type 052B Guangzhou-class guided missile destroyer, attached to the South Seas Fleet. Brand-new, displacing almost seven thousand tons, it was the first multirole, antiair-capable destroyer the Chinese had built. It reminded him of a Sovremennyy, and had a lot of the same Russian sensors, along with Grizzly surface-to-air missiles and YJ-83 long-range antiship cruise missiles. She had one 100mm automatic gun and a CIWS. Also a hangar, though his sources didn't say if a helo was routinely embarked. His only clear advantage was Aegis. *Wuhan*'s E-band radar had neither the reach nor the multiple-tracking capabilities of the SPY-1.

Still, in a medium-range engagement, it would be even-steven, YH-28s against Harpoons. Whoever fired first would have the advantage. He cut and pasted, added his own thoughts, and forwarded the collage to his TAOs, the EW chief, the exec, Chief Wenck, and Dr. Noblos. He queried GCCS for other Chinese units and got PLANS *Haikou,* another destroyer, farther west, near the Gulf.

Cheryl came in and he told her what they had. Sniffling, she blew her nose into a tissue. Black smudges circled her eyes. "Are we still boarding?"

"As directed. Nobody seems to want to own up to these guys."

"Black flagged?"

"Could be. Pulled out of a scrapyard someplace." He keyboarded around. Cameras fore and aft on the missile decks could be pivoted via joystick from the TAO's station, but they weren't stabilized, which made them not too useful at sea. He could look through the port or starboard CIWS cameras, but the mount had to point at what it was looking at, which could be misconstrued as a hostile act. He settled on the starboard 25mm gun camera. It was stabilized and he could move it independently of the gun.

Patchooli rode steadily in the gunsight, the crosshairs riding just above her fantail. He zoomed in, looking for a flag, but again saw none. The ship name was so spotty and half-obliterated he could make out only the double O, but there seemed to be another beneath it, maybe outlined with a welding stick. At magnification the image dissolved into the blurry, heaving speckles of digitization. "Let's make it after breakfast. Say, 08. Plenty of light by then. Tell Strafer we'll need Red Hawk in the air. And we'll go back to GQ."

He was on the boat deck, talking to Mytsalo before lowering the RHIB. The teams didn't load there; there weren't enough safety lines for everyone, and they'd make it too heavy for the davit. They'd drop the boat in the water, and then the coxswain would drive it to the stern. The boarding team would climb down via a Jacob's ladder. His Hydra beeped and he keyed. "CO."

"Sir, XO here. VHF transmission from Wuhan. *In the clear."*

"Read it to me."

" *'Request delay boarding until PLANS* Wuhan *is on station to assist.'* "

He let up on the Transmit key. Politely phrased, but what lay behind it? He held up a restraining hand to Mytsalo, who seemed too eager to get into the boat. "Did we acknowledge receipt, Cheryl?"

"Uh, yessir, we did."

"Anything more from upstairs? Fifth Fleet?"

She said there wasn't. Dan cleared his throat and spat over the side. "Well, we have our orders."

"Shall I answer?"

"I don't honestly know . . . not sure what a message like that actually means." He furrowed his brow. "Um, how far away is she? The Chinese destroyer?"

"Wait one . . . about an hour's steaming time."

He eyed the men loading into the inflatable. His current team wasn't as highly trained as they'd been aboard *Horn,* mostly because marine interdiction wasn't *Savo*'s primary mission. They were in black gear: helmets, flash hoods, coveralls, tactical vests, life jackets, steel-toed boots. They carried flashlights and radios as well as weapons. Aft, on the flight deck, Red Hawk's turbines were whining into life, a higher note above the deep *whoosh* of the ship's own intakes and exhaust. "Thank *Wuhan* for his interest. Tell him we're proceeding with the boarding and ask him to stand clear. And let Fifth Fleet know about the exchange. Over."

She acknowledged and signed off. Mytsalo's fresh young face glowed with windburn. "Max, no unnecessary risks," Dan told him. "Stay alert for weapons. Stay in touch on your radio. Do a thorough search, but don't split up into more than two teams, and don't let anyone wander off alone." The ensign nodded eagerly. The boatswain on the davit eyed them, and Dan nodded. "Get 'er in the water!" he yelled, as behind him the rotors accelerated and the noise abruptly became deafening. The SH-60 lofted off and her long dragonfly shape passed black above him, climbing for the clouds, then tilting and drifting toward the battered ship a quarter mile distant. Having a helo pointing a machine gun at your bridge usually returned sanity even to uncooperative captains. Not only that, if there was hostile activity along the decks, they could warn the boarding party.

Which, a few minutes later, pushed off. The engines

roared as the inflatable peeled away, throwing up a rooster tail as it bounded across the seas. Mytsalo rode with knees bent, clutching the center console, helmet bobbing as they hit each wave. Dan watched with both envy and relief, remembering his own days as a boat officer. Mytsalo had a Beretta, while Peeples, Benyamin, and VanDuren cradled shotguns and carbines. But their main means of intimidation, obviously, were the big guns of the warship behind them. He'd sent Kaghazchi along to translate if necessary, though whoever the sea lawyer had been spoke good English. Peeples was there to tend the engine and keep things running while the rest were aboard. The backup team would follow, standing off in the second RHIB unless needed.

He sucked smoky air. Had he been pushed into something he'd regret? A casus belli, like the Agadir incident? Why were the Chinese getting involved? At last he headed for his own station, up on the bridge.

Nothing about the boarding went according to plan. As the RHIB neared its stern, the freighter sheered away again, as it had the night before. The helo, hovering over its foredeck, reported men on the port side aft, but saw no weapons among them. Dan sent another sharp warning over the VHF. Then, losing patience, he fired a live five-inch high-cap round into the water a quarter mile ahead of the fleeing ship.

The crack and boom of high explosive, the burst of black smoke and white spray, seemed to have an effect at last. The old freighter slowed, slewed sideways, and lost way, starting to roll. The RHIB circled, then nestled in like a hungry piglet. A rope ladder dropped down to it as the bridge receiver crackled, *"U.S. Navy warship* Savo Island, *this is Motor Vessel* Patchooli. *Once again, I submit you are in violation of international law. I am heaving to under protest. I am requesting assistance. Legal action will follow."*

"Be my fucking guest," Dan muttered to Cheryl Staurulakis. She was staring out at the other ship, arms folded. She glanced at him out of the corner of her eye. "What?" he asked her.

"We've got another player on the board." She pointed off to port.

Through his binoculars the sky glowed off paint so much lighter, paler, than the haze gray the U.S. Navy favored that it looked almost white. The destroyer was still far off but had a bone in her teeth and, to judge by her aspect, would soon be on them. The wide-set bridge extended across the whole beam. Above it a pyramidal mack climbed like a ziggurat. A massive radar antenna rotated slowly at its apex. The smooth flattened way the superstructure met the hull told him it was designed with elements of the stealth the newest U.S. ships were bringing into the fleet.

Beside him the exec, the OOD, and the quartermaster all had their binoculars up too. "Get the photographer up here," Cheryl told Nuckols. "This is the first time they've deployed this class."

Dan passed down that he wanted electromagnetic intelligence, too, though no doubt the EWs and cryppies had already been on that for hours. Then he clicked his Hydra to the boat freq and went out on the wing for a clear line of sight. The helo was circling, trailing exhaust haze against the pearlescent cloud cover. The RHIB rode off the freighter's port side. "Matador One, this is Matador. Progress report?"

Mytsalo's slightly amped voice. *"We're aboard. They seem to be cooperating. Over."*

"Any sign of weapons?"

"No sir, not yet. But we've only checked the papers, haven't really started the search yet."

"What's the cargo? According to the bill of lading?"

"Uh, let's see . . . dried fruit . . . bolted cotton fabric, cotton yarn, tanned leather, and rice. And something called 'miscellaneous manufactures.' " A pause, then, *"We've got a really pissed captain here too. This turkey's hopping mad. Over."*

"Who's the woman? The one who speaks English?"

"Uh, I guess that would be the supercargo? Or she might be married to the captain—I'm not clear yet exactly. She's arguing with Kaghazchi in I guess Urdu."

Dan told him to start the inspection as soon as possible. "Remember to look for the signs of hidden spaces. Fresh paint. Recently moved equipment. Watch the crew, and give them a chance to talk to you alone if you can."

Mytsalo said *"Wilco"* proudly, as if for the first time. For an ensign, being a boat officer was your first taste of what command might be like. The high—and the anxiety, too.

"Breakfast, Skip?"

Longley, with a covered tray. He peeled back the napkin like a prestidigitator. Ham slices, hash browns, toast, sunny-side eggs. And coffee, of course. "Put it on the chair," Dan told him. "I'll have it out here."

"Bridge, sigs." The old signalman rate was gone, but a quartermaster still manned the signal bridge. Pardees hit the key. "Go ahead."

"Signal in the air from destroyer type to starboard."

"Go ahead."

"Flag signal . . . X-Ray. Kilo. Numeral, two."

The OOD peered out onto the wing. Dan looked back at him, a piece of jam-smeared toast suspended in the air. "Maritime code?" Pardees murmured, looking embarrassed.

The quartermaster leaned down from above, looking disturbed. "Flag hoist breaks via maritime code to read, 'Cease your present activities. Communicate with me by loud hailer.' "

Dan frowned, both at the peremptory tone, which was never used between ships of different navies, and at the means of delivery. NATO ships maintained a flag bag, but they were seldom used, except for displaying call signs, and decorating during festivities or ceremonies. He didn't understand.

Then, all at once, he did.

After consulting with Chief Van Gogh, he hoisted the November flag. Negating whatever the other's hoist had been. He held course and speed. The destroyer slowed some distance off, then edged in. Dan expected him to slide into position off *Savo*'s port side, on the other hand from the freighter. The first indication otherwise was when Pardees murmured, "Cap'n, this dude's got his rudder over. He's coming right, fast."

From the starboard wing, he saw that it was so; the other warship was canted far over in a radical turn. Its heel increased as he watched; they were cranking even more rudder on. Extending its relative motion, it would slip in not on *Savo*'s port side, but to her starboard. "What the fuck is this maniac doing?" he muttered.

"Sir, looks like he's planning to grease in between us and the freighter."

Dan glanced at the sea between with a critical eye. This sort of thing had happened decades before, in the Black Sea. As a result, the U.S. and Russia had rules in place to prevent incidents. There were no such agreements with the Chinese, though. "He won't have a lot of clearance in there."

"Should we close up? Come right and get in closer to *Patchooli*?"

He half wanted to, but doing so would risk collision. "Not now, not while he's in this maneuver. Whatever it is. Hold course and speed. And get on bridge to bridge, interrogative his intentions." He bent to the pelorus, taking a bearing on the pyramidal mack. Then Mytsalo came on the line. Dan ducked inside to take his call, but kept a close eye on the rapidly closing destroyer out the window.

The boat officer reported he'd started inspecting in the forward hold, but what was the ship that was closing in astern? Dan brought him up to date, without saying what he suspected. He was sure now part of the cargo was weapons, or other contraband. There could be no other explanation for the interest the Chinese were showing. Pakistan was notorious as the take-out window for everyone who wanted to end-run the non-proliferation regime.

Wuhan didn't answer his call. Its heel increased still more, then lessened. Its bearing ticked left. Headed between him and the freighter, all right. He had to admit, though, it was being jockeyed with a panache the U.S. surface force had long lost. When it matched his speed, and an officer came out on the bridge wing with a microphone in hand, it was only about a hundred yards away.

He ambled back out when Branscombe reported a hail. The ship opposite stretched across his field of vision, gleaming and complex, sparkling white and light gray. Crewmen gazed curiously up from its boat deck as *Savo*'s men and women drifted out to observe as well. A few essayed tentative waves. Nuckols held out the portable loud hailer.

Dan tried to recall what Barbara Tuchman had said about harbingers of war. Some had started with meetings on the high seas, not unlike this. HMS *Leopard*'s unprovoked attack on USS *Chesapeake* off Virginia had been one trigger of the War of 1812. FDR's dangling of USS *Lanikai* as bait in front of the advancing Japanese fleet. The capture of the *Pueblo*.

More than one senior officer had told Dan he had no sense of diplomacy. He rubbed his mouth with the back of his hand, hoping they were wrong. Or at least that he'd learned something since.

Across from him an officer in spotless whites, including white gloves, raised a microphone. "This is People's Republic of China warship *Wuhan*," a stentorian voice stated. "You will cease your illegal activities and retire."

Staurulakis, beside him, murmured, "Shouldn't we be at general quarters?"

"No hostile displays, Cheryl. And shut down the starboard SPY-1 arrays, so they don't get irradiated on their bridge. Check the open channel to Strike One, and get the tape rolling on the cameras, all right? Make sure Matt's feeding them what's going on. Minute by minute. And log everything."

He considered once more, then raised his megaphone and clicked it on. The portable amplifier sounded puny compared to the enormous power of the other ship's loud hailer. Well, that was fair. *Savo Island* was almost four thousand tons larger, and he was looking down at the opposite bridge. Speak slowly and clearly . . . "This is United States Navy warship *Savo Island* conducting boarding and search operations on the high seas. You are interfering with navigation, risking collision, and hazarding both our vessels. Request you reduce speed and increase your standoff distance immediately."

Deliberations on the bridge opposite. The speaker seemed to be deferring to a shorter man with gray hair. He came back with "This merchant is not a U.S.-flagged vessel. The master has refused welcome. What is the rationale for your boarding?"

Dan said, "I am investigating reported drug-smuggling activities under the United Nations Convention Against Illicit Traffic and Section 7 of the UN Law of the Sea. What is your rationale for interfering with me?"

"Satcomm secure phone, Captain," called the OOD, inside the pilothouse. "Dark Horse. From Fifth Fleet. Actual, it sounds like."

"Oh, goddamn it," Dan muttered. He was tempted to blow it off, but reluctantly accepted the handset extended from inside. "This is Savo Actual. Over."

"Dan, this is Fifth Fleet Actual. What the hell is going on there? You have a Chinese destroyer intruding on your board and search?"

"That's correct, sir. Type 052B, *Wuhan*. He's close alongside, actually between us and the intercepted merchant. Which still has my boarding team aboard. We're discussing it by loud hailer. I suspect because he doesn't want any electronic record if things go south."

The Chinese opposite was reeling off a long spiel Dan hadn't followed. He caught something about the U.S. not being a party of the Law of the Sea, and something else about Article 89. But Fleet was asking, *"What exactly is your reason for this search? This is a Pakistani flag merchant, right? And he's refused permission to board?"*

What in the . . . ? It was Fifth Fleet that'd *directed* the search. Obviously, someone hadn't gotten the word. Unfortunately, that someone seemed to be the vice admiral. "Sir, no one's been able to confirm that."

"Who have you asked? Did you bother to inquire?"

Okay, keep your cool . . . He set the megaphone down and waved a *give me a second* gesture at the ship opposite. "Sir, we've been in constant comms with your staff over the past twenty-four hours, seeking confirmation of registry. Both Bangladesh and Pakistan have been requested to confirm, and neither could." He crooked a finger impatiently at Staurulakis, who frowned, then fetched the clipboard hanging by his command chair. "Sir, I have your N3's message here stating that Karachi returns 'no response' to inquiry about registry. It directs me to carry out a hostile boarding if necessary. I have the date time group here if you—"

"Don't quote me my own date time groups, Captain Lenson."

"Ah, no sir. Over." He cradled the handset between shoulder and neck and lifted the megaphone. "Stand by, please," echoed back, reverberating between the hulls that rolled together, as if welded, over the sea. On the opposite bridge the gray-haired officer was on a handset as well.

Just . . . fucking . . . great. He was probably talking to his own Higher. One on one, he and the other skipper could probably have arrived at a face-saving modus vivendi. A joint inspection team, for example. But with the upper echelons giving them contradictory orders, they might very well manage to start a fucking war, or at least an international incident, over this decrepit freighter.

"All right, Lenson, I have my N3 on the line here and he confirms your previous direction to board and search."

"Yes sir. We have *Mitscher* on radar. She'll be here in half an hour. My intentions now are to continue—"

"However, in view of the lack of flag country authorization, I'm countermanding. Break off contact and depart the scene. Confirm. Over."

Dan and Staurulakis exchanged startled stares. "Ah . . . say again, Dark Horse? You're directing me to recall the boarding team? They're already aboard and executing."

"You already boarded? Recall your people at once."

He coughed into his fist, not believing what he was hearing. "Sir, with all due respect . . . We have a Chinese warship alongside that's just ordered me to disengage. I refused to do so. Is this a signal we want to send?"

His Hydra crackled. Dan cursed, but hit the Transmit button. "Matador. Go ahead, Matador One."

"Sir, this is Ensign Mytsalo. Forward hold's clean. But they're trying to stop me going aft."

The satcomm phone said, *"This is Dark Horse. Confirm receipt of disengage orders."*

Dan cleared his throat again. Then he held the handset out from his face, over the sea, where the wind came up against the wing bulwark, so that the moving air blustered in it. He said, "Dark Horse, this is Matador. You are breaking up badly. Say again all after, 'I have my N3 on the line.' Over."

Staurulakis blanched. She backed up against the door. He told her, "Let's get Red Hawk back aboard. He's out there burning fuel to no good purpose. And have him make a close pass over this guy to starboard on his way in." He clicked the Transmit button on the handset in the middle of an angry-sounding tirade and said, "Dark Horse, Dark Horse, this is Matador, Matador. Say again your last transmission. You are breaking up. Suspect sync problems. I am checking settings on my cards. Over."

"Sir, *what* are you doing?"

"Take it easy, Cheryl. Remember Nelson at Copenhagen? He couldn't see the recall flag. Because he was holding his telescope to his blind eye." He sighed, sorry he'd let her in on his deliberate mishearing of the order. Far better, for her, to not know.

"Sir, you can't deliberately disobey."

"I'm *not* disengaging on a Chinese order." Dan nodded to the ship that rolled a hundred yards off. "That's not the signal we want to send."

His exec had a look in her eye he'd never seen before. The kind of look Maryk must have given Captain Queeg, just before he relieved him. And the dead silence on the bridge told him that if she tried, the others might back her up. "Sir, you're not disengaging on *his* word. You're doing it on Fifth Fleet's orders."

"Fifth Fleet isn't eyeball to eyeball, Cheryl. I am. And backing down is the wrong message to transmit."

She glanced back into the pilothouse, then leaned in. "Captain, sure you're not getting some kind of testosterone thing going? And you're putting Max and his men at risk over there."

"It's my responsibility. But can we keep it between us, until we see how it all shakes out? I don't want you catching fire too, if I have to go down."

The 21MC on the wing lit. *"Bridge, Radio. Fifth*

Fleet flash message. Direct to CO. Is he up there? Shall I read it?"

Staurulakis pressed the lever. She said evenly, not meeting Dan's eyes, "He's here. Go ahead."

"From: Fifth Fleet. TO: CO, USS Savo Island. *Break off inspection of Pakistani-flagged vessel M/V* Patchooli *and resume preparations for Exercise Malabar. Confirm receipt."*

The bridge was quiet again. The helm creaked as the helmsman corrected.

At last Dan nodded, reluctantly. He turned back to the ship opposite, and raised the megaphone again. Said across the water, "We are ceasing our inspection. Please stand clear while we recover our boarding team."

"This is Wuhan. *Thank you for your cooperation. We will remain in the vicinity."*

He coughed and lowered the loud hailer, numb, detached. The U.S. Navy had backed down, at sea, in the face of a threat. He swallowed again and again, and succeeded, just, in managing not to throw up, although he located the bridge wastebasket in the corner of his eye just in case.

He was cursing to himself when he turned, and saw the chief corpsman's sagging face.

Mitscher reported in by VHF, but by then Dan was off the bridge. He was in engineering female berthing, experiencing a chilling sense of déjà vu.

The petty officer lay curled like a comma, turned away in her bunk, face to the bulkhead, where an iPod played softly. A flash flickered as a corpsman bent in with a camera. "No one's touched her?" Dan asked the master-at-arms.

"No sir. Couple of her friends came down to check on her, take her to chow. Found her like this."

"She was on the sick list," Grissett said from behind them. "From yesterday. She complained of malaise and muscle aches. Had a dry, unproductive cough and a slightly elevated temperature. A hundred and one, I think. Maybe a hundred and two. I issued ibuprofen and prescribed fluids and bed rest."

The compartment was empty except for them; the petty officer's division chief; Bart Danenhower; and McMottie, the leading chief. Dan leaned in close to examine the face he'd last seen at mast, taut with accusation and outrage. Now Petty Officer Sherri Scharner looked as if she were zonked out after an exhausting watch. Only a fleck of brownish froth on her upper lip appeared out of the ordinary. Dan reached out, then drew his hand back as Grissett cleared his throat. "You're going to take samples?" he asked the chief corpsman.

"Yessir, respiratory fauna. Urine and stool samples." Rubber gloves snapped, and the corpsman laid out tubes, swabs, and needles on a stainless tray. Talc smoked the air. Grissett added, "In view of, uh, what's been happening, we better take a vaginal swab, too."

Dan blinked, then realized what he was saying. He looked at the others in the compartment. All male. "Um, how about holding for a couple of minutes, until we can get either the exec or Lieutenant Singhe down here. No, wait, maybe Garfinkle-Henriques. I'd just feel more comfortable if there was a . . . you know what I'm saying." They nodded and stepped back. Dan jerked his head toward the door and headed that way. Grissett accompanied him.

"Chief, I've got to get back to the bridge. There's a situation I have to make sure stays sorted out. But we've had this conversation before."

"We did, Captain. In the Med. When Seaman Goodroe died."

Uncannily like this, except the previous victim had been a strapping young man. "I need your best guess as to what's going on," Dan told him. "We reported this and got nowhere. We scrubbed down all the ductwork, but that only bought us a break. How many of our crew are down with this now?"

Hermelinda Garfinkle-Henriques clattered down the ladder. Dan explained to the supply officer what was going on. She frowned and went on into the compartment. Grissett murmured, glancing back at where the supply officer was leaning over the body, "Sir, I have to caution you about drawing direct lines between whatever most of our people are reporting, which is some kind of flulike illness, and the deaths. They may be linked. They may not— Don't let her touch it! We don't want contamination."

The lieutenant flinched away. Dan said, "Okay. All right. But you're saying, what our two fatalities are from, might not be the same as the . . . *Savo* crud?"

"It might. It might not." Grissett looked bewildered for just a moment, before the curtain of professional detachment dropped again.

Dan tried again. "What did Scharner just die from, then?"

"Looks to me like some kind of atypical pneumonia. Leading, I guess, to something like toxic shock syndrome."

"Atypical how?"

"In that we didn't see the progressive fluid buildup, the other classic signs of pneumonia. High fever. Heavy mucus production. Breathing difficulty, pain in the chest, so forth."

"Instead—"

"They just wake up dead."

Dan had about three dozen more questions, but he needed to get back to the bridge. He left them there, gathered around the bunk, no one saying much. Except for a sharp intake of breath from Garfinkle-Henriques, when Grissett rolled the body over to begin taking samples.

Dan was climbing the ladder when the nausea returned. Suddenly, overwhelmingly, his stomach had to spew out something raw and dark inside him, *right now*. He clamped his hand over his mouth, barely holding it as he undogged a door and bolted outside. It was raining, a soft mist that felt like part of the clouds. Its breath cooled his face as he craned over the rail, gagging. Fortunately he was on the lee side, opposite the still-accompanying destroyer.

Above all else, he didn't want them to see that.

* * *

He stopped in his at-sea cabin to rinse his mouth. It was raining hard when he got up to the bridge. *Mitscher* rode a mile to the east, her haze gray melting in and out of the squall's skirts. The Chinese destroyer lay close to the freighter, as if protecting her from further harassment.

Staurulakis updated in laconic sentences. Mytsalo was on his way back. The Chinese had sent a boarding team to *Patchooli*. He heard her out, looking away. Scharner's death only made it worse. Something was stalking his crew. Deadly, persistent, and it was taking down more and more people. Not only that, the after-effects were worrisome: difficulty sleeping, malaise, weakness, continuing lung problems, something like asthma.

He stayed on the bridge until the RHIB was back aboard. Mytsalo saluted, but Dan was in no mood to hear his report. He leaned back in his chair, the bridge absolutely quiet. No one spoke, not even in the usual murmurs, as *Savo* slowly hauled around to southward.

He hadn't figured to get any sleep that night. Hadn't been able to eat anything; felt like he'd never be able to swallow again. He didn't need psychoanalysis to know why. The most shameful and miserable day in his career. Maybe the worst, for the United States Navy, in its two hundred–plus years. It had been surprised, defeated, stabbed in the back, and crushed—but it had never backed down.

Until now. He shuddered, a vomity taste still lingering, and pulled the blanket over himself.

The CO's buzzer woke him. He clawed up, coughing and hacking. Something was wrong with his throat. The darkened room was distorted. Larger than he remembered. *Was* this his cabin? Dark shapes loomed and leered. A sensation like rough noodles sandpapered his tongue. He fumbled a vague response to whatever the OOD was asking. Hermelinda repeated her statement, tone insistent, and Dan finally understood: a message from Strike One; the Pakistani armed forces were going to full alert. He mumbled, "Okay, got it . . . How far're we from Karachi? . . . Bearing, range to *Wuhan*? . . . Let's set self-defense condition three. Just in case. And, uh, have the chief corpsman report to me. Yeah, now."

With no transition, in the blink of an eye, Grissett was by his bedside, shining a flashlight on a thermometer. "Fever. Dry cough. How you feeling, Captain?"

"Like . . . shit."

"Afraid you've got it, sir. The *Savo* crud. Or whatever you want to call it. Take two of these. Drink this. How's that trachea? Any breathing difficulties?"

"No . . . not yet." But his lungs were wheezing and crackling, deep down, when he breathed out. He fought panic. Unable to breathe . . . back at the Pentagon, inhaling smoke. . . .

"Brought you up an inhaler, in case. Don't be too proud to use it. I'll tell the XO you're down hard."

The corpsman eased the door closed. Dan coughed

and coughed. When he got up to urinate, he staggered into the side of the little head compartment. Only its tight confines saved him from falling. Having voided, he felt his way back out into the cabin. Clicked on the shaving light and stared at the mirror.

Remembering the skipper of USS *Reynolds Ryan*, and how one wrong order, when *he'd* been sick, had killed a ship and most of her crew.

12

The Indian Ocean

He passed the rest of the night in fevered dreams, each with some aspect of frustration or terror. He took *Savo,* now a huge silver spaceship, down to land on an asteroid where she displaced all the air, leaving them unable to breathe on the surface. Yet they had to accomplish some shadowy mission . . . He didn't remember the rest, but each dream was unimaginably detailed, vivid, scary. Each time he was about to die, or the missile was about to hit, he battled to wakefulness, panting and coughing. He sucked on the inhaler in the dim light from the radio remote. Listened to distant creaking, voices. Then let his eyelids drag shut again.

Cheryl woke him at 0800. Grissett hovered behind her, with Longley in the doorway. They looked concerned. "Sir, we doing all right?" the exec murmured. Her hand hovered over his brow, but she didn't actually touch him.

"Yeah . . . still here." He coughed and cleared his throat. Tried to roll out, but found he just had too little horsepower to sit upright. "Um, maybe some coffee—"

"Right here, Captain. And some nice rye toast, with butter." Longley set the tray down, poured half a cup. Dan eyed the plate, but it made him feel like hurling.

"Try to eat," Grissett said. "Even if it comes up again, you'll get *some* nourishment."

"Look, you guys don't need to fuss over me." He gathered all his strength and hauled himself upright. Then grabbed the bunk frame just before he went down. "Where . . . where's *Wuhan*? *Mitscher*? *Pittsburgh*? What about this increased alert status?"

Staurulakis explained, but Dan couldn't get traction on the answers. Something about the Chinese task group re-forming south of Karachi. Something else about submarine activity off Singapore. He sagged back into the bunk. "I'll be up to the bridge in a little while. If anything serious goes down, Commander Staurulakis has command authority. Chief, Longley, you can witness that."

Staurulakis patted his blanket. "Stay here, Captain. There's nothing to worry about." Grissett drew a glass of water from the tap and set it and two white oval pills beside the bed.

The door closed, leaving him staring at the overhead. "Nothing to worry about." With the newly confident and aggressive Chinese moving into what might very well be a blocking position, and tensions escalating between Pakistan and India?

If only that were true.

* * *

He slept until 1030, when guilt goaded him out of bed. He felt very slightly better, or at least stronger, though every muscle ached, his head still felt stuffed with bronze wool, and his thinking was not exactly first-class. He started to shave, but his hands shook; he quit after the second sting that meant he'd cut himself. He stepped into yesterday's coveralls, made sure he had a pen and his Hydra, and lurched into the passageway.

Only to stare up in dismay at a ladder that loomed above like the East Col of the Matterhorn. He was about to turn back when one of the fire-control petty officers stepped out of the equipment room, ran a gaze up and down him, and held out an arm. Dan gripped the handrail, half-supported by the petty officer, and managed to make the top. He squinted into the light. "Captain's on the bridge," Nuckols yelled, making him flinch.

"Too loud, Boatswain, way too damn loud."

"Sorry, sir."

Dan tried to get up into his chair. Nearly fell, but made it, and sank back with a deep sigh that turned into a wrenching coughing fit that left his ears ringing. He rubbed his face, trying to regenerate the Big Picture. Headed south . . . en route to join up with the battle group for Malabar. Behind them, the Chinese. Up north, the Paks and the Indians gearing up for another go at each other.

One of the worst things about a deployment was how

distant the rest of the world began to feel. It wasn't quite as bad these days, with satellite e-mail, chat, but he still had to guess at and try to reconstruct what was going on over the horizon. If there still *was* a world out there. If *Savo*, like one of Heinlein's generational starships, wasn't all the universe that still existed. He simply had to infer, from the crumbs of information that reached them out here . . . but why was he worrying?

Hey, if you needed to know, your bosses would tell you, right?

Yeah, like they'd explained what was supposed to be in the freighter's holds, and why they'd suddenly decided to call him off, when he'd all but had his hands on it.

He coughed, levered upright, and took a fresh grip on the clipboard. He should be studying the exercise op order. But even the thought was laughable. He had barely enough energy to bite off another breath.

"Captain. Heard you were under the weather."

He screwed his head around to meet Amarpeet Singhe's dark-lashed gaze. As usual, a hint of cleavage peeped at the neck of tailored coveralls, and gold glinted deep within. But he didn't even care to squint for a better view. Just sighed. "Amy."

"Thought you might want to know how we're doing on the investigation."

"Uh, right. Yeah . . . very interested," he lied. Tried to struggle upright again, to at least pretend a modicum of interest. "You're working this with Chief Toan, right? Where is he?"

"Actually I've been doing most of the interviewing.

The chief's been concentrating on the physical evidence."

"There's physical evidence? I thought . . ."

"I didn't mean that. Just, following up on the disconnection of the light switch in the darken ship trunk."

"Oh. Right. You followed up on that? I mean, he followed up?"

Singhe came close, as if sharing something intimate. "Sure you're in shape to take this aboard, Captain? XO said you were down hard."

"I'm listening, God damn it."

"Well, it turns out the switch was disconnected, yes. But anybody could have done it—it was just a piece of cardboard slipped between the contacts."

"So that's a dead end?"

"So far. But I've been interviewing the girls, about who's been paying particular attention to Terranova, so forth and so on. There's a significant amount of fraternizing going on aboard, Captain. That the command either doesn't know about, or doesn't care to acknowledge."

He cleared his throat. "Um, I wonder if you could . . . the coffee urn . . ."

Dark eyebrows crept up. "You want me to get you coffee?"

"Um, no, I didn't mean that. Ask Nuckols to bring it over." As he coughed into his fist, then couldn't seem to stop, lights strobed behind his eyelids. Maybe he *should* be in his rack. "You said, um, significant fraternizing. Is this something we want to ackowledge?"

"Everybody knows. And I'm afraid it runs deeper

than I expected, frankly. We need to raise consciousness about this issue. Maybe a command-wide time-out—"

Dan suppressed a sigh and fitted his fingertips together. He'd always felt there was little point in cramming healthy twenty-something men and woman cheek by jowl in a six-hundred-foot hull for months at a time, and expecting saintlike chastity. As long as it didn't impact readiness, he was willing to look the other way . . . to a certain extent, anyway. "I'm not happy to hear that, Amy. We'll have to think about how to address it. But isn't a limited amount of, um, interaction between consenting adults a different issue than assault with a knife?"

"The environment generates the crime, Captain. If you stop panhandling, your murder rate goes down too. They proved that in New York."

"Uh-huh, but can we focus on one thing at a time, Lieutenant? You were going to look into Peeples, right? He had the attitude." Something else occurred then, and he added, "Also, Petty Officer Scharner, the one he had the set-to with—"

"She's dead. Yes sir. But the chief corpsman swears that was the crud."

"He's absolutely sure? She couldn't have been smothered?"

"No sir. Neat as that would tie it up, I don't think we have to go there yet. And as far as Peeples, the CMAA searched his locker and bunk area—"

"What?" Dan hitched himself upright. "I didn't sign off on that."

"He consented to a voluntary search. No knife, no stained coveralls, nothing incriminating." Singhe inspected the overhead. "So we're at a dead end. Except for one thing Terror remembered at the re-interview: the smell of limes."

"Limes, huh? She didn't mention that."

"Remember, she was pretty shaken up. Once she had time to think about it, she remembered. He smelled like limes."

"Okay, maybe that's valuable, maybe not. Do we have anything lime-scented in the ship's store?"

"Not for two years, Captain. Hermelinda remembered stocking a lime aftershave back then. But nothing recently. So it might mean, whoever our guy is, he's not a recent accession."

Behind her, Bart Danenhower lounged against the nav console. Obviously, next in line to talk. "Okay, good." Dan hitched himself once more; he kept slipping down on the slick leather. "Keep at it, Lieutenant. Sooner or later, he'll try it again. I'd rather nail him before that happens."

The chief engineer had nothing much new, just needed permission to tear down one of the gas turbine generators to replace seals. The message traffic came up, which Dan usually read on his desktop, but apparently word had gotten around that he was installed on the bridge. He ate a couple more ibuprofen. Forced himself to turn pages and initial routing boxes, skimming most, but stopping to read one.

Staurulakis had mentioned sub activity off Singapore the night before. This morning's message gave more detail. Chinese nuclear submarines had been detected approaching the Malacca Strait. To join an already robust presence in the IO? He rubbed his forehead, contemplating what that might mean for force numbers and threat level, the delicate balance of red line and boundary testing, that prevailed in the Darwinian, Mahanian world of the Indian Ocean. But generating thought felt like squeezing molasses through a strainer.

One by one, his department heads came up through the forenoon hours, and he tried his best to give appropriate responses. But he could feel his attention wandering, his responses disjointed and partial. His arms ached as if he'd spent the morning shoveling coal, and his head spun whenever he made the slightest effort. Was this how half his crew felt? Grissett had mentioned lingering effects. Longley brought up another tray, but Dan winced and waved it away.

The overcast was thinner today, the sun brighter behind the scrim of monsoon cloud. He sent his steward down for his sunglasses, leaned back, and rested his eyes.

He was asleep again when a sudden increase in the noise level roused him. He cleared his throat and stretched, then tensed as *Savo* heeled and a sudden cacophony of shouting broke the drowsy routine of the watch.

When he joined the officer of the deck out on the

wing, Van Gogh had his binoculars up, staring ahead. "What've we got?" Dan asked him. "Why'd you change course?"

"Something weird on the surface search."

"Weird? Weird how?"

"A line . . . straight line across the screen. Combat reported it; the JOOD confirmed."

Dan looked down at the sea. Out at the horizon. Then behind them. The sea heaved in all directions, shading from a slate graygreen far out to a deep cobalt directly below. Small birds darted along the crests, and bits of weed the pale hue of drowned corpses slid past, their shadows slanting down blackly into the deep blue beneath. His mind labored, but couldn't summon an explanation. "A squall line? Or some kind of anomaly effect?"

"I guess it could be," the chief quartermaster said, still peering ahead. "But that's not what I'm wondering about . . . huh."

"What?" Dan glanced back into the pilothouse. Everyone was looking out ahead, except for the JOOD, who had his face submerged in the black rubber hood of the radar repeater.

When Dan looked back at the sea, a thin dark line extended from dead ahead off to the left and the right, seeming to taper, or vanish, at the edges of vision. As he blinked at it the line extended, swiftly running out and away in both directions until it bridged the horizon. Van Gogh snapped his glasses down, turned, and shouted into the pilothouse, "Slow to five knots. Steady as you go."

"Collision alarm," Dan told him. A moment later the triple electronic tone blasted out over the 1MC. The thing was swiftly growing darker and wider. Obviously closing in. When he lifted his own glasses he saw it was a surge of sea, capped here and there with white, the overcast sun glowing and flashing off its sullenly lifted planes. It looked like the mother of all big surfing waves.

BM1 Nuckols, on the shipwide circuit: *"Now hear this! All hands, stand by for heavy seas. All hands topside lay within the skin of the ship immediately. Now set material condition Zebra throughout the ship. This is no drill."*

Doors began slamming, isolating each space from the next, subdividing the ship into hundreds of watertight compartments. The JOOD, head still down, began counting down the range as the phone talkers slammed the dogging levers on the wing doors. "Twelve hundred yards . . . one thousand . . . eight hundred yards."

Dan lurched across the pilothouse and pressed the Transmit lever on the 21MC. "Main Control, bridge. Skipper here. We've got some kind of major wave system headed our way. Anything you need to do to minimize damage, keep the engines on line, do it." Then pushed the button for Radio, and told them to put out a voice warning, alerting anyone in transmission range. "And a message to Fifth Fleet and Strike One, too, flash precedence," he added.

"Four hundred yards."

Now it was visible with the naked eye, and the lookouts were calling it in. The sea itself was lifting, as if some unseen force were peeling it up. Above it rolled a thick, pearlescent boiling, a heavy, ghostlike mist. The only thing he'd ever seen remotely like it had been the shock wave that had wrecked *Horn,* but this came on much more slowly.

He'd heard of seismic waves. "Tidal" waves, though they had nothing to do with the tides. Generated by subsea earthquakes, they could march across thousands of miles of ocean, and wreak massive destruction when they hit land. But he'd never expected to see one.

He leaned on his chair, fingers digging into leather and steel. The silence; that was scariest. The way it just came on, noiseless, implacable, steadily larger. A massive, hollow tube that might have lit up the jaded brain of a lifelong surfer, but that frightened him. Without radar, or at night, this thing could have taken them unawares. How many ships had vanished, lost at sea forever, for just that reason?

A warship was built to take heavy seas, and the usual way you met them was head-on. But naval architecture design parameters didn't factor in one-offs, monster rogues, whatever this thing was. Any ship ever built, balanced just the right way, could break its back. A mine or a torpedo could snap a keel with a bubble of gas. What might one single, massive wave do? He racked his sick, tired brain. He'd warned Engineering, so they could be ready to reset whatever tripped off the line. Gotten a message off, to warn anyone else in range. The bow lookout was sprinting for the port break, shemagh fluttering, leaving headset and cord lying on the foredeck. The *dit dit dit, dit dit dit* of the collision alarm staccatoed on, shrill and galvanizing. "*All hands brace for shock*," the 1MC announced.

"Three hundred yards." The JOOD lifted his face. The murmuring died away as men and women wedged themselves between consoles, or grabbed the hand-worn steadying cable that stretched along the pilot-house's overhead.

Another danger occurred to him. The sonar dome was "inflated" with twenty-four thousand gallons of pressurized water. If he took this thing head-on, it would compress and, most likely, collapse the dome. In effect, blowing out the ship's eardrums.

He told Van Gogh, "Back down, Chief."

"Sir? What was that?"

"All back full. Right now!"

The OOD and helmsman gaped, but when he repeated the order they obeyed. He gripped steel, trying to concentrate. Though the screws turned inboard and the rudders were small, a Ticonderoga's hull dimensions and 80,000 shaft horsepower made her extremely responsive. But dead in the water, then going astern, the helmsman would lose steerageway as they lost wash across the rudders.

Savo Island shuddered and seemed to fishtail slightly. Then, seconds later, gathered way astern.

He clung to the overhead cable, eyeing the passing sea, then the oncoming monster. They wouldn't get up totally to a full backing bell. But he'd need steerageway, in case they started to broach. His brain felt sluggish. As if thinking were a skill he'd never learned. But he couldn't stand aside, not now.

"Two hundred yards." The rising bluegreen all but filled the windscreen. It towered above the bullnose. He couldn't guess how high this thing was, but the pilothouse of a Tico-class was sixty feet above the waterline. How many millions of tons of sea water did a wave sixty feet high contain? It would lift the bow first, then the midships, and last, the stern. The point of maximum stress would be midships, as bow and stern hung unsupported by sea. The condition was called "hogging," and it had broken many ships before.

"One hundred yards," the JOOD breathed.

"This is the captain," Dan said, raising his voice. "I have the conn. Belay your reports."

Gas turbines were vastly faster in response than the steam-powered ships he'd started his career on. *Savo* could accelerate from no-load to maximum power in thirty seconds. So he waited, until it felt like he couldn't breathe. But power up too soon, and he'd hurl ten thousand tons of metal into a cliffside at thirty miles an hour. He had to catch this thing at just the right—

"All engines ahead flank three," he snapped, and the helmsman repeated the order, no hesitation now. A second ticked away. Another. The turbines began to whine, spooling up rapidly, their song clearly audible on the bridge in the creepy stillness.

Savo slowed her retreat, wallowed, then began to gather way forward again.

A foreswell reached her and the bullnose began rising. But too slowly for the massive slope that lifted ahead of them. At the same time that uncanny mist closed in, like the worst fog he'd ever seen. The helmsman cursed, fighting the wheel. Dan waited, squinting, clinging to his handhold, and as the massive wave pried the bow upward he ordered, "*Left* hard rudder."

The ship shuddered beneath them, heeling, bowing like a stressed girder as the immense wave pressed them skyward. He felt heavy, as in an ascending elevator, but the heel from his radical rudder order was counteracting the wave, which was trying to force her over to port. The sea crashed through the bullnose and cascaded up over the foredeck in a welter of deep green, turning white as it broke apart on ground tackle and gun mount and VLS hatches but still rising, hundreds of tons of it, thousands, and slammed into the flat forward face of the superstructure, shaking it like an earthquake. It whipsnapped the JOOD off the repeater, where he was still clinging, to stagger forward and slam his nose into the window. As he shook a bloody visage the whole superstructure groaned around them. Sharp cracks and bangs carried through the metal as through the bone of one's own skull.

The wave was passing; time to straighten her out. "Right full rudder . . . port engine ahead full, starboard engine back full." With this combination, the ship would pivot in place as the bow swung to starboard, ready for the follow-on waves he anticipated would emerge from the mist-murk at any moment. This fucking white stuff . . . it seethed ahead of the windscreen . . . if only he could *see*—

"Right full rudder, port ahead full, starboard back full . . . Number one engine indicates off the line," the helmsman said, voice tense.

"Christ," Dan whispered. Exactly what he'd hoped wouldn't happen.

He hesitated as *Savo* began to topple. He'd slewed her as the great sea burrowed beneath, to lessen the strain on the keel and the dome. Accepting the risk of broaching; figuring to use the engines, if she started to go, to twist her back. But *Savo*'s controls had betrayed her before, some intermittent, mysterious glitch having to do with the grounding of the back plane wiring in the machinery consoles. It could trip a turbine off the line or, worst case, cascade, and shut down power entirely. He'd hoped it wouldn't bite him in the ass when he was most vulnerable.

But of course, it had.

The 21MC crackled on through the scream of buckling aluminum and the roar of heavy water raining down, spray from the breaking crest rattling down and, along with the silvery mist, obliterating all sight. *"Number one back online . . . no . . . offline again."*

The wave passed on, under them, and *Savo* keeled over to starboard, slowly, like a mastodon toppling to die. Metal screeched and groaned as the sea surged up toward them, as she inclined farther and farther. He couldn't see the next wave. Couldn't tell if it was larger or smaller than the one just past.

In extremis, then, fuck the sonar dome. Twist her back to where, if the second wave was the killer, she'd meet it head-on. "Right *hard* rudder," Dan said, fighting the urge to scream it out. "Port shaft ahead flank emergency, starboard back flank emergency."

"Engine room . . . engine room answers, port ahead flank emergency, starboard back full . . ."

Dan clung to the chair, brain vacant now. Nothing else left to do. Only wait to go on over, capsize and break apart and go down. Trusting in the engineers who'd designed her, and the welders who'd built her, for their lives. Everyone on the bridge clung tight, some dangling like apes from the bronze cable, boots kicking in the air.

The second wave materialized from the mist. The stern dropped away, and with a screeching, exhausted cry *Savo Island*'s bow rose again, to point into the misty sky. She shuddered and quaked as the sea boiled around her.

Then, very slowly, she began to roll upright again. "Rudder amidships," Dan bit off. "All ahead one-third." She shook and snapped and groaned, yet straightened a few degrees more.

Shaking hundreds of tons of green sea off her decks, she nodded heavily from side to side. The clapper of the ship's bell rang once, twice, and again. The mist thinned, the particles of spray coalescing and falling as a light rain that pattered across the windshield. A third wave, smaller than the first two, lifted and set them back down.

"Steady up on one-zero-zero. Damage reports,"

Dan said. His knees were shaking so badly he had to grip the arm of the chair to stay upright. He coughed, head swimming, and again, kept hacking. Once started, he couldn't stop, couldn't seem to catch his breath.

"All compartments make damage reports to DC Central," Nuckols grated into the 1MC.

"You all right, Skipper?"

"Yeah, Chief. Thanks. Good work there." He controlled his coughing fit with an effort of will, tensing his chest muscles, and focused on the sea again, where another, lower line rose ahead.

A fourth, then a fifth swell, each smaller than its predecessor, rolled past. The water seethed, but it was gentling; patches of creamy spume rocked and swirled as far as he could see. "Seems to be it," the quartermaster said tentatively.

"Do these things come in groups? Or what?"

Van Gogh mused, rubbing his mouth. "There's not much in Bowditch, Captain, not that I recall. Mostly, you hear about tsunamis when they hit land. Cause a load of damage there. Low-lying ground, coastal areas . . . you know the drill."

Dan nodded. He lifted his voice to include helmsman, lookouts, talkers, the JOOD. "Set condition Yoke. Boatswain, pass 'secure from collision quarters.' Engineering . . . have the Chief Snipe call me when he has a handle on that outage. And the damage-control officer, report when he knows what that did to us."

He looked out at the sea once more, the unpredictable, dangerous sea. And summoning the very last ounce of energy he possessed, dragged himself up into his chair once more.

The messages began to stream in while they were still cleaning up. Repairing the davits, recovering the starboard inflatable, which had gone by the board, and patching four new cracks that had opened in the aluminum superstructure.

A huge tsunami had hit the Maldives, the island chain southwest of India. Fleet had a P-3 on its way there from Masirah with an OASIS II/ASIP upgrade, an electro-optical camera in a ball turret in the nose and the ability to stream pictures by satcomm. Exercise Malabar was postponed until further notice. *Savo* and *Mitscher* were ordered to the capital, Male, to render assistance while *Pittsburgh* took station to northward. Dan would be the initial task group response commander. He closeted with Staurulakis and Mills, going over the humanitarian assistance tacmemo and what would be involved in crossing the chop line to Pac-Fleet's area of responsibility.

When he was sure everything was being done to get ready, he went below. Male was twelve hours' steaming at reduced speed, with one engine still off the line for a thorough checkout of the wiring and fuel supply.

He had no doubt that when they got there, they would all be sorely tried.

13

Male, the Maldive Islands

A loft the next morning, he peered down as Red Hawk's shadow crossed a muddy, littered beach. The seawalls had been overwhelmed and wrecked. A beach road was obliterated. Streets had been turned into streams. Water was even now still draining off, scum- and debris-encrusted whirlpools circling, shimmering with the rainbows of oil and gasoline slicks. Solid columns of inky smoke streamed up to the north. Fallen trees, beached, listing boats, smashed homes, appliances, wheelbarrows, barrels, overturned trucks, uprooted poles and power lines, lay strewn across a rocky, still wave-swept strand, where the receding sea had chewed, battered, torn apart, and discarded them.

From five hundred feet up he could grasp the island's truly frightening lack of elevation. The wave had hit from the southeast, open sea, where no reefs or other barriers could break its force. For at least a mile inland, everything was gone. Houses, shops, waterfront hotels, had been smashed into a shoal of wreckage that stretched for miles, both on Male and on the other, lower islands that reached north to the horizon. A few buildings still burned; bright orange flames roasted the sky. A beachfront resort, semicircular swimming area strewn with wreckage, smoldered sullenly, one wing slumped in collapse. Puddles the size of ponds gleamed under the cloudy sky, riffled by a light wind. Where the sea had receded, the ground was a parti-color landscape that, as they descended, resolved into a panorama of shattered debris: furniture, wood, paper, metal, and here and there, limp shapes like bundles of discarded laundry.

When he lifted his gaze he could take in nearly the whole atoll, a necklace of reefs and low coral islands. According to the charts, none were more than six feet above sea level. Behind them, to the west, stretched the shallows and reefs of hundreds of square miles of lagoon.

It looked like Paradise after Armageddon. Ahead, on a slight rise, hundreds of tiny multicolored dots became human beings, milling like a disturbed hill of fire ants. *"Central stadium,"* Strafer said over the intercom, pointing to a soccer field a few hundred yards in from the leading edge of the damage.

The airframe jolted, then settled onto its struts. Dan peered out to find the helicopter the epicenter of a stampede of dark-skinned men in long pants and T-shirts, mouths open, screaming. "Keep the blades turning," he

yelled to the pilot, pulling off his cranial as the crewman dropped the exit steps. "Let's go, Stony, Chief."

He stepped down carefully, holding to the handgrips.
Staggered as he lurched off, still weak; dizzy; panting.
The chief corpsman and *Mitscher*'s CO followed. The
choking stenches of smoke and water and rot closed his
throat. He turned back to help unload boxes of canned
food and plastic gallon jugs of water, the first install-
ment of what would be many tons of aid. But the bent
backs of the helo crew blocked his way. "We got it,
Skipper." The door gunner waved him off. "Go do what
you need to. We got this."

The crowd didn't look welcoming. Someone was
shouting, over and over, "This is America's fault. This
is America's fault." Others murmured, or just looked
sullen, only slowly clearing a path. Dan handed out the
candy in his pockets, but the children took it doubtfully,
gazes lowered. The men shuffled into a queue as the
crewmen handed each an MRE and a gallon jug of
water. Past them, bodies were piled like logs inside a
goal net.

His Motorola beeped. "Captain," Dan snapped, turning to look across the flattened land to where *Savo*
and *Mitscher* rode at anchor, well offshore, just in
case whatever subsidence had raised the massive waves
hadn't exhausted itself. Two miles down the coast, *Tippecanoe* was feeling her way in.

Pardees's voice. *"Sir, First Loo here..RHIB reports
they're starting to see bodies, all around."*

He'd put the boats in the water to patrol back and

forth a mile from shore. Partially for security, but with a more grisly task as well. "Right, Noah. Collect, bring on board, be sure to treat with respect. Lay 'em out and cover 'em on the afterdeck. I'll find out where they go. I'll be sending the helo back. Maybe he can vector us to more."

Crisis response had always been a Navy mission, but it called for different skill sets than combat. He was here, the day after the disaster, to evaluate and plan the relief effort, along with providing what support *Mitscher* and *Savo* could muster. There was discussion of diverting *Vinson* to support air operations. Nor would the Navy be alone. The Air Force was planning C-130 missions in from Diego Garcia; they would land at Male International Airport, bringing far more in the way of supplies than Dan had, though the ships would be valuable in other ways—as a source of potable water and as a means, with boats and helos, to transport medical and other personnel elsewhere in the island chain.

More help was en route. PaCom advised that a French amphibious task group, and also several Indian ships, were on their way. In the longer term, six ships from Maritime Prepositioning Squadron 3 had gotten under way. They carried equipment and supplies for fifteen thousand marines for thirty days, including road-building materials, generators, and other emergency gear. They could purify a hundred thousand gallons of potable water a day and pump it inshore from miles away. By then Dan could expect to be relieved by a joint task force commander, someone with stars on his shoulders, to be the face of U.S. aid.

For the moment, though, he and "Stony" Stonecipher were on their own. He still felt nauseated, and had to force one boot in front of the other as he pushed toward the tents pitched on the far side of the field. But he had to set weakness aside. Stonecipher, in BDUs, and Grissett, in ship's coveralls and an armband with a red cross, paced him to the left. Benyamin, in boarding gear and armed with an M4, brought up the rear, just in case.

The folding chairs and tables looked as if they'd been dragged out of the school next to the field. Tent fabric billowed in a steady wind. Maps were taped on the tabletops. He was ushered toward three men in camo uniforms and a woman in a bright red sari trimmed with gold. Stonecipher eased a case of MREs off one shoulder; Grissett, a box of medical supplies. Dan shook hands and introduced himself. "So, does anyone here speak English?"

"We all speak English, sir. We were a British colony until 1965."

He sank into one of the offered chairs. "Um . . . right. Well, we can provide helo transport, boats, water, and limited food and medical care. The other ship coming in, *Tippecanoe*, has more. And many more ships and planes are on the way. Tell me how we can help, and who we should take orders from."

The military guys looked to the woman. She said, in flawless Oxbridge, "Yes, sir. I am Mariya Farih, mayor of Male. Colonel Jaleel here, of the Maldives National Defence Force, is in charge of our disaster response." Jaleel came forward, hand extended. Stocky, with a clipped black beard, he looked sleep-deprived already. "Very glad to see you." He shook Dan's hand as if he were never going to let go.

"Just sorry we had to meet like this. Is something wrong? That crowd seemed less than welcoming."

The mayor said, "We've had some internal problems, Captain. Rioting. Unrest. We actually had declared a state of emergency even before the sea rose against us. And, yes, there is resentment against the United States. Over your stance on the Kyoto Protocols." She forced a smile. "But *you* are not responsible for that. We welcome any assistance."

"I see. Is this going to be your emergency headquarters, Madam Mayor? Colonel?"

"Perhaps. At least temporarily," Jaleel said.

They went over a map of the island, to orient him; the ferry terminal, the airport, the local hospital, the petroleum storage facility on another, smaller island to the north. Dan guessed that was where the columns of smoke were coming from.

Shouting outside. He glanced through the tent flaps to see Benyamin fending off a large islander with his carbine at port arms. Dan had set up facilities at Bagram airport, at the beginning of the allied buildup in Afghanistan. Between that and a review of the humanitarian-assistance documentation, he had a fairly clear idea what would be needed. Security first, if the locals were unable to maintain order. Then emergency medical care and water distribution. After that shelter, generators, radios, reuniting families, burying bodies, food service, and water purification. "Well, if you don't mind some advice—"

"We would be happy to hear whatever you suggest," the mayor said. "Though of course we must make the final decisions. I will be talking to the president shortly, by the way."

"Absolutely. Well, to address your location first. It might be desirable to place your headquarters somewhere with better transport, better communications, and isolated to some extent from crowds . . . to prevent incidents. That would make your choice the ferry terminal, the container port, or the airport."

"On Hulhule Island," Jaleel said, placing a finger on the map. The Male International strip was across a narrow strait to the north.

"Um, might be wise. More room to stock supplies. Better security. Better communications. Most of your early relief shipments will come in by air anyway. I can arrange helicopter transport if you like. Shuttle you over, help set up a command post, and let you get a look at the damage."

Jaleel agreed quietly, saying he'd planned to go there himself, but the island government hadn't fully executed their disaster plan yet. A policeman in British-style khaki came in and handed the colonel a message. Jaleel sighed, scratching his beard. "We can't forget the other islands. This is from Kandolhudoo. Apparently it was hit hard, just about destroyed . . . the plantations, the tourist hotels, fishing villages . . . we are getting reports in by radio. Would it be possible to assist them as well?"

Dan said they'd do what they could, and repeated that more help was on its way. He laid out what he could do today: send a firefighting team to the oil terminal, supply antibiotics and plasma substitute to the hospital, and send rations and water to a distribution point at the ferry terminal via the ships' boats. Red Hawk could help the islands' own aircraft start transferring medical, sanitary, and security personnel. The water depth at the ferry terminal, unfortunately, wasn't enough for a ship to come alongside, but there was a berth at a small freight-handling facility on the other side of the island that Stonecipher thought they might get *Tippecanoe* alongside.

Dan sipped bottled water, feeling overwhelmed. Outside, the shouting was growing louder, merging with an ominous-sounding chant. "Okay, we'll head back now. I'm going to leave you this radio, all right? Or you can contact us on—what are you using for your emergency comms?"

"HF only. Everything else has gone down. That is all we have with the mainland and with the southern islands."

"Uh-huh. Okay, we'll get to them, but it looks like your main population center here is where we need to do the most work, plus getting things set up over at the airport."

Jaleel nodded, as did the mayor, and Dan added, "One other thing: we've got the Indians en route, the

French—but someone's going to have to be in charge, or we'll be fighting each other for pier space and use of the landings. I suggest you pick someone to coordinate the naval relief effort."

They conferred briefly, the woman in the bright red sari dominating the discussion. She ended it by turning to him. "I think you have nominated yourself for that position, Captain. If you will accept it."

He invited Jaleel and the mayor to go up in Red Hawk for a quick look-see. Strafer flew them south first, following the chain of reefs and islands. From on high, they were pearls in a cobalt sea. From lower, the level of destruction, in villages dotted hop-skip-jump wherever a coral outcrop rose a foot or two above high tide, was sobering. People waved desperately as they flew over, but all he could do was circle, to show at least that he'd noticed them, then fly on.

As they headed back, Staurulakis reported two Indian coast guard ships had arrived and were proceeding to the container terminal. Dan asked her to warn them that he intended to put *Tippecanoe* there, as she had frozen stores and other food. The exec said she'd pass that word, but that the Indians didn't seem inclined to listen.

Male receded down the port side, and they landed at the international airport. The end of the single strip had been overwashed, but the terminal and hangar/repair buildings looked undamaged. Strafer went to check out the fuel situation as Dan, Stonecipher, and Jaleel went into the terminal. It was thronged with strandees, German, Dutch, Indian; all flights had been diverted or canceled. Fortunately they had water, food, emergency generators, and toilets, so aside from temporary inconvenience they'd be all right. Dan reassured them help was on the way, and asked for doctors or nurses. He got three volunteers. He dropped them and Jaleel back at the soccer field, then sent Red Hawk back to the airport, to transport medical personnel and supplies to the outlying islands as soon as the teams were ready.

The messages were piling up back in CIC. He waded in with a tray and a Diet Pepsi beside him. Pulling a sample ROE for humanitarian assistance off the net, he modified it and put it out, authorizing use of force only for self-protection and reminding all hands that they had to respect local customs, and could not seize personal property for redistribution. He included this as an attachment to an update message to PaCom, along with the titles and names of everyone he'd dealt with, to give whoever took over from him a head start. Then he went to the map again. Supplies would come in at two locations, the container terminal and the airfield. They'd have to be distributed by helo and boat, and the airfield won on both counts.

Dave Branscombe came down to discuss comms with the airfield and the shortwave links with the outlying islands. They settled on a coordination net for the seaborne relief efforts. Dan said to clear it with the

Maldivians, then set a watch on that frequency and on the harbor net as well.

The harbormaster; that's who he'd forgotten. He got him on the radio for a discussion about water depths, the ferry terminal, connections with the airport. The man warned him about bringing weapons ashore, and mentioned pigs as well. Dan said he didn't have any pigs aboard, and that his crews would wear sidearms for self-protection. If he didn't like that, he could take it up with Colonel Jaleel.

In the middle of this Mills came in with the news that the Indians were on Rescue and Coordination asking to talk. After some back and forth with their senior skipper, Dan convinced the guy to accept him as the on-scene commander, subject to Jaleel's direction as host country representative. The Indians had loaded basic food and medical supplies at Goa and gotten under way hours after the first notice of the tsunami. He asked them to finish unloading and clear the pier as quickly as possible; *Tippecanoe* would come alongside as soon as they cast off.

He stayed in his seat to check in on a satellite chat room set up to coordinate relief efforts, not just for his area, but for everywhere the tsunami had hit—Sumatra, Sri Lanka, the Nicobars, even Madagascar, far, far to the west. The damage stretched a quarter of the way around the globe. The first C-130s were en route, scheduled just after dusk. He confirmed runway lights and radio beacons were operational, and that fuel service would be available.

The French reported in that afternoon. Two ships, FS *Mistral* and FS *Henaff*. A check of *Jane's* and the intel database told him one was an antisubmarine corvette, which wouldn't be of much use in this situation, but the other was a dock landing ship with a heavy helo detachment—ideal for getting aid ashore quickly. After a call to Jaleel, who sounded exhausted, Dan phoned the French commander back, gave him the coordination net frequency, and asked him to take charge of relief to the atolls to the north, Faadhippolhu, Miladhunmadulu, and Thiladhunmathee, with a zone of responsibility from 4°45' north to 7° north.

Cheryl cleared her throat, to wake him. "Captain."

He yawned and stretched. "Yeah, Cher. What'cha got?"

"202's back aboard. Both RHIBs are back for crew change and maintenance. Commander Danenhower reports the DC crew has the petrochem fire under control."

"This is the fire—"

"On the tank farm island."

"Okay. Good. What else?"

"You're due at the airfield at 2000 local. Conference of relief providers. They want you to brief on the coordination of seaborne relief. And some interesting news. The Chinese reported in."

He sat up, boots slamming to the deck, as the whole depressing, enraging business flooded back. "Fuck. The Chinese . . . *Wuhan*?"

"No, she and the other destroyer are still up north. This is the other unit in their task group. The support ship."

He leaned to the keyboard. *Weishanhu,* hull 887, was a Qiandaohu-class replenishment ship. It displaced thirty thousand tons and carried two helos, but her complement was only a hundred men, which would limit flexibility. Still, she would supply fuel, water, and enormous quantities of food and other supplies, and her onboard cranes would get them ashore quickly. He said reluctantly, "Holy smoke, this thing's enormous. How'd they get in touch?"

"HF to Male."

"Not to us? On the coordination net?"

"I tried to call them on that freq, but there was no response."

Which might mean they were declining to acknowledge him as on-scene commander. Did he need to worry about that? He decided not to, for now. "We'll need a list of—no, never mind, the colonel can ask them that." Dan ran his hands through his hair, noting that it was getting past time for a visit to the barbershop. "They could go outboard of *Tippecanoe* at the terminal. That should give even this mother enough keel depth. Pass that suggestion to the harbormaster. I don't think we need to get involved. And let Captain Hunteman know they might be mooring alongside, so he can get his fenders over and lock down his topside accesses. We don't want them wandering around. Frankly, I'd just as soon not have them moored alongside him . . . but I guess it's the most logical place to put her."

The exec put a hand on his shoulder. "Understand, Skipper. You can't have felt too great about how that all turned out."

This was the first time they'd discussed it aloud. And it still hurt. Forever after, his name would be associated with it. The Navy had a long memory for any shortcoming or error, and he had a feeling this one would turn out to be epic. He shook his head. "It's not the message we should've sent, Cheryl."

"The fleet commander had to know what he was doing. Maybe whatever they were hiding, we already knew about. And airing it in public would just put Beijing on the spot."

Dan wished he could believe that. He said irritably, "They *need* to be put on the spot. They've been proliferating missiles all over the map. Along with Pakistan, North Korea . . . but don't get me started." He coughed long and hard, doubled over the command desk. When he looked up, she was gone.

He took the RHIB in to that night's meeting, along with Amy Singhe and Max Mytsalo, just to give them a look.

They cast off after dark. The bowhook cradled a portable searchlight, scanning the water just ahead. Twice they had to detour around floating logs, and other, less identifiable debris. A small plane droned above, lights flashing, and banked away toward the field. Where, as they passed, heavier engines thundered: a four-engine transport. They motored past the riprap at the end of the runway and made for the inlet beyond. Lights glittered here and there on Male; some parts of the island had power, while others, closer to the water, were dark. They passed close to the tank farm. The fire-glow no longer flickered, but the stink of burning petroleum, dank and heavy, lay over the water, mixed with the smells of rot and decay from all the organic material that had been sucked back into the estuary.

"D'you know the route in to the ferry landing?" Dan asked the coxswain. The boatswain said he did, and pointed to brilliant orange apron lights ahead.

They ran in at dead slow, heading for two jetties. Beyond them lay the sloped roof of the terminal and a concrete pier where palms swayed and clashed beneath tangerine lights.

The bowhook raised his arm suddenly, pointing off to port. The coxswain pulled back the throttles and they drifted in, turning slightly, toward where the bowhook focused his beam.

Something floated there. Dan stood, hoping it wasn't what it looked like, right up until the smell reached him.

"Pick it up, Skipper?"

"Can't leave it out here, BM2." He cleared his throat, leaning out as the boat drifted the last few feet and the thing bumped into the rigidly swollen rubber with a faint thud. The details came through one at a time, each reluctantly acknowledged, as if his brain resisted assembling sensory inputs into recognition. Small. Face-down. Dark hair.

A child, back humped beneath thin cotton as arms and legs dangled. It had only begun to swell. He knew that from other bodies he'd picked up at sea, on other cruises. But this was smaller than any he'd encountered before. It belched gas as they got a line around it. "Careful," he muttered to Singhe. "The limbs can separate very easily."

A heave, and they had it over the gunwale. The bow-hook threw an oil-stained tarp over the slack face, but not before Dan had looked into the fish-eaten sockets of a young boy, ten or eleven at a guess. He looked away, sighing, toward the orange lights. They glimmered cheerfully on the water, as if this didn't matter. As if someone's whole world had not just died.

No one said anything else the rest of the way in.

The passenger area had been cleared of the strandees. Tables had been pushed together, and a vertical whiteboard held the by now familiar outline of the island. Another showed the northern and southern atolls, populations called out in grease pencil. A steady chain of Maldivians trudged past, each lugging a box or crate. Forklifts and trucks shuttled outside the huge windows, under the saffron light. A Fokker transport, gunning its propellers, nosed in to where white Nissan pickups waited with men standing in their beds. Dan joined a group of about thirty men and a few women, among whom he recognized the mayor, this time in a severe dark blue pantsuit. Lieutenant Singhe headed straight for her, and soon they had their heads together. He wondered what they were comparing notes on.

Colonel Jaleel, looking as if he hadn't changed his camos, welcomed them in English. "This meeting is so everyone can see who they've been talking to on the radio. So far we have representatives from India, the United States, Singapore, and Japan. French forces are providing assistance to the northern islands. And let me now also welcome China, in the person of Captain Han." He nodded to where a small man in the same white uniform Dan had seen aboard *Wuhan* stood, cupping his elbows. "We are grateful for your help. If all will take seats please . . . I will now introduce our secretary of human welfare, who is in charge of the relief effort."

There was an uncomfortable dance as they found chairs. The Indians started to settle down, then got up again. Apparently they didn't want to sit next to Captain Han. After several awkward moments, Dan found himself between the Indians and the Chinese. He nodded to Han, who bowed his head but said nothing. After a few minutes of platitudes and gratitudes, though, the secretary called on "the senior officer in charge of our naval relief efforts, Captain Daniel Lendon, United States Navy."

"The name is Lenson," he corrected mildly, standing.

"Captain Lenson, sorry. Are there remarks you would like to—?"

The scream of a landing transport drowned out his words. Dan cleared his throat and took out his PDA. "Um, thank you. First I would like to thank all present for their cooperation. We've already provided over three hundred tons of relief supplies, aside from transport, and communications, and water. I'd like to remind everyone, including our latest arrivals, to keep a listening watch on the coordination net. We need to deconflict our ship movements to anchorage and offload areas, and our helicopter operations as well, both for increased efficiency and to assure the safety of all concerned. In concert with the harbormaster, I will continue to coordinate naval efforts, including"—he looked down at the Chinese—"Captain Han's ship, with his permission."

Han said, in clear English, "We will cooperate in providing necessary relief supplies."

Hmm. Not exactly agreeing they would do so under his direction, but not disagreeing, either. Dan said, "Captain, if it's agreeable, I'd like to locate you outboard of USS *Tippecanoe,* at the freight terminal. We can use your cranes to discharge cargo from both ships."

After a moment Han said, "That is a reasonable way to proceed. If the local authorities direct me to berth there."

After an awkward pause, Jaleel said, "Would you mind?"

"I will do so," Han said, to the colonel, not Dan.

O-kay . . . He finished up with several specifics, then turned the floor back to Jaleel.

Outside, in the cool night breeze, he told Amy to have the boat stand by, and wandered over to where a U.S. Air Force C-130 blasted exhaust fumes as it churned slowly up. The rear ramp dropped, and under the queer vibrating light the forklifts grunted into sudden bustle.

One carried a gray torpedo container. Inside was not a Mark 46, despite the stencils, but the body of Petty Officer Scharner, packed in salt and ice. Consigned back to Diego Garcia, for further shipment back to the States.

Dan stood watching them unload, sagging with fatigue, but not as depressed as he had been since the incident with *Wuhan*. There was Indian-on-Chinese suspicion, French standoffishness, Maldivian pride, but as far as he could see, everyone was cooperating, coordinating their efforts to bring help to suffering people.

The forklifts backed away from the transport, burdened with sacks and boxes marked with the half-moon symbols of military rations. They rolled and pivoted in a mechanized quadrille. Crews seized the pallets and slid them into the truckbeds. Then they sped off toward the landing, where boats from three different nations waited to relay cargo along the islands.

Dan rubbed his bare arms against the cool breeze. Human beings weren't just an aggressive species. They knew how to work together as well. Maybe they just needed a disaster every day, to discover how much alike they were, how much they all needed one another.

A short man in rumpled khakis . . . no . . . Army greens was fidgeting a few feet away, looking as if he wanted to intrude but didn't dare. He wore oak leaves on the shoulders of his jacket. Two bulky satchels crouched by his boots. Dan frowned. "You aren't waiting for me, are you, um, Major?"

The officer saluted. A hangdog look, drooping jowls. "Captain Lenson? *Savo Island*?"

"That's me." Dan returned the salute. "And you're . . . ?"

"Dr. Leopold Schell."

"How can I help you, Doctor? Here to help with the relief effort?"

"I'll be glad to lend a hand if I'm needed. But I'm from Fort Detrick, Captain. U.S. Army Medical Research Institute of Infectious Diseases."

Dan got it then, though he hadn't expected Army. "At last. We've been hoping for someone like you."

"Well, two fatalities got our attention. Especially since Bethesda wasn't able to help, I understand."

Dan was shaking his hand when he remembered. "Oh shit. Wait a minute. You're gonna need the body."

"Yes. I'll want to take samples, conduct a thorough autopsy—"

With a roar like thunder the C-130 accelerated down the runway, lifting its nose to the night. Dan looked after it helplessly, and sighed. He was turning back to Schell when the VHF on his belt spoke. *"Skipper?"*

"Excuse me, um, Leo—" He fumbled for the Motorola. "Go ahead, Exec."

"Captain? You on the RHIB headed back? Over."

"Just about, the conference just broke. Over."

"You might want to get back here as quickly as you can." Staurulakis sounded unnaturally somber. *"Over."*

"What is it? Over."

"Message from PaCom. We're directed to get under way."

"Under way. Whither bound?"

A pause, then, *"I'd rather not say on an unsecure*

*circuit, Captain. But please, don't linger. I'm passing
that word to* Mitscher *as well. We'll be hot-boxed at
short stay when you get here. Over."*

Short stay was with the anchor chain straight up and
down, and hot-boxed meant with the turbines warmed
up and ready to go. And both ships . . . He signed off,
then lifted his gaze to find Schell staring at him, looking
apprehensive. "Bad news?"

"Follow me," Dan said, and turned and started jog-
ging toward the boat landing.

IV

ON STATION

14

Heading North

He coughed into one fist, grunting as the jarring re-awoke his headache. A calm yet sullen sea the color of cold iron heaved slowly, barely rolling the ship. They'd cleared the northernmost islands of the Maldives, en route to what his orders called Operation Odyssey Protector, in OpArea Endive.

He slumped in Combat, weak and lethargic. "Odyssey Protector." "Endive." Who made up these names? He ran through his traffic at the command desk, then toggled back to the same message. The one that had pried them loose from relief operations in Male, and sent *Savo* charging north at near flank speed with fuel tanks lower than he liked.

Usually cruisers and destroyers were topped up every three to four days, to maintain fuel levels above 50 percent. But obviously that wasn't going to happen. And fuel wasn't the only thing in short supply. Hermelinda

Garfinkle-Henriques had cornered him that morning at breakfast. "It could be a problem, sir," the supply officer had said. "You directed me to contribute everything we could to the Maleans—"

"The *Maldivians* . . . never mind. Yeah, we should get reimbursed for whatever we dispensed as disaster assistance. You documented it, right?"

"Yes sir. Of course. But I wasn't talking about reimbursement. Our dry and canned stores were only ninety to one hundred twenty days' worth when we left on deployment, and we only got a partial replenishment in Dubai." She'd kept her voice low, but added, "Our fresh stores are gone and the refrigerated stores are getting low. I'm going to the restricted menu tomorrow. If we're out much longer, we'll be scraping the bottom of the dry and canned stores."

Just fucking great. He scrubbed his face with his hands, coughed, and started to get up. Then sagged back, and reread the message.

Savo and her shotgun escort were to take station roughly on the Tropic of Cancer, a hundred nautical miles seaward from the Pakistani-Indian border. In other words, midway between Karachi and Jamnagar. With ringside seats at what was shaping up to be another undeclared war. Matt Mills, in the TAO seat, was double-checking their patrol area preparatory to putting it up on the LSDs, which glowed in front of him, the flat displays canted so reflections would not interfere with vision. And above them, the ever-present reminders of his weapons status, his engines, launchers, radars, other equipment.

Crap engines, low fuel, low food, and a sick ship. Well, Schell was at work, debriefing Grissett and going over the records of everyone who'd come down with the crud since day one, back in the Med. He rubbed his face again, hoping they found something solid.

"Did you see this press conference?"

"What's that, Matt?"

Mills read from the *Early Bird*. " 'State Department spokesmen announced today that U.S. forces are on station ready to shoot down any missile exchange between the two disputants.' "

"*What?* You've got to be shitting me."

But there it was in black and white, or rather, in text on his screen. "Oh, fuck me."

"This isn't so good," Mills agreed.

"Why did they have to *announce* it? This makes us the first-strike target for both sides if the balloon really goes up." He started to type a message, then restrained himself. The Navy had damn-all influence on what State put out. All he'd end up doing was coming across as a whiner. Not that he minded whining, but he'd save it for when they were running out of food and fuel. Something PaCom could do something about. Not crying over spilt milk.

He hitched himself up in the chair. A nap, he really should get his head down before they reached the patrol area. "We've got a lot to get done. Get a groom on our VLS and SPY-1. And set up a siting conference. This is a big area they've parked us in. But I'm not seeing a specific intercept station." The geometry would be critical, if he was really expected to play a spoiler role. *Savo*'s location relative to the launching point, and more specifically, to the intended impact point, would constrain their ability to intercept.

"I'll pass that to the XO. This afternoon? Thirteen hundred?" Mills lifted his Hydra.

"No. I mean, yeah." Dan coughed, then winced, grabbing his head. The crud hung on, all right. He had barely enough energy to sit upright, no appetite, and the less said about the state of his guts the better. Worse yet, he still felt like he wasn't thinking at top capacity. Not the way a CO should feel, going into a strategic-level commitment.

Before he sat down with his Aegis team, though, he went up to his at-sea cabin. Half an hour free; he climbed into his rack, sighed, and closed his eyes.

Then opened them again. Stared at the overhead. Got up, and turned on his computer.

To research the Indian-Pakistani nuclear posture and force balance.

The two nations had gone to war three times: in 1965, in 1971, and most recently, in 1999, over Kargil, in Kashmir. The big change was that now, both had operational theater nuclear weapons. Since Kargil, the tension had seesawed between moments of lull and episodes of renewed friction. Lately, the rise of al-Qaeda–linked cross-border terror had gotten more attention, but the arms buildup had continued.

Stockpile numbers were the most highly classified secrets new nuclear states guarded, but the latest estimates credited both with between sixty and a hundred weapons. Nuclear, but not thermonuclear, straight fission devices. So far as outsiders knew, neither had tested a hydrogen weapon.

The Indian Strategic Forces Command had a long-range capability in strike aircraft, backed up by a short-range missile, the Prithvi, something like the long-retired U.S. Sergeant. Mounted on transporter-erector-launchers, it was small, difficult to spot from satellites; DIA could provide no hard data on the locations of its deployment. Most sources estimated its range as about a hundred miles.

Pakistan looked even or perhaps slightly ahead in missiles, with the recent deployment of a regiment of Shaheen-1s. Also TEL-mounted, this threw a thousand-kilo warhead to three hundred–plus miles. They were deployed in the Kirthar Mountains, south of Islamabad. During the last near war, the batteries had been redeployed near Jhelum, southeast of the capital, but then moved south, back into the mountains, where, presumably, the Indian air force would find it harder to get at them.

He checked a desk atlas left by some previous skipper. That might put Pakistani missiles, at least, within reach of *Savo*'s Standards during their descent phase, depending on their targets. Hitting an Indian missile, on the other hand, might be harder. They'd be flying west or northwest, away from the ship, and a tail chase had a much lower chance of intercept.

In terms of the two sides' doctrines, not much had been published. They seemed to be where the U.S. and

USSR had been in the 1950s, holding each other's cities, command facilities, and airfields at risk. A Naval Postgraduate School thesis pointed out that Pakistan had never renounced first use of nuclear weapons. A *Defense News* editorial he accessed online implied that Pakistan might use nukes against even a conventional invasion. India had originally forsworn first use, but a recent statement from New Delhi had modified this to add, and he read this carefully, "In the event of a major attack against India, or Indian forces anywhere, by biological or chemical weapons, India will retain the option of retaliating with nuclear weapons."

Which you could read as a not-so-veiled warning that "no first use" wasn't ironclad.

He leaned back in his chair, ear tuning to the creaking of the superstructure. Bart Danenhower had identified several more cracks in the alloy, most minor, but one worrisome. The CHENG said they'd almost certainly been caused by hogging during the passage of the tsunami wave, but that didn't mean they couldn't expand. Like a crack in a car's windshield, which lengthened with time. The snipes had drilled holes and welded on patches, but Chief McMottie and the hull techs had refused to guarantee they'd stop the fractures from progressing. Not that the deckhouse was going to fall off, but any flaw in a strength member compromised the hull girder.

What he liked least was that unlike earlier conflicts, when the Pakistanis and Indians had gone at it alone, now both were linked to others. The Pakistanis had bought Chinese air defense systems and granted commercial and maybe naval access at their port of Gwadar. China, Myanmar, Pakistan, and Iran were conducting military exercises together. And both China and Pakistan had been caught proliferating advanced weaponry to even less savory regimes. The Indians, in reaction to their enemies' search for allies, had drawn closer to the United States.

He remembered the national security adviser's words in the elevator of the Rayburn Building. "War now may be better than later." They'd chilled him then, and sounded even more ominous now. Ed Szerenci had always affected a cold detachment from the human realities of war. Could he really, at the right hand of a president who too often acted before he thought, push for a face-off now, believing the balance was shifting against the United States?

Just as the Germans, in 1914, had believed they had to act, or lose the advantage to the Allies?

But no matter how hard he thought, he came up with no answers at all.

Longley brought him a tray. Before the door closed, Dan glimpsed an unfamiliar face behind him in the passageway. Then he caught Grissett behind him, and it snapped into place. "Dr. Schell," he murmured unwillingly. "Chief Corpsman. Did you have something for me? Want half of this sandwich?"

Schell was already in shipboard coveralls, which suggested he hadn't brought a change of uniform. What had been in the duffels, then? He declined the sandwich and perched on the bunk Dan waved him to. Grissett remained standing, hands behind him, head lowered. "I understand you've been affected by this syndrome too," the doctor opened with. "How are you feeling now?"

"Still under the weather," Dan admitted. "Headachy, fatigued. It's tough to concentrate."

"Medications?"

"Ciproflaxicin," Grissett put in. "And Motrin. Cough, elevated temperature, torpor."

"Interesting." Schell nodded, then said, "I, um, understand you served with a former colleague of mine. From USAMRIID."

"Maureen Maddox," Dan said. Her name brought Signal Mirror back, the covert Marine Recon mission into wartime Baghdad. Nearly everyone had died, either along the way or on the way out, along with Sarsten, their too-gung-ho join-up from the Special Air Service. Zeitner, who'd wanted to start a Firestone station. Gunny Gault, killed holding the rear for their retreat. Maddox, their biowarfare guru, had died in Level Four isolation. Leaving only the blue and white starred ribbon on his service dress to remember them by.

"Um, yes."

"Right. Any progress on the crud?" His tone came out harsher than he'd meant it.

Schell pursed his lips. "We could've used more tissue from the last, uh, fatality. But fortunately, your chief corpsman kept blood samples. We're running tests. Hopefully, we'll get something interesting.

"I've reviewed the clinical investigation results from

your first case, in the Med. Bethesda eliminated a number of possibilities, but couldn't identify a causative agent. No antibody to LP1 or LP4. The sputum isolate was difficult to type, but possibly a Portland subgroup. In particular, I see, they ruled out legionellosis, based on a negative result from a *Legionella pneumophilia* serogroup one. They suspected the ventilation system."

"Chief, you told him what we've done so far. Sterilizing the ductwork."

"Yessir."

Schell nodded. "We won't have the results for your female noncom for a few days yet. I suspect it will show pneumonia and multiorgan system failure. But if you did a thorough sterilization, I'm willing to conclude that contrary to what everyone's thought up to now, we're not dealing with an airborne fomite."

Dan blinked. "That's—"

"A fomite's an infectious agent, or a vector . . . virus, bacteria, fungus . . . in some cases, an insect."

"We might have insects?"

"I thought about it, but considering how clean you keep this ship, I don't see that as the vector."

"Thanks—I guess. So what is, then?"

"I'm hoping our cultures will tell us that. So far we have L1 and L3 antigens identified from the blood sample. In the meantime, I have suggestions for at least localizing the infection."

"I'm listening," Dan said. "I'd really like to not have to report another fatality. But even the aftereffects are hurting our readiness. In some watch stations, we're in port and starboard when we should be in four sections. Over time, that's gonna wear everybody down."

"Providing fertile ground for opportunistic infections, like pneumonia . . . which was the final cause of death in your first case, and I suspect in your second, too." Schell deliberated, looking at Dan's screen, which still read TOP SECRET at the top and was an appreciation of Indian nuclear doctrine.

"I should have turned that off," Dan said. "Aim the monitor away from you, please."

"I wasn't reading it, Captain."

"You said you had suggestions."

"He wants to secure the showers," Grissett said, and just the way his arms were folded conveyed doubt.

"Secure the showers," Dan repeated. "You think it's in our freshwater systems? Chief, didn't we already hyperchlorinate? I remember, the water tasted like a Y pool."

"Yessir, we did," Grissett said. "Charged it all the way up to 50 ppm."

"Hyperchlorination may not be effective in rooting out a stubborn infection, with certain organisms," the major said. "But we don't know the incubation period, and I understand from your chief of staff that you're on a fairly important mission out here."

"We call them executive officers. Yeah."

"Ordinarily, I'd recommend putting into port, debarking your crew, and tenting for a full-scale disinfection regime."

"We can't leave station," Dan said.

"How many have to die before you can?"

He sucked air. Schell didn't mince words. "I don't want to lose *anyone,* Doctor. But the decision to call off a mission isn't mine. I'll report anything you want me to. Endorse your recommendations. But if things go down like they might, having us out here could save a lot more lives than we have aboard."

Schell gave that a beat, then rose. "Fair enough. I'll have something more concrete as soon as the results are in. Meanwhile—"

"Secure the showers," Dan told Grissett.

"Sir, I don't think—"

"Better safe than sorry, Chief. Let's go with Leo's call. I'll tell the CHENG to secure the supply. Instruct the compartment petty officers to placard them off-limits. What about cooking water, drinking water, Doctor?"

"Cooking should sterilize any organisms. But, yes, I'd avoid drinking the water for the present."

"Secure the scuttlebutts, too," Dan told Grissett, who looked stone-faced. "How are we set on bottled water?"

"Offloaded it all in Male, Captain."

"Crap," Dan muttered. "Okay, look, get your heads together and figure out how to sterilize enough so we can get everybody a gallon a day, anyway. We can use the feed water, too; it's made from the steam evaporators and stored in separate tanks from the potable water. It's deionized, distilled. Ought to be fine to drink.

"But we can't run long that way, Doctor. Find out what's making us sick, and tell me how to fix it."

Schell just looked thoughtful. Dan glanced at his bunk. Then at the bulkhead clock, and sighed. Time to get on the 1MC and tell everybody what was going on. No showers. *That* certainly wasn't going to help morale.

The setup conference convened at 1300 in CIC, back by the digital dead-reckoning table, where they could spread out references and argue in something like a roundtable format. Though the DRT was rectangular. Present were Dr. Noblos, Chief Wenck, Lieutenant Mills, Lieutenant Singhe, and Cheryl Staurulakis. Dan opened with, "Okay, everyone's read the messages. I want to position for the best chances of an intercept, against missiles from the deployment areas the DIA specifies. But before that, I asked Matt to speculate on how this thing's going to unfold, if it does." He hesitated. "Which of course we hope it doesn't. Matt?"

Mills passed out printed slides. "I'll start with the naval picture. The Indian navy, with overwhelming numbers and the *Viraat* carrier battle group, dominates the green-water zone. But their force-projection capabilities are limited. Even if they clean-sweep the Pak navy, it doesn't win the war.

"Ground capabilities are more evenly matched. India's armored forces are larger, but their ground options are limited by two factors: first, Pakistani bases are closer to the border, so they can deploy faster. Second, India has to guard its northern border as well, against China, which is allied with Karachi. If they coordinate their threats, India won't have enough divisions to hold both borders. Especially in the Himalayas, which function as a force sponge.

"Bottom lines. First: whoever mobilizes faster gains an advantage. Second: if ground forces stalemate, the next step is vertical escalation. Third: if China weighs in, things get hairy fast. That's when a conflict could spread."

A chill harrowed Dan's back. It sounded like the Europe of 1914. Split between hostile blocs, with interlocking alliances meant to deter, but that had actually only pulled one country after another into war, like shackled-together slaves being dragged helplessly overboard to drown.

But Mills was passing around another slide. "The air order of battle clearly favors India. The Pakistanis emerged from a sanction regime two years ago. They've taken delivery of new Chinese fighters, but not enough to counterbalance the Indian air force's MiGs.

"As to how a conflict might go . . ." The blond lieutenant half shrugged, rolling his eyes toward the black-painted overhead.

"Go ahead and speculate, Matt," Dan told him.

"Yessir . . . Well, if a flare-up lasts longer than a couple days, the Indians will achieve air superiority. But it'd be bloody. Meanwhile, both air forces would be unable to support their armor, which each side depends on to gain ground.

"Depending on how things kick off, there might be limited air strikes against command and control, training areas, or nuclear weapon storage facilities. The risk here, again, is escalation."

"India will push back," Singhe put in. Dan wondered how attached she was to what had been, after all, her parents' home.

Noblos put in, "Actually, either side has the capability to escalate. You've left that out."

"We've seen that dynamic in a number of recent conflicts," Staurulakis said.

Mills nodded. "Correct. But the danger isn't escalation, in and of itself."

The civilian scientist said, "It isn't? Yes it is."

"No sir. Beg to differ. What's really dangerous is when the inferior side—in this case, the Pakistanis—run out of counter-escalatory responses. If they lack air power to respond to an Indian deep penetration, the next step up's their ballistic missile forces. There's been some indication this is their plan, if they lose the air war. India has no defense again conventional TBMs. So *their* only step left on the escalatory spiral would be nuclear."

Mills waited, but no one else commented. He nodded, then passed around the final slide. It was headed COMPARATIVE NUCLEAR FORCE POSTURES and showed that both Pakistan and India possessed airdropped bombs and theater-range missiles, though India was working on an ICBM, mainly to deter China's growing arsenal.

"That's about all I have," the operations officer concluded.

"All right, thanks," Dan said. He tried to fake a strength he didn't feel. "Now, if you'll all recall, we got a DIA appreciation after we exited the Gulf that spoke to this issue. They said India was abandoning its defensive orientation along the western border. Exercise Divine Weapon tested its new strategy: to rapidly destroy Pakistan's military, without a lengthy period of mobilization or warning.

"I don't know if anyone here is familiar with the opening moves of World War I, but the Germans had something called the Schlieffen Plan. They depended on speed and shock to occupy territory, and encircle and destroy the French.

"But the plan was brittle. When the German army didn't hit hard enough, the French and British wrecked the whole strategy.

"The Pakistanis have held counterexercises, attempting to block any Indian blitzkreig. But they also drilled own-force protection procedures on a tactical nuclear battlefield." He let that hang, then added, "So we anticipate a race to mobilize, then a series of escalatory–counter-escalatory moves. Karachi's not ruling out a nuclear counterstrike if the ground battle goes against them. It's an unstable situation. And we're going to be within range of both sides."

Staurulakis spread her hands on the glass surface of the tracer. "Captain, what exactly do they expect us to do there? Any insight, from your time in DC?"

He couldn't stifle a sardonic grin. "I don't get much insight into anything in Washington, XO. Our orders are clear as mud. Station ourselves in a position to intercept, then stand by. We have three geometries to worry about. First, that of nuclear deterrence. Second, our own geometry vis-à-vis what we're guessing to be the most likely launch sites."

"And third?" Mills prompted.

"That, I guess, is political . . . what message having us here is supposed to convey. If I had to guess, that might be something like reducing Pakistani confidence that they can carry through a nuclear first strike on Indian command and control.

"Uncertainty's always been a big part of deterrence. And it's in the U.S. interest to keep anyone from using nukes first . . . because as soon as someone does, it becomes that much easier for the next country." He hesitated, thinking about that in the context of Nagasaki and Hiroshima. What if *no one* had ever used such weapons? Would the world be safer, or more dangerous? Then shook his head and went on. "Of course, that assumes we come down on India's side, if the balloon goes up. But let's see if there's a geoposition where we could intercept launches by both sides."

"That'd be a strategic node," Mills ventured.

Dan nodded tiredly, taking his point: that such a location, if it existed, would be easy for both sides to compute. Most likely, *Savo* was already getting built into the target set for both countries. If taking her out meant their missiles would have a better chance, it would only be logical to make her the first target. "Yeah, we'll talk own-ship defense, too. But first, the geometry. Bill? Why don't you kick off. As the resident expert."

Dr. Noblos sat back on his stool, arms crossed, tilting his nose at the overhead. He looked like a large gray heron. "It isn't an attractive situation," he observed.

"Tell me more," Dan said, though he didn't like the guy's attitude. Never had, actually.

Noblos closed his eyes, as if bored with explaining the obvious to dunderheads. "Assume we pick up a launch as it clears our radar horizon. We'll have less than eighteen seconds to lock, track, evaluate, and fire. We might get a few seconds more downcuing from Obsidian Glint. But the handoff procedures aren't synchronized yet, and I don't have much confidence in the contractor.

"The Defense Support Program satellites . . . all you have is text from the joint tactical ground station. You're still not on automatic distribution from the Space and Missile Defense Command Operations Center. AWACS . . . we're on the ragged edge for Rainbow, out of Saudi. They might pick up an ascending booster out of western Pakistan, but India's out of their range."

Dan said, trying to keep his temper, "So, all in all, our probability of a successful intercept?"

"Negligible," Noblos said, not without relish.

Dan turned to Wenck. "Donnie, your take?"

Wenck agreed their response time would be counted in seconds, but seemed less pessimistic than the physicist. "Depends on the launch site. I'm guessing, for both sides, back a good distance, out of range of tacair. So . . . I calculated the baskets."

He keyboarded on a notebook, and like magic, the center LSD at the far end of CIC changed to show two pulsating hoops hanging in space. "I ginned this up with the UYQ-89 TBMD-scenario planning module. Not accurate down to the decimal point, but it illustrates the choices . . . which ain't great. I'm mainly looking at airfields here. Figure they'll hit them first. There's three down south, inside our footprint. This up here, Uttarlai, that's right on the hairy lips of our effective range. You can see here, the target body launch site, our interceptor platform position on a UTC grid, and the oval overlay is where that generates reasonable engagement conditions . . . defined as an intercept-slash-kill probability of intercept above 20 percent."

"That's a pretty damn low P-sub-K," Noblos put in.

Wenck flattened his cowlick in a familiar gesture, staring at the screen. Lost, obviously, in the numbers. "Ain't gonna get much better, Doc. No matter what, it's gonna be a crossing engagement, unless they're shooting right at us. P-sub-K goes down, ordnance expended goes way up."

Despite himself, Dan's gaze went to the Ordnance status board. It would tell him, moment by moment, what and how much he had left in his shot lockers.

But defending Indian military airfields wasn't really his mission. Unless the U.S. and India were allies, a change he didn't think he'd have missed. The Indians hadn't been exactly welcoming to the U.S. Navy since independence, though the chill had lessened since China's rise. He tapped on the glass. "So what you're saying is, we can't count on knocking many warheads down. And, goddamn it, that limited range is really hurting us." Depending on geometry, again, the Block 4A intercept envelope extended out to a little over 120 nautical miles. He rubbed his chin. "Okay, that's Pakistan. How do we look against an Indian launch?"

"Still a crossing shot. Intercept about a hundred and fifty kilometers up." Wenck circled the suspected deployment area, and drew lines from there to various ground and air bases. All five people regarded them silently. "We could knock down anything headed for Karachi," he added, sounding as if he was trying to be helpful.

"What about own-ship defense?"

Mills said, "In BMD mode, of course, we're peeking through a soda straw . . . almost blind. We'll have to depend on *Mitscher* for protection. Mainly because of that, I'd like to stay at least sixty miles offshore. That keeps us out of range of both sides' coast defenses, and gives some warning of any incoming surface or air threats."

"Shit, that really cuts down our coverage." Wenck blinked at the screen. "We can't crowd the goalposts any closer? We're gonna be way, way off base on this one. Especially if they launch against northern India."

"Exactly so," Noblos put in. "That will be a ninety-degree ground path crossing angle, and you'll have to intercept at apogee. As flyout times compress, acquisition and track, initialization and launch, all get more critical . . . probably beyond the skill level of this team, given your manning, documentation, and training deficiencies, and your interfacing problems as documented in my previous reports to you, the ISIC, and COMNAVSURFOR."

Crap, Dan thought. He said, half hopefully, "Did you

actually recommend decertification?" If ALIS and the Block 4 were no longer mission capable, he could report that and withdraw. The capability was still experimental, after all. Probably ending his own career, such as it was, but at least pulling his sailors out of a quickly narrowing crack.

Noblos quirked his eyebrows. "Don't put words in my mouth, Captain. I'm not at all happy, but your technicians are barely—just *barely*"—the rider glared at Wenck, who smiled back—"keeping it in spec. Patched and baling-wired together. So far, at least."

Dan rubbed his face, unutterably weary. What the hell were they doing here? Putting American skin in the game, if the subcontinent erupted into war again? Giving the diplomats a tiny bit of leverage over two opponents that had never actually been very responsive to outside pressure? The two nations were fixated on each other. Like two wrestlers in a cramped ring, they had no attention to spare for spectators.

Noblos sniffed. "Well, if no one else will, I'll sum up."

Dan sighed. "Please do, Doctor."

"We can intercept Pakistani launches slightly more easily than Indian, but they'll all be crossing engagements, and our chances poor. We only have twelve rounds, so at those P-sub-Ks, we *might* take down two warheads. Not enough to have any conceivable impact. So my recommendation is, Mr. Mills is correct. We should stay well out to sea, out of harm's way. If ordered, lob our rounds in there, but don't encourage Washington to expect much in the way of results."

Dan blew out and straightened. His knees shook.

Had to get off his feet, before he fell down. "All right, I think we've got to the bottom line. Thanks for your inputs. I'll take them into consideration in deciding on our patrol footprint. Remember to pass to your division officers and chief that scuttlebutts and showers are secured until further notice. The XO will pass the word on a limited freshwater issue for personal use."

They broke, and each left in a beeline. Dan was left leaning on the DRT. Looking down into the glass, wishing it were a crystal ball. *Savo* was nearly helpless in TBMD mode, especially if she had to continually scan the immense arc from Karachi to the Gulf of Kutch. That meant high duty factor at peak power, a combination guaranteed to generate a high failure rate. If it wasn't for *Mitscher,* he'd have serious doubts about ownship survivability. She'd be the shield to *Savo*'s arrows, but how were those all-too-few arrows expected to be employed? And against whom?

Pakistan?

India?

Whoever struck first?

Or both sides, equally?

He lowered his head. Doubts and questions belonged in a message. And maybe he ought to do just that. Right after he got his head down for a few minutes . . .

Once again he was awakened, in the dark, this time by a tap at the door. It was the chief master-at-arms. "Captain, got a major problem."

"What?" he grunted, rubbing grit from his eyes. Was

he ever going to get an uninterrupted hour of sleep again?

"Sir, one of the storecreatures, I mean storekeepers, reports she was grabbed from behind, blindfolded, taken into a void, and assaulted."

"Oh, Christ." He felt sick, and not just from the after-effects of the crud. As they'd all feared, the steel beach ejaculator had escalated. He sat up and coughed long and hard. Finally choked out, "Who? Is she hurt?"

"Celestina Colón, sir. Seaman storekeeper. She's in sick bay, but doesn't seem to be injured, aside from bruises. At least not that I could see before Chief Corpsman shut the door."

Dan sagged back, panting, coughing. His scarred trachea spasmed, and closed. He gagged, rolling on his side, trying desperately to clear his airway. He reached for the emergency escape breathing device, clipped to the bulkhead. It was charged with oxygen. But pulled his hand back, got the inhaler instead, and triggered a cold burst of vapor down his windpipe. Tried to calm himself. Tried to *breathe* . . .

"You all right, Skipper?"

"Yeah . . . yeah." He coughed some more, finally got a full breath, and rolled out. Planted his bare feet on the deck tile.

Then reached for his coveralls, and got dressed.

15

Tropic of Cancer

An unpleasant sense of déjà vu that wasn't déjà vu at all. Once again he was interviewing a female crew member. But this time, in sick bay instead of the exec's cabin. And this time, she hadn't just been fondled, threatened, and ejaculated on.

The victim was a stony-visaged crewwoman sliding back and forth on the leatherette of Grissett's examining table as *Savo Island,* rolling and surging in the swells thirty knots of wind from the south-southwest were pushing up, creaked and groaned deep in her steel bones. Colón didn't look shocked, or numb. Her coveralls were pulled down to the waist. She wore a white uniform-issue T-shirt sweat-stained under the pits. Chief Toan, the master-at-arms, stood behind her; Cheryl Staurulakis leaned in the corner, arms folded; Dr. Schell, who'd apparently been called in, was snapping off green latex gloves by the sink. He started to reach for the tap, but diverted in midmotion to a plastic gallon jug, to pour the rinse water from.

Dan cleared his throat and sank onto a vacant stool. "Is she all right? I mean, physically?"

"I gave her a sedative," Schell said. "Examined her. Slight bruising. No permanent physical injury."

"Thank God for that. Celestina. I'm so sorry this has happened. But we'll get to the bottom of it."

He took a deep breath. This had to be done right. "One question first. It's a formality, but the regs say I've got to ask it. We have to report all sexual assaults, but there are two kinds of reports we can make. Restricted, and unrestricted. Restricted is when you, the victim, don't want your name used, and don't want command or law enforcement involvement. That protects your name and privacy. The other is unrestricted. That triggers a full NCIS investigation." He paused. "We're going to ask you to sign a paper, specifying your choice."

"She wants an unrestricted report," Staurulakis murmured.

"XO, I need to hear it from her."

"Unrestricted," Colón said.

Dan nodded. "I think that's the right decision. All right then, I file the reports for the full investigation. So, tell me what happened. From the beginning."

He knew Colón by sight, had eaten with her on mess decks visits and greeted her in the passageways. She worked in Supply. Slight, brown-haired, with smooth olive skin and a tiny mole near her upper lip. She reported now in spare sentences of careful school English that seemed somehow separate from whatever emotional process was going on behind dark eyes. She'd been in the aft supply passageway when the lights had suddenly gone out. Someone had grabbed her from behind. She was shoved into one of the spaces—she wasn't sure which—and pushed down onto something soft.

"Then he undressed me," she said. "And used his fingers."

Dan looked at Schell, who shook his head no almost imperceptibly and held up a plastic bag containing a swab and gauze. The rape kit, Dan guessed, though he'd never seen one before. But unless there'd been penetration . . .

"Was there more than one assailant?"

"No sir. Only one."

"Did you see, or feel, a weapon?"

"I felt a point in my back. He said he had a knife, and would use it if I left before the lights came back on."

"So he spoke. What did he sound like?"

"Gruff. Deep. But it sounded false. Like he was not using his regular voice."

"And you say you weren't actually, uh, penetrated? Even slightly?"

"He had his fingers in me, Captain. I heard him grunting. But I didn't feel a dick. Then there was a clanking noise. He told me to stay where I was until five minutes after the lights came on."

Dan looked at the overhead, then to the master-at-arms. "Did you search the compartment yet?"

"Yessir, we conducted a quick search. Whatever this asshole jacked off into, he took it with him."

"I'll expect a complete statement by noon. What else, Chief?"

Toan looked away. "We'll search the compartment again, Captain. See if we can get fingerprints. And yes, we will take a complete statement."

"Not *nearly* enough, Chief. This is the second incident. And even worse than the first. You and Lieutenant Singhe were investigating that. I saw one follow-up report. Then nothing. No mess decks scuttlebutt? Nobody bragging to his buddies?"

"We have our eyes on a suspect." Toan glanced sideways at Colón, who was staring at the door as if hypnotized.

"We'll talk about that offline. Celestina, what about you? Anyone been stalking, annoying you?"

"I did have one guy."

"And who was that?"

"The Iranian. Shah."

"Behnam Shah," Dan said. One of the castaways they'd picked up in the Arabian Sea. A religious refugee, if you believed their story; an escaped murderer, if you believed the Iranian news agency. Actually, Shah was the one who'd been hanging around outside CIC, before Wenck had told him he wasn't going to be admitted. "He works in the galley, right? So he'd know the layout back there. He was stalking you?"

"Not exactly. But he kept trying to talk to me."

"Attempting to get you alone?" Staurulakis asked her.

"No, just to talk."

"Friendly? Or in a threatening way?"

"I didn't want to talk to him. I got a boyfriend back in Caguas. I don't think it was Shah. The man who did this, he did not have an accent."

Which might mean nothing, if the guy knew more English than he was letting on. Dan asked Toan, "Was Shah one of your suspects in the groping, with Petty Officer Terranova?"

"Not particularly. No sir." Toan hesitated, then added, "Let me point out one thing, sir. The fact that her attacker turned off the lights."

"So?"

"He turned off the lights in the helo hangar passageway, too. When the Terror got groped."

"Which . . . I'm a little slow today, Chief. Enlighten me as to what you're saying."

Toan said, "There's no topside access from the interior passageway on the Supply Department level. So the lights are always on, and there's no easily accessible switch. Unless someone knows how to turn them off back at the lighting panel."

Staurulakis stepped forward, arms still crossed. "So you're saying, an electrician? Or someone in charge of the compartments?"

"Could be," Toan said. "Remember, if it's the same guy, he fiddled with the darken ship switch up on the hangar deck level, too."

Dan hesitated, then patted the woman on the shoulder. "One more question, Seaman Colón."

"Yes sir." A soft voice, but with steel under it. "It isn't the first time."

He blinked. Had been about to ask if she'd smelled anything like lime aftershave or cologne, but now said, "What? Not the first . . . he's done this to you before?"

"Not him. But it isn't the first time it's happened to me. Shit like this."

She stared ahead as the ship groaned around them. "I was in a foster home . . . my foster brothers. Both of them. I thought, when I joined the Navy, things would be different. But maybe it's never going to be."

Staurulakis stepped forward and put her arm around the girl's shoulders. Looking up at Dan, she said, "We'll get this guy. And put him away for a long, long time. I promise you that, Celestina."

Climbing to the bridge level, Dan had to stop to catch his breath again. The ladderwell reeled. Weird thuds and moans echoed through the steel. With the monsoon, this wind wasn't going to stop. And given the layout of their patrol areas, they'd be steaming beam to almost all the time. Ticos didn't have fin stabilizers, like smaller ships, and were tender anyway; she'd roll nonstop.

He felt doomed. And guilty; the girl already hadn't had a great life, with foster homes and abusive families. But she'd thought the Navy would be different. Better.

Instead . . . this.

The guidelines were clear. Once the report landed on the CNO's desk, there'd be an NCIS agent en route at flank speed. Flying out from the nearest office, which was Bahrain, to the carrier, and maybe getting him or her on a helo, if the carrier was close enough. Or, if someone had planned a resupply and refuel, via the re-supply ship. They wouldn't let this stagnate. Too much chance of splatter.

And though he didn't like to think this way, he had to cover his own ass and the command's by making sure he followed the instructions on sexual assault—sending messages to God and everyone documenting every detail, everything he'd directed done, everything he'd been told to do. It would take time and command attention, time he desperately needed.

But he owed it to Colón. Her assailant must be the same guy who'd assaulted Terranova.

Or was it? He clung to the smooth steel of the hand-rail, and broke into a cold sweat just thinking about *two* sexual predators on the same ship. A copycat? No, Oc-cam's razor: Do not unnecessarily multiply entities. And the MO, which hadn't been announced, was the same: finagling the lights, then abduction at knifepoint. Their perpetrator had started with fondling, and now progressed to manual penetration while masturbating. The next step, from everything he'd read, would be rape and possibly mutilation, or even murder.

So, how to proceed. One of the castaways had been hitting on her. But he doubted they'd know the ship well enough to screw with the wiring. Also, they hadn't been aboard when Terranova had been . . . no, wait, they had. So that didn't exonerate them. Especially this Behnam Shah.

But Toan had mentioned another suspect. One he

"had his eyes on." Dan hadn't wanted to ask who in front of the others. Maybe they could identify a suspect. Isolate him, until they could offload the bastard. But he had to root this out. Before it widened the already deep chasm between the females, including the female officers, and the rest of the ship.

A damaged crew took much longer to repair than a damaged ship. Was it Jenn Roald who'd told him that? Or Nick Niles?

So he needed to address it. Not just officially, by the reporting requirements, but directly, to the crew. He lifted his head toward the top of the ladder as someone opened the door to the bridge. Cleared his throat, straightened his back, and climbed toward the light.

They cruised through the day and the next and then the next, midway between Karachi and Mumbai. The wind varied between twenty and thirty knots, consistently from the southwest, and the seas continued very heavy. Terranova picked up another strange high-altitude, slow-moving contact, like the one they'd tracked going through Hormuz. Or that had perhaps tracked them . . . On the second day a message relayed that Pakistan had both refused their refueling request and officially protested their presence within the Islamic Republic's exclusive economic zone. The government had referenced its reservation, on signing UNCLOS, that it did not authorize military maneuvers by foreign-flagged warships within the EEZs of coastal states without the consent of said states. The U.S. was asked to remove its task forces and not to intrude again.

In sick bay that morning, Dan was examining a reddish stain on a cotton pad. "I'm not sure what I'm looking at here," he confessed as the ship labored around them.

Schell, dark circles under his eyes, sagged back against the tier of bunks. Grissett sat on the lowest. The command master chief, Tausengelt, had pulled out a desk chair and reversed it. The doctor murmured, "It's a culture. The stain brings it out. From one of your hot-water heating systems."

"And?"

"We'd need an electron microscope to be certain, but I'm 90 percent sure it's somebody new in the zoo. A previously unidentified amoebal pathogen. In other words, a variation of Legionnaires' disease."

Dan held the stain to the light as the physician went on to explain that *Legionella* bacteria had evolved to infect freshwater protozoa. "Such as amoebas. Now, we may not care for the idea, but we're pretty much always surrounded by bacteria. And most of our freshwater systems—at home, in hotels, restaurants, hospitals, and so forth—are colonized by protozoa. They love warm water 24-7, same as we do, so it's an ideal habitat. In ninety-nine out of a hundred cases, they never cause trouble, because we're adapted to them. But in the case of *Legionella pneumophila*—meaning, it likes the lungs—the bacteria can jump to us, infect us, and cause the symptoms you're familiar with."

Dan nodded. He still felt exhausted, even when he got enough sleep, and too many of the crew felt the same way, evidenced by the way they dragged around. "But, a bacterium? Doc here's been dosing everybody with cipro—"

"You've obviously got a ciprofloxacin-resistant bug. Which we're seeing a lot more of, by the way."

"How, exactly, does it infect? What's the route of transmission?"

"Via the hot-water systems."

Dan shook his head. "No, you said it *bred* in the hot-water systems. How does it get from there to the crew? In the drinking water?"

Schell squinched up his face. "No, stomach acid's usually up to the job of dissolving any bacteria. It's still iffy, but I suspect your showers."

Dan frowned. "You mean *in* them, or . . . or by taking showers?"

"The latter. Unfortunately. Aerosolized and misted by the nozzle, water's easy to breathe into the lungs. Which are also wet, warm, and welcoming."

Schell droned on about how the bacterium involved was atypical, which was why Bethesda hadn't detected it in the sputum and blood from the first fatality, back in the Med. Dan interrupted. "I get all that, Doc. But how do we fix this? We thought it was in the vent ducts."

"Right, your corpsman told me that." He nodded to Grissett. "Not a bad guess, working with what you knew."

"You're certain it's our hot water."

"As I said, without an electron microscope to positively identify, no. But based on everything else, 90, 95 percent certainty. The fact that your bronchoalveolar washings came back negative makes me suspect a new strain. I plan to call it *Legionella savoiensis*."

Oh, great. But maybe this wasn't the time or place to argue over Latinate terminology. "All right, let's go with that diagnosis. What do we do about it?"

"The book answer is, have the ship recalled and quarantined. Steam-clean every hot-water pipe and heater and fixture aboard. Especially any dead legs in your system. And wherever your cold- and hot-water systems mix, like heat exchangers. If I report this to Navy Medical, that's what's going to come back. Pull you off the line and send you home."

"We can't do that." But as Dan rubbed his mouth, he remembered previous experiences with NavMed. Both professionally competent and fiercely independent, the Bureau of Navy Medicine was its own fiefdom. Pressure from outside, or even from above, merely hardened its stance. Recall and quarantine was all too possible. "We can't leave now. Not with a war about to start."

"You also can't keep the guys on a gallon of water a day, sir," Grissett put in. "Or keep the showers secured."

"I sailed with the Korean navy," Dan said. "They didn't have showers. They bathed in buckets."

All three men just looked at him. He grimaced, seeing how it was, and went on. "But, uh, obviously we can't do that for more than a couple days. So, tell me what to do. Chemicals? Hyperchlorination? How do we fix this?"

Schell looked away. In a low voice he said, "You can't use chemicals aboard ship. Not in the concentrations needed for eradication. We're not talking just upping the chlorine count here. Trihalomethane, chlorine dioxide—you can't use those in confined spaces."

"There isn't anything else?"

Schell hesitated. "Well . . . there is one thing you could try. It's called 'heat and flush.'"

Dan glanced at Grissett. "I'm listening. Doc?"

"Me too, Captain. But I think I know what he's gonna say."

The physician said, "You have to get your water up almost to boiling. At least a hundred and eighty degrees. Two hundred is better. Hold it there for thirty minutes, and you've got a sterile system. We do that with outbreaks in hospitals."

Dan said, "Okay. The downside?"

"It doesn't work for long-term infestation management. You'd have to follow up with some form of continuous chemical disinfection. The main problem for you is how labor-intensive it's going to be. We're talking isolating every section of the system, cleaning out any incrustation or scale that can harbor colonies, then charging with superheated water and maintaining it at that temperature for half an hour. The thermal expansion—"

"We're gonna burst some pipes," Dan said.

"Which means potential burns and scalding."

Dan nodded, tracing the plumbing systems in his mind. He turned to Tausengelt. "Sid, an interrelated issue. CMC, you can speak to this, maybe. We're really stressing this crew. If we break them, we can lose this ship, with or without eliminating the crud. We're seeing equipment degradation—the reduction gear assembly on number one gas turbine generator, the water intrusion on the CRP prop system. This heat and flush Dr. Schell is describing . . . can we impose this extra level of work? Deployed, at condition three, in heavy seas?"

Tausengelt rubbed his face in what might be unconscious mimicry of his CO. When he took his hand away his leathery features were contorted in what looked like extreme pain.

"You okay, Master Chief?"

"Touch of trigeminal. Comes back now and then. Feels like a skilletful of hot chicken grease on your face. Uh, basically, Captain, it's your call."

"I know that, Master Chief. My question is, what's going to be the effect on the crew?"

Tausengelt said slowly, "Basically, Skipper, I'd say they're scared."

Schell plumped down on the lower bunk beside Grissett, looking interested. He locked his fingers around one knee and rocked back.

Dan nodded. "Okay, that's something solid. Scared of what?"

"Basically, sir, of you."

"Scared of *me*?" He frowned.

"Basically, sir, you gotta understand. Now obviously I wasn't here for the previous regime, Captain Imerson and Fahad Almarshadi and so on, but it was apparently more easygoing then."

"It was slack and slipshod." Dan shook his head. "And the command climate survey showed it."

"Yessir, no argument. But some folks like it easygoing, and they haven't been happy about all the condition three and stepped-up drills. The reinspections, and so forth. There's always that element that wants the eight-hour day, even under way." Tausengelt waved that away, though the grooves around his mouth dug deeper. "But it ain't even just that. Going aground in Naples, then you coming aboard, Goodroe dying—it was like the start of a downward spiral."

"The spiral started long before that."

"Basically, no argument, sir, I'm just passing along what I hear. Then the crud, then all the shit since— it's like, fatigue's setting in. They were in awe of you at first. The Medal of Honor. How you seemed to know everything. Your, um, your command presence. But since then, it's been operate, operate, operate—only one port call, to blow off steam—and everybody getting sick—and now it's like, they don't have a clue what we're doing parked off Pakistan." The old master chief shrugged. "The deckplates know there's a war about to start, and we're supposed to stop it."

"That's not exactly—"

"Well, it's what they *think*. Sir. And those stories . . . the scuttlebutt about *Horn,* and what you did in the China Sea . . . that you hung a guy for murder—"

Schell whistled, leaning forward. "*Hung* a guy? A crewman, you mean? Actually *hung*?"

Dan said, "This is the Navy, Dr. Schell. Sea stories

get embroidered. As you know, Master Chief. Look, let's cut to the chase. Regardless of what the crew feels, we're here on a national-level mission. That means we have to stay on station unless we're totally unable to continue.

"So, Doctor, I'd like you and the chief corpsman here to huddle with Bart Danenhower. See what CHENG thinks about how many man-hours it would take to heat and flush one of our shower systems. When he's ready to discuss it, I'll be on the bridge."

Dan climbed slowly to the bridge, pausing at each deck level for a breather. Like an old man, hunched, trembling, and panting.

Legionnaires' disease. Christ! If Schell was right, they should report this. Take whatever orders NavMed came back with, most likely, return to Dubai for overhaul. The crew would bunk ashore while workers swarmed over the water systems.

But to do that, *Savo Island* would have to abort Odyssey Protector. And not just leave her station untenanted, but the Navy out of the ballpark on the missile defense mission. *Defense News* had just published a piece on the recent speedup in the sea service's TBMD program. Which, as he recalled, Admiral Niles had mentioned too. But the follow-on ships in the pipeline—*Monocacy, Hampton Roads, Omaha Beach, Salerno, Java Sea,* and *Guadalcanal*—weren't ready yet, though the first two were almost operational.

He stood by his command chair, clinging to it as the ship rolled. Heading: one-one-zero, nearly beam to. Van Gogh had the watch. The bridge team stood wordlessly, gripping handholds. The sea was dark blue, furrowed by the endless monsoon wind. *Mitscher* rode between *Savo* and the land, far over the horizon.

He was still up there when Bart Danenhower came up. The CHENG fingered his striped locomotive-driver's cap, staring past Dan at the sea as they went over the fuel-consumption figures. On patrol off the Levant, they'd evolved a nonstandard, unapproved low-speed mode, with one shaft powered and the other idled. They could loiter at six knots and still be quiet, if submarine detection ranges were a consideration. Which they were; if either Pakistan or India decided *Savo* was an impediment, a torpedo might be the most readily deniable solution. Dan made a mental note to jack up Zotcher's sonar team. "Okay. So, how many days' steaming left? Before we have to leave station?"

"Twelve days to 30 percent."

At 30 percent he had to either leave, or get a firm commitment for refuel. So far, no one had responded to Cheryl's plea for support, and he still didn't have a commitment from the USN, either. "Jeez, I don't know. And we still have to run everything from main control?"

"So if you suddenly need to crank on the knots, it'll take five, ten extra minutes."

Not all that long . . . unless you were trying to evade an incoming weapon. He massaged his eye sockets. Danenhower looked tired too; the black mustache drooped; he leaned against the navigation console with eyelids nearly closed. So Dan didn't feel good about asking, "New subject. Did Doc get with you about what they think the crud is? And this hot-water flush they're proposing. I'm really up against it, Bart. He wants to report this to NavMed. They'll order us to leave station. Which we can't, not now. Not with what's going on up north."

The Baylor grad scratched a heavy eyebrow. "Amoebas in the hot-water heaters."

"Is what they propose doable with the equipment we have? And the available manpower?"

"Well, it would've been easier aboard *Peary*."

"That was a Knox-class."

"Right, did my ensign tour aboard her. Twelve-hundred-pound steam plant. In fact, I was discussing with the Doc, it'd be easier and maybe more thorough to do this with saturated steam, not boiling water. Fortunately, we still got some steam aboard."

"From the waste-heat boilers."

"Right. We run the laundry, galley kettles, scullery dishwashers, and the lube and fuel heaters with it. Actually, potable water heaters, too. So we've already got steam lines to some of the places."

Dan asked more questions, and they discussed piping runs, cooling rates, and steam pressure and temperature curves for a few minutes before he sat back. "Okay, sounds like you've got a handle on it. How about man-hours?"

"That's where it gets hard." Danenhower glanced

behind him; the damage control assistant, Jiminiz, and Chief McMottie joined them. "Hector, what'd you come up with for labor loading?"

"It'd mainly be the hull techs, repair lockers, enginemen, with maybe some assistance from the rates that're used to handling hot water, steam . . . like the mess specialists. Disassemble, drain, pressure test, tighten all the joints. Replace any corroded piping or worn valves, as long as we've got it apart."

"That's good, Lieutenant," Dan said. "Thinking ahead."

"Apply steam and run it up to temperature. Dwell. Then release pressure, let it cool, retighten, pressure test again, and turn the water on. We got eleven separate shower sets aboard. Unit commander's cabin, CO in-port cabin, CO at-sea cabin, officer showers, first-class showers, Goat Locker, and five enlisted washrooms: forward Weps, forward Ops, Engineering, after Weps, after Ops."

"Female showers?" Dan asked.

"Their showers are separate, but the piping systems are common. Anyhow, we can't do just the showers. Gotta do each hot-water system all the way from cool-water input to the nozzle heads, or it'll just reinfect. Plus the galleys—Schell says; they're cooking with bottled water and washing up with salt water, and that's gonna give us GI problems sooner or later." The DCA consulted his notes. "For all eleven, and the galley . . . eighteen hundred and eighty man-hours."

Dan shook his head, demolished. No fucking way, out here, could they commit that level of effort. Not with a third of the crew already debilitated to the point they could barely hunch over a console. And they'd need hoses, valves, connectors, gauges, chain hoists . . . not just littering the decks and impeding passageways, but degrading the repair lockers on which they'd depend in case of battle damage. "That's too much. We can't do them all."

"Okay," said McMottie. "How about four? One forward, one aft, the one in Officers' Country, and the one in your at-sea cabin?"

Dan shifted in his chair. "Yeah. Whichever has the least feet of piping. I don't have any problem with water hours, shower hours, male/female even-odd days, whatever. And I don't need the one in my sea cabin; I'll use the one in Officers' Country. Those three, and the galley, make how many man-hours?"

Jimimiz consulted his notes. "Six hundred."

Dan ran it in his head. Working twelve-hour days, fifty days; with ten hands on it, say five days. "That's doable. If the balloon doesn't go up before then. Bart, temperature, pressure?"

The CHENG said, still looking out at the slowly passing sea, "Schell says saturated steam at 250 degrees, sixty pounds pressure, for thirty minutes will kill anything. Good or bad."

"That long? Never mind, we want a thorough job. But we need at least one set of showers back ASAP. Say, Weps berthing. Where we had our first fatality. Then the galleys, the scullery, so we can start using water again there. Can do?"

Danenhower pushed off the nav console. Looking

resigned and, somehow, twice as fatigued. "We'll get on it, Cap'n."

At noon BM1 Nuckols tapped off eight bells, stepped aside, and handed the 1MC mike to Cheryl Staurula-kis. Dan leaned back in his chair as her voice rolled out over the shipwide circuit, in every working space and berthing compartment and passageway. She started with the reminder that they were patrolling off the coast of Pakistan, awaiting developments. Then explained about the disease. *"We've been calling it the crud. Dr. Schell tells us it's a variant of Legionnaires', a bacterial infection, lurking in our water systems, probably infecting us through the showers. To fix it, our snipes and metal-benders are tearing down the hot-water systems and disinfecting them with live steam.*

"I know this will be inconvenient for a while. You can help by standing clear and assisting when appropriate. We hope to have one shower reopened tomorrow, probably in forward weapons berthing. The master-at-arms will promulgate a schedule by departments. Until then, there's a special on Old Spice and deodorant, half off, in the ship's store from thirteen to fifteen hundred."

She said it so drily he did a double take. When she signed off he beckoned her over. "So you *do* have a sense of humor, XO."

She cracked exactly one unit of microsmiles. "For official use only, Captain."

"Okay, what've we got this afternoon? I don't seem

to have much to do up here until they decide war or no war."

"I'm going down to forward berthing. Then talking to Behnam Shah."

"The Iranian. That Colón said might be the one who assaulted her. What kind of interview?"

"Don't worry, sir, ship's legal will be there. He'll get his rights."

"What's your feeling? Anything one way or the other?"

She said she was devoid of any conviction. "All I'm after is whoever dragged that girl into an empty fan room."

He believed her. Hell, he had little choice. He heaved out of the chair, then doubled, hacking. He straightened and wiped his mouth, to catch her glance. Commiserating, or pitying? Who knew. "Okay, let's see how they're doing. But take it slow on the ladders, okay?"

The galley was paved with hoses, tropic with humidity and the smells of steam and food. Chief McMottie handed them half-face filter masks. "In case the stuff aerosolizes as it comes out." Dan set his cap on a steam table and fitted the mask before following him in.

He did a slow, thorough walk-through. Steam blasted out from special bleeder caps in thin whistling streamers that condensed into white plumes. The holes drilled in them were exactly the size to let steam creep along the pipes, maintaining over two hundred degrees, before exhausting at still near-boiling temperatures. "Anything in there, we're gonna cook well done," McMottie promised. Dan attaboy'd the mess specialists standing by to finish scrubbing down; the repair team, in full-face masks, waiting for the system to bake; the chiefs and petty officers supervising.

He even complimented one of the Iranians they'd picked up, who was shoving a swab along the deck, urging the condensate into the drains, and was rewarded with one of the sweetest smiles he'd ever received. He turned away, both warmed and sobered by the reminder of strangers aboard. Strangers who might or might not be what they seemed.

He climbed up a deck and let himself into the Supply Department Office.

Behnam Shah was in blue *Savo* coveralls without insignia, stiffly upright in a folding chair, dark eyes burning, eyebrows a straight line, fingers white-clutching thighs. He bolted to his feet as Dan entered. "Captain. I do not do. You will kill me? Shoot me? I need mercy. I need to explain."

Dan closed his eyes and shook his head. He glanced at Hal Toan, who stood to the side, arms folded. "Relax, Mr. Shah. First, let's clarify something. You're not a USS *Savo* sailor. You're a foreign national, soliciting refugee status. All right? So your standing around here is . . . someplace between refugee and guest. But no one's getting shot. Whatever certain elements among the crew may have told you, they're just spinning you up, okay?"

Shah frowned. "Spinning up?"

"It means . . . never mind. Hermelinda, how's things working out with these guys?"

The supply officer said the three Iranians were good workers. After a couple of incidents, they'd understood certain areas of the ship were off-limits. While she was speaking, the ship's translator let himself in the half-door. "Bozorgmehr," Dan said.

"Captain." The deep bass was impressive as always.

Using Kaghazchi to clarify when necessary, Dan asked about the Iranian's berthing, his work in the mess, if he'd gotten adequate medical care. Did he have any complaints about how he'd been treated? Shah didn't, and seemed abjectly grateful, almost fawning. But behind those hooded eyes Dan also suspected something withheld. Something more remote, more separate, and, perhaps, more hostile. Some of the chiefs thought this guy was a spy. He thought that unlikely— only in the movies did you insert spies by floating them on a log where no ship might ever pass—but then again, maybe he shouldn't rule it out.

More to the point, though, was Colón's specific mention of Shah's interest in her. A stalker might cross the line to something more serious, given the opportunity. And someone who worked in the galley, breaking out stores, might know what spaces would be unlocked and untenanted at zero-dark-thirty.

"Do you own a knife, Mr. Shah?"

"No sir. Knife? Never. I have no knife."

"Do you know Seaman Celestina Colón?"

A visible swallow. "Yes sir. I know her."

"Attractive, right?"

A short exchange. Kaghazchi said, smiling, "He says, she is indeed."

"I could understand a guy being attracted," Dan said. "Hey, we're all guys here."

"Not all of us," said Garfinkle-Henriques from the terminal at her desk.

"Except for the lieutenant, of course." Dan eyed the Iranian again, trying to gauge not the man, but himself. Whether he, Lenson, was holding some sort of grudge. Certainly he'd suffered at the hands of torturers who looked like Shah. Iraqi, not Iranian, but emotions didn't respect boundaries. The previous exec, Fahad Almarshadi, had accused him of prejudice. Before killing himself . . . which Dan still felt responsible for. Why hadn't he seen the signs? Intervened? Instead, he'd leveled blame.

Maybe it was impossible for human beings to avoid stereotyping, or meet each new face with a complete lack of bias. All he could do was try to set in a certain tare weight against it. Try harder than usual to be objective.

At the same time, *someone* had stripped and grossly violated Colón. *Someone* was a clear and present danger to his crew. And so far, Shah was the best suspect.

"Ever been alone with her?" Dan asked.

The guy glanced left and right as if for some avenue of escape. But there was only worn gray paint, dented steel government-issue desks, finger-grimy keyboards, and plastic-housed monitors. "No sir. No."

"Never?"

"Just to . . . to talk. In the passage, the passageway. I tell you, Baha'i, good people. No violence. No rape."

Dan had made it his business to look the Baha'is up. A sort of reformed Islam that, yeah, came across as peaceful and nonviolent. Even faced with the prejudice and discrimination being reported from Iran, including exclusion from jobs and higher education, harassment of their children, and desecration of their cemeteries.

But he had no proof this guy actually was one. Escaping from prison was supposed to be a sin for Baha'is, as it meant breaking the law. And anyway, there were no doubt bad-apple Baha'i's, too. Christianity, Buddhism, Islam, hadn't exactly wiped out evil among their members. "She come on to you, Mr. Shah? Put the moves on you?" He told Kaghazchi, "Give him that as colloquial as you can."

Another short exchange. The translator murmured, "He says no. Just that he thought she was '*khosh-gheli*' . . . very beautiful."

Dan caught Chief Toan's worried glance. They weren't getting anywhere. He could ask the Iranian for fingerprints, a DNA sample, but had nothing to match them against. And he wouldn't be getting the refugees off the ship for days yet, maybe weeks. He couldn't even get refueled out here. "Crap," he muttered.

"Sir?"

"Nothing, Chief."

Dan's Hydra beeped. He snatched it off his belt. "Excuse me. Captain here."

"*Sir, TAO. EW reports momentary emitter bearing one-niner-five, consistent with Snoop Tray.*"

The Snoop Tray, proper name MRK-50 Albatros, was a mast-mounted submarine radar. "That's Russian, right?"

"Russian-built, sir, but carried on their export Kilos, too. Including Indian 877s and Chinese Improved 636s. It was operated in periscope mode for approximately fifteen seconds."

A pop-up, a look around, then submerging again. So, something else to worry about. "Very well. Give the operator an attaboy. Keep a sharp lookout around that bearing, and call me if he pops up again."

He rebelted the radio, and tried to recall where they'd been. "Chief Toan. Did you have anything you wanted to ask Mr. Shah?"

Toan looked at the guy in the chair, then narrowed his eyes significantly at Dan. He switched his gaze back and forth until Dan frowned, then looked where he was squinting. Jeez, maybe he *did* need glasses . . . Yeah. The Iranian was sweating. Moisture glistened at his hairline. Maybe not that damning, from a guy who'd probably been "interviewed" by the Iranian secret police. But not reassuring, either.

Toan said softly, "You don't own a knife, Mr. Shah?"

"As say, no knife."

"So you said. Stand up, please."

The Iranian hesitated, then got up. Toan stepped forward, and with one motion gripped the man's right arm and thrust his other hand deep into the right pocket of his coveralls.

He pulled out a brass-hilted clasp knife. When Toan flicked out the blade, it was a good three inches long.

The stainless gleamed sharp. "Good eye, Chief," Dan murmured, wondering why he hadn't caught its outline under the cloth. Well, Toan had been behind the seated Iranian.

"This isn't a knife?" Toan said.

Shah ducked his head. He looked both agitated and guilty. "Oh, that, yes. I found. I forget I have it. Only a small knife. For pencils."

"Been sharpening a lot of them on the mess decks, have we?" Dan braked his sarcasm, and rose. "I think that's enough. To restrict him, anyway. Chief, what've we got for a makeshift brig?"

"No designated space, Captain. I'll have to figure something out. Meanwhile—" The chief produced a set of handcuffs from behind him, probably hooked into the back of his belt.

Instead of submitting, the Iranian threw his hands off, shoved him away. Shouted, at the top of his voice. Toan staggered back and collided with the bulkhead as the refugee ran for the door.

But his path led right through Dan. His eyes met the Iranian's, and the man hesitated. Just for a fraction of a second. When he regathered himself and came on again, Dan braced both hands on his chest, pushing Shah back into Toan's arms. The chief master-at-arms, who'd bounced back off the bulkhead like a rubber ball, pinioned him from behind. The Iranian's right fist, still free, cocked back. His eyes gleamed feral, terrified.

Then the spark died. His shoulders slumped. Without further resistance, he allowed Toan to pull both hands behind his back. The cuffs click-ratcheted home.

"I am sorry," he muttered. "I was afraid. There is no-where left to run."

Dan said, "We're not going to hurt you, Mr. Shah. There'll be an investigation. Then a trial. A fair one. With legal counsel."

"I understand. That is the American way, yes? And if I guilty?"

"Sentencing is out of our hands. But until then, we'll have to confine you. For your own safety as much as ours. Chief, where do you recommend? The break?"

Ticos didn't have brigs. Few ships did anymore, except for carriers. Detainees, such as captured pirates, were normally restrained with flex cuffs, and either kept outside under an awning or within the forward breakers, with a 24-7 guard. Each breaker had a forward and an aft hatch and only one door to the interior. Lock those, and you had a closed space out of the weather. "Port break, I think," Toan said. "I'll set it up, sir."

"Make sure he has ventilation, water, and somewhere to piss. And once he's locked down, get those cuffs off. Remember, he hasn't been convicted of anything."

"Yet," Garfinkle-Henriques muttered grimly from her desk.

A rap at the door; two more masters-at-arms looked in. To a low instruction from Chief Toan, they escorted the prisoner out.

That night before dinner Dan sat flipping through the traffic in the wardroom. He'd looked in on Shah; the suspect was bedded down in the breaker, with a folding cot. Unfortunately, keeping a guard on him around the clock would cost three more hands, out of a workforce that was getting increasingly stressed the longer they stayed at sea.

The news was sobering. Threats and counterthreats between India and China continued to build. The biggest news, though, was from New York. Wall Street's computerized trading systems had crashed, reopened four hours later to major losses, then crashed again, at which point trading had been suspended. A massive cyberattack was suspected, and analysts feared the panic might spread to the banking system. His own modest savings were bland, low-risk, and most likely safe, but Blair's trust fund, and her stepdad's investments, would've taken a major hit.

But the Indo-Pakistani confrontation over Kashmir seemed to be cooling off. A peace conference had been organized. World leaders would meet in Mumbai, the city formerly known as Bombay, a few hundred miles southeast of where *Savo Island* pursued her lonely patrol.

Even more good news: a German oiler, *Stuttgart,* was on its way to Ballistic Missile OpArea Endive. Another two days, and they'd have full tanks again.

He sat at the coffee table, fighting a tickle in his throat and trying to feel optimistic. Maybe peace *could* be preserved. Pakistan and India had fought before, but there was a new term in the equation now. Nuclear terror had always cooled down any disagreement between the U.S. and the USSR, reminding both sides what existential horror awaited if they didn't compromise.

The tinkle of a hand bell called them to dinner. He ate with his head down, not really following the conversation. Until, when the main course was cleared, everyone shoved his chair back. Longley, looking triumphant, pushed in a cake on a rolling cart, complete with lit candles. The passageway door opened and several chiefs and senior enlisted sidled in.

"What the heck?" Dan muttered. The junior officers snickered. All, apparently, in on the joke. But what *was* the joke? It wasn't his birthday.

"Go ahead, cut it," Staurulakis said. *"Captain."*

A two-tier white cake, with what looked like orange or banana frosting. But as soon as he sliced into it with the silver knife Longley handed him, the crackle of plastic told him what mattered wasn't the cake, but what had been baked inside. Or maybe inserted afterward, in a cavity hollowed between the layers. He got a better grip, angled the knife, and cesareaned it out.

"Well, what do you know," he muttered. It was his uniform hat, encased in a heavy wrapping. "Where'd I leave it this time?"

"Down on the mess decks, Captain," said the cook, standing by the sliding door to the wardroom galley. "When you were inspectin' cleanup. We knew we had to get it back to you. In some *special* way."

They were all waiting, looking uncertain. Even the exec seemed anxious, her gaze begging him to play along. Christ, what did they think? That he was so uptight, so stuffy, he couldn't take a harmless joke? He gave them all a shamefaced grin. "Guess I better tie a lanyard on it, keep from leaving it around. Thanks,

Cookie, this looks real tasty. Now . . . who wants a piece of my hat?"

Their relieved laughter made his eyes sting. He turned away for a second, blotting them surreptitiously with the back of a hand. Then began cutting slices, one after another, onto the plates his officers and chiefs came up to hold out for a share.

16

OpArea Endive

Two days later he was in forward berthing, inaugurating the newly reopened facilities with his own first full shower since Schell had closed down the potable water. Enjoying near-scalding heat on his skin. And, not coincidentally, showing he trusted that the crud had finally been eliminated. But he flinched back when Chief Tausengelt unexpectedly stuck his nearly bald old osprey's head in past the plastic curtains. "Captain? Gonna be out soon?"

Dan covered himself instinctively, then relaxed and flicked foam off the disposable razor. "Uh—almost. Just got to finish shaving and rinse down, Master Chief. What's so blazin' damn hot I can't finish my shower?"

"Urgent, sir. Messenger's standing here."

"Okay, send him in."

"Uh, you might wanna come out instead, sir. Seein' as how he's a she."

Towel knotted around his middle, Dan pinned the makeshift loincloth with one elbow. He'd expected a radio messenger. Instead it was the Terror, chubby-cheeked, holding out a folded note. He frowned, reading. It was from Donnie Wenck, suggesting he come up to CSER 1.

"What's this all about, Petty Officer Terranova?"

"It's on television, Captain."

"We don't have television out here. What're you talking about?"

"Chief Wenck said you'd want to see it. That's all I really know, sir." The towel started to slip, and she averted her eyes as he grabbed for it.

"Well, all right, goddamn it . . . I mean, all right. Just let me get dressed."

The Combat Systems Equipment Room was in the forward deckhouse, portside aft. The work space was narrow and long, racked with spares, a coffee mess at the far end. It smelled of hot rosin and ozone. This high in the ship, in the closed space, the motion was dizzying. He wouldn't care to be locked in here all day long. Three of the ETs and Donnie Wenck got to their feet as he came in. He said, letting a little irritation show, "Okay, Donnie, what's so important you got to summon your CO to see? Instead of just telling me about it? You know, things out here can't be like they were back at Tactical Analysis."

Wenck pushed his hair back—it was really getting long—and jerked his head at the screen. Dan glanced at it, then did a double take. Not crystal clear, but the picture was there. Talking heads, then jerky footage, maybe from a cell phone, of smoke rising from a tall building. Of black-uniformed assault troops with pointed rifles. Dimly, over the hiss of static, the crackle of small arms, came the occasional boom of heavier ordnance.

"Sorry to *bother* you, Captain. Thought you'd wanna see this."

"Okay, okay, forget it. What is it? Where's this broadcast from?"

"We were farting around, see what we could pick up. Couple days ago we latched onto this English-language channel out of Mumbai. Mainly these really lame Bollywood flicks, and dumbass game shows. But then this, about half an hour ago."

Dan stared at the grainy footage as a commentator came on. The dialect was unique, but it was English. As his ear tuned he braced his fists on a work desk. *Savo* rolled hard, the spare boards and tools shifting and rattling. Probably in a turn at the west end of her long racetrack. Ought to alter that now and then; being predictable wasn't a good idea, not with a sub hanging around.

"The invaders succeeded in barricading themselves in the eastern wing, but security forces say their numbers are significantly reduced. However, the litters coming out point to heavy casualties. We have no firm numbers yet, but are told by a member of the police that well over a dozen have been killed. And as you can hear, the fighting is still going on."

Medical personnel were carrying a body out of the

hotel, surrounded by Asians in dark suits. Each held a pistol down alongside his leg. As the camera started forward, one of the men caught the movement, and pointed a gun. The screen abruptly went dark.

Dan frowned. "This is Mumbai, you said?"

Wenck said, about as somberly as Dan had heard him ever say anything, that it was the peace conference. "Somebody drove a truck in. Blew through the gate, then satcheled the walls from the inside. There were more guys outside waiting to blast their way in."

"The peace conference." Dan stared at the screen, which had cut to what looked like a service entrance, to judge by the trash containers. Men in hotel livery were carrying out litters, laying them in a row. Those with faces covered were being carried off to the side, out of view of the camera, which jerked and went black before the program cut back to the commentator. "Okay, you were right to call me. Keep notes on what's going on, okay? As things develop. Run updates to me on the bridge."

He stopped in CIC on the way and checked the air, surface, and ASW pictures. Then took the command seat, next to Dave Branscombe. The CIC copies of the Navy Enemy Threat Guide and *Savo*'s fighting instructions lay open in their red plastic binders. The comm officer was the most junior of his qualified TAOs. A little slow, but he generally reached sound decisions. A lot of the job was memorization, and being able to follow the logic chains in the pubs under tense conditions. On the large-screen display, the Aegis beam metronomed, outlining the flat land to the east, the north, highlighting the mountains rising behind it in neon orange. The air picture, digitally relayed from *Mitscher,* looked normal at first. But over the next hour, flights between cities in India began to divert, turning back the way they'd come or sharply veering south.

Something else scratched at his memory. Then crept out into the light. "Dave, whatever happened to that Snoop Tray emitter? I never heard a redetection on that."

"We never redetected, sir. Got every sensor we own up and looking, and *Mitscher*'s got her tail out too."

This wasn't reassuring. The sub might be gone, of course. Detected for just a moment while headed east, west, or outbound. But he couldn't assume it had gone away just because it was no longer emitting. Its exposure, on that first detection, had been only fifteen seconds. The hallmark of a savvy submariner, revealing himself only for an instant before going deep again. And it hadn't shown up since, not even on the GCCS, which usually carried at least a general localization and identification of every foreign submarine worldwide, derived from NATO and allied sensor chains and traffic analysis.

He rubbed his face. It wasn't good having a sub lurking around, without knowing at least whose it was.

Someone cleared his throat, and he looked up at one of the cryptographers. "Special intel, sir," he said. Dan accepted the clipboard. That hadn't taken long.

It was flash, SPINTEL to the cryppie spaces, too hot

for the general messaging system. From the Joint Chiefs. Its spare sentences detailed a terrorist suicide attack in Mumbai. The attackers had breached a security wall around the Renaissance Convention Centre, where the peace conference was being held. Wielding automatic weapons, RPGs, and satchel charges, they'd penetrated the Powai Ballroom and killed nearly twenty diplomats, security personnel, and hotel staff.

Bad enough; but the next paragraph was worse. Not only had several Chinese been among the diplomats killed, but General Zhang had been wounded. Dan hadn't even known the senior military leader had been at the conference.

3. (S/NF) NO ORGANIZED GROUP HAS YET ACCEPTED RESPONSIBILITY, THOUGH AL-QAEDA GROUPS BASED IN PAKISTAN MAY HAVE BEEN INVOLVED. CHINA AUTHORITIES HAVE DENOUNCED INDIA FOR FAILURE TO PROVIDE SECURITY, VIEWING ATTACK AS INDIAN PROVOCATION.

4. (S/NF) NATIONAL TECHNICAL MEANS INDICATE GOVERNMENT OF INDIA IS CONSIDERING MILITARY ACTION INVOLVING THOSE UNITS ALREADY MOBILIZED FOR EXERCISE QUOTE DIVINE WEAPON UNQUOTE ALONG WESTERN BORDER. GOVERNMENT OF PAKISTAN HAS WARNED ANY ATTACK WILL BE MET WITH QUOTE MAXIMUM FORCE UNQUOTE.

5. (S/NF) NSC HAS ORDERED US FORCES IN IO AREA TO COMBAT READINESS BUT DIRECTED TO WITHDRAW TO STANDOFF DISTANCES TO AVOID BEING DRAWN INTO INCIPIENT CONFLICT. EXCEPTIONS: USN USS SAVO ISLAND TASK GROUP AND SUBPAC IN-SHORE RECONNAISSANCE ASSETS, AND USAF RAINBOW, WHICH ARE SPECIFICALLY TASKED WITH MAINTAINING TABS ON IN-DIAN AND PAKISTANI GROUND MOVEMENTS AND THEATER STRIKE ASSETS. SPECIFIC ORDERS FOLLOW.

6. (S/NF) NRO AND NATIONAL TECHNICAL MEANS DEDICATED TO CENTCOM/PACFLT/ IO AOR. INTEL SUPPORT IS BEING RAMPED UP FOR THIS REGION AND MORE ASSETS ARE BEING REFOCUSED ON BELLIGERENTS AND OTHER STATES THAT MIGHT TAKE ACTION ON CURRENT EVENTS. FOR SAVO TG AND OTHER FORWARD ISR ASSETS: ANY INDICATIONS OR WARNINGS OF ANY MOVE-MENT OR ACTION BY ANY INDIAN OR PAKISTANI MILITARY ASSETS, ESPECIALLY THOSE INVOLVING POTENTIAL LAUNCH SITES OR MISSILE DEFENSE SITES, WILL BE FORWARDED IMMEDIATELY UPON DETEC-TION DIRECTLY TO WH SITROOM FLASH VIA STEL/SPINTCOM, IN ADDITION TO CURRENT THEATER NOTIFICATION PROTOCOLS. ADDI-

TIONAL INFORMATION TO BE DISSEMI-
NATED AS BECOMES AVAILABLE. SPECIFIC
AMENDMENTS OR CHANGES TO CURRENT
OPORDERS PASSED SEPCOR.

SECRET NOFORN
//BT
DECLAS OADR

He initialed the route sheet with the pen the
radioman held out. Telling Branscombe quietly to set
condition three, he went up to the bridge for a short
conversation with "Stony" Stonecipher over the covered
tactical net. He told *Mitscher*'s commander to open the
distance between the ships, put his helo in the air, and
increase his readiness against submarine, air, and cruise
missile threats.

When he went back down to Combat, Cheryl was
reading the same message at the command desk. Speculation and turnover briefings buzzed as the rest of the
consoles manned up. The exec glanced up when he
took his seat, then went back to reading, following each
line with a clear-enameled fingernail.

Dan shivered, suddenly, deeply. He examined the
large-screen display with a sinking feeling. Remembering the process Tuchman had outlined: domino
toppling domino, preliminary mobilization, full mobilization, then declaration of war. Country after country dragged in. Sleepwalking, one after the other, into
war. Please, God, not again . . . but it hadn't happened

since 1945 . . . maybe people had learned to step back from the brink. "Okay, Cheryl, what else should we be doing?"

"As I read this, we're primarily an intel asset right now. Tasked to keep tabs and report back."

"I read it that way too, but why station a TBMD-capable ship here for that?"

"Our Aegis picture, primarily, I guess. And our nice beefy cryppie assets." She blinked, looking worried. "I don't see this as anything . . . *personal*, Captain. They're just tasking us based on our gear."

Dan said, getting irritated, "I didn't say it was 'personal.' Where'd you get that? I'm just saying, *Mitscher* could hold down the air picture. Why keep us here? And where are these additional orders they mention in para five?"

"I checked the LAN in case something got by 'em in Radio. Nothing there yet either."

"TAO, air: fast movers, Indian, lifting off from Sirsa. Looks like Mirages and MiG-29s. Eight radars so far."

Dan spun around to the air picture as symbols materialized. The TAO said, "Captain, from the CTs: lot of chatter in Hindi. Something big's going up."

Dan grabbed the radio handset. "Going out Fifth Fleet Secure. ComFifth Fleet, this is *Savo* Actual. Flash, flash, flash. *Savo* holds multiple fast movers, possibly Mirages and/or MiGs departing Sirsa. Evaluate as outbound raid. Composition eight. Also a spike in HF voice traffic. Over."

The secure satcomm speaker squealed as the scrambler circuits synchronized. "*Savo, this is Fifth Fleet*

Ops-O. Admiral is en route to the watch floor. Do you have any further information?"

Dan started to key the handset to reply, but the electronic warfare watchstander shouted, "TAO, EW: Multiple airborne radars equating to Mirage F-1 and MiG-29 Strikers powering up over Halwara. Looks like six radars at this time." Before he could key to pass that, another alert came in. Multiple fast movers were taking off from Bhatinda, too.

"Savo, this is Fleet. Did you copy my last? Over."

Dan shook himself out of information overload, and keyed. *"Savo Actual. Update follows. Designate flight from Sirsa, Raid 1. Raid 2 is outbound from Halwara, composition six. ELINT holds airborne Mirage F-1 and MiG radars. Raid 3 outbound from Bhatinda. No further information at this time. Over."* He glanced at Branscombe. "Get me a distance to the closest raid. I doubt they're headed for us, but set condition one if they are."

More squealing. Someone was calling them, but the circuit didn't sync. Dan let it warble away as over the next few minutes heavy strike packages lifted off from two other Indian air bases as well.

Terranova, at the Aegis console, kept the readouts small, so Dan could keep his eye on the big picture as more and more aircraft rose and headed west. Data points winked into existence on the west side of the border as well. The track supervisor reported multiple aircraft taking off from Pakistani airbases. *"Shit, looks like the whole damn PAKAF is going airborne,"* she said over the net.

"TAO, EW: Multiple airborne search radars going active all over eastern Pakistan."

CIC simmered at a low buzz. Dan leaned back, unable to come up with anything concrete he should be doing. *Savo*'s Standards had just enough range to reach the southernmost elements of the warring air forces, but he had no orders to take sides. Pakistan was still officially a U.S. ally, though drifting toward China. India and the U.S. had been edging closer, in the same incremental, continental-drift motion, but weren't formally allied.

Staurulakis closed her terminal and stood. "On the bridge?"

"For now." Dan didn't want to stay down here, but this was where he ought to be.

He and Branscombe discussed splitting the watch, having *Savo* keep an eye on the Pakistani coast while *Mitscher* focused on India. They had to watch out for naval sorties, and any increased activity in coastal defense and naval airfields. If anything hostile to the task group were to develop, they'd see the first signs there.

Unless, of course, they'd been assigned to a sub. Either Indian or Pakistani . . . or worst of all possible cases, designated as a target to *both* submarine forces. Which might have something to do with the threat emitter. He wished he had *Pittsburgh* back. But Youngblood was far to the west, off Karachi, eavesdropping, with the tip of his sensor mast just barely exposed—the inshore surveillance the JCS message had mentioned. The carrier, of course, was far offshore, where any threat could be detected from hundreds of miles away.

While he was stuck here, sixty miles from a quickly escalating hot war. "Dave, how about you coordinate with the TAO on *Mitscher.* See how much overlap we can develop, and give me a recommendation."

"Will do, sir." Branscombe looked on edge. Dan hoped he could depend on him. Next in line was Amy Singhe, but she wasn't yet totally qualified. And even if she had been, on paper, he didn't feel absolutely comfortable giving her weapons-release authority in writing, which was what the CO had to do. Every time something happened, Amarpeet made herself the center of the fray. Good, she was aggressive . . . but that alone didn't make a skipper confident about trusting his ship to her. She was smart . . . but that wasn't all it took either. Bart Danenhower hadn't been the sharpest knife in the drawer on *Horn,* and wasn't the sharpest aboard *Savo,* but Dan trusted him. What the chief engineer said, got done. No drama. Just a smooth-running department . . . except of course for the fucking engine-controls back panel grounding issue.

"Captain?" Chief Toan, blinking at the large-screen displays. "If this is a bad time . . ."

"Hey, Sheriff. Yeah, things're a little tense just now. Is it important?"

"Well, about the investigation."

Dan looked at Branscombe; the TAO was on the line to his opposite number two miles away. "I guess, for a minute . . . what you got?"

"Well, I told you we had another suspect."

"I remember. Got a pretty good idea, but want to tell me who?"

"The petty officer you brought aboard. The retired sonarman, I mean. How much you know about him?"

Dan sucked a breath. Not what he'd expected. "*Carpenter?* Uh, he worked for me at our last duty station. Are you saying you suspect *Rit*?"

"He's been showing some pictures around that make us wonder about him."

"What kind of pictures? Of what?"

Toan said, unwillingly, "Of young girls."

Dan blinked, but believed it. All too readily. "Hardcore?"

"Well, no . . . topless . . . beaver shots . . . that kind of thing. Apparently he's got a Polaroid collection. Some of 'em from a while ago, looks like."

"And he's showed it to somebody down there in Sonar." Dan blew out. "Rit's no angel, Chief. He's gotten in trouble before, ashore. But I've never seen him be violent, or resort to force. Paying a couple hundred for a weekend shack-up, that's more Rit's style. Old Polaroids . . . you really see him as a suspect?"

The Vietnamese-American's face was carefully neutral. "He owns a knife."

"I gotta say, Chief, most of the sailors in the Navy own a knife. And all the boatswains have to carry one on the job. That make them suspects too?"

"We're confining Shah because he had a knife."

Dan shook his head, noting that fifteen of the Indian strike aircraft were closing on Masroor, a Pakistani strip near the coast. His order-of-battle information showed a suspected strike element of nuclear-capable Chinese-built A-5s based there. The callouts suggested that Masroor had a CAP aloft, identified as F-16s. As Aegis updated, they began clicking east as if to intercept. "Not exactly, Sheriff. I'm confining him because he was sniffing around Colón, by her own testimony, and because he *lied* to us about the knife. Lied sitting right in front of us, with it in his goddamn pocket."

Toan lowered his voice still more, until it was all but lost in the background rush of the air-conditioning, the mumble of voices. "So . . . are you directing that Carpenter not be considered a suspect?"

Dan sucked a breath. "Chief, I gotta cut this short and get back on satcomm. If you say he's a suspect, he's a suspect. Don't rule him out based on my say-so. But you've got to bring me more than some old snapshots. Has anyone checked out Peeples? The guy who was flipping off his female petty officer, before she died?"

"We've checked Peeples out. There doesn't seem any reason to—"

"Captain, sorry to interrupt," Branscombe put in. "You might want to look at CentCom chat."

Dan excused himself, and Toan left. He logged in on the command desk terminal and scrolled up and down, gleaning, pausing to speed-read an appreciation by an Army colonel on the CentCom staff.

The ground invasion had started. Exercise Divine Weapon had left Indian armored forces already in forward positions. The orders to advance had come shortly after the first casualties were carried out of the Renaissance Mumbai.

To the colonel, it looked like the deep offensive Indian planners had practiced over and over: a blitzkrieg-type combined-arms assault that counted on surprise, air strikes, and massive conventional firepower to overwhelm the Pakistani army. Two gigantic armored spearheads were racing west, spring-loaded from their exercise positions. He thought the Indians would most likely try to reach the Indus River, at which point they would hook left and right to encircle and destroy the surrounded Pakistanis. The seized territory would be used to bargain for action against the militant groups that had attacked Mumbai. Meanwhile, air strikes would attempt to decapitate Pakistani command, control, and communications, in a replay of U.S. "shock and awe" on Baghdad.

The Indians envision it as a limited incursion for limited goals, the colonel concluded. *But Islamabad may not see it that way.*

Dan rubbed his face, and surfed. A SEAL team had recovered a Special Forces soldier held hostage in Afghanistan, but aside from that, the news from home was all bad. Wall Street trading was still closed. The crash had expanded to the banks. The president had closed them, a step not taken since 1933, and called an emergency meeting of the Federal Reserve.

Another cyberattack had corrupted the four central servers that processed transactions for the self-service automatic pumps at gas stations, halting truck and delivery service across the country. And a major fire had shut down a smokeless propellant plant in St. Marks, Florida, one of only two in the country and the one that supplied over 90 percent of the Army's needs. St. Marks made not just powder for small-arms ammunition, but propellants for mortars, artillery, naval guns, and gas generators—like the ones in automobile air bags or, as it happened, in *Savo*'s missiles.

He sat motionless in the whirring, humming chill air as the hinges of the doors of Mars creaked and began to swing open. It wasn't clear yet, with whom. But the United States, no less than India and Pakistan, was at war. It would be waged in the shadows, before flaring into open conflict.

His mess attendant, at his elbow. "Cap'n. Gonna want evening meal up here?"

Dan tried to work the tension out of his shoulders. Remembering how Singhe had massaged them. Wishing those soft yet strong hands could dig into his muscles once more. "Yeah, I guess. From now on until further notice, Longley."

Over the next twelve hours, he slumped in the chair, or alternately paced the aisles as *Savo* pitched and rolled. The Indian spearheads advanced and the Pakistani defenses began to dent in, visible on the large-screen displays as a froth of low-level air contacts over the forward edge of the battle area. The high-side chat posted near-real-time inputs from DIA and play-by-play commentary by the Army. The Indians had also embedded TV crews in their forward elements, and now and then Donnie called to say he'd Tivo'd a clip from the front lines, rebroadcast over commercial TV.

General Zhang had left Mumbai, flown out in a PLAF transport with escorts from both the Indian air force and the Chinese. Still alive, the bastard . . . the spy who'd orchestrated, years before, the systematic theft of U.S. military secrets, and ordered the murder of an innocent young woman.

Scattered cyberattacks and sabotage were crippling aircraft production facilities at General Dynamics and the two submarine shipyards left in production, Electric Boat and Newport News. Too late now to regret the paring away of the defense industrial base. If open war came, would he even be able to get ammunition?

0510, and a message from Fifth Fleet. The replenishment ship *Stuttgart*, en route to OpArea Endive, had been instructed by her national authorities to turn back toward the Arabian Sea. "Shit," he muttered.

"Problem?" Mills said, beside him now in the TAO chair.

Dan blinked; when had Matt taken over from Dave? He was getting fuzzy. Weak, forgetful—the aftereffects of the crud. He tried to squeeze his tired brain back into something resembling alertness. "Uh, it's *Stuttgart*. Our oiler's been called off."

"Fuck." Mills rattled his keyboard, stared at the message. *"Fuck."*

"Let CHENG know. See if there's anything he can do to cut consumption even more. And query *Mitscher*, see what their fuel percentages are. They've got to be just as hard up."

He got up and paced again, hands locked in the small of his back. Stopped behind Terranova, who was worshiping at the Aegis console. Dr. Noblos snored a few feet away, the Johns Hopkins rider sleeping in a chair. *Savo* rolled, and Dan staggered before catching himself on a console.

Without *Stuttgart,* his situation was critical. *Savo* had an intel mission? Fine; the cryppies and the EWs were sending steady reports. But so far, neither the Pakistanis nor the Indians seemed to be taking the war to sea.

So where were his orders, and what was he still doing in a war zone so dangerous that the Germans refused to send a ship into it?

A hell of a lot of questions. But damn few answers. Or maybe one: with everything going down back in the States, they'd forgotten he was out here.

In which case, he'd better start thinking about when to pull up stakes and head for calmer waters. In both the literal and the figurative senses.

Pushing through the curtain into Sonar, he stood behind Carpenter and Zotcher as they scanned the amber pulsing patterns. *Mitscher,* streaming her low-frequency tail, would probably get the first indication of anyone bird-dogging them, a Pakistani Agosta or Daphne, or an Indian Kilo-class or Type 1500. But if one succeeded in getting in close, his own team, pinging active, could determine whether they lived or died.

He looked down at Carpenter's skull, the pale scalp visible between gray thinning hairs. He couldn't envision the old sailor dragging the wiry, athletic Colón into a fan room.

He closed his eyes and stood swaying to the roll. Remembering what Szerenci had said, and how the nations of Europe had been sucked, one after the other, into the maelstrom. Then took a deep breath, propelled himself back out into CIC, and seized Noblos's shoulder. "Bill. Bill?"

The physicist jerked awake. "Christ! I was napping."

"Sorry. A question. You said we'd up our P-sub-K the closer inshore we got."

"Correct. Essentially." Noblos rubbed his eyes.

"It's a straight-line relationship? Or geometrical?"

"Uh . . . neither, but your first miles closer are going to up your probability of kill more than your last." He coughed, and Dan remembered he too had had the crud. Earlier than the rest, though. "But that wasn't my recommendation. The actual recommendation—"

"Was to leave station. I remember."

"And we *should,* Captain. We really should. This isn't our war. And your chances, if you attempt to intervene, are not good."

Dan started to reply, something about not always being so negative, but bit it back. He needed Noblos. Didn't have to like him, but needed him. "Well, goddamn it, I'm going to close the range. Just in case."

"You're accepting additional risk."

"I understand that," Dan said. Keeping the lid on his temper. He strolled back to the command desk. "Matt! Tell the OOD, come to zero-four-zero. Let's get in a little closer."

"Um . . . yessir . . . how much closer?"

"Not you too, Matt. Just get us in there. Thirty miles?"

The tall lieutenant's voice was reluctant. But he said, "Thirty miles from shore. Aye aye, sir. I'll pass that to the bridge."

0530. The ship leaned and creaked, differently now, with the seas nearly dead astern. In the aft camera, up on the leftmost screen, waves towered black in the foreglow of dawn. He stood watching for minutes, mind blank, leaning over the shoulder of the surface warfare coordinator at his console back near Sonar.

At last, reluctantly, he disengaged his attention from the endless parade of swells. Went back to his command chair, but hesitated before sitting again. His butt ached like a dying tooth. His brain felt as if it had been removed, frozen for ten thousand years, then reinstalled. Half an hour until the mess line opened. He muttered, "Matt, I'm fading. You got it. I'm gonna lie down for twenty, in my sea cabin. Then—"

A digitally generated double chime bonged from the Aegis area. "Launch cuing," Terranova announced, almost primly.

Dan wheeled. "From where?"

"Link 16, from Rainbow." The Saudi-based AWACS.

"We need LPE, impact point, area of uncertainty," Dan rapped out. "Get the geo plot up."

The middle panel blanked, then relit. Eastern Pakistan. Western India. Launch point, impact-point prediction, area of uncertainty. The last two he could ignore for a few more minutes. They were only guesses, until first-stage burnout and weapon pitchover. ALIS didn't have a detect yet. Just the heads-up from the Air Force bird, orbiting hundreds of miles to the west.

Suddenly he didn't feel sleepy. But everything inside his head still seemed to be running more slowly, like a computer with too many programs open. He breathed deep, pinched his cheek. Didn't seem to help.

The alert-script buzzer went off. "Profile plot, designate Meteor Alfa," Terranova murmured. "Meteor" was shorthand for a ballistic missile in the air. "Rapid climb rate, but not as fast as a solid-fueled rocket. Size and acceleration profile consistent with Ghauri type. Passing angels fifty. Identify as TBM. ID as hostile. Stand by . . . ALIS has track . . . computing trajectory and IPP."

Beside him Mills murmured, "Ghauri's a liquid-fueled single-stage. Derived from a North Korean design. Transporter-erector launched. Nuke capable, but no one knows if it actually has a nuclear warhead. Spins early in the transonic regime, to increase accuracy."

"Very well." Dan turned the seat and sank into it, riveted to the screen. They wouldn't get an intercept angle until they had a firm impact prediction. But he was constrained, not just by geometry, but by range. If the target was north of Jodhpur, or the Indian air force base at Phalodi, no chance of an intercept. If it was south of there, he just might have a good enough probability of kill to take a shot.

If he *decided* to. But the decision wasn't just technical. After all, the U.S. hadn't taken sides. But he had no more than six or, at the outside, eight minutes to decide.

He glanced at the red Launch Enable switch near his right hand. Not really a "fire" switch, in the classic gunnery sense. The magazines were authorized and enabled via the command console. The Fire Inhibit/Enable key just allowed the command to go to the magazine. The Canister Safe Enable switch, on the bottom of the canisters, was another safety interlock. The gunner's mates held those keys, so no rogue CO or TAO could launch on his own.

But once all the keys were turned by human beings, ALIS herself ran through a built-in system test, calculated the chances of a successful intercept, matched parameters, and sent the fire signal.

He had to keep his inventory in mind too. Better than the last time *Savo* had engaged, but still limited. Twelve Standard Block 4A theater missile defense missiles. Once those cells were empty, *Savo* was no longer a national-level asset.

And they'd had only a 50 percent kill record last time.

The display jerked, then jumped forward, as if the camera was falling straight down from space. It was nauseating, and he blinked, keeping his fingers clear of the switch.

A white dot welled up, like a whale rising from deep beneath the sea. It pulsed on the center screen. The "gate," the vibrating bright green hook of the radar's acquisition function, zoomed in, corrected, and centered.

"ALIS locked on," Terranova announced. "This is a big mother."

"Very well. Manually engage when track is established."

The bracket convulsed, as if blown by a stiff gust, and strayed off the dot. The petty officer cursed. Caught it, guided it back. It circled, then locked on. The white dot grew rapidly. Not a visual picture, though it resembled one, but the digital representation of the radar data the SPY-1 was feeding back ten times a second.

Beside him Mills had begun the prefiring litany. Alerting VLS, the bridge, *Mitscher,* and Higher to what was happening. "Bring up GCCS on the other screen," Dan murmured.

But the screen was blank. Someone behind them said, "GCCS, no data."

"What? . . . Try again. There's got to be data." The center screen was still raw video from ALIS. But the left showed only a blinking caret. "Where's the goddamned big picture?" he muttered.

The voice called, "Geeks is down. No response to repeated queries."

"Oh, this isn't good," Mills murmured. Dan blew out. Without the Global Command and Control System, he was limited to what *Savo*'s and *Mitscher*'s organic sensors—Aegis, EW, sonar—could see, and, of course, what he could eavesdrop on in high-side chat and Indian television.

Tunnel vision. The classic danger for every commander in combat.

"Meteor Alfa, gathering horizontal velocity,"

Donnie Wenck called, and Noblos's voice added, "Pitchover."

Dan flinched, winching himself back to the large-screen displays. "Okay, get that info out. Now! Flash voice, ComFifthFleet and CentCom." Alfa's elevation callout, in angels, passed six hundred and was still climbing. But the white dot, gripped by the brackets, which up to now had been stationary relative to the geo plot, began to drift. Eastward, toward India. Burnout and pitchover, into the long ballistic trajectory that would end at its target.

At some point he'd missed, Wenck or Terranova had put the predicted point of impact up on the rightmost screen. The area of uncertainty overlay shrank, expanded, elongated, and shrank again, shivering like Jell-O as ALIS continually recalculated. But in general, it was a vaguely oval-shaped darkness in western India, hundreds of miles inland from where *Savo* steamed.

He leaned forward in his seat, squinting. Fifty miles in length, forty in width, it seemed to be centered west of one of the Indian airfields the air strikes had risen from . . . supporting the ground attack that was crashing through the shattered Pakistani defenses. "How confident are we on that IPP, Terror?"

"Sir, hard to say. Should be narrowing down pretty quick, though, once it's free of the atmosphere. Like I said, a humongous big return. Solid track."

Dan sat back, casting his consciousness outside the box ALIS kept trying to cram it into. Should he have Red Hawk aloft? A glance at the gyro told him they were still headed for the coast. No, *Mitscher*'s bird would provide a sensor package between them and the coast. Both the Pakistani and Indian naval air forces would be on strip alert, if not already aloft in the land strike role. Diverting to hit *Savo* and *Mitscher* would offer their opponent an opening. He couldn't let his guard down to seaward. A sub coming in from patrol, and finding a U.S. task group between it and a widening war, might not even need specific orders to attack. He clicked the IC selector to ASW and monitored. Should he prod them? He decided not to.

He looked back up at the center screen, and straightened in his chair.

The AOU was still vibrating, still shrinking with each succeeding recomputation. But with each quiver, the impact point crept west, leaving the airfield behind. "What the *hell* are they aiming at?" he murmured.

Mills cleared his throat. "Right now, looks like . . . Jodhpur."

"The city? The population center?"

"I'm showing the city center west of the strip."

Dan smoothed back his hair, glancing at the clock. His scalp was wet, which wasn't surprising. Two minutes since detection. They were locked on, but it was still too soon to fire. Standards had limited range. With a crossing engagement, far inland, their window would be very narrow. If he fired too soon, the Block 4 would run out of kinetic and maneuvering energy, fall back into the atmosphere, and self-destruct. But if he fired too late, the incoming warhead would reach its target ahead of its pursuer.

If he couldn't be sure of an interception, it was probably better not to fire at all.

But the moment he thought this, a countervailing doubt spoke up. If the Pakistanis had actually aimed the opening salvo of a nuclear war at a population center, wouldn't it be better to attempt an intercept, even if it would most likely fail?

The Lenson Doctrine, they'd called it in Washington: If the U.S. possessed the capability to prevent a nuclear strike, it was morally bound to do so.

But if it failed, who would be blamed? If he intervened, it had to be successful. Attempting an intercept, and failing, would degrade the credibility of the system as a deterrent.

And *was* it countervalue? Or *were* they aiming at the airfield . . . a valid military target, after all, even if it was only a couple of miles from a heavily populated urban center?

He wandered in a different labyrinth now. Not of dark sunken passageways, seething with the dust of ages, but of branching decision trails obscured in risk and uncertainty. He squinted at the screen. The impact prediction had halted, midway between airfield and city. It vibrated, but didn't move either way.

"TAO, what's your take?"

"If we're gonna shoot, sir, I recommend a two-round salvo."

"Concur with that. Tactically."

"Then we have weapons release?"

"I didn't say that." He half turned and caught

Wenck's gaze over the Aegis console. "Donnie? No sign of another launch?"

"No alerts, no detections."

He covered his face with his hands and scrubbed. What was the Pakistani intent? One single missile, targeted on either an airfield or a city. Was it nuclear-tipped? They'd threatened just that. Was this the follow-through? Some sort of warning? Or merely display?

Mills said tentatively, "The question is, should we get involved at all."

Dan thought of calling Stonecipher. Then, Jenn Roald. But there wasn't time. And this wasn't their responsibility, but his. "That's the question, all right. But we're here. Why? Just to stand by and watch? We have to assume worst-case. That this is a nuclear weapon."

On the screen, the altitude callout pulsed nearly unchanged from second to second. The projectile was midphase, at the peak of its great parabolic arc. Weightless. Cold; despite its terrific speed, there was no atmosphere up there to heat it through friction. But ALIS seemed to have an iron grip on the heightened radar return from its beam-on aspect.

In another minute, that would change, as the warhead headed back down. Its speed would increase even more, accelerated by remorseless gravity. Temperature would climb. It would radiate in the infrared. Then, as its ablative sheathing charred away, the warhead would grow an electrically charged ionization trail, much bigger than the weapon at its heart. The challenge then would be to pick it out from debris, detached stages, or decoys, accompanying it along the downward path through reentry.

He had to decide by then.

"Captain . . . hadn't we better let somebody know about this?"

Dan blew out. In blackshoe-speak, it was always a bad idea to be the senior guy with a secret. He unsocketed the red phone and selected satellite high comm, the voice circuit that would connect *Savo* to the highest levels of command. Took a deep breath, and keyed.

"Sit Room, CentCom, Fifth Fleet. This is *Savo Island* Actual. Flash, flash, flash. *Savo* has received launch cuing from Rainbow. Aegis holds Pakistani missile launch. Missile profile, consistent with Ghauri-type. Current IPP is very close to the city of Jodhpur. *Savo* has warhead track and engagement computed. Can engage, but only within a short window. Estimate time to engage is two minutes. Over."

The circuit indicator light went red, and a squealing screech was followed by a garble. Someone was trying to answer, but the scrambler circuits weren't synchronizing. He keyed again "Sit Room, CentCom, Fifth Fleet: Dropped sync. Did you copy my last? Over."

The circuit dropped sync again. "Fuck," he muttered. Waited two seconds, then hit the button again. "Any station this net, *Savo Island,* over . . . Screw it, we're not getting any joy here." He turned to yell past Mills, "CIC Officer: get on Fifth Fleet Secure. Start calling them and the battle group. Try until you get a response. Then put me on."

Terranova broke in, loudly but without any stress

evident in her South Jersey accent, "Meteor Alfa at apogee. Terminal phase commence. Lock-on remains solid."

Mills cleared his throat. "Captain. Request permission to engage."

Dan didn't answer. He was still staring at the area of uncertainty. A pretty accurate description of where his own mind was parked right now. In neutral. Idling.

The return blurred and began to stretch out. The ionization trail. It looked like a comet, hearted with a harder dot that must still be the warhead itself.

Behind him Wenck said, "Skipper?"

Dan stared at the geo display. Had the quivering oval started to move? Yes. It had.

Only about ten miles across now, it was slowly, slowly tracking northwest.

Directly over the city.

Mills touched his arm. "Permission to engage? Roll FIS to green?"

The Firing Integrity Switch. Essentially, the safety catch on the ship's main battery. Dan muttered, "Not yet . . . not yet. CICO, joy on the Sit Room? CentCom?"

"No joy, sir. Circuit keeps dropping sync."

Dan said, "Stand by on permission to engage. Set Zebra."

Mills said into his mike, "Bridge, TAO. Pass Material Condition Zebra throughout the ship. Launch-warning bell forward and aft."

"IPP's moving again," Terranova noted.

"I hold it," Dan said. "Moving away from the airfield, toward a population center."

"Concur," Mills said instantly.

Dan opened the order of battle and hastily searched it as the 1MC announced hollowly, *"Now set Circle William throughout the ship. Secure all outside accesses."* The A/C sighed to a stop. Doors thudded closed. The air base. An army base, too, though no specific location. Within the city limits? The database held little on Jodhpur itself. Population, nearly a million. A tourist destination. An old fort.

When he looked back up, the IPP was at the western edge of the city, on the far side from the airfield, and the AOU was five or six miles. If they were aiming at anything, it wasn't the strip, unless the missile was off course. He didn't have hard numbers on the Ghauri, but the circular error, probable for most second-generation liquid-fueled theater-range weapons, the Al-Huseyns and the Scud derivatives, was around two miles. But even given that generous estimate of its probable accuracy, this thing wasn't aimed at the airfield. "It's definitely meant for the city," he muttered. "Or if it originally wasn't, it's now off course and headed for it."

"Concur," Mills said again. "The IPP is clearly west of the city, but close enough for major damage."

Dan glanced at the CIC officer, who was still clutching the handset. He shook his head slightly, looking scared.

"Okay, FIS to green," Dan said.

Mills touched his mike. "Launchers into 'operate' mode. Set up to take Meteor Alfa, two-round salvo. Deselect all safeties and interlocks. Stand by to fire. On CO's command."

Dan clicked up the red cover over the switch. ALIS was computing trajectory, intercept point, probability of kill. Mills was tapping away at his terminal, entering a backup order in case Dan's glitched.

He took a deep, slow breath, watching the ionization plume waver and grow. Taking his time. Thinking it through. But knowing, too, he'd never be sure. And over time, interpretations and stories and maybe even legends would grow around this moment. Like Sarajevo. But all that was out of his hands.

He reached out and unsocketed the red handset of the uncovered high-frequency command net. Bowed his head, then pressed the button. "Flash, flash, flash. This is *Savo Island*. I pass in the blind: Pakistani missile targeted on Jodhpur. Have consistent drop sync with all commands, this and other nets. I assess that the missile must be engaged to prevent massive loss of life. Engaging at this time. Out."

He socketed the handset without waiting for a response. Took one more deep breath, then said, in as confident a tone as he could manage, "You have permission to engage."

17

The Devil and the Sea

A heart-stopping pause, during which the toxic-gas-vent dampers whunked shut. Dan tensed, hunched, finger still on the switch. Wait . . . had he inserted the Fire Auth key? Yes, he had. The steel chain lay close to his hand. But was ALIS going to initiate? Or were they already too late?

The endless moment stretched.

Then a roar vibrated through the hull. "Bird one away," Mills intoned. A pause, then a second roar. ". . . Bird two away. Firing complete."

On the LSD two small bright symbols detached from the circle-and-cross of *Savo Island*'s own-ship. Morphing into blue semicircles, they headed rapidly inshore, leaping ahead with incredible speed from sweep to sweep of the Aegis spokes. They were already at full speed, almost four kilometers a second, as the dual-thrust motors of the first stage boosted them into exoatmospheric flight.

Dan blew out, with a strange sense of déjà vu. He'd dreamed this, years before, though he couldn't recall exactly where. Which meant something, he wasn't sure what. Maybe that time didn't exist, or that it all existed at once . . .

He scrubbed his face, trying to deny fatigue. "Matt, get a message out. Short and sweet, but make it clear we stood by until we were certain the TPI was over a population center. Ten Block 4s remaining. Continuing on station, but fuel state critical."

"Coffee? Just made a fresh pot." Chief Zotcher set a mug by his elbow. The heavy Victory style, with the ship's crest on one side and a sonar system logo on the other.

"Uh . . . thanks. But, Chief, I'd rather have you nailed to that screen. That emitter's still out there. And there's gotta be a sub attached to it."

"We got our best young eyes on it, Captain."

Dan forced himself to his feet and carried the mug over to the EW stack. He inspected the screen over the operator's shoulder. "That Snoop Tray, day before yesterday . . . no, day before that. Nothing since?"

"Nothing radiating out there, Captain."

"How about from shore?"

The EW petty officer said there was intense air activity over the Pakistani naval air base nearest them. "A major attack. Heavy jamming, AA radars, and the cryppies are reporting a lot of air-to-air chatter."

Dan regarded it for a few seconds, then was drawn

irresistibly back to the large-screen displays. He'd been away less than a minute, but the blue semicircles of *Savo*'s outgoing rounds were already closing in on the red caret-symbol of the target. He gripped the back of his chair, hardly daring to breathe. "Stand by for intercept," said Wenck, words eerily uttered at the very same moment by Terranova, baritone and soprano, an ominous duet. "Stand by . . ."

The symbols met. Aegis's lock-on brackets jerked, apparently snagging its own terminal vehicle momentarily instead of the target, then recentered. Dan leaned forward.

The radar return blurred, widening, elongating. A second later it began to pulse, then all at once glowed much more brightly.

"Intercept," Wenck called from the Aegis console. "That winking is rotating debris. The debris is spreading . . . spreading out . . . ionization trail growing . . . it's burning up."

The radar return showed what Dan assumed was the smaller debris field left from the explosion of the Block 4's warhead. Not a gigantic payload, but anything hitting at fifteen thousand miles an hour carried a punch. The Ghauri was single-stage. Its payload remained integral with the airframe, like the old V-2. Once it was destabilized, they could depend on the atmosphere and its own speed to tear it apart. As he watched, the speeding dart of their second round hit as well. The radar return expanded suddenly to five times its previous size, like a bursting firework. Then, slowly, faded.

"Payload detonation," Wenck intoned. "Both Standards connected."

The CIC crew rose at their consoles, cheering, clapping. The trail faded, widened, glittered, as the lock-on brackets began to hunt back and forth, uncertain what to lock onto. ALIS's eagle eye continued to show ever-tinier pieces of debris, the blaze of ionization as they turned to metal gas. But there was no longer a central contact.

He stayed hunched forward, watching the last fading falling sparklings. Then blinked slowly. Even as the vent dampers clunked open, and the air-conditioning whooshed back on, he couldn't shake the feeling that this it wasn't over. Not at all.

It had only begun.

The morning resumed. Longley brought up scrambled eggs and toast and limp too-pink ham, but Dan only picked at it, then set it aside to slide up and down the command table until it dove off during a bad roll. *Savo* set flight quarters, nosed around into the wind, and launched Red Hawk to relieve *Mitscher*'s SH-60. The ETs came down every half hour with updates from Mumbai news. And the high-side chat was still up, so he was getting DIA analysis, press releases, and reports on the UN's efforts to arrange a cease-fire. But they weren't getting anything from Pakistan, and Mumbai seemed limited to reporting bellicose statements rather than actual news.

Of course, in the middle of a war, no one knew what

was happening. No news agency had reported on the Jodhpur missile, making him wonder if the Indians had even detected it. So far, there'd been no official notice.

He sucked a breath. Maybe, just maybe, the Indians *hadn't* detected it. If so, and it was a signal, intercepting it had been exactly the wrong thing to do. If one side thought it had sent a warning, and the other didn't respond, what was the natural conclusion? That the warning had been brushed aside.

He shivered at the most chilling thought yet: that *Savo*'s presence, and his attempt to protect innocents, might *lead* to escalation.

But that was speculation. The one clear fact was that Indian armor had achieved a massive breakthrough. Eight battle groups, over a thousand tanks, had penetrated the Pakistani lines in both the north and the south, and the remaining Pak army was being enveloped. The Indians had speeded up their advances toward Multan and Sukkur. The BBC, which still had reporters in Karachi, reported a government source as saying the Indians' lead elements were across the Indus and racing for the capital.

He wanted to put his head back, catch a few seconds' rest, but instead called up a geo of Pakistan. He was no master of ground strategy, but this looked familiar. Two breakthroughs, near the country's narrow waist. Once they reached the river, the forces could wheel toward each other. When they met, they'd seal the remnants of Pakistan's forces between them and isolate the capital. Islamabad would have to sue for peace.

Cheryl was in the TAO seat, giving Mills and

Branscombe a break. Dan knuckled his eyes, wishing he could massage his brain. Or put his head on a pillow. But if he was responsible, he wanted to be physically in the seat. He sighed and called up his traffic.

Routine, routine. One requested further data on his Iranians, and recommended that he isolate all three, instead of just Shah. He hesitated—the others hadn't given the slightest trouble—then forwarded the message to Chief Toan, asking him to take the others into custody as well. It wouldn't mean any additional manpower; they had to keep a guard on the breaker anyway. He had to get rid of them. Innocent, guilty, whatever, they had no business aboard. He scratched furiously at what felt like bugs burrowing under his scalp. And he hadn't taken anything stronger than caffeine.

At 0900 GCCS came back up, all at once, pouring data over the leftmost LSD. "Freeze it and save, in case it goes down again," Dan told the exec. Her manicured nails tapped keys as he studied it. Two great salients pointed west. The southernmost had almost reached the river. Another Indian air strike was returning from a Pak air base west of Sukkur. In ruins now, no doubt, runway cratered, hangars demolished, fuel burning, aircraft wrecked and shot up. He glanced to where Singhe sat, headphones to her ears, running a scenario for her strike team. The screenlight lit a downturned scowl.

He zoomed out, looking for anything from the ASW tracking and fire control system. The closest subs were a French unit in the Arabian Sea . . . and, sending his eyebrows up, two Chinese nuclear attack boats transiting the Malacca Strait westbound.

But what struck the eye was a vacancy. Most shipping, particularly tanker traffic to and from the oil-rich Gulf, stuck to a hundred-mile-wide bottleneck at nine degrees latitude, north of the Maldives and south of Cardamom, before going on to round the southern tip of India and then Sri Lanka. The whole time they'd been in the IO, ships had been spaced along this route. A few were still headed east, but only two now lay between the Lakshadweep Islands and Socotra, and six off the Horn of Africa. But when he looked at the course/speed readouts, two of those were headed south, not west—diverted to other destinations. The sole remaining vessels headed east were all Chinese-flagged.

"Sea-lanes are emptying," Cheryl muttered, beside him. "In response to the Indo-Pak conflict?"

Dan reared back, speaking to the black-painted overhead. "That shouldn't stop international energy traffic. And I don't like the looks of those subs coming through Malacca. That's one of the redlines the Indians always drew: a Chinese nuke in the IO, they go to full alert." He rubbed his face. "Uh, I've had my head in this for the last twenty-four. How's our crew doing? And we're getting desperate on fuel. I don't want to have to hoist our bedsheets and sail back, like that sub in the twenties. Never mind, I gotta get with CHENG on that. But how are we holding up otherwise?"

Staurulakis shook her head. "We're keeping stations manned, but we're losing our edge. People were tired going into condition three. Half of 'em are still recovering from the crud, then we dumped all those man-hours for steam-cleaning on them. We're tasking the watchstanders, the ETs, and the Engineering people hard, and we can't keep Red Hawk up four on and four off for long."

"Right, Stafer's got maintenance issues too."

Staurulakis muttered, "I'm concerned about you, too, sir."

"I'm all right. Never mind about me. Stick to the crew."

"Well, then, they're in a steep decline in operational readiness. And we still haven't heard back if we're actually still supposed to be here." The exec picked at her lip, frowning; the skin around her eyes looked translucent, almost green. "You never saw anything about our taking down the Jodhpur strike?"

"The Indians didn't release that there *was* a strike. And I haven't seen anything responding to our shoot-down report."

Dan got on the Hydra for a discussion with Danenhower. The chief engineer reported soberly that they were already below 30 percent fuel. *"We're squeezing her tits down here, but the bridge keeps upping turns. What's with that?"*

"Probably just maintaining steerageway, Bart. Below five knots, every one of these heavy seas pushes the bow downwind. And we're powering only one screw. That makes it even harder. Nothing else we can do? Shut down housekeeping?"

The CHENG said glumly that it wouldn't make much difference. *"Most of that comes off the waste heat boilers anyway. If we shut down the radars, though—"*

"Not possible, Bart."

"*Then there's not much more I can do. My question is, at what point do we turn and run for Al Hadd?*"

Dan swapped quizzical glances with the exec. "Al Hadd . . . what's Al Hadd?"

"*The closest possible fuel point,*" Danenhower said patiently. "*There's a commercial airfield there. They'll have jet A1. It's not milspec, but we can burn it. Four hundred and twenty nautical miles. If we leave now, we might make it before we suck the last tank dry.*"

Dan clicked to acknowledge, catching Staurulakis's pointed glance too. He hadn't realized they were that close to bingo fuel. Which triggered a thought: "How about our helo gas? We can burn JP-5 in the LM-2500s, can't we?"

Danenhower said sure, JP-5 was just an eight-cent-a-gallon-more-expensive version of Navy distillate, with a lower flash point. "*But there's not that much left of that, either. Maybe a day's worth. After that, we're gonna have to hang off the stern and kick our feet.*"

Dan signed off. He was twisting his neck when a half-familiar voice said, "Is that giving you pain?"

"Hello, Doc. Old injury."

Leo Schell squatted at his side, bringing his face close to Dan's left elbow. In that position, with his voice lowered, it was impossible anyone else could hear the major's murmur. "How're you doing, Captain?"

"Still here, Doctor."

"What I'm hearing makes me wonder."

"Oh yeah?" Dan hitched up in his chair, suddenly angry. "What the fuck is it you're hearing? That we're parked in a war zone without clear orders? Exactly . . . what?"

A steadying hand on his arm. "Take it easy. Easy! When's the last time you got any sleep?"

"I don't know what business that is of yours. And who's telling you I'm no longer fit to command?"

Schell tilted his head. "Actually . . . you're the first to say anything remotely like that. Which is interesting, don't you think?"

Dan gripped the desk edge. "Who's feeding you this bullshit? Who've you been talking to?"

"I'd be breaking confidence to say."

"And I'm ordering you to tell me."

"I must refuse to do so, Captain. Remember, I'm not under your command."

"Wrong, Major. Anyone on my ship's under my command."

"Listen to yourself." Schell stood. Shifted a hand to Dan's shoulder. "Some free medical advice? Don't push yourself too hard. Or when your people really need you, you won't be there for them."

The really bad news arrived that afternoon. Around lunchtime, the EWs reported increased radar and jamming, associated with a major Pakistani strike package out of the air base at Peshawar. Dan followed it southward. Over thirty aircraft. They avoided Indian interceptors forward-staged over the border, doglegged west, angled back east. Then crossed the battle lines south of Multan.

Twenty minutes later a Navy red flash message forwarded a CIA appreciation that "national sensor assets" had indicated detonation of three or possibly four kiloton-range nuclear devices in south central Pakistan.

"It's started," Mills murmured.

Dan blinked, coming out of a daze. Maybe Schell had a point. "Matt. Where are we? I mean, what's our status?"

"In our oparea. Speed six. Course three-one-zero. Two Block 4As active and green. Aegis at 92 percent. *Mitscher* riding shotgun. Red Hawk in the air, currently to seaward monitoring sonobuoy laydown."

"Uh-huh. Okay. The Iranians . . . where are they?"

Mills dropped his gaze. "Iranians, sir? You mean the prisoners, in the breaker?"

"No, no. Never mind. Just a little brain fart, for a minute. I meant Indians. Indians and Pakistanis." He got up and paced, digging fingernails into eye sockets, from the gun fire control console aft to the tactical data coordinator station at the forward end of the compartment. The rubber-covered metal plates grated under his boots. *Savo* rolled, and something cracked far away, eased with a metallic moan, cracked again. Not more fractures, he hoped.

Sleep backed away a step. Was he being stupid? Cheryl was qualified to command. No man could stay alert forever. He could take an hour. Put his head down and close his eyes . . . He fought it back once more and grunted, "Why the hell did this have to start on our watch?"

"We did all we could," Mills said, watching him

with an expression Dan didn't much like. "Hey, Skipper, you okay? You look . . . tired. Sure you don't want to take a break? I can handle it here."

"Sure you can. I know. I just can't be out of the loop right now."

"Yes sir." The operations officer returned his attention to his terminal.

Wenck, at his elbow, pushed a lined tablet toward him. "Don't fucking *poke* me with that," Dan snapped. "What is it?"

"Just took it down. Mumbai television. You might want to look."

He scanned it with irritated apathy, then bewilderment. The Indian minister of defense had released the information that a ballistic missile had been fired at the city of Jodhpur. It had disintegrated during descent, but enough radioactive debris had been recovered to make clear it had carried a nuclear warhead. The Indian government had announced this to make clear that their actions henceforth would be undertaken in retribution.

"Zero kudos to us for shooting it down," Wenck observed.

"A lot gets overlooked in war, Donnie," Dan told him. "And to be fair, they might not even know it was us. But this isn't good. They're saying the gloves are off. From here on, anything goes. And it's interesting they're withholding the news about the Pakistani nuclear strike on their armored forces."

Terranova called over her console, "Ya think it really was a nuke that we shot down? Sir?"

"Dunno, Terror. But that's what the Indians are saying."

Another ET came through the door from forward. Wenck bent to listen, then turned to Dan. "They're putting that out now. On Mumbai news. Three air bursts, over the 33rd Armored Division. No numbers yet, but heavy casualties."

Dan sagged into the chair, the realization hitting at last through the fatigue and apathy. It had started. The first theater nuclear war. Not in Europe, the way everyone had expected during the Cold War, or even on the Korean Peninsula, but on the subcontinent.

After all, not unlike the war that had started in the Balkans, with the assassination of an Austrian archduke.

He was still trying to take it in when the cuing signal chimed. Mills read off from his screen, " 'Defense Support Program Sat detected launch bloom, Thar Desert.' "

"Cuing, Obsidian Glint," Terranova called. "Suspected launch."

On the LSD, she steered the beam to the location the satellite had just downloaded. It clicked back and forth, searching desert, then quivered as the brackets snapped on, snagging the dot that had suddenly materialized at the center. "Pefect fucking handoff," Wenck muttered. "Doesn't get any sweeter than that."

Terranova stated, "Profile plot, Meteor Bravo. Matches alert script. Matches cuing. Altitude, angels fifty. Correlates with Indian Agni medium-range ballistic missile. In boost phase. Designate hostile?"

Dan nodded. "Make it so." He picked up the red phone again. Tried it. Then hit the worn lever of the 21MC. "Radio, Combat. Why isn't the satcomm syncing?"

"You heard it, right? It almost syncs, at first. But then there's like a microsecond delay that cuts in. That scrambles the rest of the transmission?"

"Okay, so where's the problem? Can you retune?"

The voice turned patronizing. *"It's not a tuning issue, Captain. It's like there's an extra bit in the transmission somehow? Anyway, it's not on our end. Sir."*

"I've got to talk to Fleet. There's no way to get through?"

"Not on a covered circuit. We checked with Mitscher. *Their RTs can't break it either. Which means it's on the transmitting end, or somewhere in between."*

Dan double-clicked off, and caught a worried glance from Mills. "Captain . . . you planning to take this one, too?"

He didn't answer right away. Squinted up at the LSD. But a silhouette loomed between him and the displays. A tall, angular, birdlike silhouette.

Dr. Noblos's. The Johns Hopkins rider was professorial in slacks and a white shirt with a knitted vest. He leaned over the console. "You're blocking my view, Bill," Dan said.

"I understand the Indians are saying that was a nuke you shot down, Captain."

"Can we have this discussion later? Right now we have a cuing incoming."

Noblos half turned, to stare at the geo plot, then the Aegis picture. "Out of our geometry," he observed dismissively.

"You can tell that by one look at the screen?"

"Of course. It's perfectly obvious."

"Captain?" Mills, beside him, looking anxious. "I need an order."

Dan studied the screens. From where he sat, true, it didn't look good. The Thar Desert, western India, was far inland. Too soon to tell what the target was, with the missile still in the boost phase, but it would have to be aimed either west or north.

"Complete the setup," Dan told the TAO. Mills bent to the mike, passing commands to the bridge, then to *Mitscher.* Dan half turned in his seat. Shouted across the compartment, "Sonar? One last check. No contacts?"

Rit Carpenter, over the 21MC. *"Clear scope here, Skipper."*

Mills was still speaking. "Launch-warning bell aft and forward."

Dan reached into the neck of his coveralls and fitted the firing key once more. "This will be a two-round salvo."

Noblos frowned. "Why waste rounds? Launch point's two hundred miles away. And it'll be a stern chase. Ten to one, it'll never catch up."

"I'm aware of that, Doctor. Which is why I have to fire early, before pitchover."

Noblos reached across the console to squeeze his shoulder. "Refer to your rules of engagement, Captain. If your P-sub-K's below point two, you don't need to fire. And if you shoot before pitchover and IPP identification—"

Dan pushed the hand off, catching, as he did so, a whiff of something minty, aftershave or mouthwash. He lifted his head, trying to pierce the fog of fatigue and uncertainty, and the aftermath of infection, to penetrate to the core of what was right to do. Maybe it wasn't doctrine. Maybe it wasn't even possible.

But he had to try.

He'd defended it at a congressional hearing. Risked his career on it.

But he still wasn't sure it was right.

He had to balance not just capability, but intentions. And beyond even that, anticipate the most distant ramifications of his decisions. He'd shot down a missile from one side. Didn't he owe the same responsibility to the other?

"Matt, help me out," he muttered. "Take it down? I'm wondering about the message we're sending if we don't."

"We don't have the aim point yet, sir. If it's on a military target set, we should let it go."

"You heard Dr. Noblos. By the time we know, it'll be too late."

"You've been reading the news from home, Lenson," Noblos said, bending close, like a confiding son. "Every round's going to be irreplaceable. Don't waste them. Not on some kind of political statement."

The Terror's voice: "Commencing pitchover." And on the screen, the brackets quivering, quivering, then starting to move.

Headed north. Dan glanced at Mills, but got only a dropped gaze.

It was up to him.

But why should that be a surprise?

He was the captain.

"Ah, fuck it," he muttered. He snagged the clear plastic cover of the switch with a thumbnail. Flicked it up, and snapped the toggle to Fire.

Once again, that agonizingly stretched-out pause. The dampers whunking shut. The ventilation easing to a stop, leaving harsh, tormented-sounding breathing. His own.

A roar built forward. Singhe sang out, "Bird one away . . . standing by . . . bird two away." The symbology winked into existence on the display. "Two birds, dual-thrust ignition, seekers activated, on their way."

On the center screen, the Indian missile, Meteor Bravo, was into pitchover and starting to track north. No, northwest by north. Mills grimaced. "Headed away, Skipper. Target's someplace up around Islamabad."

"I told you the geometry would be disadvantageous," Noblos pontificated. "Didn't I?"

"Yeah, Doctor. You did." Dan quelled the impulse to reach across, grab that stupid knitted vest, and punch the shit out of him. "What I'm wondering is, why everyone has an opinion on what I ought to do. Who exactly's in charge here?"

The moment the words were out, he realized they were a mistake. The horrified glances from Mills, Wenck, and the CIC officer were testimony to that. "Sorry, didn't mean that the way it sounded," he amended, passing a shaky hand over his forehead. "Guess I'm burning a short fuze here."

Noblos said loftily, "I'd like it recorded that I officially recommended against this launch."

"You're not in the chain of command, Doctor. But sure, we'll document it." Dan lifted his head. "Get that down in the CIC log."

From the pure hatred in the scientist's eyes, he'd mortally offended him. Well, too fucking bad. He had other fish to fry . . . and other birds to follow.

Like the ones on the screen. They'd dropped their boosters and were now propelled by the Block 4's extended-range motor. Nearing four miles a second and still accelerating, they jumped forward across southern Pakistan with each ten-hertz rescan. The steering-control sections were still receiving midcourse guidance from ALIS, fed automatically unless overridden by Terranova. Once they were out of the atmosphere, the last finned stage would be jettisoned, and the warheads, guided now by their terminal homers, would fly on. Each warhead was propelled in the exoatmospheric phase by a small sustainer engine, then maneuvered to collision in the final milliseconds by infrared sensors coupled to gas generators and reaction nozzles spaced around the airframe.

"Stage-two burnout," Wenck announced. "Commencing terminal homing."

Onscreen the target was still boosting, perhaps by its own second stage, headed northwest. The blue semicircles of *Savo*'s missiles were closing from astern, but more and more slowly as their quarry accelerated. Dan coughed and coughed, trying to suck air past the obstruction in his throat. His inhaler . . . in his cabin. He clutched the desk, panting. "Do we have an IPP yet?" he grunted. "Get it up on the screen. Now!"

"ALIS is calculating," Terranova said. "She seems a little slow . . . Coming up now."

The area of uncertainty was a quivering blob far inland. Past where the last, frozen frame from GCCS had placed the northernmost Indian spearhead. Dan squinted. "Where . . . what's the nearest city? Can you read that?"

"Peshawar." Mills cleared his throat and repeated, a little louder, "Peshawar. Where the Pak air strike launched from."

"That makes sense." A scent of sandalwood, and Singhe's soft tones, hardened now. "They took two separate nuclear attacks before deciding to hit back."

It wasn't quite that clear-cut, Dan thought, but didn't say. "Lieutenant, I need you back on your console."

"The strike team's ready, Captain. If you have a package for us?"

"I'd just like you in your seat," Dan told her, and got a smoldering scowl back. She turned on her heel and stalked away.

When he looked back, the three symbols were only

a short distance apart on the display. They hung there, pulsating, red and blue. Speeding across the face of the earth, a hundred-plus miles up, at nearly orbital velocity. Across the broad fertile plain of the ancient Indus, where Darius and Alexander, Chandragupta Maurya and the British Raj, had marched and conquered. The earth seemed to turn perceptibly beneath them. Speeding stars, as fast as meteorites. Locked now onto their target, mere miles ahead.

Their lead Standard flickered.

It slowed. The callout beside it flickered and began to drop.

Terranova said quietly, "Terminal guidance burnout. Shall I send destruct order?"

"I told you so," Noblos observed.

Dan took a slow, deep breath. "Maybe you were right, Doctor. Technically. But that's not all I have to take into account. Terror, Donnie, if we hit the abort button on the first bird, will that decoy the second?"

"Number two's starting to lose velocity too, Dan. I mean, Captain."

When he lifted his gaze again, it was true; the callouts for the second bird were flickering downward as well. Both his missiles were falling back into the atmosphere. At the speed they were traveling, atmospheric friction would probably cook off their high-explosive warheads, but he couldn't count on that. "All right. Send the destruct order."

The lead symbol winked out first, followed within seconds by the other. By which time the red caret of Meteor Bravo was a hundred miles ahead of them, still on its way north. The area of uncertainty around its target had shrunk to seven miles across, centered west of Peshawar. Where, Dan assumed, the air base lay. He picked up the satcomm and just for form's sake tried again to report in to CentCom. Again, he got the start of a sync, then a deafening squeal before the transmission cut off. "What in the hell is wrong with our fucking comms?" he muttered, half to himself, half to Mills.

Savo rolled so hard, binders and pencils began to slide, picking up speed to vault off desks and consoles. The air-conditioning came back on in a sighing rush. He plucked sweat-soaked coveralls away from his sweat-soaked skivvy shirt, extracted the Fire key from the lock, and looped the chain around his neck again.

A moment of blackness. He came to with his head on the command desk, a foul taste in his mouth, and someone shaking his shoulder. It was Dr. Schell. "Turn over your seat. Or I'll inform my reporting senior, copy to yours, that in my judgment, the CO of USS *Savo Island* is unable to continue in command."

Cheryl Staurulakis was staring at him over the doctor's shoulder, her own face etched with fatigue and worry and something very like horror.

Weary.

So unutterably weary.

It was done. For better or worse.

The results remained to be seen.

He lay in his at-sea cabin, alternately dozing and calling the exec, the bridge, and Radio for updates. Over the next hours, news trickled in. Not via the message traffic, and not via GCCS, which had gone down again, but eavesdropped from news programs and shortwave BBC broadcasts.

The airfield and much of the city of Peshawar had been destroyed by a nuclear detonation.

Pakistan, its forces still reeling back despite the kiloton-range airbursts over the southern Indian spearhead, and now with a city burning behind them, blamed the United States for taking sides.

The Chinese ambassador to the UN had announced that units of the People's Liberation Army were moving into Bhutan, on India's northern border. India, in turn, had announced a blockade of all Chinese merchant traffic through the Indian Ocean.

The ship lurched and swayed, carrying him, high in the superstructure, in great swoops that pressed him against the bunkstraps. Gray light levered through the porthole. The second hand on the bulkhead-mounted captain's chronometer jerked, paused, jerked ahead. He looked up from the clipboard, past the radioman, at the copy of Tuchman on his bookshelf. It sounded so familiar. The names had changed. That was all.

At last he couldn't stand it any longer. He got up and pulled on the same smelly coveralls. Climbed to the pilothouse, clinging grimly to the handrail as the ship rolled around him like some funhouse ride. "Captain's on the bridge," the boatswain's mate shouted.

"Belay your reports," Dan said, cutting Mytsalo off. The ensign looked barely able to keep his feet. His face seemed longer, leaner, shadowed by stubble. He clung to the radar repeater as if without it he would fall to the deck. The quartermaster, the phone talkers, the helmsman, all looked haggard in the hoary light. And outside, the gray steep waves rolled past under a gray sky. Dan staggered to the captain's chair, then lacked the force to haul himself up into it. He clung, blinking, brain empty yet still reverberating, like a too-often-rung bell. He coughed into a fist and sucked air.

The 21MC lit at his elbow. *"Pilothouse, Radio: Cap'n up there?"*

Mytsalo pressed the lever. "This is the OOD. He's listening."

"Captain? We got a jury-rigged hookup on satcomm. Not sure what's wrong with the regular circuit, but we got the maintenance freq to sync. CentCom duty officer's trying to call you."

"Got it," Dan told the ensign. He clicked the red phone on and waited for the beep. *"Savo Island* Actual. Over."

"This is CentCom duty officer. Where are you right now, Captain?"

Dan enunciated clearly and slowly, so as not to have to repeat himself. "This is *Savo* Actual. I am on assigned station, Ballistic Missile OpArea Endive, off the Pak-Indian border. Over."

"This is CentCom. What are you still doing there? GCCS has you en route to rejoin the task force."

He blinked. Most commanders knew GCCS wasn't exactly real world, but some—especially some with stars on their shoulders—seemed to think that if it showed up on the screen it was right there, right now.

Even though with the recurrent glitches over the past twenty-four hours, they should trust it even less. But more worrisome than that was *why* they might think he was somewhere else. "Uh, this is *Savo*. No, we're in our assigned oparea. Have you been getting our intel reports? We had to launch on two ballistic missiles. Intercepting strikes. Over."

A squeal like grinding brakes with worn-out pads. Then "*—getting them. But the intel function's not worth the risk. Over.*"

"This is *Savo*. You're desyncing. Can you enlighten me as to commander's intent? Over."

"*This is CentCom. You're breaking up on this end, too. How copy? Over.*"

"*Savo*, copy that, over."

"*This is CentCom. We're backing away from the Indo-Pak confrontation. Letting it burn out. That's a national-level decision. In light of developments elsewhere. How copy? Over.*"

Dan grabbed for a handhold as *Savo* corkscrewed like an old, cunning bronc. Stared out at a massive sea as the bow lifted, then plowed deep, blasting loose a long veil of wavering spray that dimpled the rolling pools on the forecastle like a heavy downpour. Letting it "burn out"? With China invading Bhutan, an Indian ally? Or were those the "developments elsewhere"? "Uh . . . copy that. Backing away. Over."

"*You should be headed south to meet up with Strike One to fuel. Then you'll be detached for further duty. At least, that's the plan so far. Could change. You heard, about the Indian blockade announcement?*"

"This is *Savo.* Affirmative."

"The latest on that. Hasn't hit the open media yet. But the Chinese announced they're not recognizing it. Over."

Dan hesitated, then clicked Transmit. "This is *Savo.* Not sure I got that right. Not 'recognizing' it? Over."

"That a blockade is illegal under international law. So they'll break it, quote, by any means necessary, unquote." A pause, during which the sync hissed, then, *"Zhang says he's only supporting Pakistan, but . . . Any means necessary. So, you can understand—a lot of our plans are in flux right now."* A pause. *"How copy? Over."*

He took a deep breath, fighting a sense of doom. Most of China's energy, oil and liquefied natural gas, moved through the Indian Ocean. The Indians had threatened to sever that pipeline. And the Chinese had just announced they'd fight to defend it. "*Savo.* Copy all. Do you know where they intend to send us? Over."

"This is CentCom. It is possible satcomm has been compromised. Minimize transmissions on this net. Over."

Dan lowered the handset, shocked. If voice satellite communications were no longer secure, all fleet comms were endangered. He wanted to ask why they suspected compromise, but the other wouldn't say, even if he knew. Not on a no-longer-trustworthy circuit. "This is *Savo.* Roger all, but we have no orders to leave oparea. Over."

"This is CentCom. Check message traffic and comply ASAP. Minimize voice comms. We're also seeing

crashes on GCCS and the SIPRNET. Check your re-dundancy. Request confirmation via another channel if you receive orders that seem doubtful. Confirm. Over."

Dan's mouth was suddenly dry. The Navy ran on communications as much as on distillate fuel. If something, no, *someone,* was corrupting encrypted voice and GCCS, and even SIPRNET was no longer secure, the effect would be devastating. He muttered, "This is *Savo* Actual. I confirm. Over."

"This is CentCom, roger, out."

He reclipped the handset and met Mytsalo's gaze. The ensign looked shaken. "Did you copy all that, Max?"

"I—I think so. That's not good. Sir."

"No, it isn't." Dan blinked past him, then remembered what he hadn't seen when he'd looked out over the forecastle. "Where's *Mitscher*?"

"Off the port quarter, sir. In a squall."

Right, they were still in the monsoon season. Which explained the everlasting overcast, the eternal wind. And the never-ending seas, stiff and jagged, breaking and toppling as they cannonballed past.

"Captain?"

The radioman chief this time, instead of the messenger. But the same clipboard. Dan swallowed sudden nausea. Now what? He took it reluctantly. Ran his eye down it, disbelieving, then stared at the last line.

CO USS SAVO ISLAND REPORT NONRESPONSE
TO ORDERS, REF A. INTERROGATIVE WHY

SAVO TASK GROUP NOT EN ROUTE TASK
FORCE POSIT. REPLY ASAP VIA MULTIPLE
COMM PATHS.

He snapped, "What the hell's this about? What's
Ref A?"

The radioman chief's Adam's apple pumped. "Captain, we have no record of that date time group."

"I don't understand. No *record*?"

"No sir. I mean, that's right, sir. We never received
a message with that date time group."

This was baffling. Higher was referencing a message
that, so far as *Savo*'s always-competent communicators
were concerned, didn't exist. "Did you check with
Mitscher? Do they hold it?"

"Yessir, first thing. They don't have it either. We
requested a retransmit. Still waiting for that."

Dan stood turning it over in a foggy, slow brain. A
voice transmission that said, "Don't trust voice messages." That expected him to leave station, citing a
broadcast message that didn't seem to exist, or that, at
least, they'd never gotten. Then a message reproaching
him for being on station, and referencing a previous
message that he didn't hold. He muttered doggedly,
"There's got to be a record. A way you can check what
you have and haven't received."

The chief consulted his wrist, which Dan saw wore
two watches. "That's the daily date time group summary message, Captain. Comes in at midnight Zulu.
We're in Echo."

"Okay, but we can request a retransmit, can't we? Since we have the date time group of the missing message . . . the one they referenced. Have you done that?"

The chief looked ill at ease. "Soon as it came in, Captain. I, uh, I already told you we did that. Asked for a retransmit. Which we're waiting for."

"Okay, sorry. You did. But this isn't reassuring, that messages seem to be slipping past us. I don't want to get down in your pants, but could we be out of timing? Missing parts of the scrambled broadcast?"

The chief seemed to be starting to protest, then quelled himself. "That used to happen, yessir. With the old KW-37s. They got out of timing. But with the 46s, it's pretty much impossible."

"So what's wrong?"

The ITman hesitated. "I'm just not sure, sir."

"Well, get to the bottom of it! Our satellite voice comms are degrading, Chief. We have to be able to depend on broadcast."

The chief said yes sir, waited a moment, then saluted and turned away. Leaving Dan leaning on his chair, still too weak to get up into it.

So he checked the nav console. Took a range and bearing to the nearest land. A queerly shaped, low-lying peninsula poked out toward them, shaped like a flaccid, drooping penis. It didn't seem to have a name, at least that the software knew.

The own-ship symbol glowed at the inner edge of his oparea, which the console was displaying outlined in yellow. The area he should have already left behind. All right, if he was supposed to rejoin the task group . . . He recalled the last GCCS picture, estimated a course. "Officer of the deck."

"Yessir, Captain." Mytsalo straightened. "OOD, aye."

"Come to one-nine-zero. Tell Main Control, secure low-fuel-consumption maneuvering regime. When they're ready, increase to fifteen knots." He slewed the cursor, guesstimated their time to rendezvous at the most economical speed. "And have Mr. Danenhower contact me." He'd need to make sure he actually had enough fuel to get there, maneuver, wait in line, and get a drink off the tanker. *A lot of our plans are in flux right now.* "Pass that to TAO. Secure from condition three ABM. Set condition three self-defense. Have Sonar continue maintaining a sharp watch. And let *Mitscher* know, so she can follow us around. I'll call their CO in a minute, bring him up to speed."

He sagged into the console, coughing from deep in his chest while the bullnose dipped, rolled, and precessed around to the new course. Maybe Higher was right. Nothing more for USS *Savo Island* to do here. In his eagerness to help, he might even have made things worse. Helped trigger what the world had hoped never to see: a nuclear war.

He'd tried his best. But hadn't all the diplomats, generals, kings, and prime ministers done theirs, too? In August of 1914.

The leaden seas surged in. The cruiser headed into them, pitching until sharp crackles and bangs crepitated aft, ghostlike and unsettling. Far off on a shrouded horizon the silhouette of a Burke-class destroyer, *Mitscher*, mirrored their turn.

Leaving it all behind. But taking it along, too.

Well, he had his orders. *Let it burn out.*

He only hoped it would.

V

AUGUST 1914

18

Carrier Strike Group One: The Eastern Indian Ocean

Two days later he stood with lids clamped tight, fists buried in the pockets of his coveralls, swaying as the deck beneath his boots rose and fell. Spray cooled his uplifted face, and from his lips he licked the salty kiss of the sea.

He opened his eyes to a bright sky. The monsoon ceiling was wearing thin as *Savo* charged eastward, revealing blue above it, and here and there high wind-strained cirrus like shredding gauze. Her turbines sang at full power. Her intakes susurrated a continuous rush of intaken breath. Her wake tumbled and burbled like bluegreen and white wildflowers blooming on a heaving heath.

The fantail was cramped with equipment. Mount 52 in the middle, with the Harpoon launchers to port. The HF receive antennas nodded over the wake like tuna sticks. On the missile deck, the gunners' mates were doing lift checks on the aft module hatch and plenum covers. Fresh paint gleamed glossy, spray-beaded. Looped cables snagged sliding sheets of moisture in tidal pools.

After an economical-speed transit, they'd joined the battle group at dawn. After *Savo*'s deep, satisfying drink from the tanker, with Cheryl in the driver's seat while he got some much-needed kip, orders had come in. After replenishing, take station as directed by the ISIC—immediate superior in command, in this case, the rear admiral commanding the *Carl Vinson* battle group—and accompany it east. Their track lay past Sri Lanka, for the Malacca Strait. No one had yet mentioned a destination, but it was self-evident.

The South China Sea.

Boots braced against the heavy roll of a beam sea, he couldn't help remembering other fleets that had deep-graven this same route toward the sunrise. Rozhestvensky's Baltic Sea fleet, the Russians doomed to annihilation at Tsushima. *Prince of Wales* and *Repulse,* pride of the Royal Navy, the great battleships foredoomed to destruction by Japanese naval air.

He shivered. Not reassuring. So many empires had set out to conquer, and fallen in the dust.

But his orders didn't spell out things like that. They were markedly more laconic than in what he was already starting to think of, almost nostalgically, as peacetime. Only where to go, and how fast to get there.

Beyond that, he had no need to know.

In the night past, the group had threaded the Nine Degree Channel, the choke point near Cardamom

Island, and bent their course south, to clear the sub-continent. *Savo Island*'s station was on the left flank, farther out than the usual antiair screening station. The high-side chats, even the battle group nets, had gone silent, and most of the screen had their radars off, leaving *Savo* and *San Jacinto* to maintain the air and surface pictures.

He wondered, too, why no one had yet called to ask "what the fuck?" about his shootdowns. He'd sent the reports, a formatted message for every round expended, to Navsea, AmmoLant, Jenn Roald, Strike Group One, Dahlgren, and practically everyone else with a routing indicator. But heard nothing back.

"Captain?"

He sucked a brine-laden lungful and returned the salute of Angel Quincoches, the chief in charge of the VLS. Back in the Med, the swarthy, bowlegged E-7 had charged in while a rocket engine was still burning, ig-nited in its cell for a hot run. Along with Tausengelt and Slaughenhaupt, Quincoches had pushed back against Amy Singhe's "leveling management" initiative. Which had put Dan in the position of trying to balance his most innovative and aggressive junior officer against his Goat Locker. Not that they deserved equal consider-ation; when you came down to it, it was the senior en-listed who got the blueshirts working in the holes when you were prepping for an inspection—or a war, for that matter. Piss them off, and *Savo* would fall apart. But he also didn't want to step on someone who was only trying to improve things, as she saw it.

Or was he paying her extra slack because of those

dark eyes, those unexpected, yet so welcome, shoulder massages?

"They come out with a helluva big plume, the Block 4s," Quincoches was saying.

Dan tuned back in. "Sorry?"

The chief pointed at the fresh paint. "Hell of a big plume. Scorch the hell out of the paint. Sometimes, detemper the lift springs in the hatch."

"That's the high-thrust booster. You checked 'em? We don't want a hatch not to open."

"No spares," Quincoches said gloomily. "Deleted 'em from our onboard allowance. That's the problem with this just-in-time shit. They keep cutting onboard repair parts, but out here, by the time it's just in time, it's way too late. We better hope one of the controllers doesn't crap out." He looked off to where *Mitscher* still accompanied them. They would pick up *Tippecanoe* again as they passed the Maldives, giving them both an oiler and an ammunition ship. "Shed any light on where we're headed, Captain?"

"Don't know a hell of a lot more than you do, Chief. Just that we're steaming east with the strike group."

The chief shaded his eyes and peered ostentatiously around the horizon. "Ain't seen 'em. Who we got with us? Sir?"

Dan explained that the *Carl Vinson* battle group comprised *Savo* and *San Jacinto,* the two Tico-class cruisers, along with *Mitscher, Oscar Austin, Donald Cook, Briscoe, Hawes,* and *Rentz.* "And two subs, *Pitts-*

burgh and *Montpelier.* Loggies from *Tippecanoe* and *Kanawha,* and maybe pick up some more en route."

"I heard *Franklin Roosevelt* sailed early. From the West Coast."

"I'm not sure how you got that, but it's possible. *George Washington* and *Nimitz* are already out here. In WestPac, I mean."

"Who we gonna fight? Bets in the Chief's Mess are on China."

Dan forced a painful half smile. "I'm hoping it doesn't go that way."

"The Paks and Indians still going at it?"

"Far as I know, they're still fighting." In fact the Indian navy was at full wartime mobilization, with units deploying to cover the *Wuhan* task group, at the western end of the vast ocean, and others heading to the Malacca Strait.

In the same direction as the *Vinson* group, in other words. But the IO was vast; they'd most likely never come in sight of each other.

"What about the North Koreans? They're making trouble again."

Dan studied the chief's face, realizing he wanted something solid to put out to his guys. To be able to say *I talked to the CO, and here's the straight skinny.* "Chief, I'd just say that we're heading east, and the situation's confused. China's acting nuts. India's acting nuts. The exec and I are busting our asses trying to get some answers for all of us.

"But we know how to fight, and we're ready. We

proved that at Hormuz. So tell your troops, don't sweat it. We won't leave anyone holding the bag. Whatever comes over the horizon." Dan slapped the man's back. "Gotta get back to Combat. Keep at it."

"You know we will, sir," Quincoches said. "Us *middle management*."

He reeled forward along the main deck, bent into the wind, putting out a hand from time to time to a bulkhead or a lifeline as *Savo* gyrated. The sea rushed past in a continuous roar, and now and again a spatter of spray trailed over the ship, glittering in the wind. He came out of the starboard break onto the forecastle, slogged up to the bullnose, and stood facing the empty sea ahead, the wind ruffling his hair and rippling his coveralls. Channeling Kate Winslet in *Titanic*. Then faced aft, and strolled down the port side. The break was empty. They'd offloaded the three Iranians to the carrier, a big relief. Dr. Schell was still aboard, to make sure the crud was vanquished, but the plan was to offload him in Singapore. He undogged the weather deck door aft of the port refueling station. Climbed a ladder, another, and let himself into CIC.

His seat fitted him like a major leaguer's glove. The smells of warm leather and coffee and old sweat mingled with the glacier-breath of air-conditioning. He shrugged on the foul-weather jacket hung over the chair, and ran his gaze over the displays. Dave Branscombe was on, but on his far side, in the CIC officer's chair, brooded the goddesslike profile of Amarpeet Singhe.

Dan nodded to them both. "Dave. Amy. What's current?"

"Trying to get Amy up to speed, be able to slot her in on TAO if we have to."

"With your approval, of course, Captain," Singhe added. "And we'd have to put in for a waiver to BUPERS."

"Uh-huh. Well, I want the senior watch officer's and the exec's input on that. And you'd have to sit for a TAO board." Dan wasn't entirely comfortable putting her in the hot seat, but he couldn't deny they needed depth on the bench. He had only three qualified TAOs, which meant he had no backup if one took sick, or couldn't pull duty for some other reason.

It was his decision, in the end. As long as she didn't screw up, it'd probably slide on through a paper drill. But if she did, and his enemies up the chain found out . . . No, screw that. He couldn't start thinking in those terms.

The TAO situation was just the tip of the iceberg; the same problem was surfacing in his other departments. He couldn't steam in hostile seas for days on end without a fully manned watch. Yet he didn't have enough bodies to man his strike, self-defense, Aegis, sonar, and TAO seats. The only solution was to step up their efforts to qualify lower-rated personnel. And that meant deferring maintenance, so *those* personnel could spend their time training. "Okay, fine. I'll tell Matt to set up a board. So, what's happening?"

"Well, not that much since you were last here, Captain." Branscombe glanced at the screens. "Still air defense coordinator. Still getting spotty, slow updates on Geeks. But the HF jamming's stopped. Or maybe we're just out of range now."

Dan examined the leftmost screen, which showed the battle group's steaming formation. The carrier was far to the south, with the logistics ships tucked under her wing and her helicopters probing for any submerged adversaries. The next sphere out were the cruisers and destroyers. The frigates were a hundred miles ahead, tails streamed, searching the long-range, low-frequency bands for the telltale beats of submarine screws. Disagreeable to think of any ship as of less value than another, but when you came down to it, frigates were low-manning and low-cost. That made them the whiskers a strike commander liked to poke out ahead of more valuable platforms.

Also out ahead, and ranging all around the moving force, antisub fixed-wings were laying sonobuoys and working surface surveillance. In this situation, and even more so as they closed in on the strait, the group commander would be sweating bullets about threats in the area of approach.

As to their own submarines, they weren't on the radar. Obviously. The task force commander's staff, and SubPac of course, knew where they were, but no one else. Which was how they liked it.

"Merchant traffic?"

"Pretty much stopped, Captain. Everybody who's in port is staying in port."

He examined the center display, a fusion of GCCS and task force data, including *Savo*'s own picture. The

ew Chinese merchant vessels still under way had either
urned around or diverted to neutral ports. An Indian
destroyer had intercepted one, in the Arabian Sea, and
was escorting it into Jamnagar. "When do we hit chop
ongitude?"

"Midnight, sir."

As they steamed east, the strike group was leaving
Central Command for the Pacific Command. Another
clue to their destination. "And we're ready?"

"The exec was going over it with us."

"Us being . . . ?"

"The TAOs, the CIC officers, and the watch team
supervisors."

"I conducted a review of the relevant pubs and
ROEs," Singhe said.

"That's right, Amy did part of the brief. To help her
get up to speed."

"Good, that's good." Dan sighed and massaged his
cheeks. He needed a shave. And a shower. And more
sleep.

The red phone beeped. Branscombe answered.
Listened. Glanced at his watch. Said he'd pass that
information, and signed off.

"What is it?" Dan asked.

The TAO started writing in his log. "COs' conference, on the carrier, sir. Uniform is wash khakis or
ship's coveralls. Helo'll be here in an hour."

Following his escort down the vanishing-point passageways of the supercarrier, he fought the urge to throw

up. Eighty thousand tons of steel and machinery move
in a seaway, but it didn't move much, and the change
from *Savo Island*'s faster roll was disorienting. The
helo, from *Vinson,* had hopscotched from ship to ship
before returning to the carrier. He'd left Cheryl in
charge, feeling a twinge as *Savo* shrank to a gray dot
on the wide blue. But on the whole, confident she'd do
as well as he could. Maybe better, without the self-
doubt and occasional paranoia he seemed to harbor
like a malignant growth in his gut.

The conference wasn't in the wardroom, as he'd expected. His guide led him and the others from his helo
up ladder after ladder until they were far above the
flight deck. Headed for the flag level, he guessed.

Two armed sentries scrutinized his ID, checked each
CO against a list, and at last ushered them into the
tactical flag command center. The TFCC was a conference room and operations center, where the strike group
battle watch officers stood duty and conducted planning
and briefings. It had red phones, computers, large-
screen displays, projectors, and unclassified and classified videoteleconferencing capability. The other skippers
were at the far end, gathered around a mess nook with
the usual pastries and doughnuts. He valved coffee
into bone china, complete with saucer. Shook hands,
and introduced himself to captains and commanders
he didn't know. They all seemed to know him. Or at
least his name. Which might be good, or might not.

He tucked a hand under the arm holding the cup
and slouched, tuning in to the talk and speculation.

Picking up bits that could be jigsaw-puzzled together for a general picture, at least, of what was happening.

Since World War II, the Navy had been built around carrier battle groups, or strike groups, as they were latterly called. Each supercarrier was accompanied by its bristling guard of cruisers, destroyers, and submarines. In peacetime, the groups relieved one another at sea, in port, and in the yards in a rotation planned many years ahead.

In wartime, those in port could be pulled back together and put to sea, and those in the yard reconstituted. Unfortunately, there was no real reserve anymore. Since the end of the Cold War, appropriations had gone into maintaining the active forces, with the Navy Reserve almost entirely a manpower pool. The Coast Guard was behind them too, but in anything resembling a real war, their lightly armed, sensor-deficient cutters would be just inviting targets.

Now the whole vast machine was groaning into action, and millions of tons of metal and hundreds of thousands of seamen were on the move. *Nimitz* and *Washington* were already in the western Pacific. Strike Group Eight, *Eisenhower,* had been ordered out of the Gulf into the Arabian Sea, to replace *Vinson* as she headed east. In like manner, Strike Group Ten was getting under way from Norfolk to move into the Med. Strike Nine was moving up its deployment date, and Strike Four and *Franklin D. Roosevelt* had—as Chief Quincoches had mentioned—gotten under way early from San Diego.

A familiar face: Jenn Roald. Her pixieish, sharp-nosed profile homed in through the throng. She looked up and patted his sleeve. "Dan."

"Commodore. Good to see you." They shook hands. "I see you're the screen commander."

"And you're our ABM escort. You really shot down a Pakistani nuke?"

"That's what the Indians say it was."

"I want to hear about it. Everything you couldn't put in the message. But not right now. Your crew's okay? No recurrence on your Legionnaire's disease?"

"The doc's still aboard, running tests. But we might just have it licked."

"And how's the groper case coming? You've got NCIS over there, right?"

"Trying to make the arrangements. Nobody yet, though."

"Meanwhile, you're keeping your women safe? Warning them to stay in pairs, and so forth?"

He was about to say "of course, as much as I can," but a lieutenant wearing a gold aiguillette stepped in. The "Flag Loop," as the aide was called, lifted his voice. "Attention on deck."

"Please carry on, gentlemen, ladies," Tim Simko said. Short, dark-haired, round-headed, the commander, Strike Group One, looked amazingly unchanged from when Dan had played lacrosse with him at Annapolis. Yeah, the Naval Academy, when they'd dreamed of battle and glory. Now he hoped they could avoid it. Only fools dreamed of war, and only the ignorant thought it glorious. But he wasn't sure if that meant he'd grown wiser, or if he'd just seen too much. "Everyone got coffee? If you'll take seats, we'll get started."

Dan found a chair next to Roald. The admiral remained standing in front of a large-screen display. The aide handed him a clicker and dimmed the lights as the Strike One logo popped.

Simko said, "This will be a short brief, as I know you all want to get back to your units. Which is also where I want you. Thanks for coming, and greetings especially to our sub commanders, who are attending via teleconference." He nodded to a camera on a tripod. "I'll kick off, then turn it over to the chief of staff and my N-heads for the details.

"Just got off the line with Fleet, to make sure I was clear on the commander's guidance and how things are developing in the AOR. So what you'll hear today is up-to-the-minute."

Click. A map of Southwest Asia. "The nuclear exchange between Pakistan and India has stopped the invasion, but the Pakistani army has been forced back past the Indus. China has issued an ultimatum to India, to halt in place or face consequences. They've taken Bhutan, and are massing more forces at the northern border now. So India's facing a two-front war, maybe even three; Myanmar has asked Indian diplomats to leave. New Delhi's asking for our support. So far, we're trying to get both sides to the conference table, but our clout with the Pakistanis is less than it used to be."

Another image: the Indian Ocean. "Chinese, Pakistani, Iranian, Nigerian, and Burmese—what I've heard called the 'Axis' powers, though I don't know if that's

going to stick—merchant traffic through the IO ha
basically stopped; any vessel under way has been take
into custody. Beijing's assets currently in theater ar
limited, two subs and the *Wuhan* surface action group
but it's possible we could meet their forces surging wes
through Malacca while we head east. Which could turn
into a meeting engagement.

"Incidentally, we already detected those two sub
marines, Song-class, passing to the south of us. USS
Montpelier trailed them while we kicked the deci
sion upstairs, whether to attack or not. Orders came
back down to let them go, but continue tracking. The
Indian navy's been notified of their positions, courses
and speeds, using a back channel into their submarine
command."

A new slide. "As you've guessed, Strike One's
headed for the South China Sea. China's moved ai
and naval forces to the Paracel Islands, breaking a forma
agreement with Vietnam. We may head north toward
the coast; depends on how things play out. If cooler
heads prevail—and I hope they will—we'll turn around
and head back to our previous stations. If not—well
then we'll see."

In rapid succession, now, other images flicked up
"The Japanese are protesting a Chinese landing in the
Senkaku Islands, and are asking for backup. North
Korea has seized the Kaesong Joint Industrial Zone.
which it's offering to China. That would give them a
major air and naval base just north of the DMZ, and
seriously threaten allied ability to operate in the Yellow
Sea. ROK forces are going to full alert. There are also

diplomatic indications the Chinese are trying to set up other forward airfields in Timor and Brunei. Plug in long-range maritime patrol, some fighter/attack, and they could control a lot of airspace. Even if they just "persuade" some of those smaller countries to deny overflight, that increases our problem set significantly."

Simko clicked again, and the Strike One logo returned to the screen. "So we see chess pieces starting to move. And a lot's probably going on in the sub world even I don't know about . . . spooling up, moving C3 assets forward, ponying up assets from Italy and Germany and South Africa to take over as we rebalance from the Gulf and the Med."

He looked at the overhead. "Finally, we can't talk about a major conflict without addressing Taiwan. If the fat goes in the fire, the mainlanders will ramp up to get that settled once and for all. Carrier access denial in the strait would affect our operations tremendously. Meaning a lot of our surface and potentially subsurface assets not being able to break out of Yokosuka or Guam."

He beckoned to a four-striper who Dan assumed was the chief of staff. "However, it's important to remember: we're not yet at war. Right now, we're just redeploying to support our allies. I don't want to get into internal politics, but the wounding of General Zhang in Mumbai has brought the hawks in Beijing out in force. China has been beating the drums about being isolated and surrounded for years. They may see this as the opportunity to break out.

"More immediately: as we move east, our major choke point will be the Malacca Strait." A new image came up, zoomed in, and Dan recognized the narrowing northwest-to-southeast slant. "South of Kuala Lumpur, three hundred miles of narrow passage, ending at a melee of islands and the Singapore Strait. I won't kid you, we're vulnerable in close quarters." Simko searched faces, found Dan's. "But not helpless. As Captain Lenson showed us recently in the Strait of Hormuz. Dan, good to see you again."

"Good to see you too, Admiral."

"As most of you know, Captain Lenson commands USS *Savo Island,* the first of our TBMD shooters. If this mess goes hot, he'll be our umbrella. Dan, stick around after this breaks up. Got some things I'd like to go over with you." Simko turned away without waiting for an answer, and beckoned the four-striper up.

His first slide read: POLITICAL ALIGNMENTS IN SOUTHEAST ASIA. "All right . . . negotiations are ongoing, as you might imagine. Right here, right now, is where we find out who our friends are.

"Burma—Myanmar—is firmly in the Chinese camp. So far, we have commitments to provide facilities and protect our passage from Indonesia, Thailand, and Malaysia. Also, interestingly, an offer of refueling and logistics from Vietnam.

"As to Singapore. As many of you know, we've had a repair and logistics agreement there since '92, in Sembawang. But they have a large Chinese population and a lot of investment. The mainland's their largest source of imports, especially food. So far, indications are we'll probably get unmolested passage, but no fuel or other services. They might give us back-channel

I and W and contact reports. I've got the naval attaché working it . . . but right now, they're trying to play both sides. Can't really blame them, given the pol/mil geometry.

"The Europeans sound like they're going to stand clear too. Especially since the Russians are making trouble again over gas deliveries and eastern Ukraine." The captain looked at the slide. "We may get lip service from the Brits, but that's all. New Zealand's announced its neutrality. On the other hand, the Australians are with us, though it means they'll lose a lot of their raw-materials exports. We had to promise to buy their whole production for the next three months."

Dan shivered. Why did this still feel so much like 1914? The fire wasn't burning out. If anything, it was spreading. The nations were separating into opposing camps, and not always on the side they'd seemed to favor in prewar calculations. Each with its own ambitions and humiliations, throwing them onto the growing bonfire.

The briefer glanced at the sealed door, and the sentry beside it. With one outside, at the ladder landing, too, no doubt. "All right. Gentlemen, ladies . . . Everything from here on out is classified TS."

The group stirred; notepads and PDAs were turned off and put away. The first slide read:

This Briefing Is Classified
(TOP SECRET/SACHEL ADVANTAGE/IRON NOOSE)
OPLAN 5081
CHINA

Dan blinked, recognizing the same op plan Niles had showed him at the Pentagon. The next slides backed up and amplified aims, intents, and threats. The slide after that read

---

This Briefing Is Classified
(TOP SECRET/SACHEL ADVANTAGE/SABER POINT)
OPLAN 5027
NORTH KOREA

The four-striper pressed the back of his hand to his mouth. "OPLANs 5081 and 5027 have been activated. 5081 is operations against China. 5027, against North Korea. After a good deal of to-and-fro with civilian leadership, JCS has managed to get the trigger pulled on the time phased force and deployment orders. Which is why we're headed east.

"Obviously, we're never going to invade and conquer mainland China. For one thing, they have a thermonuclear arsenal. For another, we couldn't defeat the Chinese army in 1953, so we sure aren't going to now.

"The side that strikes first will gain a significant advantage. When the light turns green, we will move rapidly to disrupt command, control, and communications, breaking the kill chain that allows hostile forces to localize and target us. That includes deep strikes by Air Force stealth . . . and other measures to degrade space and cyberspace assets and sensors."

For some reason, Dan got a glance then too.

"Meanwhile, we take, hold, or neutralize offshore assets that threaten the inner island chain, while our allies mobilize and we bring up additional battle groups from the States and the Med.

"Incidentally, the cyberattacks against the continental U.S. have been traced to China. We also expect major efforts in anti-access areas and area denial, along with a push to degrade and compromise our own C4I."

The briefer shrugged. "There may be initial confusion, minor initial losses, but once we're fully mobilized, have sealed off their exits and mined their ports, we can sit tight and wait for them to come out. The East and South China Seas and the Sea of Japan will be kill zones.

"The biggest factor in our favor is economic. The U.S. and most of our allies are self-sufficient in food and energy. But China has to have imports, *and* exports. Our estimates are that they'll run out of oil and food within six months. They'll have to lay off millions, and ration food. Unemployment, inflation, food shortages: either the Zhang regime falls, or it has to deal. Economic exhaustion, hunger, plus force attrition . . . leads to the conference table, and conflict termination."

The chief of staff looked to Simko. "That concludes my briefing. Admiral?"

The battle group commander flicked to a final slide, with bulleted points. "Our terms are: regime change; renunciation of their claims to Taiwan, the Senkakus, and in the South China Sea; an end to support of North Korea; and a significantly reduced conventional order of battle. Leaving us in control in the western Pacific, and China weakened and with a more democratic government."

Simko inspected the overhead again. "Faced with those choices, we expect—or maybe it would be more accurate to say, *Washington* expects—their leadership to back down. Withdraw from India, and de-escalate with Japan. If they don't, a short war, with a compressed time frame and limited aims.

"But success will depend on speed and coordination. Strike Group One has to be ready. We will conduct a combined exercise en route to Singapore." He glanced at the door. "Your go-home packages contain a training schedule and briefings outlining the OPLANs just discussed. Restrict access and read-in to TAOs, intel, comms, strike, and AAW officers. A supplement specifies what crypto to draw and which broadcasts, settings, and other terminations to set up for follow-on data. Also, expect unannounced MDUs and practice strike operations."

Simko clicked the display back to the group logo. "All right, maybe we're getting ahead of ourselves, but I wanted you all to have the SI picture as we see it at the flag level. So there won't be any doubts, or surprises. Questions?"

Dan sat knitting his fingers. A war without doubts or surprises? The Air Force was going to conduct deep strikes, and the Chinese weren't going to retaliate? What if they thought their nuclear deterrent was being targeted?

A hand, in the back. "You mentioned the Russians, Admiral. Any idea where they're putting their chips?"

Simko shook his head. "Russia and China have been close over the past few years. A lot of arms deals. But Zhang's also mentioned a Chinese claim to Siberia. My sense is, Moscow will try to profit from both sides. . . . No other questions?" He caught Dan's eye again. "Captain Lenson, come back to my in-port cabin before you fly off."

A petty officer wheeled in a cart and began handing out sealed packages and getting signatures. The aide called "Attention on deck," and everyone rose as Simko left.

Dan blew out and stood. Even if escalation could be avoided, why should the Chinese, with the biggest army on the planet, sit on their hands until they ran out of oil and food? That didn't sound like Zhang. He was already feeding troops and support into the Chinese periphery—Pakistan, Bhutan, Myanmar, maybe North Korea. His cyberattacks had crippled U.S. transportation, financials, and security markets. Actual hostilities hadn't even started, and already both sides were wrecking each other's economies.

Brinksmanship. Bluff. And if they failed, a "six-month" war. The optimistic phrases echoed all too familiarly.

But there didn't seem to be anything concrete he could object to. And no one else had any more questions—or at least any they voiced. Leaving in the enclosed air only a stir, a subdued murmur. Above it, the aide called out the order in which they should report to the flight deck.

Trying not to look as doubtful as he felt, he started to follow the others out. Then remembered: Simko. He turned in midstride, and went through a back door into the admiral's cabin.

19

The South China Sea

The sun roared, sundering the sky. The sea shimmered flat in a burning summer heat. Already over a hundred degrees, and not yet 0800. Dan leaned over the splinter shield of the bridge wing, careful to keep his bare skin off broiling-hot steel. Looking down into a bright, deep blue, heart-stopping, sight-inviting, pulling the gaze and the mind down along the slanting shadows *Savo Island* cast like the beams of black searchlights. And here and there, every so often, a sea snake lifted its head, trailing a glittering V.

He was contemplating, once more, the advice Tim Simko had had for him, before Strike Group One had begun threading the strait. His actions off Pakistan were being viewed with disapproval in Washington.

"*Grave* disapproval, or so Fleet says," Simko had told him, the two classmates alone in the in-port flag cabin, high in *Vinson's* island. "But in view of the situation, I asked to hold on to you. There's no one else I can slot in to command my only antiballistic missile unit. They can fight until the cows come home about whether you should've shot or not, but you're still maintaining a 50 percent knock-down record. Which I gather is better than anyone back at Dahlgren expected."

Dan had rubbed the back of his neck, where it usually hurt. Actually, where it almost always hurt, if he was honest about it. "Uh, that's due more to my team than to me. I wouldn't count on those numbers every time. But . . . you stonewalled them?"

Simko had grimaced. "Yeah. I stonewalled, Dan. And not just because you were a good midfield back at the Boat School, or because we have the same class number on our rings. I've absolutely got to have *Savo* at 4.0 readiness if the shit hits the fan. Anyway, if this situation goes hot, they'll have a lot more on their plates at JCS than disciplining one trigger-happy officer."

He'd sat forward, gripping his knees. "*Trigger-happy,* Tim? I took down those missiles to protect civilians. Just like it says to, in my ROEs."

"Take it easy! I'm not saying *I* think that. Or even that it's DoD. Just that certain elements, I gather on the congressional side, have a real hard-on for you."

He'd known then exactly whom Simko meant. Who was behind the push for his disciplining and recall: Sandy Treherne. And probably others who hadn't liked his response at the congressional hearing. The hardliners. Like Ed Szerenci? Maybe. His old professor had always believed in overkill. "The last side to make the rubble jump will be the winner." Had he really said that? Well, something a lot like it. "Tim, I heard you saying the administration expects the other side to back down. And those terms you mentioned—they sound like an ultimatum."

"They do, don't they."

"I worked in the West Wing. I've seen the disconnects there, between what they wish they could do, what they eventually persuade themselves they can do, and what we can actually pull out of the fire for them. Just between us old Second Batt guys, how realistic is it that the Chinese will just . . . roll?"

Simko had just lowered his head. Not said anything. Until Dan had gotten the message, and stood. "Thanks, Tim. Guess I'd better catch that helo. Thanks for the vote of confidence. *Savo* will be there if you need her."

Simko had risen too, and shaken his hand, and said he was confident she would be. And wished him well. But in a tone Dan wasn't sure he liked. There'd been that ever-so-faint, yet unsettling, the-lights-are-going-out-all-over-the world ring to it.

Now he lifted his head, scalp baking in the burning sunlight, to survey distant clouds over islands that shimmered like fever dreams, with names from a Joseph Conrad tale. Pulau Mapur. Pulau Repong. Kepulauan Anambas. The morning sun slanting down to the east illuminated what looked like more of them, though these weren't really there. Just mirages. Illusions. Quivering chromium islands afloat on molten, glittering gold.

The Sunda Sea. The Asiatic Fleet had died here. USS *Houston* and her aged cruisers and four-pipe destroyers, the cobbled-together ABDA command. Poorly prepared, badly led, outnumbered, outgunned, and outmaneuvered, they'd gone under in a hail of fire. So completely wiped out that even their fates had been matters of conjecture, until the few surviving POWs had emerged from the hell-camps at war's end.

He looked back at ship after ship emerging between low, shockingly green islands. Destroyers, cruisers, and far behind them, like a thundercloud, the immense square bulk of the carrier. Specks glittered and swam around her; helicopters, searching the shallow seas as they negotiated the channel out. A submarine could lie doggo, hugging the bottom, to all intents and purposes part of it. Until it rose, and struck.

But so far, the screen had discovered nothing. Strike One had threaded the strait at full alert, but detected no threat. Now *Savo*'s Aegis, reaching out three hundred miles north and east, over one and a third million square miles of the South China Sea, outlined a watery prairie as empty as if they were the only navy that existed.

He'd steamed these tropic seas before. In the old *Oliver Gaddis,* when an order that hadn't really been an order had sent him to find, and destroy, a ship most said didn't exist—

"Captain?" The exec was rubbing her eyes and studying her ever-present BlackBerry.

"Cheryl. What've we got?"

"I'd like to put Amy on the watch bill. I know she's not school-qualified, but she's studied hard. And served six tricks under instruction, during the transit. She's ready."

Dan cleared his throat, searching for a reason why not, but couldn't come up with one. At last he said that was all right. Staurulakis made a note. "Next, our urinalysis quota—"

"Drop it," Dan told her. "No more pee tests. Administrative requirements, reports, inspections—draw a line through them. Fully manned watches, essential maintenance, last-minute training. That's all I want on tomorrow's plan of the day."

"Yessir. We got a response on those extra eductor fittings you wanted. None in the system."

He grimaced. "Just great. Okay, a complete check of the firemain system. Isolation valves, auto and manual, and drill each of the repair parties on bridging them in case of rupture. Check all the jumpers—"

"Banca boat to port, Captain." The JOOD, binoculars to his eyes.

One of the small craft native to these seas. Dan twisted, to make sure the remote operating console on the 25mms had it hooked up. The operator met his eye and winked. "Keep him outside a mile," Dan told the OOD. "Warn him off with the loud hailer if he looks to be headed this way." Then went back to discussing the schedule. "That's what we want to drill. Damage control, dewatering, restoring power. And medical— get Dr. Schell to help Doc Grissett update our first aid and battle dressing training. With particular attention to burns. Everything else, we drop. From here on in, it's real world." The exec jotted again, then shifted to her Hydra.

"Bridge, CIC—Radio. Skipper there?"

He leaned to depress the 21MC lever. "Lenson."

"Captain, flash message. Warning order from Pa-Com. Message board to the bridge, or will you take it on the LAN?"

"I'll take it in CIC." He sucked air and swung his legs down. What now? Staurulakis stepped aside, still on the Motorola, but shot him a worried frown as he brushed past.

In Combat again, in the same worn chair. The same displays, the same flicker from the rightmost status board, which seemed to be slowly dying. Dan told Mills to have it checked out, and logged into the CO's terminal.

The news wasn't good. USS *George Washington* had hit not one but two mines coming out of Yokosuka, warping her shafts and shutting down one of her reactors. The carrier was experiencing power loss and was limited to five knots. No one had claimed responsibility, though it was easy to assume the mines had been submarine-laid. The Japanese were resweeping the channel.

The second flash described a civilian airliner crash on the main runway at Osan Air Base, effectively shutting down Seventh Air Force operations in South Korea.

The third raised U.S. readiness condition to DEF-CON 3, with PaCom and CentCom at DEFCON 2, immediate readiness for nuclear war. He read this three times, incredulity deepening with each perusal. U.S. forces hadn't gone to condition two since the Cuban missile crisis, when SAC had been placed on fifteen-minute standby.

The final flash was to *Savo Island.* Halfway through, he twisted in his chair. "Donnie. Chief Wenck!"

"Present!"

"You read this, Donnie?"

"The SAR? Just got through it, boss. Writing up the ack message. The Terror's setting up the laptop."

It was a satellite acquisition request, directing the SPY-1 to steer its beam to a given volume of space, setting up its sensor parameters . . . in essence, telling it where to look and what to look for. In this case, according to the tasking order, that "something" was nearly a hundred miles up and moving at an ungodly speed. He scanned down the rest of the message. "What's the nomenclature on this? Let's get Bill Noblos down here. We may need him on this one."

"It's in a low polar orbit. Period about ninety minutes." Mills flipped pages in a red-covered pub titled *Draft Tactics for Engaging Ballistic and Orbital Targets,* then riffed on his keyboard. "NORAD catalog number 20404, for what it's worth. And ephemeris data. But that doesn't tell us what it is."

Dan reread the order. *Acquire, track, and prepare to engage.* A polar-orbiting body, or technically speaking, a ninety-degree inclination orbit, moved north to south, or south to north, while the earth rotated beneath it. The item they were directed to look for circled the globe every hour and a half. So that over twenty-four hours, it crossed over, or at least within reasonable slant range of, every point on the planet.

The ideal orbit for a reconnaissance satellite, whether its sensors be cameras, radars, or something more sophisticated, like the far-infrared detectors of the Obsidian Glint early-launch warning satellites. "It's a recon bird?" he asked anyone who cared to answer.

"That'd be my guess." Noblos settled into a seat on the far side of the CIC officer. He wore civilian slacks, a *Savo Island* light blue nylon running jacket, and a soft wool cap. "In a low polar orbit? Probably synthetic aperture radars, for ocean recon. Like our Lacrosse series."

Mills added, "But all we actually have is object number and orbital parameters."

"Could be some kind of comm relay," Wenck put in.

"Doubtful," said Noblos. "They put those in a synchronous orbit, so they're always over the same spot."

Dan lifted his eyebrows. Was it really possible they were being asked to acquire a satellite? "Uh, how long to acquisition? Until it's overhead?"

Wenck said patiently, "By then it's too late to do anything about it. We gotta hop on it the second it pops over the horizon, clears atmospheric lensing effects."

"All right, and how long is that?"

"That's gonna be"—Wenck peered past Terranova—"two minutes, fifteen seconds."

Dan sat back, reviewing the order. It was to acquire and, yes, "prepare to engage." The SPY-1 output was focused into a narrow, coherent beam by the phased arrays. The octagonal antenna faces were made up of dozens of radiating elements. Since waves from nearby sources interfered with each other, shifting the phase of the signals pointed the beams left, right, up, and down, within certain stops imposed by the physics of interference phenomena. To detect something as small, as fast, and as far away as their target, the beam had to be both extremely narrow and aimed exacty where it would appear. Like trying to track a fastball with a laser pointer . . . you had to start with the laser on the ball the moment it left the pitcher's hand.

He twisted in his seat, fighting the urge to go over and kibitz. "Donnie, Terror, we set to acquire?"

"Not yet, Captain." Wenck was busy on the Dell laptop that connected to the Aegis console by a cable, an arrangement that had always struck Dan as absurdly ad hoc. But, hey, off the shelf was popular . . . regardless of whether it was milspec, shock-hardened, or EMP-protected. The chief frowned at his screen. "Getting an error message. Fuck."

"What kind of error message?" Dan asked him.

"Delta AM on the array face. Hot weather like this, you get thermal distortion on the edges of the array faces."

"You can tune for that," Noblos observed. "Apply a bias correction factor. Haven't you been doing that?" He dragged his stool noisily to the console, where he was soon deep in the weeds with Wenck, Terranova, and the assistant SPY-1 petty officer.

Dan knitted his fingers, getting apprehensive. At the tremendous speed this thing was moving, much faster than the suborbital projectiles they'd engaged to date, they had to take it head-on. Otherwise the Block 4 just wasn't fast enough; its target would zip past unharmed as the seeker fell back into the thermosphere, ablated, and burned.

But he couldn't, not with two minutes to set up. They might acquire, but they couldn't fire on this first pass. Ninety minutes from now was the soonest they'd be set, when it came around again.

"And . . . there it is," Noblos announced drily. "Be sure to log that correction. That's the tweak you need when the array gets unevenly heated. We saw a lot of that at the test site in Kwaj."

"Target acquired. Designate . . ." The petty officer's voice trailed off. There was no proword for "satellite." "Uh, Satellite Alfa."

Wenck muttered, "Man, this thing is struttin'. Look at that range gate. Five miles a second. That's . . . eighteen thousand miles an hour. And the cross section fluctuates, fuck's with that?"

"Maybe rotating," Terranova suggested.

"A recon bird, rotating? Probably just the antennas changing their angle to us."

No one said anything for several seconds, as Wenck or maybe Terranova turned up the audio on the signal going out. For some reason the unsteady, low-frequency rattle sounded eerie today. "Okay," Wenck muttered. "Noodge the range gate a little more . . . got it. No, wait, lost it . . . lock on. Intermittent. This thing's really fucking small. And it's way out there, slant range four hundred miles . . . out of engagement range on this pass, anyway."

"Put it on the screen," Mills said.

It came up, not video but the range gate brackets, vibrating as usual, clamped around the contact, and the data readouts flickering, and at the bottom of the display a blank black area that Dan guessed was the sea horizon. He leaned back again.

Object 02-4064 was a recon bird. Most likely Chinese. It made sense to take it out, if a war was starting. But no one had ever shot down another country's satellite. Only their own, falling out of orbit, or in tests of the few antisatellite interceptors that had ever existed. Reaching out to this one was going to be at the very outside envelope of Block 4's and Aegis's capabilities. In a sense, it was astonishing he could even consider trying.

He remembered how impressed he'd been, back at the start of his career, at how far out the old *Reynolds Ryan*'s dual-purpose five-inch 38s could reach. Now their eighteen-thousand-yard range seemed laughable, primeval . . .

. . . No, goddamn it. He pinched his cheek painfully, catching a doubtful glance from the CIC officer. He'd gotten maybe four hours a night, going through the Singapore Strait, alert for air strikes or the lurking submarine, maybe a sub-laid mine. What had he been thinking about . . . oh yeah. That no one had ever shot down another country's satellite. Would it be an act of war? Did anyone even bother to *declare* war anymore? Maybe the whole idea was passé, like dueling.

Okay, time to let everybody know what was going on. He picked up the red phone and waited for the sync.

The comm problem, whatever it had been, had gone away, or been fixed; anyway, the circuit didn't squeal, just synced smoothly. The tasking message had come from Pacific Command, but Strike One and Fleet would be monitoring too, and logging the conversation for history. Alert for any more Dan Lenson screwups . . . He said slowly and clearly, "PaCom, this is *Savo Island,* over." On covered nets, there was usually no need to use call signs, though sometimes you did, depending on what the SOP directed.

A hiss, a crackle. *"Savo, this is PaCom. Over."*

"*Savo Island* Actual. In respect of your order to track and prep to engage NORAD catalog 20404, low polar orbital object 02-4064. Over."

"This is PaCom. Go ahead. Over."

"This is *Savo.* We have lock-on at this time. Over."

"This is PaCom. Cleared for autonomous engagement. Intercept and terminate. Over."

Dan swallowed. "Um . . . This is *Savo Island.* Unable to comply at this time. We have radar track and lock-on, but due to range and speed limitations, the target is too far east and too far above the horizon to engage. The next opportunity will be on its next orbit, ninety minutes from now."

"This is PaCom. Copy all. Interrogative: Can you intercept and terminate at that time?"

Dan cupped the handset, keeping his finger off the Sync button. "Donnie, before I answer him, homer on the Block 4's infrared, right? Is it even gonna home on an ice-cold satellite?"

"It's not purely infrared, Captain. That's just part of the decoy-penetration algorithm."

"So that's a yes, it'll radar-home?"

"Hey, I ain't guaranteeing it's gonna do shit," Wenck muttered.

"What's that, Chief?"

"Nothing, sir. But you also gotta . . . gotta remember, this thing's moving in longitude, too. Like, the earth turns under it. So it's not gonna pop above the horizon at the same place as before."

"Wenck, I'm on the phone to PaCom. Are we gonna be able to knock this thing down or not?"

Wenck turned those blue blue eyes to Dan without seeming to see him. As if a million calculations were streaming past behind them. He didn't answer for a second. Then said, "Sir, I don't know. Gonna be damn close, all I can say. A diagonal speed vector along with the crossing geometry. And if there's any maneuvering juice at all on that thing, any smarts built in so it can dodge once it knows somebody's trying to hit it, the answer's definitely gonna be no."

Dan blinked, still holding the phone. Met Noblos's lifted eyebrows, folded arms, his half smirk. As if their failure would prove, in some way, his own superiority. But he had to put that aside. For now. "Bill, what's your call? Can we knock this thing down?"

"*Savo, this is PaCom. Over.*"

He didn't answer, waiting for the civilian physicist. Who at last drawled, "Well, now that I've got it tuned for your technicians, Captain . . . it *might* be within the outer edge of the engagement envelope. *Theoretically.* If everything worked *perfectly.* But I'd have to say . . . the odds are against you."

That seemed to be all they were was going to get. He pressed Transmit. "PaCom, *Savo.* Our intercept capabilities against satellites are . . . marginal. How badly do you want this guy taken out? That will impact salvo size and any refires needed. Over."

"This is PaCom. We need it taken down. ASAP. On its next orbit, if at all possible. Expend what ordnance is necessary. Over."

Dan exchanged glances with Mills. The TAO was frowning, pointing up at the weapons inventory board. "This is *Savo.* Two issues. First: This is a Chinese satellite, correct? We had not understood here that hostilities had gone hot. Interrogative tasking. Over."

The distant voice turned hard. *"Far above your pay grade, Captain. But for your information, an Air Force Rivet Joint recon plane is missing east of Hainan Island. We suspect shootdown. Execute your orders. Over."*

Okay, that was clear enough. "This is *Savo.* Roger on execution. However, important to make clear we have only eight, I say again, numeral eight, TBMD birds remaining. Interrogative: Will there be resupply? Interrogative: How many should I commit to this mission? Over."

"This is PaCom. I say for the last time: expend what is necessary. Report results ASAP. PaCom out."

He blew out, resocketed the handset, and exchanged

astonished looks with Mills. "Okay, that clarifies things."

"They really want this thing off the board."

"If it's synthetic aperture radar, it can track forces anywhere in the Pacific, and pass targeting on our battle groups."

"But if we do, it legitimizes their shooting down our satellites too," Noblos put in. "Which they definitely can. A multistage solid-fuel kinetic-kill vehicle from Xichang Satellite Launch Center—"

Wenck said, "But they already shot down our recon plane, right? I'd say, it's game on, and we're ten points behind."

Dan glanced at his watch. "Like the man says: above our pay grades. All right, eighty-two minutes until it comes around again. We've got an orbital plotting function in GCCS, right? Get that up where we can see it. Also, dig out what exactly this thing is, and get the EWs tuned in if it's radiating. Donnie, if we shoot a two-round salvo, will we have time to refire? Or have to wait until the orbit after that? Sounds like this is getting urgent."

But Wenck was shaking his head. "We can't refire on the next orbit, Dan—I mean, Captain. Each pass, the track moves west, remember? Or the earth rotates out from under it . . . whichever way you want to put it. If we miss on this go-round, we're not gonna see this thing again until tomorrow."

Dan blew out again. Right; with a period of ninety minutes, that would be about . . . twenty-two degrees of longitude with each pass, or, here near the equator—

"Fifteen hundred miles," Wenck supplied, apparently doing the same calculation, but faster. "*Way* out of range. So this coming up is gonna be our one whack at this piñata."

Which also explained why PaCom had been so insistent that they fire *now*. They were isolating the battlefield; taking down the sensors the other side needed to fight an over-the-horizon battle. Just as Simko had predicted.

But he was the guy with his butt in the crack, squeezed between astrophysics, operational necessity, and emptying magazines. He felt for the Fire key, on its steel chain around his neck with his Academy-issue dog tags. "TAO, set up for three-round engagement. Pass what's going on to the battle group commander. Give somebody else the air defense mission. Do we need to steam west, Donnie? Will that improve our geometry?"

He glanced at the geo plot, overlaid now with the green curved lines of the satellite track function. They didn't have a hell of a lot of sea room before slamming into the Malay Peninsula, but he could run in that direction for eighty-two minutes.

"Thirty or forty miles is not going to make a difference," Noblos sniffed.

"But it can't hurt. Let's come to two-seven-zero and kick her up to flank. Prepare for three-round engagement." He stood, stretching the pain out of his back and neck, staring at the GCCS. Taking in the whole vast bowl of the China Sea, and the increasing number of air and sea contacts up to the north, off the coast.

So both sides trudged toward war. Like sleep-walkers . . .

An hour later, they were fully manned. Two watch sections, including Cheryl and Amarpeet, crowded CIC. Dan wanted them all in on this. Not just for training, but so they could say they'd been here when it started—the first offensive step of the war that now seemed unavoidable, though chat kept reporting UN efforts to avert it. No further news on *George Washington,* but another civilian airliner had attempted an approach, to Yokota Air Base. A Japanese F-16 had brought it down short of the runway, unfortunately into a heavily popu-lated part of Tokyo.

The customary litany of warning bells, dampers be-ing shut, main decks being sealed, streamed past but barely registered. He leaned on one elbow, wondering if he should fire three missiles or four. Four would cut his inventory in half. But PaCom had made it clear this thing had to come down. Finally he told Mills to make it a three-round salvo. "I know it's not doctrine, but let's just shoot, shoot, shoot. Then look, and maybe shoot again. Maybe."

"The numbers aren't there, Captain," Noblos put in. "You could go with two. Or even one, and save the taxpayers from throwing away more money. I don't believe you have decent P-sub-K on any of them."

Dan waved Longley and a sandwich off, then re-lented. He picked at chips and a pickle in between scrolling down intel updates. Japan had just announced mobilization, and the Diet had approved conscription, for the first time since World War II. The Republic of Korea was already mobilized, and Seoul, only a few miles from the DMZ, was being evacuated.

He shivered, recalling the eerie wail of the sirens there during the weekly drills. Both halves of that divided country had been on a near-war footing since the armistice. Now they were preparing for a rematch.

He'd read through OPLAN 5081. He had to keep reminding himself that GCCS wasn't always accurate. But it looked like the first stage, positioning forces behind Taiwan and in blocking positions in the passages out of the Sea of Japan and the East China Sea, was almost complete.

Once Strike One joined up with its Australian contingent, it would neutralize and bypass the Spratly Islands, off the Vietnamese coast. The Vietnam People's Navy would occupy and hold behind them. They'd claimed the Spratlys for centuries, and only lost them to the Chinese in 1988; he suspected their repossession would be Hanoi's reward for joining the allies. Strike One could then continue north to seize or at least neutralize the Paracels.

At that point, an iron ring of sensors and weapons would encircle the Middle Kingdom. The allied advance would stop there, hold whatever counteroffensive the Chinese could mount, and contemplate the next step. If one would be necessary; the administration seemed to assume the blockade would force war termination, in and of itself.

Just as the British had thought, in 1914, that their

naval blockade would force Germany to the peace
table. He shook his head, comparing the GCCS display
to the deployment chart in the op order. Everything
seemed to be moving into place, except for the hole
south of Kyushu where the *Washington* battle group
should've been. Losing the carrier's airborne sensors
and ASW aircraft left a huge gap in the defenses.

"SAR complete."

"Stand by for sunup . . . counting down . . . five . . .
four . . . three . . . two . . . *one*."

"Satellite Alfa above the horizon. Still in atmospheric distortion . . . Target acquired." Terranova's
soft, determined voice. "Stand by . . . lock-on, Satellite
Alfa."

Dan got up and stalked through CIC, back to the
electronic warfare stacks. Put his hands on the operator's shoulders from behind, and studied the green
flicker of the SLQ-32. "What have we got?"

"I'm not picking up anything, Captain." The tech explained that if it was an ocean recon bird, it would be
putting out power in the X band, giving its radar a res-
olution of about a meter. "That'd be adequate to pick
up aircraft. Even something the size of a tank. If it's a
comm relay, we'd copy that, too. But—"

"But what?" Dan glanced back to the command
desk.

"We're not picking up shit, sir. Maybe a very faint,
intermittent transponder emission. That's all."

"Captain," Mills called. Dan wheeled and jogged
back.

They had track again. The same tiny contact as

before, creeping above the artificially generated black cutout of the radar horizon. Cupped by the vibrating brackets of the Aegis lock-on. "Permission to engage?" Mills murmured.

Dan nodded. It didn't matter what it was. Their orders were clear. "Released." He flicked up the red cover and hit the Fire Auth switch.

Next to him, Mills murmured, "Confirm, batteries released for three-round engagement. Shifting to auto mode."

Out of the corner of his eye Dan noted Mills lifting his hands from the keyboard, like a pianist finishing a demanding piece. Wenck and Noblos had set the no-fire threshold to .1, one-tenth. If ALIS calculated a lesser probability of kill, she wouldn't fire. A hush the space of a drawn breath stilled the compartment. His gaze darted to the ordnance status board, to the surface radar picture, to the GCCS; then flicked back to the Aegis display.

The bellow of the rocket motor sounded muffled, more distant this time than usual. For a second he wondered if it was some sort of misfire or abort. Then Mills reached for the joystick, and pivoted the camera on the aft missile deck.

The picture came up center screen. A solid white wall whirled, thinned, illuminated from above; then blew off, gradually revealing a calm green sea. Then it was blotted out by a harsh illumination so brilliant the camera blanked, before opening its eye again to more smoke. "Bird one away," Terranova announced. "Bird two away . . . bird three away. Rounds complete from after magazine."

Mills joysticked the camera to follow pinpoints of flame until they winked out of sight. "Stand by for refire. Select and authorize missiles eleven and twelve in forward magazine."

They'd agreed on a shoot-shoot-shoot sequence, with three in the first salvo, then a look, with two missiles prepared for a refire. Dan doubted they'd have time for a second salvo, fast as this thing was traveling, but if PaCom needed it shot down, *Savo* wouldn't fail for lack of trying. As to what would happen after that . . . he put that aside. The fog of war was shrouding the whole Pacific.

"Twenty seconds to intercept," Noblos announced.

On the right-hand screen, the white dot crept steadily higher. The horizon was out of sight now, below the beam. The brackets pulsed, not so much vibrating as swelling and then shrinking. Probably a reaction to the varying reflectivity they'd noted on the first orbit. Terranova had posited it might be rotating, presenting different faces of an irregular body. But why would a recon satellite *rotate*? There had to be some other explanation.

Unless this wasn't a recon satellite . . .

"Stand by for intercept . . . *now*."

The white dot suddenly novaed. It wobbled, pulsating much more wildly, brightening and dimming. The brackets slewed back, slipped off, steered back on. But their grip seemed less certain. Off-center. "What's that mean?" Dan called. "Donnie? Bill?"

"Not sure."

"Could we have a hit?"

"More likely a near miss," Noblos called back. He didn't sound excited, or even involved. Once more Dan wondered why the guy seemed so pessimistic about the system he himself had helped engineer. He really ought to have inquired more closely into the relationships among the Missile Defense Agency, the Navy Advanced Projects Office, the Johns Hopkins Applied Physics Laboratory, the Commander, Operational Test and Evaluation Force, and Boeing, Lockheed Martin, and Raytheon. All had taken part in the design of the Block 4 and the thrust-vector-control booster. He'd met some of the monsters that lurked in the Navy's development labyrinth, back when he'd worked with Tomahawk. Not everyone wanted a new program to succeed. But he couldn't believe Noblos actually wanted them to fail. More likely negativity was just part of his personality.

"Second round intercepts . . . *now.*"

The radar return pulsed, but didn't strobe this time. Actually, Dan couldn't see any effect. "Are we calling that a miss?"

The EW operator called, "Transponder ceased emitting."

The CIC officer walked back, and returned. "The signal was intermittent, but he was hearing it. Then it stopped."

"Stand by for impact, shot three . . . *now.*"

The blip smeared across the screen, so sudden and

bright the watchers flinched. When the trace dimmed, it left only the by-now-familiar returns of spinning debris. The shrapnel from their TBM shootdowns had been incandescent hot. This chaotic, random flicker expanded across the screen like galaxies in a cooling, aging universe. "Direct hit," Wenck said.

"Concur," muttered Mills laconically.

"Good job, everyone. I really wasn't sure we were going to make that basket. Report it on covered voice." Dan leaned back, cradling aching kidneys with both hands.

Mills resocketed the red phone. "Strike One says Bravo Zulu on the shootdown. *Savo Island,* return to formation. Launch helo and sanitize Sector Hotel before the strike group passes through it."

"Anything from PaCom?"

"They acknowledged." Mills hesitated.

"What else?"

"Nothing, sir. They acknowledged the report. Asked how many rounds were expended. I told them, three."

"Very well. Make it so," Dan said. "Bravo Zulu" meant "well done." But the lack of any comment from PaCom was less reassuring. Oh, well. They probably had more on their minds than patting *Savo*'s back. Though it would've been nice to have something to pass on to the team, over and above his own congratulations.

The ear-piercing shriek of the boatswain's pipe made him plug his ears. *"Now secure from condition three TBMD. Set condition three wartime steaming. Now flight quarters, flight quarters. All hands man your*

*flight quarters stations for launch of Red Hawk 202.
Stand clear topside aft of frame 315. Smoking lamp is
out throughout the ship. Now flight quarters."*

Strike One scrubbed that evening's exercises, and set
EMCONs, emission controls, which restricted both radars and communications. *Savo* ran silent, except for
her sonars. They were headed north as quietly as possible, then. He guessed taking down Object 20404 had
been intended to help cover their advance. The Chinese
had to know they were out here, but without a more exact localization, the battle group would be impossible
to target. Red Hawk was out again after refueling and
crew rest, taking turns with *Hawes*'s helo "sanitizing"
the intended track for submarine threats.

He was sitting at the coffee table in the wardroom
that night, holding a copy of *Undersea Technology* but
not looking at it, just sitting blankly staring at the big
Tom Freeman painting of the Battle of Savo Island,
when Staurulakis plumped down next to him. "Hate to
interrupt, Captain."

He sighed. "What is it, XO?" Then, seeing "Sheriff"
Toan behind her, he put the magazine aside.

Leaning in, the exec told him one of the female petty
officers had reported she'd been raped. "She was on the
way to her berthing area when the overhead lights in
the passageway went off. Someone grabbed her from
behind, pressed a pointed object to her neck, and steered
her into an equipment room." Staurulakis paused, then

added, "He made her undress, and raped her. He's gone all the way now."

"Oh, no," Dan said. "So, it *wasn't* Shah, or the other Iranians. Is she okay? I mean, not is she *okay,* but he didn't wound her, did he? This knife—"

"Superficial cuts. But she's in shock. Grissett and Dr. Schell are treating her. Hermelinda's there too." Staurulakis looked at the magazine, and turned it facedown on the table. Added, softly, "It was the Terror."

For a second he didn't understand. Then, to his horror, did. "You mean, Beth . . . Petty Officer Terranova?" She nodded. "My God, I . . ." He abandoned the sentence. There was nothing adequate to say. "I'll come right down."

"If you don't mind, Captain, better to give her some privacy. It might just be the shock speaking. But let's let the medical people handle this for now. Get her calmed down, gather the evidence—"

The wardroom door banged open. Amy Singhe, cheeks livid. She stalked toward them between the tables, fists clenched. "I told you this would happen, Commander!" she shouted at Staurulakis. "I told you we weren't safe aboard this fucking ship."

Staurulakis bolted to her feet. She was smaller-boned than Singhe, but not much shorter. "Not here, Lieutenant. And watch your language."

Singhe looked past her at Dan. "You're telling *him*? Nothing changes. The chiefs still treat the women like peons. They still get groped, down in the working spaces. They come to me, not the command. Because the *command* does nothing. This has been on the way for a long time. And now it's here."

Another slammed-open door; Chief Tausengelt's leathery visage was stormy. He rolled in fast, only to be whirled on by a furious Lieutenant Singhe. "Here he is. Tell the captain what you said, *Master Chief.*"

"All I said was—"

Singhe curled her lip. "All he said was, 'She shouldn't have been alone." That 'they all deserve it.' *Tell him!*" She was almost screaming, jabbing a finger in the old chief's face.

"You heard me wrong, sir. I mean, ma'am. That's not exactly what I—"

"Amy," the XO said warningly. "Better cool it. Lieutenant."

Dan was on his feet. "We are *not* doing this here! My cabin, *now!*" This was getting out of hand. "We don't have time to split the crew up over this. We're headed for a hostile coast, coming in range of enemy air. We could be in action at any time."

"You think the crew's not already split, sir? That the chiefs can do no wrong? As if they don't know who's doing this. And maybe, even, *shielding* him?"

Dan kept from shouting, but not by much. "You're really disappointing me, Lieutenant. Are you alleging some kind of conspiracy? That some people *know* who the fondler, I mean, the rapist, is, and aren't sharing that with the command?"

Singhe just shook her head and looked away, folding her arms. "I'll save it for the NCIS. That's our only chance to get the maggots out in the sunlight." She glanced at him, dark eyes both angry and, somehow, pitying. "It was part of the command climate, before you arrived. But now it's taking place on *your* ship. Sorry if the fallout hurts you. I tried to tell you. But you wouldn't listen. So now it's all going to hit the fan."

She wheeled and stalked out. Tausengelt grabbed Dan's elbow. "That bitch . . . I mean, the lieutenant . . . she's gone over the edge, Captain. I swear to you, if any of the chiefs knew anything about this, we'd have the guy in irons. We know this shit is tearing the ship apart. Taking it to the NCIS isn't going to help."

Another woman had come in: Petty Officer Redmond, hair up in braids; one of Terranova's friends, Dan recalled. Deathly pale, she met no one's eyes. "Sir? Ma'am? I heard, I heard that Terror—"

"Just a moment, Redmond. Only one thing will help," Cheryl Staurulakis said. "Finding out who did it. Until then, everybody's a suspect. And we don't have any choice about calling in the NCIS. They'd have been here already if we hadn't been in wartime steaming, with ship-to-ship transfers limited to operational necessity."

Dan barely restrained himself from covering his face with his hands. "Shut up, all of you!" he shouted. They went quiet instantly, turning shocked faces to him. "Now listen up. I'm going down to see Terranova. Exec, draft a message to the carrier, requesting they send their agent at the first possible opportunity."

"Aye aye, sir."

"Master Chief, we're locking down. Everyone who doesn't need a knife in the performance of his work, turn it in to the chief master-at-arms. I don't care what the regs say, I want *all* knives turned in, *all* lockers searched for compromising materials. All unmanned spaces will be locked when not in use. Passageways outside berthing spaces will be random-patrolled by the master-at-arms force."

"Got it, Captain."

"Have Dr. Schell see me as soon as he's done treating his patient. Any other measures to prevent this happening again that you can think of, bring them to me, and I'll approve them." He stared at the stony faces, their sidelong glares, and despaired. How could he fight his ship, when the lead Aegis petty officer had just been raped? Take *Savo* into battle, with the chiefs and the female officers at loggerheads? While some faceless evil slithered among them, anonymous, unknown, corrupting morale and trust?

For a moment, he contemplated just giving up. But that was futile. No one else could fill his shoes. Perhaps Singhe was right. Maybe he *hadn't* listened closely enough. Been proactive enough. Whatever had happened, he was to blame.

He was the captain.

He looked at their faces again, at Staurulakis's rapidly blinking eyes, the old chief's leathery careful nonexpression, the female petty officer's trembling outrage, the master-at-arms' dropped gaze. Cleared his throat. "Now go. And let's try hard not to make this even worse than it is."

20

Off the China Coast

GCCS crashed again at 0130 the next morning. Dan learned about it when the TAO called an hour later. *"We thought it'd come back up again. But so far it hasn't. And, to be honest, we figured you needed the shut-eye, Skipper."*

Dan cupped the handset against his pillow, in that singular half-awake state where his brain could give rational answers while the rest of his body stayed asleep. "Uh, that's fine, Dave. But . . . it never came back up, I take it."

"Not yet, sir. And now our last satcomm path's intermittent. Unless it gets well, that takes down VTC, SHF, EHF, UHF. That's POTS, e-mail, chat, video, browsing. Essentially, everything."

He sat up in the bunk, grinding sleep off his eyeballs. Remembering, with a sinking heart, last night's conversation with Petty Officer Terranova, in sick bay.

She'd avoided his eyes. Saying, in flat sentences, that she didn't know if she'd be able to go back on duty. He hadn't tried to persuade her. Just told her to take what time she needed. For now, Donnie and the assistant radar system controller, Eastwood, would have to share the watch, with Noblos backing them up. Though not being military, the physicist couldn't do military things.

But . . . no chat, no data? Emission control had silenced radar and bridge-to-bridge radio, but usually commanders left satellite-mediated comms up. The servers were almost always ashore, and signals basically just went up and down from individual ships to the satellites. It would be difficult for an enemy to pick up such highly directional, ultra-high-frequency signals. And of course data and voice transmissions were scrambled.

Unfortunately, the Navy hadn't drilled in a non-data-linked environment for so long, it was an open question whether they could operate without it. It had meant less independent operations, more hands-on control by Higher, and a zero-tolerance mentality for any misstep.

But, philosophy aside, without satellite data, the fleet wouldn't have a threat picture, or over-the-horizon targeting capability. "We still have receive-only comms, right?"

The comm officer sounded uneasy. *"Problems with that, too, sir. Chief's speculating TADIXS, the strike data system, may be getting jammed or phase-shifted. We're trying to get up on the old HF broadcast, but it's a goat-rope. The pool of people who remember those legacy systems is pretty small. And it's only about a thousand-baud data rate."*

"Okay, well, press on. Oh, and check the Inmarsat—we might be able to use commercial comms, at least, if the military systems go down. Status of Red Hawk?"

"Relieved on station by Hawes's bird. Crew rest and maintenance."

Dan signed off. He hung up and lay back, but after a few minutes sat up again, clicked the light on, and reached for the J-phone. The watch supervisor in Radio had a different explanation for the comm problem. She said they actually were getting transmissions from the satellites, but couldn't break them. *"All we get is a hiss, as if we've got the wrong key. But we've checked eight or nine times. Something's off, but we don't know what."*

"We had problems with scrambled voice before . . . that delayed-sync issue. Could there be a common point of failure?"

"If it was only on our end, the other ships'd be receiving. And they're not."

"How do we know that, Petty Officer? If we can't talk to them?"

"We're reading maintenance discussing the issue, sir. It's not just Strike One. It's PacFleet. Maybe worldwide. Something even weirder—staff comm-oh got Strike One to send Mitscher out to the east, she's already pretty far out there toward the Philippines, to see if she could upload, without revealing our location.

Guess what? Mitscher *uploaded fine. It's the download that doesn't break into clear data, when we get it."*

Just peachy. Approaching the Paracel Islands, two hundred miles off the Chinese coast . . . where coastal radars, air defenses, and cruise missile batteries would be waiting for them . . . and they couldn't talk to each other, or pass targeting data. Other than by signal flags or flashing light.

"Sir? You there?"

"Yeah. Thanks. Carry on, and call me if anything changes."

He lay there worrying. A Vietnamese naval infantry brigade was joining the strike group, embarked in a World War II LST, to provide the ground assault force. They were being escorted by Vietnamese light units, frigates, corvettes, and missile boats. But they couldn't carry out a landing in data silence; the American covering force would be blind to any riposte from the mainland.

Which meant that sooner or later, probably sooner, *Savo* was going to get the order to light off her SPY-1 again, and report what she saw.

Which would make her the target for every enemy aircraft, ship, and submarine in the South China Sea.

At 0500 his Hydra chirped. This time it was Danenhower, calling from Main Control with the news that the machinery control system was being flexed. Dan muttered, "Okay, CHENG, it's 'flexed.' Tell me what that means."

"Okay, well, you know each system's controlled at three levels: on the bridge, in a central control station, and locally, in each machinery space. MCS lets 'em all talk to each other. So if we lose control on the bridge during battle, say, we have to press throttle commands and steering down to the local level."

"We're going to have a slower response time, again? Is that the bottom line here?"

"Not exactly. I'm saying we got bugs in our software, sir. We'll have additional asses in the chairs down here, to be ready to take over if you lose control. I'm not saying it's gonna happen, just that we're making sure we're ready, if it does. Since . . . we are at war, right?"

Dan said they seemed to be, and he appreciated the thinking ahead. He hung up, then looked at the bulkhead clock. Almost dawn. No point trying to sleep any longer.

Since almost everyone was at his or her battle quarters, the exec had arranged for breakfast on station. Dan made the rounds as gritty light oozed over the edge of the world. He drank coffee and ate sausage and egg patties clamped between fresh-baked biscuits, perched on a stack of wooden dunnage with one of the damage-control teams in the passageway outside the forward five-inch magazine. They were suited out, with tools, helmets, and masks ready to hand. No one mentioned the rape, and he didn't bring it up.

A paper-cup refill in hand, he strolled aft the length

of the ship until he reached the huge enclosed drum on which the low-frequency tail spooled. Discussed replacing one of the transducer elements with the sonar tech getting the tail ready. Then walked forward again up the port side, greeting everyone he met, and let himself down one deck for a chat with Chief McMottie in Main Control.

That complete, though little the wiser, he sallied out onto the main deck, clutching his cap against the wind.

Savo charged unpityingly forward at twenty-five knots, blowers roaring, stack gas a fading stain on a cloudless sky. He could just make out the whale-call of her sonar. The sea rushed past, a bleached-looking, light-filled blue, dotted with knots of sallow floating weed. No one else was out, except for the lookouts, who lowered binoculars and nodded as he passed.

He lifted his face to the sun and closed his eyes, relishing the heat-lamp glow, the scarlet flare behind his eyelids, the bluster of the wind. In the old days half the crew would've been out here, manning AA guns, passing ammunition, hoisting flag signals. Now their battle stations were inside the skin of the ship, in front of consoles and digital displays.

As was his. When he opened his eyes again a bird was hovering, a motionless speck so far above, so disappearingly infinitesimal in the immense blue, he couldn't make out exactly what it was. He blinked up, wanting to linger, to drink in the beauty of the passing sea one last time.

Instead he turned away. Dogged the door behind him, and clambered up to the CIC level, placing each steel-toed boot heavily and carefully on the next gritty, dusty tread.

He shivered in the arctic blast of the A/C. A glance at the LSDs told him GCCS was still down. Staurulakis got up from the command chair. "All yours," she said, not meeting his gaze. "Course 010 at twenty-five. A hundred and twenty miles to Point Charlie. One hour to *Vinson's* launch of the main strike."

At Point Charlie the battle group would shift into attack formation, to cover the Vietnamese landing. As sole antimissile asset, *Savo* would position between the mainland and the carrier while the initial Tomahawk and then air strikes went in. But until then, there wasn't much to do with the sensors down, so he climbed the last ladder to the bridge.

He was reclining in his chair, mind vacant, when a petty officer handed him an envelope. "Mail, Captain."

"What? How in the hell—?"

"Red Hawk hot-refueled on the carrier. Brought it in on their bounce last night."

Mail. It seemed like something from the Neolithic. He ripped the envelope open. Laser-jetted, with Blair's signature handwritten at the end.

Dear Dan,

They tell me your communications are shut down, but that there's a chance mail might get through. I still have contacts I'm working in DoD, so maybe you'll get an e-mail from me before this, or we'll get to talk on the phone. But just on the off chance, I'll drop this in the box.

We're in Maryland, at Dad and Mom's, since they're worried DC might be a target in some way. They broke in like kidnappers, hustled me and the cat into the car. Half an hour to pack—I could hear you laughing! The campaign is on hold right now. Fundraising's a moot issue—since the banking system's frozen, and credit cards don't work anymore. But everyone seems to think this will all be over by election day. Surely China and the U.S. aren't crazy enough to think a war will settle anything.

The stores are getting empty, though. If you see anything you might need, you buy it then and there, since you might not see it again. We're stocking up on canned food, Scotch for Dad, Mom's meds, and toilet paper. Also we bought new tires. Anything that depends on the Internet, sometimes it works, but mostly it doesn't. Everyone who had anything in the cloud has lost it. Cash is still good, but you can withdraw only $200 a day. Dad has multiple accounts at multiple banks, but not all the terminals work. There was a program about rationing in World War II on NPR yesterday, which Mom thinks is some kind of warning.

By the way, Nan says hi. Heard from her on Facebook before it went down. She said, "Tell Dad not to go anyplace dangerous." I told her you had the seniority now to stay out of trouble. Just didn't want to worry her.

Anyway, I'll write again. So far we're all right, is the main thing I wanted to say. We don't hear much about what the military's doing. The administration's slapped censorship on the networks. All you hear is patriotic bullshit about how we have to defend our old ally Japan, and noble democratic India. How North Korea's set to bomb and invade the South. We do get some actual news from the *Post* and the BBC, but we're mainly just in the dark about what's really going on. Has Vietnam really come down on our side? Dad can't believe that. You know he fought there in '67, in the Marines.

Anyway I'll write again. E-mail me when you can. I'll watch the news for anything about *Savo Island*.

Much Love,
Blair.

PS—Tom's checking on your boat every couple of days. He says the bilge pump is working. Whatever that means.

Midmorning. He was rereading Blair's letter when the duty radioman presented the clipboard. Dan ran his gaze down it, then started again at the top.

After taking the Spratlys, Strike Group One was to remain in the South China Sea, holding the islands and intercepting remaining commerce. *Savo* and *Mitscher,* accompanied by *Pittsburgh,* would detach to head east. Off Luzon, they would rendevous with USS *Curtis Wilbur* and two Japanese destroyers. Dan would command the Ryukyus Maritime Defense Coalition Task Group as something like a temporary commodore.

The joint U.S./Japanese surface strike group would fill the blocking position behind Taiwan that the *George Washington* battle group had been intended to occupy. A second TBMD-capable cruiser, USS *Monocacy*, was en route from Guam. The third ALIS-capable cruiser, *Hampton Roads,* was finishing a hasty fitting-out in Pearl Harbor and would be under way to join shortly.

A separate SI message advised that the U.S. submarine force was leaving the exits to the Pacific, where it had patrolled so far, and moving closer to shore. There, the subs would clear the path for future offensive operations. But Intel cautioned that much of the enemy sub fleet—like, Dan thought, the Songs that'd passed them on their way out of the IO—had already vanished.

Almost as an afterthought, the message said the allies and the "Opposed Powers" were now in a de facto state of hostilities. All satellite comms and data links were down, reducing the Navy to HF radio and UHF/VHF line of sight. On the other hand, all Chinese reconnaissance assets, at least that the U.S. knew about, had been taken down as well.

He kneaded his neck, understanding, reluctantly, the repositioning of *Savo* to the east. Only one day's steaming distance. But they'd be entering a wholly different theater, against a wholly different threat.

The South China Sea would be a battleground, but strategically it was secondary. Even if China broke out here, it would expand into empty sea. Its logistics would be vulnerable to submarine operations, as Japan's had been in an earlier war. The allies—Vietnam, Indonesia, the Philippines, Malaysia—would fight back, to defend their own claims in the area. If Zhang pushed south, he'd lose the war.

But a penetration of the eastern, Philippines-Taiwan-Japan line would let China pincer Taiwan and isolate South Korea, crushing two of America's oldest and best-armed allies. The next step would be to break out, threaten the second island ring, and neutralize Japan. If that happened, the U.S. could find itself pushed back so far it might never be able to return.

The world would look very different then.

"Captain."

Chief Van Gogh, looking worried. Dan coughed into a fist, initialed the message, and handed it back. "Yeah, Chief?"

"GPS is acting up. Says we're in central Luzon, four hundred feet up a mountain."

This wasn't good. "We've got an inertial nav system, Chief. Can we run on that?"

"For a little while, sir. But it's going to degrade over time."

Dan squinted out the window, at the sun sparkling on the waves. What was going on over their heads? *Far* over their heads, hundreds of miles up. No one had reported any shootdowns of U.S. satellites, but their comms and data links were all but useless, and now their navigation was screwed too. *Something* was going on. "We've still got a sextant, right?"

Van Gogh brightened. "Oh, yessir! A sextant, and a chronometer."

"Get a time tick and pull out the reduction tables. We'll shoot a sun line at noon, and do evening stars.

We can run on Aegis and dead reckoning in between." He paused, glancing out at the glittering sea again. "Now lay a course for the Bashi Channel."

Mitscher joined that afternoon. She crossed his bow and settled on his port quarter. "Stony" Stonecipher was riding shotgun again. They raced northeast at flank speed, tails out and pinging, short-range nav radars on. The helo buzzed around ahead, laying sonobuoys. He kept the lookouts alert; you wouldn't think binoculars would be that useful, but he'd seen from the SATYRE exercises how often a sub would get caught visually when he upped scope.

That evening the sky turned lurid and ominous: a deep russet, with high bands of gracefully scalloped cirrus hung like gaudy bunting above heaped piles of cumulus, clotted low and dark where the hidden sun was perishing. The scarlet light seeped into the gently rocking sea, as if—and he tried hard not to think this, but couldn't help it, leaning over the splinter shield and looking aft, past the Harpoon launchers canted out from the stern—as if their wake were drawn through blood.

He was stepping out of his coveralls when the bulkhead phone chirped again. He answered it this time to Dave Branscombe's excited voice.

The comm officer read from the message. *"Para One. Mainland jets have swarmed ROCAF F-16s patrolling the Taiwan Strait, shooting four down and dispersing the rest. China now has air superiority over the strait.*

"Para Two. Premier-General Zhang Zurong has made the following, quote Four Peaceful Announcements, unquote. First: China seeks no wider war. Second, no country will be attacked unless it attacks China, or refuses to help build a lasting stability and order in Asia and the Pacific Rim.

"Third, in order to build a peaceful, orderly Pacific free of weapons of mass destruction, any foreign force capable of delivering nuclear weapons will be dealt with by any means necessary, to prevent escalation.

"Fourth, any aggression against Chinese soil will be answered by a similar or greater level of destruction visited on the American homeland." A moment of silence, then, *"So far, no response from the White House. That's the message, Skipper. Being run up to you, but thought I'd better call, soon as I saw it."*

"I'll be on the bridge," Dan said.

He rezipped his coveralls and climbed to the pilot-house, mulling the attack on the inner island chain's keystone. The allies couldn't hold the center, between Japan and Taiwan—Okinawa, the Senkakus, the Ryukyus—without air defenses and antiballistic missile coverage.

Which meant *Savo Island,* and her sister cruisers, would be the last line of defense.

If they failed, the inner island chain would fall. And the war would be, if not lost at the outset, enormously long and bloody.

Maybe even . . . like World War I.

He stumbled over something soft, and had a bad moment. Then realized, not a body; not yet, anyway. Just the watch team's life jackets and flash gear, rolled and ready. He edged forward in the dark, arms outstretched, struggling against a sense of doom as overwhelming as the nausea that also threatened.

They weren't ready for this. A beta-test system. Five antimissile rounds left, against hundreds of weapons poised across the strait. And a silent, faceless evil driving wedges into his already sick, exhausted crew.

His hands quivered, his neck ached, flashes seared his retinas. He stood silent for a long time, one hand spasmodically gripping the back of his command chair, reluctant to climb up into it.

The nations groped lost in the labyrinth. Once more, the god of war demanded sacrifice. Once more, human beings had miscalculated, and brought down Armageddon.

But his duty, and that of his ship and crew, was clear.

ACKNOWLEDGMENTS

Ex nihilo nihil fit. I write from a braiding of memory, imagination, and research. For this novel, I resorted again to references and interviews accumulated for previous books about Navy and joint operations. I interviewed the master chief who inspects BMD cruisers, whom I knew from previous duty, and a commodore who skippered one cruiser and now commands a strike squadron. I sailed aboard an Aegis cruiser and did on-site research in several of the various locales.

The following background sources were also helpful. The list of Dan's decorations in chapter 4 was submitted by longtime Poyer Crew member Bruce James. The congressional testimony owes much to an unclassified presentation by John H. James to the Tidewater ASNE. The information on monsoons in chapters 6 and 10 is from NRL Monterey, Marine Meteorology Division. The discussion of boarding regimes owes a lot to "Broken Taillight at Sea: The Peacetime International Law of Visit, Board, Search, and Seizure," by Commander James Kraska, JAGC, USN. Chapter 13 was loosely based on U.S. Navy History and Heritage Command's "U.S. Navy Relief Efforts After the Indian Ocean Tsunami, 26 December 2004," and on "Multi-Service Procedures for Humanitarian Assistance Operations," a tactical memorandum I edited while at the Surface Warfare Development Group.

For part 4's discussion of nuclear deterrence, I read "Red Lines, Deadlines, and Thinking the Unthinkable: India, Pakistan, Iran, North Korea, and China," a CSIS study by Anthony Cordesman. Also consulted were "What Might an India-Pakistan War Look Like?" by Christopher Clary, MIT, and *Deep Currents and Rising Tides* by John Garofano. The discussion of "no first use" was informed by Scott D. Sagan's "The Evolution of Indian and Pakistani Nuclear Doctrine," and a posting by Joshi Shashank of Harvard, "India and 'No First Use.' " The operations plans and contingency plans are my *fictional* fabrications after reading *Naval Operations Concept 2010* and William M. Arkin's "National Security Contingency Plans of the U.S. Government." I have never seen any actual operations plans for such a contingency. For chapter 19, I'm indebted to "U.S. Navy Missile Defense, Yesterday, Today, and Tomorrow," by friend and fellow author George Galdorisi.

The information about infections was developed with the help of Dr. Frances Anagnost Williams, and T. J. Rowbotham's "Legionellosis Associated with Ships: 1977 to 1997." Weapons specifications are from various open sources.

For overall help, thanks also to Charle Ricci of the Eastern Shore Public Library; the Joint Forces Staff

College Library; Matthew Stroup of the Navy Office of Information, East; Commander, Naval Surface Forces Atlantic (Sylvia Landis and Kevin Ducharme); and very much to the crew, chiefs, and officers of USS *San Jacinto,* CG-56. They resemble the crew of USS *Savo Island* only in the positive ways!

I'm especially grateful to Mark Durstewitz and Bill Hunteman, who put in many hours reading chapters and commenting in detail. Queried from time to time, Joe Leonard also supplied invaluable perspective from the points of view of a cruiser captain and a squadron commander.

Let me emphasize that all these sources were consulted for the purposes of *fiction.* I'm *not* saying that anything in these references, or derived from these interviews, leads to the conclusions my characters reach or voice in the story. Likewise, the specifics of personalities, tactics, and procedures, and the units and locales described, are employed as the materials of fiction, not reportage. Some details have been altered to protect classified capabilities and procedures.

My most grateful thanks go to George Witte, editor and friend of over three decades, without whom this series would not exist. And also to Sally Richardson, Kenneth J. Silver, Kate Ottaviano, Sara Thwaite, and Staci Bua at St. Martin's. And finally to Lenore Hart, anchor on lee shores, and my North Star when skies are clear.

As always, all errors and deficiencies are my own.

Coming soon . . .

The world war with China takes a desperate turn
in the next Dan Lenson thriller
by *USA Today* Bestselling Author
DAVID POYER

ONSLAUGHT

Available in hardcover, in December 2016,
from St. Martin's Press